TRAPS

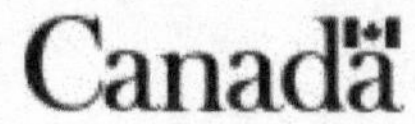

We gratefully acknowledge the support of the Canada Council for the Arts and the Ontario Arts Council for our publishing program. We also acknowledge the financial support of the Government of Canada.

Cover design: Val Fullard

Traps: A Robin MacFarland Mystery is a work of fiction. All the characters portrayed in this book are fictitious and any resemblance to persons living or dead, is purely coincidental.

Library and Archives Canada Cataloguing in Publication

Title: Traps / Sky Curtis.
Names: Curtis, Sky, author.
Series: Inanna poetry & fiction series.
Description: Series statement: A Robin McFarland mystery | Inanna poetry & fiction series
Identifiers: Canadiana (print) 20190147814 | Canadiana (ebook) 20190147822 | ISBN 9781771336697 (softcover) | ISBN 9781771336703 (epub) | ISBN 9781771336710 (Kindle) | ISBN 9781771336727 (pdf)
Classification: LCC PS8605.U787 T73 2019 | DDC C813/.6—dc23

Printed and bound in Canada

Inanna Publications and Education Inc.
210 Founders College, York University
4700 Keele Street, Toronto, Ontario, Canada M3J 1P3
Telephone: (416) 736-5356 Fax: (416) 736-5765
Email: inanna.publications@inanna.ca Website: www.inanna.ca

TRAPS

A ROBIN MACFARLAND MYSTERY

a novel by

Sky Curtis

INANNA PUBLICATIONS AND EDUCATION INC.
TORONTO, CANADA

To my lovely family

1.

I UNFOLDED THE MONTH-OLD NEWSPAPER beside my plate and flattened it with my hand. I loved reading while I ate. I was going to enjoy my breakfast of boiled egg on whole wheat toast, no butter, and look at the paper. Yes, I knew one shouldn't do this; one should pay attention to one's food, but who was watching? My dog?

I checked in with him. "Do you mind if I read while I eat, little Lucky?"

He barked twice. I thought that meant no. I also thought I should get out more.

I sliced off the top of the egg, spooned out some yolk and mushed it on the toast, still no butter. I was dieting. I was always dieting. And I was always still fat. If I've offended the word police who want us all to accept our bodies, let's just say I was still *round*. Not large. Not obese. Not a heart attack waiting to happen. Certainly not fat. *Round*. Round as a big fat honking beach ball. *Hahaha*. So, no butter.

While reaching for my toast. I looked at my fingers. Geezus. Ink. Not that I'm a germaphobe, not like my perfectionist brother Andrew, the asshole, but I got up and washed my hands. I didn't want ink on my fingers as I was stuffing food into my gob—or rather, daintily nibbling my toast. It was the first time I'd seen my article in the paper. I didn't read newspapers. This was sort of bizarre given that I'm a journalist, but I was allergic to the ink. It made my asthma kick up. Hence the handwashing. So,

I got all my news online. My father had saved the paper from the end of May for my records and given it to me at our last Sunday family dinner. It had mostly off-gassed by now. I gave it a sniff and only coughed twice. Not too bad.

When I sat back down, I picked up the toast by the corner and wolfed down a bite. It had been a long time since dinner. I'd save some calories and give a bit to Lucky, who was prancing around the table smiling at me. I wondered briefly if he would like the toast with no butter.

I turned my attention to the somewhat yellowed newspaper. What a fantastic headline: ABUSIVE ACTOR KILLS VICTIM USING BEAR BAIT. In all caps no less. And there was my byline below the head, *by Robin MacFarland*. And below that, *with files from Cynthia Dale*. Cindy was my best friend. Most of the time. She and Diane Chu, although I didn't see Diane much these days. We were drinking buds. Yeah, well, what could I say? Still fat. Still drinking.

Such a wonderful photograph. Cindy had snapped it while up in a tree, looking down at the scene of a giant bear charging through a forest towards a police officer. His face was twisted in terror, eyes wide, his mouth open in a silent scream. The caption read: "Robin MacFarland, an investigative reporter for *The Toronto Express*, deduced that a police officer had inadvertently sprayed himself with bear pheromones contained in an insect repellent bottle."

I continued reading. The first paragraph of the article summarized the situation up pretty nicely:

> The fingerprints of David Sparling, the well-known stage performer, were found on an insect repellent bottle that had belonged to Darlene Gibson, a female stagehand whom he had allegedly sexually assaulted and who was in the process of a lawsuit against him when she disappeared. Ms. Gibson's dismembered body was found in a forest near Huntsville, Ontario, by Robin MacFarland and Cynthia Dale, *Toronto Express* journalists. Gibson had been

> mangled by a bear, apparently attracted to the young woman by bear bait that had been poured by Sparling into her insect repellent bottle.

That time at my cottage was the worst. Cindy and I had headed to Muskoka in the hopes of writing a fluff story on land development and ended up examining body parts in partial decay. It was going to be a long time before I went back to my cottage.

As I munched on my breakfast, I reread the photograph's caption: "investigative reporter" my ass. I wrote for the Home and Garden section. My speciality was flowers, cutlery, scissors, pitchforks, and other fascinating topics to do with the home. Since May I had written not one, but two articles on Vise-Grips. I looked down at my legs and thought about Ralph, my boyfriend. Maybe I should do some scissor kicks or something to enhance my grip. Oh, Robin, get a grip. I gave the paper a shake, held it at arm's length so it would come into focus, ah, the joys of aging, and admired my piece. I had, after all, figured out how a bear had been manipulated to kill.

This was my second front-page article in less than a year. This didn't quite qualify for being on a roll, but the trajectory was good. It's not that I was ambitious, nor was I competitive, but honestly, bamboo pillows? Laminate flooring? The shit I knew about. I'd been on the inside pages of the paper for decades and it was sort of depressing that my career had been so stagnant. So, two articles on the front page about murders that had been basically solved by me? Not bad. Not bad at all. I could feel my self-esteem knitting together.

I thumped the paper. And look at that! Front page. My name! I was a hot property. The chaotic days after the arrest of the actor in May went on all the way through June. My phone buzzed constantly in my purse. All the major TV networks wanted to interview me. CBC. CTV. Global News. It was awful. It was grand. But still, now that I was back in the Home and Garden section of the newspaper, I was much happier. Well, maybe. Today, my job was to write about early spring flowers, now that it was June. To be specific, peonies and ants. Back to the things I was an expert on. Sad really. Not sad that I was expert on these sorts of things, but maybe sad that I truly liked these things. They were about life. About how people lived. Maybe I was helping people with their journeys on earth. Naw, who was I kidding? Rhubarb? Keyless remote entries? And now ants, for heaven's sake. So trite.

My phone pinged. A text. I brushed my hands off on a tissue and saw it was from Maggie, my oldest child. What now? She wanted to know if we were going to have a week at the cottage with the whole family. No way. We usually had a week together at the end of August, including Labour Day weekend. That way everyone could maximize their time off work without taking too many holiday days. Her request grated on me. I was torn. They loved the cottage, and I couldn't go. Plus, for heaven's sake, it was only the middle of June. The end of August was weeks and weeks away. How the hell did I know what I would be doing in two months? That Maggie sure was a planner.

I texted back to her, *Let's make a plan. Get back to you later. xoxoxox*. What a good mommy I was, showing absolutely no sign of irritation.

But really? No way was I going to that cottage for a holiday. Not me. Nopers. I needed to think about this. After that horrific time in Huntsville, that torn body and the bear attacks, the last place on earth I wanted to be was up north. Being Thursday, I had a few days to figure something out before our next family dinner on Sunday. Maybe Ralph would have some ideas. Or Cindy. Or Diane. There were tons of people I could consult. Even Shirley Hay Hair, my editor. But one thing I knew for sure. I was not going to go to the cottage for a holiday this summer. Nope. Not after what happened in May.

Severed neck bones skittered across my mind. That headless torso was going to haunt me for a long time. I would have to go somewhere else this summer if I wanted to relax and enjoy myself. I had enough money saved to pay for the kids to join me, wherever. Maybe PEI. They all liked that Anne of Green Gables story, even the boys. Maybe we could go there. Or maybe to Nova Scotia and look at some Maud Lewis folk art. They all liked art. I counted this as one of my achievements, instilling a love of art in my kids. They loved nature too, but shit, I just couldn't go to the cottage. I gagged on my egg as I thought about a finger bone buried in the earth. No, better to go east.

I glanced at my watch. Damn. It was almost nine o'clock. So late. I had to get cracking. I brushed the crumbs off the article into my hand and gave Lucky the last corner of toast. He sniffed it, gave it a tentative lick, poked it with his nose, and looked at me questioningly.

"I know. No butter. Well, that's the way it is. I'm too fat."

He barked once.

"I know, it has nothing to do with you. You're nice and thin, but I'm not and now I need to take steps to lose some weight. About ten thousand steps a day. That's all the rage these days. I should keep track on a Fitbit. More like a Fatbit. *Hahaha*."

Lucky barked again, head tilted.

"Oh, I didn't translate your first bark correctly? Silly me. You didn't want me to call myself fat? Right. Okay, I'm *sturdy*." I grunted as I bent over to pick up the uneaten piece of toast off the floor. If it hadn't had Lucky's spit on it, I might have been tempted to eat it. Yikes. That was disgusting. I tossed it into the organic bin along with the crumbs on my hand. "It's time to go to work."

Lucky barked and wagged his tail, looking at me expectantly. Every morning he did this.

"Work. Not *walk*. Work." You'd think he'd know that by now. "I'll *walk* you when I get home. Promise."

Was it pathetic that I talked to my dog like this? No, lots of people talked to their dogs. I stroked his head. "Bye-bye.

Love you." I grabbed my keys and briefcase, and rushed out the door, leaving Lucky standing in the middle of the kitchen, looking at me forlornly.

Last night, I'd gotten great parking, right across the street. I lived in a semi-detached Victorian in Cabbagetown that I'd bought for a song after Trevor, my husband of two decades, had suddenly been killed by a drunk driver, leaving me with four kids, five pets, and a huge mortgage. Of course, we'd had no insurance. That would have required planning. And Trevor had not been a planner, unlike Maggie. So, I sold the big house in the nice part of town near where Cindy lived in North Toronto and bought a rundown piece of crap at Carlton and Parliament. Being a Home and Garden reporter, I had good contacts and soon the place had been replumbed, rewired, and re-drywalled. It had turned into a respectable house with the old character retained. I was proud of it. The kids had finished up their schooling while living there, the smaller mortgage was paid off, and here I was, six years later, alone in a rambling old place with my dog. Given that Trevor had been killed by a drunk, it was pretty ironic that I now drank like a fish. I loved my wine.

As I crossed the street, I looked at my little Nissan with exasperation. Maybe if I stopped drinking a bottle of wine a day, I wouldn't have to drive a shitbox. I would be able to afford the monthly payments on, let me see, a BMW? Maybe even a Mercedes. My brother drove a BMW. His wife did, too. *Plus,* they drank wine. Maybe not a bottle a day, but still. Life was unfair. I yanked the rusty driver's door open and stuffed myself behind the wheel while tossing my briefcase into the back seat. No, I hadn't locked the car. Who on earth would steal it? Cindy always got impatient with me for not locking my car. I pointed out to her that no one in their right mind would want a tape deck. My darling Nissan Sentra was really, really old. Almost twenty years. It had almost five hundred thousand kilometres on it. And I loved it. I gave a little pat on the dusty dashboard. Maybe it was unhealthy to be attached to a car. I really didn't care. I turned the key and it purred to life. I smiled as I gassed it and threw the gearshift into D, for Devil, spinning the wheels and racing towards Parliament Street. I squealed at the corner and headed south towards the lake and my office.

I guess I shouldn't have said "my office." I had no office, per se. Only the editors had offices. We underlings had spaces. We didn't even have cubicles. There were no office dividers for us. So, I headed to *the* office and parked my rust bucket in the underground parking lot. At least we had free parking. In fact, the columns and the wall in front of my parking space made it more private than my desk. Maybe I should work in my car.

On the way up to the fifth floor, I struck a pose in the elevator, looking at myself in the brushed steel doors. They were like funhouse mirrors and shaved about twenty pounds off my hips. I was so pleased. Unfortunately, they also made my head the size of a baseball, which, although disconcerting and unattractive, I thought I could live with, given the weight loss. The elevator doors opened at Editorial on the fifth floor, and I saw Cindy hunched over her computer, tapping away, her red curls vibrating. Derrick Johnston, the asshole sports reporter who I couldn't stand, was flipping a toothpick around in his mouth with his tongue while he made a show of looking at his watch. Yeah, so I was a little late. I was always a little late, and I didn't give a shit. Actually, I did. Guilt was my best friend. I just acted *as if* I didn't care. I'd read a book that had said, "Act *as if*." The theory was if you acted *as if* long enough, eventually the *as if* would become the reality. So far, it hadn't worked for me. I still felt guilty. But I was willing to keep at it. I shook my head and rolled my eyes as I stepped around his desk on the way to mine. I muttered, "Neanderthal" as I passed by him, and none too softly either. I knew he wouldn't know what it meant. Too big a word.

Cindy looked up as I pulled my chair away from my desk and dumped my body into it. "Hi," I said. "What are you working on? Guns in Toronto?"

Her green eyes widened, "How did you know? Did you hear about that shipment that came over the border in a car's gas tank? I'm going to go to the police station later and talk to the guys if they let me in. I'd love to know how the woman got the guns into her tank and whether or not the gasoline wrecked the guns."

The cops hated Cindy. As a crime reporter, she was always in their face. Rude, aggressive, demanding, strong, and usually right. Nobody liked someone who turned them into a fool. She wasn't purely an investigative reporter, the paper had two of those: Karen Marumbo and Stanley Wong. No, my Cindy liked action. Crime. The minute she heard a siren, any siren, she catapulted out of her chair and chased it. She probably had an app for following emergency vehicles. Maybe it was called Appulance. To be fair, every now and then, she did some investigative reporting, like her great series on gangs last spring. But Cindy liked exploits. We were so different. I liked roses. And the cops liked me. In particular, Ralph Creston, a senior detective, liked me. A lot. In fact, a few weeks ago he'd told me he loved me. Why he had to ruin a nice relationship with the "L" word was beyond me.

I said, "Probably not. Gasoline is a solvent and guns do need to be cleaned. Plus, they are metal. Gasoline would be great for that." Cindy was staring at me with that look on her face. I had stepped into her territory. And after she had been told to stand down from writing the story about the actor, she was probably sensitive to my interference into her area of expertise. I knew I needed to lighten things up. "Although you wouldn't want to use one of those guns near a fire. *Kaboom.*" I laughed as I peered at her computer. What? She was on the Air Canada site. "I thought you said you were working."

Cindy tapped her space bar and up came her story. "I am. I'm multi-tasking. I'm booking my holiday. This year I'm heading to the east coast."

"Get out. That's exactly what I was thinking I'd do this summer. With my kids."

She furrowed her brow. "But don't you usually go to your cottage?"

"Not this year. Not after that.... You know...."

"Well, I've booked a flight to Halifax and I've rented a car. I'm going to drive around Cape Breton. I always wanted to look at that Bell Museum. Want to come with me? *Ding-ding*? Bell?"

As much as I loved Cindy, and I really did, I was hoping that Ralph would be able to come with us out east, and they positively hated each other. It just wouldn't work for her and me to have a holiday together. Besides, when we'd been at my cottage in May, there were times when she really bugged me. Like when she climbed huge trees, scaring me out of my wits. Mind you, she did get that great picture of the bear charging that officer. Anyway, it would be best if we didn't hook up out there.

"Really? There's a museum about bells?" I thought for a minute. "Well, there's a museum about shoes in Toronto, so I guess bells could have a museum as well. Now that I think about it, bells are pretty interesting. There are all kinds of bells. Big bells, little bells, different notes and tones. Singing bells. Bowls that sound like bells. Yes, now that I think about it, a bell museum would be full of information. I should write an article about bells."

Cindy was watching me with a small smile playing around the corners of her mouth. "The Bell Museum is in Baddeck. Alexander Graham *Bell*," she said, emphasizing the guy's last name, "invented quite a few things. Underwater sonar, air conditioners, hydrofoil boats, airplanes, you name it. He was unbelievably creative."

Chastised, and turned into a fool, as only Cindy could do, I sort of laughed. "Oh. I see. When are you going?"

"The last two weeks in August."

Oh no, not then. "That's when I think I'd like to go." I tried not to sound disappointed.

"Maybe we'll meet up somewhere," Cindy said.

No bloody way. "That would be fun."

"Where are you thinking of going?" she asked.

Far away from Cape Breton. "I don't know yet. We might even go to PEI. I have to talk to my kids about it at our Sunday dinner this weekend. Who knows. Maybe they're so entrenched in the tradition of going to the cottage they won't even entertain the idea of travelling to another province. I'll see."

"Well, if you do end up deciding on Nova Scotia, let's get together."

"Sure, sounds like fun," I lied.

2.

RALPH AND I WERE ENJOYING A LEISURELY Sunday morning brunch. He'd shown up around midnight after his shift of being a cop and saving the world. Last night, we had both been exhausted, fell into bed, and then made up for lost time this morning. So, now, well-exercised, we ate heartily. Or rather, he did. I was bravely trying to enjoy a bowl of translucent low-fat yogurt topped with three wrinkled blueberries. It looked like camel cum garnished with dead flies.

"Why don't you have some pancakes, sweetie. They're great." A bead of maple syrup was slowly making its way down his chin, through the bristles of his five o'clock shadow. On one hand, I was revolted. On the other, I wanted to lick it off his face.

"Um, well, I need to protect my girlish figure."

"You don't have a girlish figure."

I gave him a look that said, "Screw off."

He smiled. "No, you have a beautiful woman's figure. Soft and mature. Real."

"Good save." I laughed and then gathered up some courage. "You don't think I'm fat?"

He grinned. "God, no. I think you're beautiful. So many women are way too thin. There's nothing to hold on to. I like the way you look. There's enough of you to love."

There was that stupid "L" word again. He had been using that a lot lately. What was I supposed to do with *that*? Maybe he was vocabularically challenged and only knew one alternate word for "like."

And now, on top of everything else, I was faced with a dilemma. Did I continue with the yogurt so there was less of me to love, or did I drown some pancakes in syrup and go hog-wild? And why was food associated with love anyway? Food should just be fuel for the body, not fuel for the soul. Right? Was I overthinking this? As I contemplated all this, I was also staring blankly at that bead of maple syrup on Ralph's chin.

"What? Do I have something on my chin?"

I came back to earth. "Just some maple syrup."

As he wiped it off with a napkin, he said, "What's on the agenda for today?"

"Well, the first thing is to take the napkin fluff out of your stubble." I licked my finger, leaned over, and rubbed the lint off his chin. "There. Much better." I took a breath, trying to ignore the *zing* that coursed through my lower body. "Everyone is coming over for dinner tonight, and I was hoping you would, um, join us."

I was going to say "come" but after touching his chin, I didn't want to give him any ideas. I needed to get today's show on the road as it was already well past ten. I still had a ton of stuff to do and that didn't include another romp in the bedroom.

Ralph pushed himself away from the table, leaned back and looked at me. "Really? You want me to come to a family dinner? Well, that's a first. Are you sure you want to introduce me to everyone? Are you ready for that? I mean, I know we've been seeing each other for almost a full year, but I know how skittish you are. I was prepared to wait awhile for things to move along, if they were going to."

"*Skittish*? You think I'm skittish? What do you mean?" I sounded shrill. In fact, I sounded skittish. I was trying to keep my voice calm and reasonable, as if I were relaxed. The *as if* game wasn't working that well.

Ralph looked up at he ceiling, thinking. "Well, for example, if I tell you I love you, you sort of gurgle. Like you're being strangled or something. You don't know what to say. It makes you really uncomfortable. But I do love you. I love your sense of humour. Your feistiness. Your smarts. Your talent. How we are together."

Geezus. He should just shut up. My throat constricted, and I made a strangled noise.

Ralph laughed. "There. That's what I mean. You gurgle." He leaned forward, making a point. "Anyway, I'd *love* to come for dinner and finally meet your *lovely* family."

"Really? Are you sure? There's definitely some weirdness there."

"Oh? You surprise me."

What did he mean by that? Was I weird? I thought for a second. Yeah, probably.

"Anyway, we all need to talk about our summer holidays. The kids and I like to take a week or so together at the end of August and go to the cottage, but I just don't think I can handle that this year. That bear business in May was really upsetting."

"I understand." Ralph's eyes were so kind. "It's not every day you see a head severed from a torso."

We both looked away for a second, contemplating headless torsos. I felt blueberry pancakes rise up in my gorge. Yes, I had discarded the slimy yogurt, and chosen the delicious pancakes. Of course I had. I wasn't stupid.

"So, what are your thoughts, Robin?"

"I was thinking maybe we could go out east or something. Check out Anne of Green Gables or Maud Lewis. Walk on some beaches. Swim. I don't know. What do you think?"

Ralph peered at me. "When you say 'we,' are you including me in this plan?"

I told myself to be brave. Act *as if* it was no big deal. I took another deep breath, "Well, yes, if you could get the time off. That is, if you wanted to come with us."

"I would love to." He resumed eating his pancakes. "Do you

think your kids would mind? I mean, they're just meeting me tonight for the first time."

I'd thought about it. Ralph had been in my life since the end of last summer, and I liked him. A lot, actually. I wouldn't go as far as the "L" word, but still, it looked as if he was going to be around for a long time, so I might as well get my kids used to the idea that I was now part of a couple.

I was completely honest for a change. "I have no idea how they'll react. But you and I are together, and we might as well be together, if you know what I mean."

Ralph took a deep breath, looked at me straight in the eye, and said, "Thank you, Robin." He suddenly stood up and bustled around the kitchen, rinsing off plates for the dishwasher and putting food away. And *I* was skittish?

As I watched him move around my space, I thought about how I felt about him. He was certainly part of my life. It was time that my children met him. But was I doing the right thing? Who knew? But I did know that if he didn't meet my family soon it would be insulting. A year was a year. Any longer and he would think I was ashamed of him or something. Or ashamed of them. The only family I was ashamed of was my pompous prick of a conservative brother Andrew, who Ralph had already met. And my parents.

"It's so nice that we have the day off together. Do you have things you need to do?"

"Not really," he grunted.

A grunt? What was going on with him now? He sounded upset.

"Well," I chirped, "I have to go to the No Frills on Parliament Street and get some food for dinner. I was thinking a chickpea curry on rice tonight, for the vegetarians in the family, and maybe roast chicken for the rest of us. Broccoli. Strawberries. They're in season now. Also, I would like to garden for a bit and of course, walk little Lucky. Want to do any of that with me?"

Ralph didn't turn around and was briskly running water over already rinsed dishes. What was up with him? I got out of my chair and put my arms around his waist.

"Hey," I said. "You okay?"

"It's just..." He paused. "It's just that I'm so happy with *us*, and I don't want it to end."

God, men were so stupid sometimes. I had just asked him to meet my family and he was worried about the relationship ending? What a dip. "We are moving forward here, Ralphie. Not backwards."

"*Ralphie?*"

I laughed and grabbed a tea towel by the corner and snapped it at his bum. "Hey Ralphie, big detective, take this." Snap went the towel. "Assault with a deadly weapon." Finally, he turned around and grabbed the towel as it flicked near his thigh and pulled me towards him with it.

He held me in a tight embrace and kissed the top of my head. "Where do you want to walk Lucky?"

I mumbled into his shirt. "I was thinking the Brick Works. Want to go there? Or are you thinking somewhere else?"

"The Brick Works would be great. Close to us and maybe it won't be that busy there today. It's not exactly a beautiful day. How about doing the food shop now, then a little gardening, lunch, a walk, a nap, and then dinner."

This was exactly what I had in mind, right down to the "nap." "It's a great plan." I snuggled deeper into his chest. "Do you think it will rain?"

He let go of me, pulled out his phone from his back pocket, and scrolled down. "Probably not. Only a thirty percent chance."

The front of my body felt cold where he had been pressed against me. "Okay then, let's get a move on. Lots to do!"

Seven hours later, we were back in the kitchen. We had shopped, walked, and happily napped. Lucky was snoozing by the back door, all tuckered out from chasing squirrels in the backyard while we weeded the garden, and Ralph was fishing around in the cutlery drawer for knives and forks. "How many people are coming?"

"Well, let's see." I counted on my fingers. "You and me, my mother and father, my brother Andrew and his wife Jocelyn, Maggie and her boyfriend Winchester, Evelyn, Calvin, and Bertie. So, eleven."

He laughed, "Just eleven?" Silverware clattered as he gathered up knives and forks. "No wonder you wanted three cans of coconut milk for the curry and two chickens." He walked into the dining-room area while sniffing the air. "Smells great."

As six o'clock approached, I was finally making a cheese plate and cutting the stems out of the strawberries. They were glistening with juice. But the season hadn't been great tastewise, so I squirted lemon juice and honey on them. As I put the cheese and crackers on the pine blanket box, my makeshift coffee table in front of the couch, the doorbell rang. Ralph plunked a bottle of wine next to the cheese platter and beetled into the kitchen. Was he shy? I wagged my finger at Lucky as I walked to the door. "Leave that cheese alone." He wagged his tail and licked his chops. I smacked my lips together and imitated him. Yup, I was weird.

I opened the door and saw that all the kids had arrived together. They were poking each other and laughing away. "Hi everyone. Come on in." They parted around me like a tsunami and swept into the living room, grabbing chairs and jostling for places on the couch. "Help yourself to cheese and crackers." As if I needed to tell them.

I ducked into the kitchen to check on Ralph. He was determinedly stirring the curry. "I was worried it was going to scald," he said.

I knew I had turned the heat way down under the pan. "It's okay, Ralphie, you can come out and meet them. They won't bite."

He sort of grimace-smiled, eyebrows raised. "Don't call me Ralphie." *Stir stir stir*. "What if they don't like me?"

"They will, don't worry. Come on. It'll be fine."

Just as he was wiping his hands on a tea towel and getting ready to face the music, the doorbell rang again. The rest of the family. He quickly grabbed the wooden spoon and started stirring the curry again. I said to his back, "Oh-h-h-h, the big strong detective is frightened of my vicious family." He half-turned towards me and shrugged. I held up my finger and said, "I'll be right back."

My father and mother were already sitting in the living room, tucked together on the couch between Bertie and Calvin. Andrew and Jocelyn, my asswipe brother and his eye candy, were perched on the arms of the easy chairs. "Here, you two, sit on these." I dragged two chairs from the dining room table and put them in the grouping around the blanket box. "Here you go." I gave the chairs a pat. "Nice to see you."

Not really. My brother was an asshole, and his wife? Just as bad as he was. They were the kind of people who looked you up and down, examining your hairstyle, assessing your wardrobe, putting a price tag on your looks. Pursing their lips if you were wearing brown shoes with black pants. They would never shop at IKEA or The Home Depot. Even their house paint? Farrow & Ball. God forbid the neighbours should see them opening a can of the Canadian Tire brand. Not that they ever painted anything themselves; they would hire professionals. And not that their neighbours could see them—their house was lodged behind an eight-foot cedar hedge in Rosedale.

Was I resentful because they were rich? Sour grapes? Maybe a little. I'd had a hard slog, but still, they rubbed me the wrong way. They were more interested in themselves than anything else. Everything the two of them did was for their benefit only. Narcissism was the name of their game. Even if they invited me for dinner, I knew it was to parade me as a journalist in front of their guests. And if one of their guests happened to be in manufacturing, it was to make a contact. After that weed killer fellow, I now made a point of clarifying who the other guests were before I accepted an invitation. Last thing I wanted to do was endorse weed poison.

And Jocelyn? She was always perfectly coiffed with the latest style of blonde-ombre hair, which cascaded down her back. I personally thought the look was ridiculous. Who wanted to look like they'd forgotten to touch up their dark roots? She often wore white slacks and a polo sweater, which she always tossed casually over her shoulders, the sleeves loosely tied around her neck. She was L.L. Bean personified. Jocelyn was whiter than white, blue-eyed with a dazzling smile. Maybe a touch of Botox here and there. Pearls. And worst of all, thin. I used to think Jocelyn was a nice person in a friendly American kind of way, until I figured out that she was complicit with Andrew. Every anti-community decision he made was agreed to by her. So, no, I couldn't like her. She was a bitch. A well-dressed bitch, but a bitch.

I was a practicing Nichirin Buddhist—sort of—and one of the tenets of such practice was to find the goodness in everyone. Compassion was a big word at the Soka Gakkai International. I did my best, but geez, sometimes it was hard to do. As I looked at the two of them sitting in my living room, knees crossed, well-clad feet dangling, patronizing smirks around the corners of their mouths, I tried very hard to feel compassion for them. To be inclusive. To rise above my dislike. To hope for their happiness. But family was family and I had to invite them.

"So glad you could come. And how nice of you to bring Mom and Dad." I turned to them on the couch. "Hi Mom, Dad. Help yourself to cheese and crackers."

My mother looked so thin and fragile. Her eyes were taking on that empty stare that people with macular degeneration got. And my father? He was trying to look in charge, but I wasn't sure he knew where he was. His marbles were scattering all over the floor, and he kept slipping on them. Even as I felt sorry for them, a flash of anger bolted through me. Where the hell had that come from? I told myself I'd think about it later. I opened the bottle of wine, poured several glasses, and handed them around. "Cheers," I said, as I guzzled my glass, putting out the fire of fury that burned in my chest. What was my problem?

Oh no. I had forgotten about Ralph, stuck in the kitchen, stirring away. Is this what they meant by "stir crazy?" I tried not to turn into a hysterical hyena because of my private joke.

I called over the din, "Ralph, I wonder if you could bring in another bottle of wine. Thanks, sweetie." "Sweetie" was as close as I could come to the "L" word.

Suddenly, the chatter stopped, and all eyes turned expectantly to the kitchen. Ralph made a red-faced entrance into the silence, carrying a bottle of red wine as if it were a life buoy. It was certainly mine. I could almost hear my kids' brains whirring as they assessed this man of mine.

"I'd like everyone to meet Ralph, my boyfriend." There, I'd said "my boyfriend" in public. "He's the cop who saved my life when I was forced to eat almonds by a woman who had murdered her husband. Remember? It was not that long ago. About a year."

Now that was what I call a good credential. The kids kept staring at him. I couldn't believe how rude they were. He had a frozen smile on his face. This was so awkward.

My mother, bless her, broke the silence and piped up in her reedy voice. "And who are you, young man? You're not Maggie's boyfriend, that much I know. He's the black man over there. Sitting beside her."

Maggie and Winchester were snuggled up together in my reading chair, oblivious to the rest of us. Young love.

Ralph leaned forward and extended a hand to her. "Nice to meet you, Janice. I'm Ralph Creston." He turned to my father and said, "And you must be Robin's father, Duncan. I've heard so much about you."

No, he hadn't. I never talked about my parents to Ralph,

except to tell him their names. But my father puffed his chest up and beamed at Ralph. Obviously, Ralph had said the right thing. Ralph then shook my brother Andrew's hand and said, "Nice to see you again, and in much happier circumstances." He turned to Jocelyn, his hand extended. "Andrew and I met a month ago at the cottage. Nice to meet you, Jocelyn."

Jocelyn had obviously heard about the cottage fiasco where her husband's client, Dave Sparling, had been arrested for murder. Andrew had been adamant, right up to the last minute, that his rich client couldn't possibly have done anything wrong. He was rich! I watched Jocelyn as she tried, unsuccessfully, to mask her displeasure at meeting the man who had contradicted their core belief that the rich were all-powerful. She shook Ralph's hand, but I could tell from the angle of her wrist that it must have felt like holding a used condom. Poor Ralph.

"And here are my kids," I said. I pointed at each one as I said their names. "Evelyn, Maggie, her boyfriend Winchester Elliott, Calvin, and Bert."

Ralph looked at each one and smiled as I went around the room. I could tell he was feeling self-conscious so I asked him to follow me into the kitchen to help me get the food on the table. As I was scooping the curry into a serving dish he said, "Well, at least that's over. Everyone seems nice enough, except your brother and that Jocelyn. What's up with her?"

"She has a pickle up her butt. Don't worry about it. Here, take this and put it on the table." I handed him the huge bowl of curry, threw the chicken on a platter, dumped the broccoli into a serving dish, and followed him out, my arms full as well.

"Hey everyone," I said, "food's going on the table. Let's eat. Calvin, it's your turn to be on the end of the table. Ralph, you can sit between my father and mother. Everyone else, grab a seat." I went back into the kitchen and got the rest of the dinner. As I carried food into the room everyone was taking their places. Once we were seated, Andrew cleared his voice and started to pontificate.

Dickhead.

"We need to talk about the cottage."

Oh God save me, here we go.

3.

ANDREW CAREFULLY LAID HIS KNIFE and fork on his plate so that they were perfectly parallel to each other. Then he dabbed at his lips with his napkin. He was preparing for a speech. He thought that just because he had the most money of anyone in my family, he was the big boss of the cottage. I wondered how my father felt about that and looked at him. He was struggling with his chicken and seemed to have no awareness of what was going on around him.

Andrew cleared his throat to make sure he had everyone's attention. "The new owners of the land next to us are going to do some logging. They'll start the actual cutting in the fall, but there will be ATVs and lots of noise this summer." He tossed me a priggish look. "And don't you usually use the cottage until Labour Day? That's what you booked with the family in January. I'm sure they'll start the logging on the first day of September. Won't be that relaxing of a holiday."

Did I detect a smidgen of glee in his voice? Was he pleased that our peaceful summer holiday was going to be ruined? Perhaps he had trouble controlling his revenge gene and needed to get back at me for the David Sparling arrest. I'm sure he was angry about that. He didn't like being wrong, and he certainly didn't like his assumptions about his class of people to be turned upside down. The rich, in his mind, were infallible and could do no wrong. I squinted under my eyelashes at Jocelyn. She was smiling. At what? Our misfortune? She truly was a bitch.

But I was smiling too. Little did they know that Andrew had delivered great news. It was so wonderful. I now had a perfect excuse to go somewhere else this summer. Now I wouldn't have to expose any weakness by saying I couldn't hack being at the cottage after the discovery of that dismembered body. I wanted my parents to think I was strong. Ralph knew the truth, and so did Cindy, but I just didn't want my parents or Andrew to know I was vulnerable. My pride, I guessed.

"Hmm," I said, nonchalantly, grinning away. Andrew was watching me carefully. He seemed a tad puzzled. Good. "Maybe we should plan a family holiday somewhere else this summer."

Maggie brushed some of her raven-black hair back from her forehead. "I'd love to go to Nova Scotia. Maybe the South Shore? That's where Winchester's family is originally from, although he grew up in Halifax."

This was falling into my lap!

My mother shook her head. "I don't understand, Evelyn. Isn't he from Africa? Where black people come from?"

Maggie didn't bat an eyelash at being called "Evelyn," the wrong name, or at the inappropriate history lesson. "That's true, Gramma, but just like the MacFarland's are from Scotland, way, way back, we now say we come from Toronto. Winchester was born in Nova Scotia, so that's where he says he's from. He came to Toronto when he got into the University of Toronto." Maggie was clearly proud of him, and so she should be. Getting into UofT was tremendously difficult. The admission standards were very, very high.

My father looked at Winchester, his mouth agape. It was almost comical, if it wasn't so patronizing. "*You* went to UofT?" He was incredulous, the racist prick. Oh no, I grew up in his house. So, did that make me racist as well? I certainly hoped not.

Winchester smiled broadly, displaying all his gleaming white teeth. Then he opened his eyes so wide the snowy whites were like neon lights. He looked left and right, magnifying the effect. I was sure he did that on purpose. "Why yes, sir. Electrical Engineering."

"Did you hear that Janice? The boy went to UofT."

"Yes, Duncan. Who would have thought?"

My father turned his filmy eyes to Winchester. "What did you say your name was, young man?"

"Winchester. Winchester Elliott. With two 't's.'"

"Elliott, huh? An English name." He said it as if Winchester was a thief.

But Maggie was smiling happily, and Winchester was certainly enjoying himself. Maybe he'd been taunted all his life and this was a tame game for him. I had to admire his self-confidence.

"So," I said, dragging the topic back to where I wanted it, "let's go to Nova Scotia. Do you want to travel around and look at stuff, or do you want a beach holiday?"

My sensitive child, Bert, looked upset. "I'm not sure I can take that kind of time off work, but if I had a say, I'd want to hang on a beach."

Glad that the focus of the conversation was now off Winchester and the colour of his skin, I said, "Oh, Bertie, even if you could only come for a few days, I'd fly you down and you could stay for as long or as short as you can."

Evelyn looked up. "You'll fly us there? That's so expensive." Evelyn, the ever-practical one, was already calculating the cost of the airfare in her head. "It'll be thousands. We could all chip in."

"Oh, honey, that's so nice of you to suggest that, but I've been saving for a family vacation for a while."

Andrew sniggered. He wouldn't have to save up for a trip. He'd just take it out of a single day's revenue from his investments. He flew here and there all the time.

My father spoke up. "I'd be happy to contribute. Janice and I have some money set aside for travel, but now with her eyesight going and my diminishing faculties, I doubt we'll be going anywhere."

Whoa! My father was flat out admitting he had dementia? Well, wasn't that a step in the right direction. On top of that, he didn't look sad or angry, he looked as if he were accepting his lot in life. "That's very kind of you Dad, but maybe you should save that money for other things."

"Like what?" he yipped. "My coffin? Now he was angry. "You can't take it with you, Robin. Take the damn money."

"Well, thanks, Dad. It would be helpful." Hopefully he'd forget about his offer by the end of summer. I didn't want his dirty money. His career was in investments like Andrew's, and I was pretty sure not all of it was honestly come by. I wanted no part of that. Nonetheless, he was offering me a gift.

I studied Andrew to see how he was taking all this. He was enormously competitive with me in our relationship with our parents. Everyone had always acknowledged that he was the favourite in the family. My parents pretended that wasn't the case, making sure all gifts were virtually identical in cost and believe me, I knew he'd be offered some money to match whatever my father wanted to give to me for my trip. I didn't mind he was the precious one. Who wanted that kind of attention? However, Andrew did have a look on his face that I couldn't place. What was it? He didn't look at all ashamed that he hadn't offered to help his sister. If narcissism had a look, that's what was on his face. Like he'd gotten away with being a greedy pig. If he'd been a kinder brother and followed my father's lead, he would have offered to help. He was almost as rich as Midas.

My mother pitched in, "And we could take care of Lucky while you're gone."

Damn. I hadn't thought of Lucky. No way was I going to leave my precious dog with them. "That's so kind of you, Mom." I'd figure it out. Maybe Cindy would take the dog. No, she was going travelling then too. Whatever.

Calvin was chewing slowly, his head tilted on its side, his thoughts percolating. "Listen, Mom, I think I have enough points on my credit card for a car rental. We could do one car if we rented a van."

I hated vans. Trevor and I had fought about the kind of car I should have, with him always saying we needed a van. I could still hear him whining about it now. "We have four kids, you need a van." But I couldn't be the soccer mom type. No vans for this secret Wonder Woman. I would drive anything but—and that was clear, given my ancient Sentra.

Winchester interrupted my thoughts. "Why don't Maggie and I drive down in my car? We can take Lucky, and then we'll have a large vehicle and a smaller one there. It would probably be helpful to have two cars."

I resigned myself to a van.

My father nearly choked on a grain of rice. "You have a *car*? Did you hear that Janice? The boy has a car."

"Yes, Duncan. Who would have thought."

Oh, for heaven's sake. I wanted to punch them. I did a little internal Buddhist chant.

"Really Winchester? You'd drive all that way? It'll take you a couple of days." I checked out Maggie's face. Was she on board with this?

She saw me watching her. "No problem at all, Mom. It will give us a chance to see Quebec and New Brunswick. I hear the drive along the Saint John River is spectacular. And I love Lucky. We'd take good care of him."

Winchester was smiling. "I've done the drive lots of times, don't worry. It's not too bad. And I can share it with Maggie." Winchester looked at her adoringly. They were so cute together.

Andrew was listening to all this with a leer on his face. "Now that you've worked out all the details of the car costs, do you know where you'll go?"

Naturally, he would know the best places to go; of course he would. Probably some five-star resorts. No doubt he'd stayed in all of them. Jocelyn was looking at him expectantly, smiling and waiting for his words of wisdom. I was sure their relationship was complicated. Two narcissists getting together? All that me, me, me. It was a wonder they got anything done at all.

"Well, Andrew..." I had found that one way of dealing with his bullying was to be condescending back. I didn't like how it made me feel, but survival of the fittest and all that. "...We have to decide what kind of holiday we want, first of all."

"I think we all vote for beaches and swimming, Mom." That was Evelyn. Everyone was nodding. "It would be the most relaxing."

Andrew looked affronted. "Oh. Well. I was going to suggest Trout Point Lodge, near Kemptville. I've stayed there. Rustic yet luxurious."

"I think, Andrew, we would prefer renting a cottage near the ocean for a week. We want beaches. Kemptville is pretty much inland." At least I knew that much. Or was it Kentville that was inland?

"Well, then," he spouted, not to be deterred, "The Quarterdeck. It would be perfect. Just outside of Liverpool. Right on a beautiful beach. Summerville, I think it was called. We've been there as well." Andrew had been everywhere in the world. "Beautiful, wasn't it, Jocelyn?"

She smoothed down one side of her treated tresses. "Oh Andrew, do you remember? The restaurant?" She lifted her eyes to heaven. "Divine. Just divine."

She was the kind of person who used the word "divine."

"And not that much, given the luxuriousness of the place. We had a two-storey condo with a hot tub and barbecue looking right at the beach. The weekly rate was so reasonable." He named a price that was my whole holiday budget. I tried to keep my eyes from bugging out.

"What a great recommendation. I'll be sure to check it out online." *Hahaha.* Never.

The kids were trying not to laugh. Calvin was tapping away

on his phone. "Okay, if we want to go to the South Shore, we need to go to somewhere near Liverpool. Or Shelburne. Or somewhere in-between. That's where the beaches are."

"Thanks Calvin. I'll take a look and rent us something. Now put your phone away. No phones at the table."

He sheepishly tucked it into his back pocket. "Sorry, Mom."

I turned to Winchester. "Where exactly in Nova Scotia is your family from? I mean, where did you grow up?"

He was chowing down on the chicken, smiled, waited until he'd swallowed, and said, "We were from Port Mouton, but I grew up in the North End neighbourhood of Halifax."

My mother looked up. "North End? A black community. Am I right? And isn't there a community of black people outside of Halifax?"

I interrupted. "Do your parents still live there?" I directed my question to Winchester and ignored my mother. Not nice, and a trick I learned from my father, but I didn't want her travelling down a racist road at my dining-room table. A quick glance at her reassured me that she hadn't even noticed she'd been sidestepped. The joys of the MacFarland family.

"Sure. Maggie and I could stay with them when we get there."

"How are they with dogs? Would Lucky be welcome?"

"No problem at all. We always had a dog. My mother's allergic, so a hypoallergenic dog like Lucky would be fine. We always had poodles."

"Yappy things," said my mother. She was being so social today. I wish she'd keep her mouth shut in that grim line she usually wore. Meanwhile, my father and Bert were lost in their own little worlds.

The table was cleared of the main course and the strawberries were ladled out. Finally, everyone left in a flurry of excitement, chatting enthusiastically about the summer adventure. I stood at the door and watched Andrew take my mother's arm as she hobbled down the porch stairs. He could be nice. My father was gripping the banister and following slowly, deliberately placing one foot in front of the other, as if he were walking on ice.

Ralph and I were doing the dishes, or rather, he was doing them and I was clearing up. "So," I called to him as I was sweeping crumbs from the blanket box into my hand, "what do you think?"

"About what?' He called back.

"About my family?"

"Early days yet."

So, I was right. We were weird. He just didn't want to say so.

"Do you like them?"

"Your kids are great. Open and fun."

"And my parents?" I said as I walked into the kitchen carrying empty wineglasses.

"Well...."

I put the glasses on the counter beside him, and he loaded them into the dishwasher. "They're a different generation with different values," he said.

"I know, I know," I sighed. "Not the most enlightened."

He turned around and gave me a hug. "Don't worry about it, Robin. I know who *you* are. You're nothing like them."

"I didn't treat my mother that well tonight. Just like my father."

"She had to be stopped before she really put her foot in her mouth. You accomplished that. So really Robin, don't worry about it. They might be your parents, but you've made a kinder path in your life than they ever did. Andrew on the other hand? And that Jocelyn? They're more like your parents."

I could feel the tension seeping out of my body as he enveloped me in his arms. "You're right," I said, "But I hope Maggie and Winchester are going to be okay."

"They will be." He let go of me and started using a metal scratch pad on the curry pot.

"Thanks, Ralph."

"It's the least I could do." He scrubbed harder at a stubborn burnt bit on the bottom of the pot. He'd been right—the curry had needed stirring. "This pot is a mess. But I'll get it. Great dinner, by the way."

"No, I meant for supporting me with my family. I really appreciate it."

"Do you think your kids like me?"

"Are you kidding? Of course they do, Ralphie."

"Don't call me 'Ralphie.'"

I laughed. "So, do you think a holiday with them will be okay?"

"Let's see if I can get the time off. How long did you want to go?"

"I know the kids are all talking a week, but I have five weeks holiday this year. I've used up two—you know, one last January after Christmas and I want to take one off this December before the holiday season. So I could take up to three off. What about you?'

"I think I could take three. Maybe we could fly out, spend a week with the kids, tootle around the province for a week, and then drive slowly back with Lucky in a rented car."

"Lucky doesn't know how lucky he is. Everyone's vacation plans revolve around him."

As if on cue, Lucky started barking at me, tail wagging. I looked at Ralph and said by way of an explanation, "He always gets a treat after dinner."

Ralph wiped his hands on a tea towel. He was finished with the dishes. "We better not forget his treats, then."

I threw Lucky a biscuit and asked Ralph, "Do you like that plan? Three weeks off and split up that way?"

"I think it would be wonderful, Robin. I would love to do that. It sounds like a great holiday in a place with a slower pace of life. I could use some downtime. I need a break from what's going on in Toronto."

The police department had been under fire for the rapid rise in the murder rate. "I personally don't think all the criticism is fair, Ralph. First of all, our population is far larger than the last statistic almost twenty years ago, so really the rate is down. And secondly, ten percent of the murders happened all at once with a mentally ill man driving into a crowd. That has never happened before. So that skewed the figures."

"But still, numbers are numbers, and the public is worried."

"I know," I said, sighing. "I know."

"Anyway," he said, cheering himself up, "A fun time in Nova Scotia would be just the ticket."

It was going to be a perfect holiday away from the cottage. I was so happy that my dignity had been preserved because I hadn't had to admit that the murder of Darlene Gibson had knocked me sideways and that my love for my own cottage had been poisoned by a headless torso.

"Yes," Ralph said, "it's going to be a really relaxing holiday."

If we only knew.

4.

SHIRLEY PAYNE, MY HIGHLY SEXED EDITOR, was perched on the edge of my desk—as she was fond of doing—and tapping the plastic top of my computer monitor with a blood-red manicured talon. *Tap tap tap*. So irritating. The sound wasn't quite as bad as nails on a blackboard, but it was close. Her legs were tightly crossed, making her red pencil skirt ride up high on her thigh, exposing way too much toned flesh. I knew she wasn't younger than I was, so how did she accomplish that smooth skin? My thighs looked like bubble wrap.

The males in the room had their heads down, but moments before, I had seen their widened eyes surreptitiously travelling down her thigh to the foot that she'd been slowly swinging back and forth. Each time she did this, the thin gold chain around her ankle flashed in the overhead fluorescent lighting. Her spike-heeled fuck-me pump swayed in the air. The shoe was an exact match to the skirt. All this showing off wasn't for the boys at their desks, oh no. She kept admiring her shapely ankle and gazing at the open door of Doug Ascot's office, Cindy's boss. The two editors had a sizzling on-again, off-again, relationship that kept everyone guessing.

But Doug wasn't playing the mating game today and had swivelled his chair around so his back was to the door. The bald spot on the top of his head shimmered in the light, and the pen in his right hand rapped on his mouse pad. He had a hard job as Crime Editor, plus there was Shirley. He was no doubt seeking solace from the magnificent view of the lake below him. The vista was spectacular. Tiny triangles of white sails floated across the vast lake below the office building. He was gabbing on his phone. All the clues added up. His relationship with the Life Editor was off-again.

"So, vacation days," Shirley was saying, just a little annoyed as she glanced at Doug's back. "You want the last week of August and the first two of September? Three weeks?" *Tap tap tap* on the plastic edge along the top of my monitor. It sounded like a parrot scraping away at a cuttlebone. She was thinking.

"My family thought we'd go to Nova Scotia, and apparently that's the best time of year, weather-wise. Lots of sun. We were thinking a beach holiday." I hated begging.

"A beach holiday. For three weeks." *Tap, tap, tap*. "Pretty long holiday."

"I get five weeks a year now." I really hated begging.

"And Cindy is going to be away then, too. You going with her?"

I almost said "God, no," but muttered, "No. As I said, it's a family holiday."

"I don't know. I just don't know. It'll be sort of empty around here with the two of you gone. Doug has already given Cindy permission to take off the same three weeks that you want. With the two of you gone, who's going to be writing articles for the paper?"

Oh, for heaven's sake. It wasn't as if the two of us were the backbone of the paper. "Well, there's Derrick, something is always happening in the football world." I wanted to add, "Something to do with pigskin and balls. You know, him being a pig with no balls." But, of course, I didn't. "Plus, there's your investigative reporters. Maybe they're working on something that will break at the end of the summer. Karen is good at digging stuff up. And Stanley has lots of contacts. Informants."

I knew I was scraping the barrel here. The end of summer was about the only time of year when there was absolutely no news. In August, the paper was filled with the topics I wrote about: putting ponds away for the fall, planting bulbs, cleaning out gutters. Shirley would miss me. That's why I had to resort to begging.

She slid off my desk, patting down the straw nest on top of her head that had earned her the nickname "Hay Hair." Every time she slid off my desk, her legs made a farting noise on the Formica. And every time this happened, I did my best not to laugh my head off. I was so immature. I thought it was hilarious. I needed to grow up. I turned my head, pretending to scan the room for something interesting, hoping I wasn't squeaking.

She straightened out her skirt as if nothing had happened and tugged down her black satin blouse, rearranging the inadequate darts to sort of match up with her formidable chest. As she did this, she glanced again at Doug's open door. He was still looking at the view, his back to us, yapping on his phone. A spark of infuriation flared across her face. Definitely off-again.

She tried to hide her emotional reaction to Doug's rejection by twirling some hair in her finger. But I knew. Her fake eyelashes were doing jumping jacks every time she looked at the back of his chair. The plastic beads around her neck vibrated on her magnificent chest, beating out a salsa dance. She was beside herself.

"Okay," she said, "you can take all that time off, but only if you promise me that if anything, *anything* at all, happens out there that's the least bit newsworthy, you tell me. You write it up. As you know, news is dead in the summer, and I expect you to be a team player and a loyal employee by always being on the job, even on a holiday. Journalists don't sleep."

"Yes, Shirley." I rolled my eyes, forgetting that she could see me doing this in the reflection on my black computer screen.

"I mean it, Robin. Don't do that. It's unbecoming. Don't ever forget it's a long time to take off from a newspaper that's operating on bare bones in the summer." As she said "bones," she looked again at Doug.

"Yes, Shirley." I sounded as contrite as I could although I thought she was full of shit.

"Even if it's news far away from Toronto, there are a lot of people in this city who have Nova Scotian roots, or at least maritime ones, and they would be interested."

"Yes, Shirley." After all, she was right. Winchester came to mind.

"So, keep your eyes and ears open for anything that seems off to you. I don't know what issues they have down there, but I know ocean pollution is a hot button topic these days and so is lice in farmed fish. Plus, poverty and health care need attention down there. Not to mention the systemic racism." Shirley dug a pointed nail into her hair and wiggled it around on her scalp. There was a scraping sound. I felt my stomach lurch.

"Yes, Shirley. I'll pay attention to what's going on."

"And you'll write it up. After all, it is a *paid* vacation."

"Yes, Shirley." Geezus. I was getting fed up with all this yes-man stuff.

"Okay. Good. I'm glad we got that settled."

Doug was finally off the phone and Shirley sashayed over to his office, shoulders swaying as she walked. On-again? It was hard to keep up with these two.

As soon as her back was turned and her perfume of eau de cigarette smoke had faded away, I texted Ralph. *Got the last week of August and the first two of September off. You?*

Ralph replied immediately. I guessed he was at his desk. *I had to finagle a bit, but it's looking like a go. I'm just waiting for the higher-ups to sign off.*

Fantastic. *Great! Do you want me to order your plane ticket while I'm booking the others?*

Yup. I'll email you the money. Love you.

I felt my ears burn. I wished he'd stop saying that shit. I sent him a thumbs-up emoji and immediately felt guilty, but it was the best I could do.

I counted on my fingers how many tickets I had to buy. Calvin, Bertie, Evelyn, me, and Ralph. Winchester and Maggie would be driving. So, just five. Ralph and I needed one-way tickets because we would be driving home. I logged on to the Air Canada website hoping my credit card wouldn't self-destruct in billowing smoke. Wow! There was a seat sale. I couldn't believe the deal I got. Maybe the new cheaper airlines were giving Air Canada a run for its money. Whatever the reason for the low prices, there was now some budget left over for eating out. Fish and chips! Lobster! Local wine! Blueberry pie! I couldn't wait. This trip was going to be great.

I texted the kids that I'd bought their tickets for the last week in August plus Labour Day Weekend, to return the Monday night, for a total of ten days. Anyone who had to change their flights could do so easily, and I would pay for the change. Tonight, when I got home, I would search the web for a great place to stay on the South Shore. In the meantime, I had to get back to my thrilling article on peonies and ants.

I was deep into the article, describing the symbiotic relationship ants have with the nectar peonies secrete, and giving hot tips on how to get ants off the blooms if you wanted to bring them into the house, when Cindy grabbed my rib cage with two hands. I was so used to her trying to shock me that I was no longer reactive. I lazily spun my chair around.

"Hiya. What have you been up to?"

"What? I didn't scare you? Not even a little?"

"Old hat, Cindy."

"What are you working on?" She leaned over my shoulder, trying to read what I had been writing. Her breasts pressed against the side of my neck. I was used to that too.

"Stop it." I leaned forward, away from her body.

She leaned forward, pressing harder, and laughed, reading my article. "'If you turn a bloom upside down and immerse it in water, the ants come off.' So thrilling."

"Cindy." I hadn't used my warning voice since the kids had left home. She took the hint and backed her breasts away. With a *harrumph,* she folded her almost six-foot frame into her chair beside me. The air *whooshed* out of the plastic-covered seat. Cindy was a big woman.

I said, "So ... what's up?"

"The usual. Shootings. Knives. Snapped off bottle necks used as weapons." Cindy looked over at her boss's office door, which was now shut. "And I'm guessing, Doug Ascot."

"I think they're on-again. They had a rough few minutes there while I was talking to Hay Hair about my vacation days."

Cindy's eyes widened with interest. "Oh? Did you get what you wanted?"

"Last week of August, first two of September."

"Hey, that's fantastic. Same as me. What flight are you on?"

I told her while hoping we were on different flights. We weren't.

"Holy smokes!" Cindy clapped her hands together. "Maybe we can take a limo together to the airport."

Maybe not. "I'll be travelling with Ralph and three of my kids. The taxi will be stuffed as it is."

I tried to let her down gently. No way would she be having a holiday with her family. Cindy's kids were a little angry at her because she had divorced their dad, and then, outrageously, came out as gay. Their attitude was so unfair. He was the one who'd had an affair, not her. She'd been loyal to a fault. He was a dentist who'd developed a keen interest in his hygienist's mouth. He'd also treated Cindy badly for years, and the kids thought that was the norm and followed in his footsteps. I'd had the same problem with Trevor. He'd been dismissive and degrading to me as well, but I had made a great effort to tackle the kid's attitudes and have them treat me with kindness and respect. The number of times I'd had to say to them, "I expect to be treated with kindness and respect at all times" could fill a book.

"You're going with your family?" Cindy was trying to sound upbeat, but the corner of her mouth twitched down.

At first, I didn't reply and just patted her arm. Cindy was lonely. She hadn't been able to find an intimate partner in her age group for the past three years. Plus, her two best friends were busy. Diane Chu, our mutual friend, was taking off to Vancouver for an extended stay to take care of her mother. So now, without her kids around and me with Ralph, she was often at loose ends. I felt badly for her and wanted her to know that I understood. But I didn't feel badly enough to be dishonest and downplay my pleasure of travelling with my kids and Ralph. I wasn't going to crow about it, but I wasn't going to hide it either.

I replied, "We always have a family holiday at the end of the summer. It's our tradition."

"Three weeks of tradition?" She was looking at me sideways, half-focused on her screen.

"Oh, no. The kids will be there for just the first ten days, and then Ralph and I will drive around the province a bit for a week, maybe go up to Cape Breton, and then take a week driving home."

The silence stretched between us. Cindy rolled her chair back to her computer and turned it on with one of her very long fingers. Everything about Cindy was long. Except, of course, her hair, which was short, red, and curly. Right now, her head was bent over her keys. I knew she was upset, but what could I do, short of inviting her to spend some time with us? I wouldn't mind that much, but Ralph? He had trouble with Cindy. That was putting it mildly. She was just too, just too, well, she was just too much for him.

On the other hand, what would it hurt to have a dinner with her or to offer to meet up in Cape Breton for a hike or something? Ralph was going to have to get used to the idea that she and I were good friends, most of the time. I'd have to talk to him about that. Kindness and respect. My theme song.

Cindy's back was hunched as she tapped at her keyboard. Finally, breaking the tension, she said, "Sounds like fun."

She sounded so sad. I took a chance. Ralph would have to lump it. I couldn't bear the thought of my friend being sad and lonely. "Maybe we could meet up in Cape Breton for a hike. A picnic. A kayak."

Did I really say that? God forbid. I'd never fit into a bloody kayak. I tried to imagine it: Me lifting rolls of flab and tucking them under the fibreglass shell while ocean waves slurped at the side, sucking me under, rendering me unable to extricate myself from the boat when it turned turtle. Forever stuck upside down, my body trapped, waiting for sharks to smell blood. This was not a pretty picture.

"That's okay," she sniffed. Her voice sounded as if a boa constrictor had wrapped around her neck.

Before I could reply, reassuring her that it was a heartfelt invitation, she suddenly got up and strode to the glass doors of the office, yanked one open, and hightailed it left. She was going to the washroom. Derrick, the sports writer, leered after her and waited for me to follow as I always did during one of our tiffs. At that very second, Shirley flounced out of Doug's office, lipstick smeared, skirt twisted, two blouse buttons undone. She was heading over to my desk.

"No sign of Cindy yet? She's pretty late." She glanced at her watch and then tapped it.

I couldn't tell her that Cindy had arrived and was already in the washroom. Shirley would guess that Cindy was upset and that just wouldn't do. We couldn't show any sign of weakness to the head honchos. "Must have got stuck in traffic. So much construction on Jarvis these days."

"She comes down University."

Right. My bad. "Well, there's traffic everywhere. "

"You don't have to cover for her, you know."

I did too. She was my friend. My upset friend. I stood up. "I'm going to get some coffee. Want some?"

"Sure. Thanks. Not that I need it." She threw back her head and made a sound like a flock of Canada geese taking off. She was laughing. "I'm hot already." She tossed me a conspiratorial look. "Men."

Yeah, right. Men-o-pause. "Be right back. Double cream, no sugar?"

"Already sweet," she honked. She licked her finger, touched her hip, and made a sizzling sound. "Hot with sugar."

Geezus. I hurried past Derrick's desk and turned left to the washroom. As I pushed open the steel door I heard, rather than saw, Cindy. Oh God. She was sobbing. My tall brave friend was crying her heart out. My chest ached. What could I do? She was sitting on the edge of the day bed in the small room before the cubicles, her head in her hands, red curls escaping through her fingers. I grabbed a box of Kleenex off the shelf in front of the mirror and sat down beside her. I put an arm around her shoulders and crooned, "I'm so, so sorry about everything. It will be okay. Really it will."

What "it" was I wasn't completely sure.

"I'm just so tired of doing everything on my own," she said, sniffling. "It's wearing me down. First my husband. Now my kids."

"And now me," I said softly. "You feel abandoned by everyone."

"It's not your fault, Robin. I want you to have a nice time. You deserve a kind man like Ralph. You deserve your wonderful kids. It's not your fault."

Her heart was breaking and she was trying to reassure me? "I feel badly nonetheless." And I did. I felt so awful that she was crying. I had never seen her cry. Mad? Yes. Plenty of times. But crying? Never. It was really upsetting me.

"I know how it is, Cindy. I know how brave you are, chasing after people with guns. Showing up at crime scenes, seeing awful, awful things. You've made such a name for yourself and you are so good at your job."

I was rambling a bit. I didn't know what to say to make her feel better. She leaned into me and took a shuddering breath. I stroked her head as gently as I could. It was like patting a poodle that had been licking an electric socket.

I continued, "We are such good friends. I love you from the bottom of my heart. Please, please join up with Ralph and me in Nova Scotia."

Oh no. What was I doing?

"But what about Ralph? I know he doesn't like me."

"Ralph will just have to get used to the idea that you and I are really good friends. And I think he'll like you once he gets to know you a bit better. It's just because you're a journalist."

"But so are you. And he clearly likes you."

I snorted. "I write about feathers and petals and kittens. You write about people killing each other, the fentanyl crisis, war lords. You are a crime writer and he's a cop. Of course, the two of you will tussle. But that's because of your jobs. Maybe on holiday you will get along."

Probably not. Only a few months ago, at my cottage, they were at each other's throats. I thought about it. But that wasn't true all the time. In fact, I could remember a few times where they actually talked to each other without raising their voices. Maybe it would be okay. "Please join us? The kids are leaving on Labour Day. You could join us after they're gone. Travel around. I would really like that."

"Really?"

No, not really. "Absolutely. We will have fun. You could tour around the province with us for a week. Our details aren't settled about destinations, but we could coordinate. You could even drive home with us. If you wanted to. If you can change your airplane ticket."

How did I go from a hike in Cape Breton to a week or two? I needed better boundaries. But I felt so badly for her.

"Really?"

"Please?"

"Oh Robin, that's so kind of you."

"I'm not being kind. I would really enjoy your company." It was a begging kind of day.

"Oh. Thank you. Okay. I will. Thank you."

"No, thank you."

Ralph was going to flip.

5.

CINDY AND I WERE SURGING THROUGH the desks on the editorial floor to our stations when Derrick hissed at me. "Hey Chicky, where's your boss's coffee?"

Christ. I'd forgotten. "Mind your own damn business, Derrick." This was a knee-jerk reaction, but still, I would never be grateful to that dickface. I grabbed Cindy's arm, turned on my heel, and dragged her back out the glass doors to the elevator. I could hear Derrick snickering behind me.

"Coffee for Shirley," I explained to her as I marched her to the elevator doors. "I told her I was going for coffee when really I wanted to follow you to the can."

"I could use something hot," she said, pulling her arm into her chest so my hand touched her you-know-what.

She laughed as I elbowed her in the ribs. "Hey, get yours from someone else."

We struck poses in front of the polished steel funhouse mirrors in the elevator for three floors. I was fat. I was thin. I was tall. Cindy was short. Cindy was fat. Cindy was thin. It was our morning exercises.

In the cafeteria, we joined the daily ten o'clock lineup. Of course, we had arrived when everyone wanted coffee and a muffin. As we shuffled past the cash register, I saw Alison Trent, the paper's researcher, sitting at a booth. Her beaded dreadlocks clacked as she forked in a piece of blueberry pie. I wanted it.

"Hey, Alison. How are you? Any summer plans?" Her pie looked delicious. Why hadn't I got some?

She held up a forkful. "Want some?"

Cindy laughed. She knew me better than that. She knew I would never share a fork. Never. Cindy bent over, stuck out her tongue, and slurped up the morsel. She looked at me while she fake-chewed long after it was gone. "Delicious."

Alison blithely continued eating. Was there something wrong with me? I never shared a fork, not even with Ralph, who I kissed on the mouth. My mind briefly wandered to that maple syrup dripping down his chin.

"*You* got any summer plans?" Alison was looking at me, deflecting my question. She liked to be mysterious, that girl.

I hauled my thoughts into the present, away from Ralph's lips. "Ah yes. Cindy and I are heading out to Nova Scotia for the last week in August and the first two in September."

"South Shore? Or Port Hood? Melmerby?"

I was surprised. Did she know the province? "South Shore. Do you know Nova Scotia?"

"Not really. But the South Shore has had a drought the past three summers. By August, everyone's wells are dry." She chomped away on her pie. Flakes of pastry flew off her fork and dotted the tabletop. I resisted picking them up with a wet fingertip and putting them in my mouth, which was watering.

"I didn't know that." I'd have to make sure I rented a place with a nice deep well.

"Yup."

Cindy was impatiently tugging me towards the elevator. I said, "Thanks for the info, Alison. Got to get this coffee to Shirley." I held up one of the cups in my hand to make my point.

Alison waved and said, "Systemic racism," to our retreating backs.

What? As we stood in front of the elevator, I whispered to Cindy, "What was that about? 'Systemic racism?' Shirley just said the same thing to me."

Cindy shrugged as she contorted her body in front of the polished steel. I laughed at her attempts.

"You'll never be short Cindy."

Cindy meandered through the labyrinth of desks to her work station, and I trotted over to Shirley's office with the coffees. As I got closer, I could smell the stench of cigarette smoke seeping under her door. Who did she think she was fooling? There had been a ban on smoking in public places for over a decade and yet Shirley persisted with various sprays and plug-ins, hoping to mask the smell, which never worked. When I got to the door, I put one of the coffee cups I was holding on the floor so I could knock.

"Come in." Her voice sounded like the underwater burble of a diesel boat engine.

I turned the knob and stifled a grunt as I bent over to pick up the coffee from the floor. I really needed to lose some weight. I pushed the door open with my shoulder and breathed shallowly in the smoke-filled room. She had stubbed the cigarette out on the metal side of her garbage can. A piece of paper in the can was smouldering, the edges glowing red. As I was registering "fire" in my brain, it burst into flames. I watched it with fascination. As it licked the paper beside it, I suddenly realized this could be a catastrophe. Hands shaking, I put down one cup of coffee on a stack of files, peeled the lid off the other, and threw coffee on the blaze, dousing it.

Shirley looked at me with amusement. This had obviously happened many times before. "I told you I was hot. And sweet. I'm assuming you threw *your* coffee on the fire, not mine." She held out her fist for the cup. I dumbly handed it to her and quickly exited her office, shutting the door tightly behind me.

As I entered into the relatively fresh air of the office, I took a deep breath and scurried over to my desk. Derrick was laughing behind his hand, and Cindy had turned from her monitor and was giving me an exasperated look. I maintained as much dignity as I could, sat down, shook my mouse to bring my screen to life, and immersed myself in peonies and ants. This was not shaping up to be a good day. For hours and hours, I glanced at the office clock hundreds of times. There must have been something wrong with it.

The first thing I did when I finally got home was head straight for the fridge. I flung the door open amidst a clinking of bottles and pulled out the super-sized one I wanted. A perky Pinot Grigio from the Niagara region. I could have kissed it. I grabbed a tumbler from the cupboard and smelled the sweet liquid as it poured from the bottle into the eight-ounce glass. I was going to have a party. All by myself. Oh, and with Lucky, who was prancing around my feet, and then running to the kitchen door. Of course. Silly me. He needed to go out. I downed several large slurps as I opened the back door for him and licked the spillover off my hand. Lucky raced for the herb garden, lifted his leg on the basil, which I made a note to feed to my brother Andrew, and then cantered, head held high, back into the kitchen.

"Such a good boy. Did you water the peesil?" I tossed back a few more gulps and laughed at my joke. "Peesil? Get it, Lucky? So funny." I bent over and stroked his head. Lucky just stared at me. "What? Why are you looking at me like that? I know I like my wine, but what a day. Peonies and ants." Another slurp. "I ask you Lucky, what sort of career is this? Peonies and ants? Geez, you'd drink too."

Lucky barked.

"Okay, so maybe you wouldn't. But I would." Lucky barked again. "You think I should stop? Well guess what?" I did a sloppy pirouette, holding my glass out as I swung around in an oblique circle, only spilling a little. "As fun as it is, I think I should stop too." With that, I placed one foot deliberately in front of the other, opened my purse that I had tossed onto the kitchen counter, and scrabbled around until I found my cell. "Watch this." Lucky obliged. I held it in front of my face, squinted, straightened out my arms, squinted some more until the letters came into focus, scrolled down a bit, and punched a number. Sally Josper. My naturopath.

I got her answering machine. "Sally," I shouted, my volume knob turned up by wine on an empty stomach. "I still have that pesky little problem we were talking about." I hoped I was pronouncing my words correctly. "Time for it to go. Do you have an appointment available this week sometime?" I winked at Lucky. I was proving that I could do it. "Send me a text and I'll confirm back."

"There, see Lucky? I'll stop. One day. In the meantime, what should I eat?" He ran to the cupboard and wagged his tail. "You want your kibble?" I poured him a bowl and then opened the fridge door.

"I'm really hungry. M-m-m-m. Eggs. Right. I'll make an omelette. A gooey cheese omelette with salad on the side. A nice light meal. Lucky, you're not listening to me." Lucky was rooting around in his bowl for the bits of kibble he liked. "And after dinner, I'm going to rent us a cottage. On the South Shore of Nova Scotia, somewhere between Liverpool and Shelburne."

Lucky looked up briefly and then went back to his feast. I poured another glass of wine from my large but now half-empty bottle of Pinot Grigio and whisked two eggs, grated some cheese, diced some peppers, and mixed everything together in a bowl. While it was frying, I opened up a box of salad, stuck in my hand, and tossed a handful onto a plate. "Do you think I should wash the lettuce, Lucky? It says prewashed on the box. But still. *E. coli* and all that. I've heard some of the workers aren't screened for diseases. And you know how I feel about germs." I briefly wondered if I had washed my hands lately.

Lucky wagged his tail. He was a scintillating conversationalist. Plus, he always agreed with me. As I sat down to eat, I entered into my phone's search bar, *South Shore NS cottages to rent*. Oh look, only about five hundred hits. I sucked in some omelette and thought. I needed to refine my search. How many bedrooms did I need? I drank some wine to lubricate my brain cells. One for each kid, plus one for Ralph and me. Five. Probably not that many five-bedroom cottages for rent. That would narrow it done. I plugged in *Five bedrooms South Shore NS for rent.*

I laughed. I had a choice of two. One was in the town of Liverpool and the other was in a place called Hunt's Point. Both looked a little decrepit. Peeling paint and curling shingles. We had left it kind of late to book for the summer, so our pickings were slim. I soldiered on. I read the descriptions of both, quickly scrolled through pictures, thought about wells drying out versus town water, and the proximity of beaches versus close-by restaurants. I decided that the one in Hunt's Point was the better bet, despite it being on a well. It was available for the week we wanted and was described as a large salt box. I wasn't familiar with this style of architecture, but it looked like a large square box, painted white. I briefly wondered where the term "salt box" had come from.

I leaned forward to look at the photographs. Just how dilapidated was it? There were twenty images, both interior and exterior. One thing my career had taught me was how to assess a house from pictures. I paid attention to ceilings, looked for watermarks and saw no stains, meaning it wouldn't smell of mould. This was important to me, having asthma. Both bathrooms looked as if they were at least from this century, although I couldn't see a shower in either. The kitchen was large with a long, battered pine table running down the centre, surrounded by mismatched wooden chairs all painted different colours. The fridge and stove were avocado green, so from the seventies. Each bedroom had a double bed covered in a quilt, a braided rug beside the bed, curtains, and a painted chest of drawers. There were no closets anywhere. No one would accuse the house of being too fancy, but it looked clean enough, and had a certain wholesome charm.

There were only three exterior pictures. One showed the view from the back door off the kitchen. There was a small sliver of blue shining in the distance, running along the top of some fir trees. I guessed this was the ocean view the ad had crowed about. Ralph, at six feet, four inches, would have a better view than I would, at five feet, two inches. In the next year or two, the view would be lost behind the growing trees. Another photograph showed the yard. It was dotted with large rocks and random patches of daisies. The grass was cut and it looked as if someone had taken the time to trim around the rocks with a weed eater. No fence anywhere, meaning I would have to take Lucky out on a leash. I didn't really mind; I was used to doing that at my cottage in Huntsville, Ontario. The last picture was of a firepit in the middle of the yard. That would be fun. We could sing songs around a bonfire in the evenings if the mosquitoes weren't too bad.

I expanded the image of this last photograph by spreading my fingers and it looked like there was a rusty pipe sticking out of the ground beside the firepit. What on earth was that? I expanded the picture some more and saw that the pipe had some sort of gizmo on it. What could it be? I searched my mental Home and Garden database and decided it must be a pipe to a drilled well. So, it wasn't a dug well, which would likely have a flat cover on it of some sort. I knew that drilled wells, unlike dug wells, were usually very deep, meaning it probably wouldn't run out of water.

The house looked good enough. It wasn't a five-star hotel, not by any stretch of the imagination, but it had a quality about it that I liked. It seemed friendly. Despite my job, I didn't like granite countertops and stainless steel appliances. The avocado green appliances were pushing it, but at least the fridge and stove hadn't gone into a landfill and so obviously still worked. Besides, the house was close to a long, sand beach in a park called Summerville. Wait. Hadn't Andrew mentioned a fancy hotel with a good restaurant near Summerville Beach? I google-mapped the address and saw that it was, in fact, almost walking distance to that hotel. Well, if we wanted an upmarket meal, we could have one.

As I ate my omelette, I typed a one-fingered email to the owner of the house. I detailed the time period I wanted it, which just happened to be when it was being rented out, described my family, and asked if a smallish, cute, non-shedding dog was okay. I gave my phone number, address, Facebook link, and crossed my fingers as I tapped, "Send." If Lucky couldn't go, neither could we. The more I thought about this house in Hunt's Point, the more I wanted it. It had such a nice peaceful feel to it. I flipped through the pictures again. It was a true Nova Scotian house, clean, not renovated to the nines, with lots of real things in it. A well-used table to eat at. Durable braided rugs, probably made from rags that someone's children had eventually outgrown. It felt calm. Plus, the location was perfect—it was close to lots of beaches and high on a hill, away from rising ocean levels. Not that this would happen overnight, but one had to be prepared. I was such a worrywart. I took another slug of wine while I gazed at the main photo of the house. It was so handsome.

Suddenly, my phone rang. I jerked back and it flew out of my hands, skittered across the table, and slid to a stop just an inch before falling off. I reached for it before the fourth ring, hoping I'd catch the caller before it went to voice mail. It was an unknown number with a 902 area code. Nova Scotia! Wow, that was fast.

"Hello?" I tried to modulate my voice and enunciate my consonants. This drinking had to go. Sally Josper hadn't texted me back. Maybe she was away.

"Hi dear, just got your email. I understand you'd like to rent my house for ten days at the end of the summer?"

The woman sounded as if she were in her early seventies, and nice. Her accent wasn't the drawl that I expected from a local Nova Scotian. She did say "hoose" for "house," but that was my only clue she was born and bred in the province. "Is it still available?" I asked hopefully.

"Well, yes, it is. I just this morning decided to visit some relatives in New Brunswick for a few weeks and someone suggested I rent my home. The ad's been in for only a few hours. I've never done this before, so I'm being careful. It's important to me that I rent to the right people. Energy, you know. I need the right energy in the house. Nothing too jarring. It's for your family, you say?"

Energy, huh? I knew all about that from an article I wrote on feng shui last year. "Yes, I have a rather large family and your house seemed perfect for us. We need a peaceful place where we can play board games and sit by a bonfire, looking at stars." I hope I didn't sound too Pollyanna. "My kids are all working adults now, and we are looking for a place to wind down, for a week. We just want a quiet holiday, close to beaches." I wasn't lying, this was all true, although I felt like I was lying. Maybe I was trying too hard.

"It doesn't sound like you're a bunch of yahoos who would drink all night long and disturb the neighbours."

"Oh no, we aren't drinkers. Far from it." I stopped my hand in mid-air while it was reaching for my glass.

"Now tell me about this dog."

"Lucky."

"Why? Did it survive falling in a well or getting lost in the woods?"

"Oh no, we just like the name. Lucky. He's a cute little thing. Well-behaved, quiet. Non-shedding." I patted Lucky's ears with one hand as I was talking about him, hoping he wouldn't start yapping.

"Not a yapper? I had a dog that was a yapper that died about seven years ago, and my neighbour is only just talking to me now. So, I can't have a yapper."

I wrapped my fingers around Lucky's muzzle and gave him my sternest look. "Oh no, Lucky is a very quiet dog. Rarely barks." Now I was lying through my teeth.

"Well, you sound just fine. Send me an email transfer for half the rent and use the password 'house.'" *Hoose*. She gave me her email address.

"Oh, thank you very much. We will take good care of your home."

"I know you will, dear. And if you decide to rent it for longer, just let me know. I might want to stay some additional time at my daughter's."

We said our goodbyes, and I quickly sent her an email transfer. I nearly danced around the room. I couldn't believe it. My whole trip was coming together so easily. I was finishing off my omelette and glass of wine when my phone rang again. Ralph.

"Hi," he said. "I managed to officially get all that time off, so we are good to go."

"That's fantastic, Ralph. And I've just got off the phone with a very nice woman in Nova Scotia who's going to rent us her house."

"Oh?" He sounded a bit perturbed. "It's a done deal? You didn't send her money already, did you?"

"What? I shouldn't have?"

"I would have liked to vet her, you know, make sure you weren't being taken for a ride. But I guess I could do it now. What's the name?"

Good question. I had no idea. I dithered, "Oh don't worry, Ralphie. She's very nice and I'm sure it's all on the up and up." I was trying to lighten the situation up and buy some time.

"You didn't get her name?" He sounded incredulous. I needed to change the topic, and fast.

"Did you get some dinner?" Saved again by food. While I was trying to divert him, I put his call on speaker and shot off a new email to the mysterious woman in Nova Scotia, asking her name. God, I hoped I hadn't been scammed. Hopefully, she would answer as quickly as she did my initial query.

"Yes, I ordered some fried chicken from that new place on Parliament. Near you, actually. And don't try to change the subject."

My inbox pinged. I quickly read her email. "You're so suspicious. Her name is Nancy Littleton." I could hear his fingers tapping his computer keys.

"And where is this house?" He tapped again on his computer. "Hunt's Point? Or Yarmouth? There are two Nancy Littletons." His voice was clipped.

What was with him? His knickers were in a twist. "Hunt's Point. It's on the South Shore, near beaches. Why are you so crabby?"

"She seems okay. Not even a traffic violation."

I asked him again, "What's up?"

"I ran into Cindy, your friend, at a drug O.D. earlier tonight. As I was leaving she said, 'See you in Nova Scotia, big guy.'"

Oh no. I had wanted to break that news to him gently, couched in glowing terms, as I kissed him, and played with his willy-nilly. Just shit.

"Oh, it's nothing." I bent the truth. "She's going the same time we are, on the same flight. She'll be touring around Cape Breton for a week." I didn't add that she'd be joining us in the second week. That tidbit of trivia would wait until I had Ralph in hand, so to speak.

6.

SIX WEEKS LATER, WE WERE ALL STANDING in line at the Air Canada booth when I heard, "You whoo-o-o." Cindy. Her short red curls bounced as she jogged over to us. I gave her a hug while Ralph rolled his eyes.

"You made it," I said. "I was getting a little concerned."

"I wasn't," said Ralph.

Cindy ignored him and looked at the kids. "Where's Maggie? Getting something to eat?"

"No," I replied, "She and her boyfriend are driving down with Lucky. They left yesterday." I showed her my phone. "You can see where they are on my Find Friends app."

Cindy took the phone into her hand. "Wow, that's so cool. They're just passing Sackville, New Brunswick." She frowned thoughtfully. "But isn't that app an invasion of privacy?" And then she frowned again. "Well, I guess not if she allowed you to follow her."

"You can always turn the location finder off if you don't want people to know where you are."

"That's good feature. Especially if you're somewhere where you shouldn't be." She peered at the phone. "Oh look. You can actually see the car moving. This is so neat. Hey Robin, let's you and I do this. I'll download the app. What's the Wi-Fi password here?" It was a rhetorical question—everyone knew that airport Wi-Fi was unsecured.

Did I really want to share my location with Cindy? I guess

it could come in helpful. I did worry about her when she was out at crime scenes. Yeah, it seemed like a good idea. Even today, I could have seen where she was and not been worried she was going to miss her plane. And I could always turn my location off, if I wanted privacy. So, we tapped away on our phones as we shuffled to the check-in counter with our luggage.

A few hours and a smooth flight later, my family were all seated in a large red van that had been rented by Calvin on his credit card points. I tried not to pout when I shoehorned myself into the front seat beside Ralph. I didn't like being in a van. It was so suburban. Cindy had taken off to destinations unknown, although now I could have known them if I wanted to. I resisted the urge to spy on her with my Find Friends app. Ralph, our driver, found his way down one highway to Highway 103 West that followed the South Shore.

I was completely befuddled. Why were we travelling westerly when we were heading south? Calvin tried to explain it to me, but with, "Well, we *are* heading west. That's why."

"West? But don't we want to go south?"

"That's how the province works," he said, as if that would explain everything.

Finally, Ralph came to my rescue. He knew how my brain computed information, what my inner visual landmarks were. "Picture your keyboard. Nova Scotia is a forward slash from north to south. It's on a slant, so heading south is actually heading west."

"Oh," I said, turning around and giving a sideways look to Calvin sitting in a middle seat. "*Now* I get it."

He shrugged. Normally, he was such a happy-go-lucky sort of kid. Maybe he didn't like to travel. Bertie, on the other hand, was usually miserable, and yet, there he was, behind me, contentedly playing a game on his phone. Evelyn was napping on the other side of the van behind Ralph, her head leaning against a window and her mouth slightly open. Calvin saw me looking at her and pretended to jab her in the ribs. I fake-scowled at him and he laughed. My kids were so playful. That was more like my Calvin.

I turned back around and looked at Ralph. I was so lucky to be with such a kind man. And given that he was a cop, I was constantly amazed at how open-minded and flexible he was, except when he was driving. He never went a kilometre over the speed limit, which drove me nuts. I resolved to do most of the driving on the way home. In a proper car. Not a van.

We turned off Highway 103 just past the pretty town of Liverpool and took the Lighthouse Route the rest of the way to Hunt's Point. We travelled past a few wooden houses painted bright colours, a storage place, and tons of short spiky trees. At a sharp corner, Ralph slowed right down, obeying the twenty kilometre per hour sign, as we passed a billboard for a resort that had a golf course, not that anyone played golf. But I'd read it had a decent restaurant. Suddenly, there was ocean on our left and cottages sandwiched between the two-lane highway and seaweed-covered rocks. We finally reached Hunt's Point with its cute half-moon beach behind a seawall. We turned right on Maple Hill Road and arrived at what was going to be our home for the next ten days. I loved it at first sight.

The van crunched up the gravel driveway, and as we drew closer, I could see two cars parked in front of a sway-backed garage. One, an old Honda Accord, was Winchester's. They'd made good time, arriving just before us. But the other car? I had no idea. It was an old Toyota Corolla about the same vintage as my Nissan Sentra, but with more rust. Salty ocean air, I guessed. As we were unloading our bags from the back of the van, Lucky bounded out of the house and ran across the lawn to the car. I picked him up and threw an angry glance at the back door. Maggie knew better than to let Lucky out. The stupid dog did not always come when he was called. The last thing I needed after this long day of travelling to the other side of the country was chasing after a dog that was excited to be out of a car. My frayed nerves blistered as I slammed the van hatch down, one-handed. I was furious.

A very large woman waddled rapidly out of the house, waved, and called heartily, "Welcome, welcome. I hope you like the place." She swept her arm around her, encompassing the house and yard. "And that Lucky is the cutest dog ever. She bent over and snapped her fingers. "Come Lucky."

Lucky squirmed in my arms and jumped out, running to this stranger who then picked him up and laughed as Lucky licked her face. "No kisses, you silly thing," she said as she turned her cheek so Lucky could lick her some more.

I was flabbergasted. In just a few minutes, this rotund grandmother had trained my dog to come when called. My boiling temper simmered down as the woman jiggled over to me and gave me a big hug, squishing the dog between us. "So nice to meet you. I'm Nancy Littleton, but you can call me Nan." She turned her head as Ralph and the kids were trudging up the path, burdened with suitcases and shouted, "The kids can take the stairs up with their luggage. You, handsome man," she smiled at him when he turned around, "I'm assuming you and your wife will want the downstairs bedroom."

Ralph gave her a thumbs-up with his free hand as he entered the house and didn't correct her assumption. I looked the woman over, trying to gauge how open-minded she was. She hadn't said anything about Winchester and Maggie being together, so hopefully she wasn't racially prejudiced. And if she wasn't prejudiced, hopefully she was open-minded about unmarried couples sleeping together. One never knew in rural areas, and I didn't want to create bad feelings.

Nan peered at me through clear blue sailor's eyes, "Frankly, I don't care if you're married or not, but that neighbour of mine? Mr. Henshaw? He's a stickler for that kind of shit."

Ah! She swore. I was going to like this woman. "But what about Winchester?"

"Oh, nobody around *here* cares about *that*. A little further up the shore it's a different story. But here? There was a boatload of blacks dumped here, or actually in Port Mouton, three hundred years ago—*three hundred*—and lots of them have intermarried." She laughed merrily. "So many beautiful tawny children with green eyes."

She looked truly delighted. I was *really* going to like her.

Nan lowered her voice. "But homosexuals? Watch out. That Henshaw? Totally homophobic. He'd spit on one if he could. I hate the man, but have to be civil, you know what I mean? He's my neighbour."

I was worried about Cindy. "Are most people around here homophobic?"

"Oh God, no. There aren't enough of us to have a hate on anyone. Henshaw? He just doesn't care about community. He lives alone. Probably killed his wife," she said, laughing. "But most people couldn't care less. We have to get along." She patted Lucky behind his soft ears. "This is the finest little pup. But what am I thinking? Come in, come in. Let me show you and your partner around the house." She put Lucky down who stood quietly at her feet.

Was this my dog? Nancy Littleton was a magician.

She plodded up the path, and Lucky trotted obediently behind her. I felt a pang of jealousy. How had she trained him? The ground vibrated with her every step. This woman was a force.

Nan continued to chat while I meekly followed. "I'm off to New Brunswick to visit my daughter and grandchildren. Told her I'd be there later tonight. That I wanted to make sure you were settled."

"That was nice of you to wait to let us in." I panted, keeping up with her.

"Let you in? Not even I have a key to the house. I never lock it."

Really? "Aren't you afraid?"

"Of what?" Nan looked at me, her blue eyes wide with curiosity.

I shrugged. Good question. I was stumped.

Nan opened the door and said, "The stairs are straight ahead, as you can see." I looked up the flight and could see into a bathroom at the top. "There are four bedrooms up there, two on each side. Here, on your right, is the living room, and on your left is the dining room. Down this hallway..." Nan said over her shoulder as she took off past a pile of coat hooks on a long board, "is the kitchen. There is bathroom over here and beside it, through this short hall," she gestured, "is the downstairs bedroom."

As she was pointing down the short hallway, Ralph emerged from the bedroom, saw her, and held out his hand, "Nice to meet you. I'm Ralph Creston. You must be Nancy Littleton, the owner of this beautiful house."

I looked around at the mismatched chairs in the kitchen with their chipped paint and the ancient appliances. The bare light bulb in the ceiling with the upside-down lampshade on it. The missing bits of tiles on the floor. The plywood cupboards. The fake wood panelling. But the house had a feel to it, a quiet presence. It even smelled as if it were good. No doubt about it, I loved this house, and I was glad and somewhat amazed that he did too. Ralph lived in a steel-and-glass, granite counters, floor-to-ceiling windows kind of condo in downtown Toronto. I wasn't sure he would be comfortable in an old house. But here he was, smiling away at her and she? She was smiling back, head tilted to one side. Oh, my heavens. She was *flirting* with my boyfriend. And he was enjoying it. Somehow, it felt just fine.

Lucky sensed things were going well and chose at that moment to race around the table in circles, yapping away. The windows were wide open in the summer heat, and I was worried about Mr. Henshaw. Nan smiled indulgently at the dog, whose ears were flapping, and said quietly, "Now Lucky, no barking. We've had this conversation before."

The dog immediately stopped and looked at her, tongue hanging out, grinning all over his furry face. This really wasn't my dog. For years my family had shouted, "No barking" at Lucky, and he never once stopped. And now this woman quietly told him to be quiet and he was? She was a dog whisperer.

But Nan was continuing to talk. "The well for the house is a good one; in fact, a really good one. We haven't had any rain for six weeks, since the third week in July, so lots of people's wells are running dry." She probably sensed my alarm. Where was she going with this? Would our well run dry? "Now, don't worry. This well won't ever run dry. It's very, very deep and tapped into an underground stream. Clear and pure and cold. Don't worry about it at all. The only reason why I'm mentioning it is because every now and then you might hear the outside tap running. Neighbours coming to get a jug or two of drinking water. Now, I've told them to use the well in town while you're here—there's taps just past the fire hall on the road to Milton—but you know, old habits die hard, so you might hear the outside tap going."

"No problem," I said, although I wondered about complete strangers wandering up the hill to pilfer some water. "We're pretty flexible."

Ralph stifled a laugh. He knew just how flexible we both were. His cop ears were always on high alert. And ever since I'd been attacked by a murderer in my home just over a year ago, I was a trifle vigilant. But Nan didn't catch the lie, or chose to ignore it. She patted down her short hair, and said, "Well, that's about it. I'll be off now."

She looked around the kitchen. "Oh right. One last thing. I left on the table a list of things to do around here. I've written directions to some of the beaches, as you said you really wanted a beach holiday, and the weather looks good for that. Also, there are a few fairs where you can see chainsaw carving and horse pulls. There's a folk art show in Lunenberg coming up. People come from all over the Maritimes to see it. There are rides and performers at the Bridgewater Fair. It's usually lots of fun and kicks off with a parade. There's bingos to raise money in the Port Mouton Hall and, of course, lots of suppers. There are pie socials and bake sales as well." Food events? Now she was talking. She smiled at me, probably guessing my thoughts. "Anyway, there's a list on the table. If you get tired of the beaches, or if it rains, you can always find something to do."

I walked over to the list and picked it up. She had obviously spent some time researching and typing out the things. "That's so nice of you to do this. I'm sure we'll have a great holiday here. Thank you for everything." I could hear the kids upstairs opening and shutting drawers and calling out to each other. I knew we would have a wonderful holiday.

Nan walked over to me and gave me a big warm hug. "You have a nice time, dear. I've googled you, and I know you've had a rough go this spring. Bears and all." She let go of me and hurried down the hall to the front door. "Have a great time. I'm off." She waved jauntily in the air and left a wake of silence behind her. Lucky looked longingly at her retreating back.

Ralph rubbed his hands together. "I love this place, Robin. Everything about it is perfect. You found a real gem. We're going to have a great time." He wrapped me in his arms and began a slow dance around the kitchen table. Lucky ran around us, happily yapping.

"Lucky, no barking." He didn't stop. "Ralph. The kids. Don't. Stop." I could hear them banging around upstairs. I hooted as I was swung around, "Don't Ralph. The kids. Stop it."

He laughed and put his hand on my bum, pressing me closer. "Oh-h-h-h," he said in a falsetto voice. "Oh-h-h-h, don't ... stop. Don't stop." He laughed again, twirling me around while Lucky yapped.

"Ralph. Stop." He didn't and was nuzzling my neck. I gave up. "You are impossible." It was so good to be in his arms.

"Hey, Mom. Hi, Ralph."

Maggie was standing at the door. How long had she been there? What had she seen? We flew apart as if a bomb had gone off between us. "Hi Maggie," we said, in unison.

"What's this?" Maggie sauntered past us to the kitchen table and picked up the list of things to do that Nancy had left.

"Oh, it's a list of activities and places for us. Nan made it."

"She's great, isn't she? So good with Lucky. And I love how her house feels." With that, she walked over to a cupboard, got a glass, filled it with some water from the tap, and took a tentative sip. "So nice to drink water that doesn't taste like chlorine. Toronto tap water is very safe, but that chlorine taste has got to go." She drained the glass. When she was finished, she looked around for a dishwasher. "No dishwasher?"

"One of the main attractions of the house," I joked. "Now we have to do dishes together, like a family. Get those microbiomes juiced up."

"I don't mind," said Maggie, as she headed out of the kitchen. "And by the way Ralph," she teased as she called over her shoulder, "no means no."

He looked at me and made an embarrassed grimace. "She's right. Sorry. It won't happen again."

"Oh, Ralphie."

7.

THE NEXT WEEK WAS GLORIOUS. The sun beat down, the wind was calm, and the sand was soft and warm. We hung around on Summerville Beach from late morning to late afternoon, day after day, gorging on elaborate picnic lunches and periodically strolling the long, white sand beach. If no one was around, and I had a pocket of dog treats, I would let Lucky off his leash to run. And he did. Almost every time I called him, he came back. That Nan Littleton had somehow ingrained in my disobedient dog the benefits of returning to a person. If he didn't come, I just had to shout, 'Wanna a treat?' and he hightailed it back to me.

Wearing a bathing suit had its challenges. Despite my lofty goals of losing some weight—that never happened—I always wanted a treat too. *Haha.* But I tried to minimize the situation, despite Ralph's opinion of me having more to love. I did my best to hold my head up proudly in my all-black, hopefully slimming, suit with its ruffled skirt that concealed an issue at the top of my thighs. When I sat down in my beach chair, I artistically draped my towel across my belly, making sure it covered what I tried to pass off as a wine stain on my leg, which was actually a spider vein. I would plonk Lucky on my lap, hopefully hiding the rolls of the personal bakery that was my stomach and that specialized in muffin tops. With all the nubile creatures around cavorting on the beach with their long gazelle-like legs, I tried not to feel embarrassed by my thickening body. I tried to place myself beside other over fifty women, who were all, it seemed, dealing with the same alarming events tossed our way by time.

Ralph, on the other hand, his paunch hanging out over the edge of his bathing suit, didn't give a shit. Every now and then he looked at me, his eyes travelling down the length of my body, his smile lascivious. When I caught him doing this, I would pull the towel around me tighter and fake-frown at him, causing him to laugh and put the book he was reading on his lap while waggling his eyebrows at me. The two of us lazed in beach chairs while the kids flopped like beached whales around us on their towels. It was all so good. I could feel myself unwinding in the soft ocean breezes.

Evelyn, always the curious one, had discovered that the water flowing out of Broad River at one end of the beach warmed the icy sea water up enough that swimming was possible for longer than a few minutes. Calvin, the adventurous one, saw some kids leaping off a railway trestle running above the river and decided to give it a try. The locals warned him to only jump off at high tide, when the water below the bridge was deep enough to prevent his feet from hitting the sand below, breaking his back. The things we learned about tides. I wasn't that enamoured with the idea of my kids hurtling through the air into water that might be a smidgen too shallow, but they were having a gas, and I just looked out at the horizon and pretended it wasn't happening.

After our seventh night of eating delicious fish and chips and huge seafood platters at a local restaurant in Port Mouton, we sat around the campfire outside the house, drinking hot chocolate, roasting marshmallows, and singing away as Ralph played his guitar. The roaring blaze shot sparks into the air and our voices lifted as we sang some old folk songs like "Four Strong Winds," and "Leaving on a Jet Plane." Everyone's face had a rosy glow from the day's sunshine and the fire's flames. I looked around at my lovely family, and I knew we were all finally rested and in holiday mode. Even Bertie was smiling and teasing his sisters. But I knew that boredom might soon seep in. I myself needed a change of scene. I also needed a drink. Why hadn't I slipped a little hooch into my hot chocolate? What went with hot chocolate? Certainly not wine. Maybe Bailey's. I decided I'd get some from the liquor store outlet beside the Port Mouton restaurant.

I tossed an idea out to the crowd, "How do you feel about doing a few of the things that were on Nan's list? I mean, we've been here a full week. It's Labour Day weekend, and we haven't really done anything but eat and sleep and swim."

"Yeah, it's been perfect," Bertie said, laughing.

"Like what?" asked Maggie, the ever-practical daughter, leaning forward, her mouth full of marshmallow. Winchester, beside her, was looking at me expectantly.

I had the list with me as I had anticipating this discussion. I pulled it out of the back pocket of my jeans and with the light of my phone's flashlight, I silently read. When I got to the local suppers, I stopped at a lobster dinner that was being held in Liverpool at the fire hall. Nan had starred the dinner with an asterisk and written in pen beside the typed entry: "Always a big success. Huge Labour Day fundraiser for the fire hall. Well-attended."

I read Nan's addendum to the group and said, "This looks good. It's tomorrow night. Saturday." I checked out the cost before Evelyn started worrying. "And it's reasonable too. My treat. Want to go?"

Ralph stopped strumming on his guitar and said into the ensuing silence, "Sure. Sounds like fun. I love lobster. But let me cover it. I'd like to treat everyone."

Bertie spoke up, "Well, that's nice of you Ralph. I think it sounds good. Let's do it."

If even Bertie was up for it, then I knew the rest of the kids would want to go. I was right. The vote was unanimous.

Suddenly, Lucky lunged at his leash towards the edge of

the property, barking ferociously. "What is it little Lucky? A squirrel?"

I peered into the dark but could only barely make out the silhouette of some bushes. Suddenly, they parted and in the gloom I could see a very little but wiry man in short sleeves and jeans stomping over to us, thwacking on a newspaper in his hand as he approached. Long white hair fell in oily strands over his high forehead and a yellowed mustache hung over thin lips tightened into an angry slash. Was this the notoriously crabby Mr. Henshaw? Ralph and I stood up simultaneously.

Ralph took three giant steps away from the fire towards the man and held out his hand. "Ralph Creston. How can I help you?" He was making an effort to sound pleasant, but I could tell he was pissed at the intrusion.

"Henshaw." He slapped the paper into Ralph's outstretched hand and sputtered. "Read this." His face warped into a feral scowl that in the firelight made him look evil. White bushy eyebrows glowered over slits for eyes and he spat out venomously, "You stupid people. There's a fire ban. No rain for weeks and weeks. What do you think you're doing, putting us all at risk? You people from Ontario think you're the centre of the universe." His voice scraped against my skin like barbed wire. He was bouncing forward on his toes, as if wanting to get in a punch.

Ralph held up his palms in a placating gesture. He lowered his voice to almost a whisper. Slapped a friendly smile on his face. These were de-escalating techniques he had learned from the police force's sensitivity training classes.

"I am very aware of the fire ban, Mr. Henshaw, sir. The ban is only for daytime burning. And we've got three buckets of water here." He pointed to the buckets standing to the side of the fire, the flames reflecting in the shimmering surface of the water. "We will put the fire out when we go back into the house. No one is at any risk. You don't need to worry."

But Mr. Henshaw was not be placated, despite Ralph's calming efforts. Henshaw yelled into the night as he turned his back and marched away, his spine stiff with anger, "I'll report you to the authorities. First thing tomorrow. I have contacts, you know."

Lucky barked madly at his retreating figure, his yips high and piercing. Oh God. What would Nan say if I aggravated her neighbour with my barking dog? I loved it here and was already planning on coming back. I tugged at the leash, trying to reel Lucky in. Mr. Henshaw suddenly stopped mid-stride, turned on his heel, marched back, and aimed a kick at the dog. He missed by a mile, but the intention was there. The kids were frozen to their seats as they witnessed this act of violence against a defenceless little dog. I was paralyzed with the shock of it. How dare he?

Ralph took four long strides and caught up to Mr. Henshaw, grabbing him by the elbow and propelling him through the gap in the bushes. Henshaw's feet barely touched the ground as he was escorted off the property. From the other side of the bush I heard the words "barking" and "police" and "bylaws" in Henshaw's vicious growl. Next, Ralph's low voice floated over the foliage, and I wondered what he was saying to the obnoxious little prick.

When Ralph returned, he was wiping his hands together as if trying to rid himself of poison. He sat down, placed his guitar on his lap, and started picking at the chords for "Stairway to Heaven." We all relaxed and started humming along as the fire died down into glowing embers. After a while, the kids started drifting off to bed, finally leaving just Ralph and me warming our hands over the coals in the cool August night.

Ralph looked at me. "He won't be bothering us again. Or Nan Littleton."

Oh? How had he accomplished that? "What did you say to him?"

As Ralph smiled, I could see the creases around his eyes crinkle in the fading light of the fire. "I just talked about community spirit and being kind to others. About letting people simply be. To control urges to harm. To always be pleasant. Don't worry. He'll be better behaved from now on."

That was it? That was all he did? Yeah, right. "You showed him your badge, didn't you? You told him you'd take him in if you ever heard a bad word about him or from him ever again. Am I right?"

Ralph beamed innocently. I was right.

We threw water on the remaining coals and watched the steam curl into the dark sky. As we walked hand in hand over the dew-dampened grass into the house, I knew I would have trouble falling asleep. I don't do well with confrontation. Plus, I needed a drink. A whole day without a drop was not my idea of a holiday. That wholesome hot chocolate shit had to go. Ralph put the newspaper on the kitchen table and went down the short hallway into the bedroom. "You coming?"

Not yet. Maybe in the morning. Although frankly, I hated morning sex. Smelly breath, gritty eyes, needing the bathroom. This was not a winning combination for me. Now sounded better. But I needed a drink. Oh Robin, you'd think you were a sex-starved party-crazy fifteen-year-old.

I eyed a bottle of wine on the kitchen counter. Ah ha! The glistening red fluid was beckoning to me. Should I go to bed? I thought about my chilled skin being warmed up by Ralph's cozy body. Then I thought about my insides being warmed up by a nice glass or two of wine. I paid attention to how I felt. I was jangled. That event with Mr. Henshaw had upset me. Poor Lucky. I needed a drink or three.

"No, I'm going to stay up and..." I thought quickly and eyed the paper on the table. Rescued. "...I'm going to read the paper."

"Okay. Well, I'm bushed." I heard the bed springs squeak as he climbed in. "Night." His head landed on the pillow with a soft whoosh.

I settled Lucky into his crate in the corner of the kitchen, reassuring him that he was safe from the bad rat-faced man, and then tiptoed to the wine on the counter and grabbed a tumbler from the cupboard. I lifted a neon pink chair out from under the table as quietly as I could, sat down, and poured myself half a glass. Who was I kidding? I'd have the other half shortly. I held the glass to the light, admired the deep shimmering red, and took the largest gulp I could. It slid down my throat like a slow lazy river and started a comforting heat in my belly. I slouched backwards in the chair, tilted my head back, shut my eyes against the single light bulb dangling from the ceiling. I sighed deeply. This was more like it.

"Mom? You okay?"

I snapped my head forward and sat upright in my chair. Oh, it was Calvin. Geezus.

"Oh hi, honeybun. Just catching up on the local news."

He stood in the doorway to the kitchen, his hair tousled, his pyjama bottoms hanging around his hips, and his feet bare. "Oh, I thought you were sleeping." He was looking at me, head tilted as he looked at the almost gone glass of wine.

At least he didn't say he thought I was passed out drunk. I shook out the paper and quickly glanced at the headline. "No, just thinking about what I'd read. It seems fish farms are destroying the oceans." I read the article quickly—speed-reading a skill I had mastered from my job. "In fact, in particular, the farms are affecting the lobster industry." I was pretty sure I wasn't garbling my words. "There was a study. When the farm in Port Mouton is functioning, the catch is down significantly. The females aren't reproducing at the same rate either. It has something to do with the odour from the plumes generated from the food. And the antibiotics."

He padded over to the tap. "I came down for a drink of water. All that sunbathing makes me parched." He drank thirstily from a glass and then washed it. Well-trained, that boy.

"I know what you mean." I took a dainty sip of wine to illustrate the point.

He looked at me, eyebrows raised. I wasn't fooling him.

This drinking thing had been going on for six years now. Ever since Trevor had been hit by that stupid drunk driver. The fact that the driver was now in jail for vehicular manslaughter and a host of other charges didn't help. Of course, the kids were aware of my love affair with wine. I often wondered about the long-term impacts. Would they be typical adult children of an alcoholic? Vacuuming at four in the morning? Lining glasses up in their kitchen cupboards in order of size? Rearranging book shelves alphabetically? Trying to maintain order in their worlds that had become an unsafe chaos? Sally Josper had told me all about the harm I was doing to my children. It didn't stop me.

"It's good to relax, Mom." Calvin was smiling at me, his lopsided grin warming my heart.

With these few words, my eldest son had let me know that he knew what the wine was about and that he accepted the situation for what it was. I was one lucky mom. "Thanks, sweetie. I hope you have a good sleep."

"You too, Mom," he said as he climbed up the stairs to his bedroom.

After I heard his bedroom door shut, I refilled my glass, slugged back more wine, and took a deep breath. The one yoga class I went to years ago had emphasized that deep breathing could be very cleansing. I had stopped going to the classes because my yoga pants had split up the back during one of the positions, which I had renamed, "the downward hog." Now, I was leaving all animal poses to Lucky. I took another cleansing breath. I was trying to cleanse the snake of anxiety that was hissing in my ears. Maybe I needed to wash it out. Yes, that's what I needed to do. I took another huge gulp of wine, swirled it around my mouth, swished it between my teeth, enjoyed the foam I'd created, and finally swallowed. There, cleansed.

I was so ridiculous. Now that the snake of anxiety was gone, I listened for a bit to the wind peacefully rustling the leaves outside, took another gulp, and refilled my glass. Again. I was starting to have fun. I'd been so good all week, only having a glass or maybe two with dinner. It wouldn't hurt to go backwards for one night.

I reached for the paper and was mindlessly flipping through it when I spotted a big ad for the lobster supper at the fire hall tomorrow night. There was a line of photographs of the local figures who were going to attend. I glanced at them briefly, my eyes blurring. It started at five o'clock, and there was a little map showing exactly where it was. Being a little tipsy, I tried several times to expand the map by spreading my fingers on the paper before I clued in that this only worked on electronic devices. Silly me.

I read the ad copy and it looked fantastic. Apparently, all sorts of bigwigs were going to be there. The recently elected Member of the Legislative Assembly, the Mayor of Liverpool, the owner of the new cannabis grow site, a couple of environmental people from Dalhousie University, the director of Liverpool hospital, the scientist who had done the study on Port Mouton fish farm's effect on the lobster industry, and surprisingly, the owner of the fish farm. I spent a little time trying to match the names to the photographs but was only semi-successful. Well, well. Wasn't that an interesting kettle of fish. I then cross-referenced the names with the ones in the front-page article and saw they were pretty much the same. Small-town politics.

Below the ad for the lobster supper was a lithograph print of a black man holding a smoking musket. It was advertising The Black Loyalist Heritage Centre on the South Shore, in a place called Birchtown, near the town of Shelburne, and looked interesting. I wondered if Winchester would like to go to it. He'd said his family was from Port Mouton. Maybe some of his relatives would be featured in the Loyalist Centre. I took out my phone and googled the location. It was close enough to get to in half an hour or so—we could go and be tourists if the weather became a little unsettled.

I pulled Nan's list from my jean's pocket and saw the Centre was on it. Good, now I wouldn't have to find a pen and add it to the list. I put her recommendations on the table, stared at the newspaper's front page, watching the words dance around. My mind wandered around in circles. What did I know about lobsters? They moved backwards and were caught in traps. Not much. I'd learn more at the dinner. Finally, I finished up the bottle and felt like I could fall asleep.

I stumbled up off my rickety neon pink chair, lifted it carefully back under the table, tidied up the newspaper, and toddled across the kitchen with the empty wine bottle. I put it in the recycling bin under the window. When it clinked against another bottle in the garbage, I put my finger to my lips and shushed it. Yup, drunk again. I was definitely moving backwards, just like a lobster into a trap.

8.

THE NEXT DAY DAWNED BRIGHT AND CLEAR, again. Another beach day. Ralph and I were sitting at the kitchen table in companionable silence while we ate our oatmeal and fruit. Sun filtered through the wavy glass in the wooden-framed windows, casting shimmering shadows on the table. I snuck little peeks at him as I savoured my breakfast. What a guy. How lucky was I to have found such a decent man? Someone who treated me well, someone who listened and valued what I said. Someone who didn't dismiss my point of view. Someone who took good care with all things pertaining to me. Someone who was so good, so morally aligned with my positions on things that bugged me. Someone who made perfect oatmeal.

How had this happened? I wondered why I was so astonished. Did I truly believe I deserved to be treated like I was a subhuman, or a piece of shit? Was it because of my father or brother or mother? Had I been programmed to accept being treated badly? Was it in my DNA to be emotionally beaten up? Why did I drink so mucht? Was this in my DNA as well? Was it baggage from my past? I could puzzle about this forever, but it was all too much for me at this hour of the day. I was nursing a small hangover. Maybe when I got back to Toronto I'd talk to Sally, my naturopath, about all this. She'd been away when I called her for help. I had to stop the melancholic thoughts, and just eat my breakfast.

Be in the present, Robin. I was sitting at a lovely harvest table across from a great guy who treated me like spun gold. I savoured the maple syrup on the oatmeal and made hand shadows in the sunlight on the table. Ralph looked up from his breakfast and smiled at me. My heart melted. I was so lucky.

"The kids are flying back on Monday."

"Mmm-hmm. What time?" Ralph was talking with his mouth full. Nobody's perfect.

"Later in the day. Around dinnertime."

"Maggie and Winchester?"

"Leaving very early Monday morning. They're going to arrive in Toronto around midnight."

"That's a long drive." Now he was slurping the dregs from the bottom of his bowl. God.

Winchester had assured me it was just a seventeen-hour drive, if you set your cruise at one hundred and thirty. I told him to hide that information from Ralph and to keep a watchful eye out while zipping through Quebec.

"I'd like to do something different tomorrow. Kick up our heels a bit."

"Sounds good." Now he was licking his fingers after buttering his toast.

I checked the weather app on my phone and saw that some rain was predicted to blow in Sunday morning, so at least the dinner tonight wouldn't be affected. Maybe we could head down during the rainy weather to the Black Loyalist Heritage Centre in Birchtown on Sunday and check it out. We really had gone nowhere, just the beach and a few local places with a couple of trips to Liverpool thrown in for food shops, and I found that a bit embarrassing.

"There's some rain coming tomorrow. Maybe we could go down to that Heritage Centre in Birchtown."

"Sure, if you like."

"I could stay here in this peaceful house for another week. At least. That would be so lovely." I had no idea I had been so wound up and it felt so good to unravel a bit. That pesky snake of anxiety had faded into the background.

"Yeah, me too. But it's good to get out and do stuff."

My phone dinged. A text? Or an email? Oh, it was Nan Littleton. She was asking how our week had gone and giving a few instructions on closing the place up—she was going to stay at her daughter's a bit longer. Really? Now there was a temptation.

"Who's texting you?" Ralph was talking, now with his mouth full of toast.

"Nan, the owner. She's staying away for another week. I know we had plans to travel around Nova Scotia and then to mosey on back to Ontario, but how do you feel about staying here for another week? I could use a bit more beach time."

"With Cindy?"

I'd almost forgotten about her coming.

He was picking something out of his teeth. "I don't know about that. Travelling with her and staying in different rooms is one thing. But having her with us all the time...?" He shrugged.

Oh right. I hadn't thought about the logistics of staying here with her. He didn't look pleased. "You got along okay at the cottage in the spring."

"No, we didn't."

"Maybe it will be better?"

"It won't."

He was teasing, sort of.

I was certainly getting some pushback, and I didn't want to argue. That would be a fast way to wreck a beautiful day. "Okay, no problem. I'll text Nan back saying we will make sure the place is perfect before we leave. We can all can travel around, as planned."

"I didn't say that's what I wanted. I'd like to stay here for another week as well. I've had a great time. It's good to unwind, and I could do more of it. I think both of us lead very busy lives and doing nothing much is a good thing to do."

I was confused. He'd changed his mind? "But what about Cindy?"

He shrugged and took a sip of his coffee. "You're very good friends. I will try harder to get along with her. She has her good points. If I get too bugged by her, I'll just go for a walk. Hardly a hardship in the most beautiful place on earth."

"Oh Ralph." I knew what he was sacrificing for me. "You are such a kind person. Thank you for accommodating my family and my friend."

He looked up from his last square of toast. "I really want you to be happy. I love you, Robin."

I gurgled.

He laughed. "What? Acid reflux?"

"Okay, I'll text Nan back and ask if we can stay another week, just the two of us. And Lucky."

"And Cindy," he added.

"Right. And Cindy. So, three of us."

As I was texting, Bertie entered the kitchen and stretched while looking out the window. "Another crappy day," he said and laughed, scratching at some itch. "I can't wait to get to the beach. Some local kids told us about this great place to swim called the Bear Hole. It's just up the river after the bridge."

"Bare hole?" The name conjured up all kinds of images—none of them good. "You have to skinny-dip there?" I looked at my phone waiting for Nan's reply.

"Mom. No, 'bear' as in the animal. Not 'bare' as in naked."

"Oh, that makes me feel better. You're going to swim where bears swim. Great. I'm a bit nervous of bears after last spring."

He ignored me. "What's for breakfast?"

"It's a make-it-yourself breakfast. Grab what you want." I pointed at the fridge with my spoon. My phone dinged, and I read the incoming text. I held my phone up to Ralph's eye level so he could read the good news. We could stay for another week at half the cost as there were just the three of us. That was so nice of her.

One by one, the kids filed into the kitchen and sat at the table, eating heartily. Ralph announced he would take Lucky out for a pee, and I threw things out of the fridge onto the table to make lunches. An hour later, we all piled into the car and drove to Summerville Beach for our last family day on the soft white sand. When we got there, I let my eyes rest on the far line of the ocean, and every now and then, took a deep breath, clearing my Ontario life and work out of my body and mind. It was such a gorgeous day that I was tempted to swim in Bear Hole but quickly changed my mind when I looked down and saw parchment-like skin wrinkling around my knees. Best not to shock the beachcombers.

That night we stuffed ourselves into the van and headed to the lobster supper in the town of Liverpool. Highway 103 was virtually empty—only one car headed in the opposite direction—and I thanked the very kind Canadian government for providing me personally with such a great road. Ralph was driving and I was the navigator, following the directions of the little blue line on my Google map. We turned off at the first exit to the town and almost immediately took a sharp left on Old Port Mouton Road. We cruised down a long hill, past a church, a government building, what looked like a brand-new school, and some pretty houses that dotted the side of the road.

A well-tended cute bungalow on the left was particularly stunning with its raft of orange Canada lilies waving slowly in the soft summer breeze. A nice-looking middle-aged man was mowing the grass, and his energetic wife was knee-deep in a rock garden lining the ditch in front of their house, enthusiastically pulling out weeds. They probably started working outside in the cooler evening after the heat of the day. Both were bronzed a golden brown, and no doubt were enjoying their retirement sitting on beach chairs during the day. I didn't recognize them from Summerville Beach, so they likely had a secret beach that only the locals knew about. She looked up at the sound of our car and lifted her hand in greeting as we passed by. People sure were friendly around here.

There was quite a tricky corner at the bottom of the hill—a three-way intersection—and then another odd corner. At the second one, although there wasn't a stop sign, Ralph stopped anyway. No one honked as we figured out which way to turn. Again, I marvelled at the kindness of the people. I could live here forever, I thought, as I flashed back to the noisy ongoing construction in Toronto and the bad-tempered drivers who impatiently leaned on their horns as soon as a light turned green. We took a left and the fire hall showed up on the right side of the street. We had arrived.

Ralph cruised past the low cement building looking for parking. From the passenger window, I saw that the concrete pad in front and the parking lot to the side of the three-bayed garage housing the fire engines had been cordoned off with a rope of jaunty, multi-coloured flags that flapped in the breeze. There was an opening on the far side where a man in a red-plaid flannel shirt sat behind a grey metal box on a desk. I guessed this was where we paid for the dinner. Inside the boundary of flags were twenty or so long tables covered in plastic tablecloths that had been secured by silver pegs at the corners. There was a plate of sliced lemons on each table, big bowls of salad, baskets of buns, beer mugs filled with silverware, and jugs of ice-cold water, condensation dripping down the sides. Plastic bibs in front of each place setting were weighted down from the breeze with lobster cracking tools. Local kids ran out of the fire hall carrying plates of bright red lobsters that they plonked down in front of chairs. We were a bit late, and I glanced around for a parking spot. My mouth was watering.

One of the tables was extra long and ran in front of the garage. I could see a bunch of people milling around that table and heard loud guffaws through my open car window. It sounded like the goofy noise politicians made when they were in a crowd. This, I guessed, was a head table. I wondered if there were going to be speeches. After reading the paper last night, I had gotten the sense that the fish farm in Port Mouton was a contentious issue. I recognized from the newspaper photograph, the owner of all the local fish farms. He was slapping backs and hee-hawing with anyone and everyone. I didn't like him on sight. He reminded me of my brother—an arrogant and pretentious prick who thought he was above everyone else

We parked the van at the first place we came to about half a kilometre up the road behind a shiny black Dodge Ram and slowly walked back to the supper past more late model vehicles. The car dealerships in Liverpool and the next large town along the highway, Bridgewater, must have a heyday at the end of lobster season. Looked to me like a great deal of fishing income was spent on fancy cars. Obviously, with my ancient rust bucket, I did not adhere to those priorities. Though, a sporty pearl-grey Miata caught my eye as I walked along the highway shoulder to the fire hall. Maybe that's what I should get next. I tried the image on. Me, the feisty feminist in a sports car, versus me, the middle-aged soccer mom in a cranky crate. Which was it, Robin? You could mix and match, right? Right! I could be the zingy feminist in an old clunker. Of course, I could.

We stood at the end of a long line at the opening in the roped-off area. I worried for a moment that we wouldn't get to sit together, but then I saw that the table in front of the head table was wide open. Perhaps people were shying away from the big shots or perhaps from the owner of the fish farms. What was his name, anyway? I tried to dredge it up from the murk of my brain but had no luck. That sure was fun drinking all that wine last night. Too bad it had erased my neurons.

The line finally inched along, and Ralph cavalierly paid for our tickets. I quickly corralled everyone to the empty table right in front of the head table. I met with some resistance from Evelyn who felt we would have a better time as a family away from the hoi polloi, and God forbid, speeches. But no back seat for me. I wanted to see the head honchos of the town close-up. I wanted to hear everything they had to say.

Maybe I had been away from my job too long. Maybe three weeks holiday was a bit much. But no doubt about it, my curiosity was piqued. What an interesting crowd. What on earth could go wrong? Or, more to the point, right?

Comfortable in my seat, I zeroed in on the owner of the farms. Statten. That was his name. Frank Statten. Tall and thin with a runner's build, he was a good head above everyone else, making it easy to follow his almost white-blonde hair as he worked the crowd. I watched him hobnobbing with the MLA of Queens County, an earnest-looking black woman in her early forties. I wondered if she was a descendant of the Black Empire Loyalists. Apparently, she had won the election in a landside and was very popular even a year after her appointment. The mayor of Liverpool, a short round man wearing leather sandals, and whose picture had also been in the advertisement, kept dodging her if she happened to wander his way. I wondered what his issue with her was about. Something political I assumed.

On the other hand, Statten kept touching her arm as he followed her around like a puppy. She kept yanking her arm away from him, back to her body. When he didn't give up his overtures, she finally clasped her hands behind her back, whereupon he dropped his eyes to her now more visible breasts. He looked up and smiled at her. She shook her head. God, what an asswipe. The MLA periodically looked around, probably hoping desperately that someone would rescue her from this primate.

It wasn't going to be the mayor, who was hovering next to an energetic thin woman who had pressed her lips tightly together as she glanced at Statten. She, I remembered from the advertisement in the paper, was the author of the study about the negative impact of fish farms on the lobster industry. Anger vibrated off her whole body whenever she looked at him. Behind these two was an older rangy fellow wearing cords and a ratty sweater. I figured him for the representative of the environmental studies program at Dalhousie University in Halifax. He was jabbering his academic nonsense to whom I guessed was a young student doing his best to appear interested.

The ancient chairperson of the hospital in Liverpool leaned on his cane behind this unlikely duo and was engaged in a conversation with the young CEO of the cannabis grow operation, Weedlot. I guessed it was a pun on "woodlot," something many around here harvested for their wood stoves. They were no doubt arguing about the addictive qualities of weed. The CEO's voice buzzed like a chainsaw over the older man's. He was angry about something.

Definitely an eclectic group of people with an interesting dynamic between them.

One by one, everyone in the crowd sat down while the smiling volunteers continued with carrying out plates of steaming lobsters. They were all such a nice bunch of kids, polite and respectful, wearing white aprons and chef's hats on their heads, hurrying to get the food on the table before it cooled.

I recognized one of the waiters. Who could forget this beautiful boy of about fourteen? He'd been our server at the restaurant in Port Mouton. He had shining blue-green eyes, light brown skin, and dusty brown curls that escaped from his cap. He made a point of placing a nice fat lobster in front of the MLA. It was certainly larger than any other lobster around by at least a pound, maybe two. I wondered briefly if she was his mother. She must have had him early in her life if she were.

Statten had manoeuvered his way so that he was sitting next to her, smiling like a shark. In front of him was a scrawny lobster, a one-pound canner it looked like, and he eyed it with a grimace. I had a bird's-eye view of his exchange with his neighbour. He was pointing at his feeble excuse for a dinner and comparing it with hers. She, embarrassed, offered to trade plates with him. He, pretending to be polite, held up his hands. No, he was implying, you keep your juicy lobster. She, impatient, with no time for this sort of game, just grabbed his plate and exchanged it with hers, slapping it on the table. I inwardly rolled my eyes. Politics.

In this pantomime, it was quickly revealed that he had the greedy personality of a conniving and manipulative capitalist pig. She, on the other hand, appeared to be a diplomatic politician. The beautiful young boy walked by carrying two plates of lobster and saw immediately what had happened. He whisked the small lobster away from the MLA and replaced it with a larger one, although nowhere near the size of what was now Statten's. The small lobster ended up in front of the scientist, who was a thin brittle woman who probably only ever ate lettuce and likely didn't want or care about the size of her lobster. When she looked at her plate, her mouth puckered like a cat's ass.

I inspected the dishes placed in front of my family. We had all received good-sized lobsters, although it was hard to tell Maggie's and Winchester's, as they had already been torn apart. Everyone was soon sucking out the soft white meat from the claws and digging away with their various tools. I dipped every morsel into the bowl of butter in front of my plate. God, I loved butter. Who needed lobster? I controlled my urge to pick up the bowl and siphon off a mouthful.

Halfway through the meal there was a clinking of a spoon on a glass and everyone looked at the head table. Slurping noises subsided and lobster tools thunked on to the tables. The mayor was standing up and gesturing for quiet. He was a squat unattractive man, fleshy and sweaty. He reminded me of Toronto's old mayor, the crack cocaine king. This guy had the same furtive look, the same entitled white man attitude. His jowls shook as he cleared his throat. What was this jerk's name?

"I'd like to thank everyone for coming here today to help raise money for the new MRI machine at the hospital. This cheque," he waved a pale blue cheque in the air, "represents the advance sales of tickets. We still have today's admission tickets to calculate. Dr. MacKenzie," the mayor held out his palm to the director of the hospital, "could you please come forward to receive the cheque for just over eight thousand dollars?"

Everyone clapped as Dr. MacKenzie shuffled around the table and took the cheque from the mayor in his left hand while shaking the mayor's hand with his right. Their smiles were pasted on and aimed to a back corner of the patio. I turned my head and saw a young woman standing at the far reaches of the cement pad, near the rope of flags, holding a camera. I guessed she was a reporter from the local paper, *The Breaker*.

"Thank you, Mr. Bradley, Dave," Dr. MacKenzie said to the mayor. "Every little bit helps."

Right. The mayor's name was Dave Bradley. I made a mental note.

I briefly wondered if I should be documenting this scene for *The Express*. But then I saw Calvin was filming the whole thing on his phone. If Shirley wanted, I could snip a still from his footage. But why would she want it? No one in Toronto would be interested in a lobster supper two thousand kilometres away. I sat back and relaxed.

Frank Statten pushed out his chair and stood up, unannounced by the mayor, and smiled at the crowd like he owned the floor. "And I will match every penny that was donated today," he crowed.

He haughtily nodded his head at his own achievement, a cheque in his hand, and marched around the table to where the mayor and the hospital director stood. Statten extended his left hand across the table and handed this cheque to the hospital director.

Dr. MacKenzie received the cheque in his left hand as before and shook Statten's hand with his right. Given the tight choreography, it was my guess the doctor and Mr. Statten had done this dance many times before. Maybe that's why he wasn't dead. So many people hated what he was doing to the ocean, but did they hate him enough to kill him? Well not if he was giving them money. I was so cynical. The chairperson and Mr. Statten both smiled toothily at the photographer from *The Breaker* while their hands were clasped together.

After the photo op, the doctor sat down and Mr. Statten stood his ground in front of the crowd. He interlocked his sinewy fingers in front of his non-existent belly, which frankly made me look twice, and rocked back and forth on his heels.

"It is my great pleasure to help the people on the South Shore of Nova Scotia. I have spent all of my adult life, up until this very moment, and hopefully for years to come, employing the good people in Queens County and feeding the nation with my fish. It has given me great pleasure to be instrumental in first funding the hospital's new wing, and now, helping to supply it with the equipment it needs."

The MLA was beaming at him. What the hell? She supported him? But as soon as I witnessed her grin, she wiped the smile from her face and looked around guiltily.

I looked at Ralph. He tilted his head and I could see his hand under the table giving the man a one-fingered salute. He hated fish farms as much as I did. The thin scientist at the far end of the head table was clenching her jaw so tightly I thought her fillings might crack. The Dalhousie scientists were ramrod straight, seemingly paralyzed as they stared at this man who was destroying the beautiful ocean. The younger one's leg was bouncing up and down under the table. But there were some people in the crowd who clapped. Their livelihoods depended on this man's entrepreneurial adventure into fish farming, and they wanted him to know how pleased they were with his efforts.

I watched the MLA carefully. It looked to me as if she was now doing her best to appear neutral. She'd wiped the broad smile off her face and replaced it with a thoughtful frown. She no doubt knew how bad fish farms were for the environment, but she also knew people needed jobs.

Statten continued to sway on his heels, and I saw he was gripping the edge of the table in front of him. The phrase, "dizzy with success," popped into my mind. I looked at Ralph with raised eyebrows and tilted my head at Statten. What was happening? Ralph looked back at me and then focused on the fish farmer. I watched his eyebrows knit together. Statten's hands were stiffening up, and his face seemed frozen in a grimace.

Beads of sweat formed on Statten's brow as he opened his mouth and tried to speak. "Than yeh fu..."

I watched in fascination. He was having trouble formulating his words. It was as if his mouth was paralyzed. Was the man having a stroke? Surely not. He was tall and thin like an athlete. But these looked like stroke symptoms to me. I had read up on them because of my ancient parents. Suddenly, Statten pitched forward onto the table and hurled semi-digested pink lobster pieces all over the plastic tablecloth. The crowd gasped. This was awful. The vomit ran in rivulets over the edge of the table and splattered onto the cement pad. As I looked under the table to survey the progress of the barf, I saw his right knee collapse and then his left. With a clatter of lobster tools and water glasses, he tumbled to the ground.

9.

THE SOUR STENCH OF VOMIT HUNG OVER the crowd. Everyone was momentarily shocked into silence. I could see Mr. Statten lying on the ground under the table in a tangled heap between the chair legs of the mayor and the MLA. I squinted my eyes to see what the fallen man was doing, if anything. His hair was matted in chunks of his own vomit, and I could feel bile rising in my chest. When the kids were little and spewing at the slightest stomach upset, I often spewed along with them. I averted my eyes and saw Ralph pushing his way through the crowd to the fallen man. The smell wafted all around me. I turned my head away, trying to find a pocket of fresh air. I was pretty close to tossing my lobster and swallowed twice.

As I looked to the right, I saw that Calvin, at the end of our table, was holding his phone up and taping everything. Hopefully, he had been taking a video of the whole dinner, including Statten's speech, and had caught the actual fall. But because he was at the end of the table and not directly in front, I knew he couldn't capture what was going on under the table.

I pulled out my phone, aimed it downwards, and started filming. It didn't look to me like Statten was breathing at all, but then maybe he was breathing shallowly. It was hard to tell. I didn't know why I felt it was important to get all this documented, but I did. Maybe it was journalistic instinct or something.

By now, Ralph had reached him, and I saw his strong hand reach down to feel the side of Statten's neck. Taking a pulse? He removed his hand, and when I followed it up above the table he was punching into his phone. Probably 911. So, the guy wasn't dead? Some strokes were so severe, the person died immediately. Despite what I thought about fish farms, I hoped this wasn't the case. Nonetheless, he'd have a long road to recovery from what was clearly a very bad stroke.

I looked around the head table to gauge everyone's reactions to the sudden collapse of the owner of the fish farm. I was shocked to see that the scrawny scientist had a pleased look on her face. Really? She was happy that a human being had been taken seriously ill? I aimed my camera at her to video the look. Beside her, the Dalhousie scientists were gaping, horrified. The mayor was loosening his tie from his fleshy neck. The MLA was breathing rapidly and searching the crowd, probably looking for her son. Or at least who I thought was her son. Ralph bent over again, and I filmed him rechecking Statten's pulse. When he looked up, he caught my eye and gave his head a small shake. Whatever sign of life that he had felt before was now gone.

Mr. Statten was dead.

A siren was wailing in the distance and coming closer. It crossed my mind that the ambulance for the dead man had probably been paid for by him. So ironic. At the same time, a stocky fellow rushed out of the fire station carrying a defibrillator. He pushed through the crowd and slid on his knees to the man's head. Ralph bent down and spoke into his ear. The man stood up, wires dangling from the open casing of the defibrillator, and walked slowly back into the station. Dead was dead.

Two paramedics leapt out of the ambulance and dodged under the flag-covered rope with their own defibrillator. The crowd parted as they forced their way to Mr. Statten. Tossing chairs aside, they knelt beside his head and began working on him. They were mandated to try and save a life until that life was officially pronounced gone. Mr. Statten's corpse bucked with each electric shock. I almost threw up again, with every morsel of my being screaming to leave the poor man alone. The female kept zapping his heart while the male gave him artificial respiration.

The mayor cupped his hands and called out a name over the sound of a second siren approaching the fire hall. I think he shouted for Dr. MacKenzie. The director of the hospital, who had been seated almost at the end of the table and was now behind a group of onlookers leaning on his cane, started to make his way forward.

I looked back down under the table and watched the impotent rescue effort. With every jolting arch of Statten's back, I gulped down bile. Even though he was using a barrier device how could the paramedic put his mouth on a mouth flecked with bits of vomit? But I pointed my camera under the table and kept filming the action.

Ralph stood over the two paramedics, his arms spread out, keeping people from crowding the situation. Dr. MacKenzie tapped him on the shoulder with his cane, probably harder than he needed to, and Ralph turned around angrily. But when he saw who it was, he stepped aside to let the old man get through to the fallen man on the ground. Again, I aimed under the table and filmed Dr. MacKenzie painfully getting down on his knees and then touching the victim's throat and then wrist. He touched his throat again. He then laid his hand on the arm of the female paramedic as she was gearing up for another zap and shook his head. There was no point. Mr. Statten was dead. She could stop now that it was official.

I dropped my hand so the phone was now at my side. The audio feature was still on, but there was now no need to actually film. Audio taping would do just fine. What happened from now on was really neither here nor there.

The far-off siren was now blaring in our ears, and what I assumed was a police car screeched to a halt in front of the fire hall. When I looked more closely, I saw it was a ghost car, the word "Police" barely discernible on the side doors, a painted holograph. A very young female cop slammed the car door with authority, strutted to the rope, ducked sharply underneath it, and began clearing the cement pad of all attendees of the supper. Like a sheep dog, she herded the crowd to the exit. Her right arm rotated in a wide circle, stopping briefly at the gap in the rope before continuing on its circle, her left hand steadily pointed to the exit, her meaning clear. The party was over. Fixed on her face was a permanent frown that she probably thought made her look powerful, but in reality turned her into a sourpuss. She didn't fool me for a second. I knew her type, and so did Ralph. A bully. He looked at me and rolled his eyes.

People stumbled around overturned chairs and headed to the exit, leaving behind them half-eaten lobsters and scattered crumbs of bread on the tables. Their plastic aprons rustled in the breeze as they walked to their cars. I signalled to my kids that they were to remain. We had seen, up close, the whole crisis. We were witnesses.

The rookie now stood with her feet spread by the opening in the rope, circling her arm and indicating the exit with her knife-like hand. She was unsmiling and determined with this most serious duty. There was no need for her behaviour. People were very upset—some of them were crying. Watching Statten die had been a terrible thing to see. Her lack of compassion was astonishing, and I thought she'd do well to sit in on a seminar in Nichiren Buddhism about the benefits of treating others with care and dignity. Sure, Statten was disliked and had caused a great deal of harm, but he was a human being with a Buddha nature, deep down. I tried to convince myself of this.

Soon everyone had left, except a few of us, including my family, the head table, some random servers, the paramedics, and Ralph. The cop marched over to our table, her mouth a jagged slash, her eyes little piss holes in the snow. I knew what was coming and braced myself.

"You are to leave," she commanded, her hand chopping the air and pointing to the exit.

To my credit I didn't say, "Says who," but simply looked at her. I didn't bother smiling. I sensed the kids behind me were waiting to see what would happen next. Although I appeared to be a somewhat frumpy middle-aged woman, a timid flower, they knew I had some cactus spikes. They had all been impaled on one over the years. Consequently, they had developed a sixth sense of when the spikes would poke through my petals. They knew that this was one of those times.

The woman had mightily pissed me off.

If there was one thing I couldn't stand, it was the abuse of power. My temper bounced like a kangaroo around in my chest. It would have cost this cop nothing to be kind, empathetic, and respectful. There was absolutely no reason for her to be so officious after what was certainly a disturbing event. Despite Mr. Statten being a very unpopular guy, except perhaps to those whom he touched with his money, no one liked to see a person fall to the floor and not get up.

"Perhaps you didn't hear me. I said you are to leave." Her face was very close to mine.

Big mistake.

I read the name tag pinned to her chest. "You can back off now, Mizz Branson." I emphasized the "Mizz" for no reason other than I liked the buzz saw sound of the word. I made a pushing gesture in the air with my hands, warning her to take a step back.

She looked at my hands, and then, at me. Something flickered in her eyes. Her head tilted to one side, as if she were sizing me up. Could she take me on? But perhaps the look was one of confusion. I opted for the former interpretation of her stare, self-preservation being at the top of my survival-as-a-person list. Yes, she could take me down in a fight, no doubt about that, even though I outweighed her by about thirty (or fifty) pounds. I watched her eyes carefully. They weren't leaving my face either. But there was that flicker again. Maybe she *was* confused. Maybe, like all bullies, she was perplexed by someone who defied her commands. She didn't take her eyes off mine, but she did take a step back.

"The scene needs to be cleared." This was said as a peace offering.

I nearly hee-hawed. I loved winning. I said, "We are witnesses to what happened." I broke the stare and gestured at the devastation around us. "We were just feet away. Perhaps you'd like to ask us a few questions. Perhaps you'd like to ask us what we saw." I was on a victory roll.

She was thoroughly baffled by now. She was being told what to do by me? A short, overweight, middle-aged mommy? By someone wearing white sports socks with sandals? I watched her eyes dart this way and that, her neurons randomly flashing, trying to wrap around this turn of events. The officiousness drained out of her, leaving her like a deflated balloon. She knew I was right. She took out her notebook and said, "Anyone here have video of what happened?"

I shot Calvin a look and shook my head slightly. He tucked his phone into his back pocket. Good boy. My phone was already in my jeans. My kids, bless them, all shook their heads.

Ralph strode around the table and introduced himself to the cop. "Detective Creston. Toronto. How are you?"

He was making small talk while he figured out what was going on.

She was watching the paramedics stow their gear. After Dr. MacKenzie's pronouncement of death, they had stopped trying to bring the very dead Mr. Statten back to life. The fledgling cop now had ammunition to shore up her authority. "Well, this is a sudden death and all sudden deaths need to be investigated. I need to protect the scene. He was a young, healthy man, suddenly dead." She held herself stiffly as she tried to justify her earlier behaviour of controlling the crowd before she even knew the man was dead.

Ralph let her off the hook. The young woman was obviously still an insecure traffic cop who spent her days pulling motorists off the highway and conducting breathalyzer tests. "I see. And what do you think happened to Mr. Statten?"

She was grateful he hadn't pushed her on her pre-emptive behaviour, and I watched her sagging somewhat with relief under his questioning gaze. He had that de-escalating effect on people, most of the time, disarming them to get at the truth of the matter. She said, "I'm not at all sure, but maybe Mr. Statten had a stroke. A sudden fall like that? And then death? A stroke for sure."

Ralph smiled at her. "Good detective work," he said, peering at her name tag. "Officer Branson. Well done. It looks like a stroke to me too. Classic symptoms, really. We could even see his face and fingers stiffening up. I was sitting at this table here with my partner's family. We're here on a holiday."

Ah. So, I was a "partner." I rolled the sound of that in my head. *Partner*. It bumped up against the word "love," and I felt my chest lighten and then constrict. And then lighten. What was I was going to do with this relationship? Why was I so reticent to commit, to fall into love, to be loved? Why was I like this? Why did I have these deep-rooted issues? Why couldn't I just accept that Ralph loved me, was totally committed to the relationship, and only wanted me to be happy?

But with the scent of vomit lingering in the breeze, and the sound of car doors opening and shutting, I knew this was not the time to sit down, even metaphorically, and have a *tête-a-tête* with myself. Something dreadful had happened here and I needed to deal with it.

She said, "Well, thank you for staying as witnesses." She actually smiled at me. Ugh.

What a two-faced bitch. I didn't smile back. I knew her type. Once she saw she was outranked by Ralph, she grovelled. Or maybe she was just young and I shouldn't be so quick to judge. Maybe the word "partner" had opened doors. It didn't really matter what meaning she put on the word. The detective and I were together.

I said to her turned-up nose, "Even Dr. MacKenzie thinks this is a stroke, right, Dr. MacKenzie?"

Dr. MacKenzie ambled over and huffed twice. "I didn't say any such thing, not yet, young lady, but yes, it was a stroke." He turned to the cop. "Classic symptoms. Paralysis. Slurring. Loss of coordination. Vomiting." He nodded at Officer Branson. "I know it looks suspicious, he being so young and definitely healthy, but I had a youngster, a lad of fourteen, die of a stroke just a few days ago."

Branson looked thoughtful. "So anyone can have a stroke. Poor boy. Poor family. Who was it?"

"It was the Schnare's second oldest, Billy. He died at his birthday party."

"Oh right, I heard about that. Unbelievable. How awful, and at his own birthday party."

Two strokes of healthy people in three days? That sounded suspicious to me. But then, I had a suspicious mind. Did no one else think that was odd? Speaking of odd, that old geezer had called me "young lady." Didn't he know better? Not politically correct these days. But I looked at his stooped frame and gnarled fingers tightly gripping his cane. He was ancient. Probably ninety or more, and everyone must look young to him.

Officer Branson did a little victory shake of her fireplug body. I wasn't sure why, given she was wrong about needing to protect the scene. There was obviously no crime here. "With everyone saying this was a stroke, including the good doctor," she gestured at him and he smiled, showing teeth the colour of putty, "there can be no question about cause of death. The nearest coroner is in Halifax, two hours away, and she is so busy with the current rash of waterfront homicides—stabbings you know—that there is no reason to call her down here if it's obvious he died of a stroke. I'll make that recommendation to my boss."

Ralph replied, "Oh, it was a stroke alright. As I say, we watched the whole thing up close. He seemed to lose control of his body, it was as if he were paralyzed, and then, of course, there was the vomit. Never a good sign in stroke victims."

Branson was mystified. "Really? Why not?"

I wondered myself but was nodding as if I knew.

If Ralph was surprised that she didn't know what vomiting in stroke victims meant, he didn't show it. "If someone vomits while having a stroke or before a stroke, they usually die. It's a pretty clear indicator of the outcome of a stroke victim. Those who don't vomit have a far higher chance of surviving the stroke."

"I didn't know that," she said while tapping on her phone. She looked up at him. "Just notifying the funeral home."

I didn't know that either, despite my stroke research. Vomiting was a sign of stroke and indicated the seriousness of the event? Was I about to have a stroke? I was a perfect candidate. Overweight, middle-aged woman who ate tons of butter and was about to throw up. Maybe I was going to have a stroke. That was the last thing I needed right now. Oh, calm down Robin. I knew I was as healthy as an ox, and I looked like one too. I had to stop talking to myself like that. I was not an ox, I was a comfortable middle-aged mother. Speaking of being a mother, how were my kids doing? I looked down the table as Branson was making her call and then back at the officer. I was surprised that a town the size of Liverpool had a funeral home.

"Liverpool has a funeral home?" I asked while she was tapping.

She looked up from her phone. "Since 1893. It might be a small town, but we've been here a long time. It's on Union Street. I imagine he'll be cremated. Just searching for their number now."

Once she found the number she backed away and held her

phone to her ear. It seemed that just a minute later a black van pulled up and two men got out. They opened the double doors at the back of the van and pulled out a gurney. They sidled over to the dead man and sized up the situation. Ralph was helping them figure out the best way to place the gurney so that they could roll Mr. Statten onto it. I turned my attention back to my kids.

Evelyn, my ever-practical daughter, was fidgeting with her hands in her lap. Her shoulders were shaking. Oh no. My tattoo-covered daughter was crying. I made my way around the chairs and knelt beside her. "It's okay sweetheart, it's okay." I rubbed her shoulder.

She looked at me with her tear-stained face, mascara smudging black tracks down her cheeks. Her Doc Martens were banging against her chair leg. She'd dressed up for the dinner. "I just watched a man die," she sobbed. "It was horrible. He fell down. He hit his head on the pavement. He's dead." She choked out the last word.

"I know honey, I know. It was awful to see. But he's already on his way to his next life."

She contemplated my words as the two men rolled Mr. Statten's still warm body onto the gurney. They were being surprisingly gentle.

"I know you believe in lives recurring, Mom, but I'm not so sure. Dead looks pretty dead and gone to me. And he's gone. How can that be? One minute he's giving a speech, and the next minute he's gone?"

"Strokes are like that sweetheart. They can be viciously sudden. Sometimes, people are okay after a stroke, but sometimes..."

"They are not." She nodded as if to confirm to herself this awful truth.

"And this is one of those times. But watch. See what's happening now? Those two men are taking good care of his body. Do you see how gently they are buckling him on to the board? They are honouring the dead. That's what we need to do, sweetie. He was not a good man in many ways, polluting the ocean the way he did, but he did some good. He employed people, and he gave some of his money away to help society. There was a Buddha nature in him as well as being a polluter of the ocean, and we need to remember that."

"I don't know, Mom," said Bertie, who was listening in. He leaned closer to Evelyn and brushed some hair out of her face. They'd always been tight. "I just don't know about that. Polluting the ocean on such a scale is pretty criminal. Sure, he affected people's lives but not always in a positive way. Yes, he paid people to work for him, and yes, he gave away some of his money, but he decimated the lobster fishing industry with his fish farming. He ruined just as many people's lives, if not more. He polluted the ocean in a big way."

Calvin leaned forward. "I agree with Bert. I'm glad he's dead. Maybe his fish farms will fade into obscurity."

I didn't admonish Calvin for being glad someone was dead. I understood it. I myself was mostly glad my husband had died in a car accident. He'd treated me terribly. So, everything my sons said was true. I personally was also struggling with this concept of being happy someone was dead. Truth be told, I was siding with the scientist, who, I saw, was still looking mightily pleased that a scourge had been removed from the face of the earth. The mayor Dave Bradley wasn't looking too distraught either, and the MLA was texting on her phone, the picture of capable professionalism. I could tell she was determined to reign in her emotions. But on the other hand, I had been taught by my mother to not speak ill of the dead. Well, why the hell not? He had been a horrible human being who had left a path of devastation behind him a mile wide. But my Buddhist practice insisted that all people had a buddha nature, even if it were really deep down. But, sometimes, I didn't know about that. I'd think about this later.

I looked Calvin straight in the eye. "You're right. He was

disgusting. But now he'd dead, so let's all go home." I waved at Ralph from across the pavement and walked my two fingers in the air to indicate it was time to go. He nodded and headed around the table to us.

He asked, looking around, "Where are Maggie and Winchester? I saw them a while ago but have lost track."

I scanned the mess around us and saw them in a corner talking to the boy who had served the head table their lobsters. The boy was beside himself, his head in his hands, and his body swaying. Maggie was comforting him the best she could, leaning towards his face, and Winchester had put an arm around his shoulders, holding him up. I signalled to them it was time for us to go. They quietly led the upset boy to the MLA, who I had guessed correctly, was his mother. She put down her phone, stood up, and thanked Winchester and Maggie for their help. He'd be okay. But she didn't hug him.

Everyone who was still remaining stood up to go, and I wondered about the clutter left behind. Who would clean it up? Shouldn't we make a little effort? "Hey kids, lets tidy up a bit," I shouted.

They all half-heartedly grabbed a few plates and looked around for a garbage can. There was none to be found. I remembered I had a plastic bag in my back pocket that I was going to recycle as a poo bag for Lucky and pulled it out. I scraped some of the vomit off the head table with a clean paper plate and stuffed it into the bag. Then I held it open for them to dump their trash in. I tied a knot with the handles, and carried it gingerly by the knot. It smelled like barf. When I got into the van, I gave the garbage to Calvin, who was sitting behind me. I said, "Here, toss this into the back hatch, thanks." He flung it high over his shoulder and Ralph shook his head, his eyes mock-glaring in the rear-view mirror.

Calvin said, laughing, "You did say, 'toss.'"

"Calvin. You can gently place it in the rubbish bin behind the house when we get home. After all this talk of pollution, I want to set a good example and not be seen pitching garbage around." I said this pointedly.

We reversed our route into town and stopped at a convenience store on the Old Port Mouton Road where we purchased ice cream cones. They were a third of the price of Toronto cones. Half a lobster wasn't going to last us until morning. I hungered after some potato chips but contained myself. Maybe there was some cheese at the house. As we drove along Highway 103, clouds gathered over the horizon. No campfire tonight, I guessed. It looked like it was going to start raining any minute. A kilometre later, fat greasy drops splattered on the windshield, and the wipers swished back and forth, the only sound in the silent van.

10.

AT THE CRACK OF DAWN THE NEXT MORNING, around ten—we were on a summer schedule—Ralph and I sat at the breakfast table talking over the sound of rain pelting against the windows. Wind howled around the house, and trees rocked back and forth. Fog swirled across the lawn in smoky loops, and Lucky stood at the window, his paws on the sill, growling at what must have looked to him like ghosts. The weather was terrible and fascinating. And what a shame. It was the kids' last full day here in this lovely cottage, and there would be no swimming today. Even still, I loved weather. Perhaps I felt a kinship with chaos. I'd have to think about that later, when I wasn't eating pancakes smothered in whipping cream and maple syrup.

And right now, the rain was a blessing. After seven weeks of drought, the water levels in rivers and wells had dropped alarmingly low. Some rivers had shrunk to rocky pathways with intermittent stagnant pools of rust-coloured water, topped with yellow foam. My kids had reported that even the famous Bear Hole in Broad River had been reduced to a shallow kiddie pool. Perhaps this rain would fill up everyone's wells and all the rivers on the South Shore.

From where I sat in the kitchen, I could hear laughter and muttering coming from the living room. Calvin, Bertie, and Evelyn had already scarfed their pancakes, taken one look out the window, and were now hanging around the front room in their pyjamas, playing on their phones. In a way, it was a good thing to have a crummy day. It was a nice break from the routine of going to the beach.

"Hey, Mom," someone called from the front room. It was Calvin. "There's a CBC article on Frank Statten's death."

Already? That was fast work. And the CBC? They must have thought he was pretty important, or maybe it was a slow news day. Should I be writing up his death? Shirley, my nympho editor at *The Toronto Express*, had wanted me to contact her if anything newsworthy happened. But would *Express* readers in Toronto be interested in a Nova Scotian death? Probably not. But fish farming? That might be of interest. It was so controversial and ridiculously stupid. Maybe I should call or text Hay Hair. I'd think about that later too. I didn't want to ruin a peaceful start to my morning. Today, I was the queen of procrastination.

Calvin called out, "They say it was a stroke, and that he was the owner of the Port Mouton fish farm and other fish farms around the South Shore. It also said—get this—that he'd been charged numerous times, under the Environmental Act, but always got off. Did you know that?"

He wasn't waiting for an answer, and no, I didn't know that.

"Shouldn't you be writing about this, Mom? I mean, *fish farms*." He made a gagging sound.

I called back, "Thanks for the hot tip, Calvin. I'll think about it. Maybe talk to my editor."

That was the last thing I wanted to do, even though he'd practically read my mind. What a way to wreck a holiday. I'd come all this way to get away from work. Besides, was it a story? So what if another immoral, disgusting, pompous guy was dead? Ah, but Robin, don't think like that, have compassion.

Calvin was still shouting. "I should sell them my video of him barfing. Or sell the stills to you for your story."

"Calvin." He knew *that* tone of voice, and I heard nothing

more from the peanut gallery. He must have gone back to his phone.

Winchester and Maggie stumbled into the kitchen. They were so cute together with their arms interlocked as they made their way over to the oven where the pancakes were being kept warm. Maggie took a deep breath. "Smells so good, Mom. Thanks for the pancakes."

"Ralph made them."

Ralph looked up from his dish of blueberries and smiled. "I like to cook, every now and then."

Maggie turned and beamed at him. She had such a beautiful smile. "Your kids were so lucky to grow up with a dad who cooked."

Ralph stiffened and quickly focused all his attention on his fruit. Maggie frowned at me, one eyebrow raised. What was this about? I lifted a shoulder in a "let-it-go" shrug. I had, in the course of our year-long relationship, only mentioned his family once before. It was at the very beginning, I don't think we'd even started to date, and he had fused his lips together and clammed right up. The response from him had been so extreme that I hadn't dared to mention it again. Of course, I was curious about Ralph's past, but I wasn't going to push it if he didn't want to talk about it. He was scrooched down over his dish. It was time to move on and change the topic. I smiled at Winchester as if nothing had transpired. But he was no slouch and was watching this interchange carefully.

I said, "Since it's such a rainy day, I thought we'd go to that Black Loyalist Heritage Centre in Birchtown today. How do you feel about that, Winchester?"

Winchester looked at me, puzzled.

"We don't have to go there," I said, hurriedly. "We could go to Lunenburg and look at the Fisheries Museum. Or, we could go to Digby to see the replica of Maud Lewis's house. She was a famous folk artist. There are also some fairs and stuff like that around in various towns. Lots of interesting things to do. Nan left quite the list. It's completely up to you people what you want to do today." I watched Winchester's body language carefully.

"Why would I mind?" he asked, confused.

"I don't know." I could feel my face flushing. I didn't know how to talk about this. I blurted, "You're black."

He smiled, looked at his naked arm with wide eyes, and pretended to be surprised. "Oh, look. My skin is black. What a shocker."

I wasn't quite sure how to respond to his joking. It felt like my foot was an inch from my mouth. "Maybe you don't want to see how Black Loyalists were treated."

He looked away. "But Robin, I already know how they were treated."

Of course he did. Stupid me.

"Have you been there before, to Birchtown? To look at the Heritage Centre?"

"Well, no, but I have a grandmother who had a grandmother who had a grandmother. The treatment of blacks in Nova Scotia is not news to me. I don't need to go to a museum to find out about my cultural background. We've heard all about it. Africa. Enslavement. Fighting for the British. The underground railroad."

I had clearly dug myself into a hole. The last thing I wanted was a conversation about racism that I was obviously ill-equipped for. I danced back to firmer footing and focused on the day's agenda. Just the facts. "So," I said carefully, "you'd rather go to Lunenburg? Or Digby?"

"Oh no, I'd love to go to the Heritage Centre in Birchtown. It would be interesting to see how it jives with what I've heard. I'm totally fine with it."

What? I was not doing well in this exchange.

Maggie could sense my discomfort. "Don't worry about it, Mom. We're cool." And that was that. She bent over to spear some pancakes from the oven and put them on two plates. She used her fingers to knock them off the fork and withdrew her hand as if she'd been burned. "Piping hot," she whispered to Winchester.

He laughed.

Geezus, now I had to listen to my daughter make sexual innuendos? A headache was stirring just behind my eyes.

They grabbed their plates and headed out to the living room to join the others. I didn't know how Winchester would feel about going to a place where he might bump into some of his heritage. Sure, he'd sounded pretty nonchalant, and he certainly looked as if he could handle it, being so solid, so confident, but I just didn't know. He said he'd be fine with it, but he might have been posturing. On the other hand, I wanted to go. The Centre had favourable write-ups and it would be good to have some intellectual stimulation after lounging around on a beach for the better part of a week. I had to take him at his word. I couldn't second-guess the situation. I made a decision.

"All right," I said to Ralph, "if the rest of the kids think it's okay, let's go to Birchtown."

Ralph was fishing the last blueberry out of his bowl with his fingers. "Sounds like a plan," he said, licking his fingers. I frowned at him. I couldn't stand bad manners. He looked me straight in the eye and then wrapped his tongue around his finger, slurping upwards twice.

I ignored the buzz in my hooey, cast him a glance which he smiled at, and shouted in the direction of the living room: "How do you guys feel about going to the Black Loyalist Heritage Centre in Birchtown today?"

Evelyn called back, "We're good with it. If it doesn't bother Winnie."

Winnie?

Winchester said, with a touch of impatience, "I'm fine with it."

I said, "You don't like to be called 'Winnie?'"

"Whatever," was his response.

I guessed he didn't. Or maybe he did. I wasn't good at interpreting "whatever."

"Okay," I said to no one in particular, "Let's go to Birchtown and check it out."

An hour later, all seven of us were jammed into the van and heading down the highway. We passed through heavy rain, light rain, fog with drizzle in it, and patches of no rain. With Ralph driving carefully, of course at the speed limit, I stuck my nose to the window and looked at the passing scenery. There were lots of scrubby spruce trees, some of which seemed to grow out of massive rocks that looked like they'd been scattered like overgrown marbles across the landscape by a huge hand. Their roots spread across the tops of the rocks like long fingers, holding on as if their life depended on it, which I guess it did. There was so much wind. Every now and then, on the left side of the highway, there was a sliver of ocean, splashing close to the side of the road. It must have been high tide. We passed over Sable River, and I saw the rocks in the stream were already being submerged in rainwater. Twenty minutes later, Shelburne came and went. Shortly after that, Ralph slowed down, turned off the highway, and found Old Birchtown Road.

We drove by houses that were in a variety of conditions—some newly painted and some were faded and peeling. Some of the front yards sported old tires and bathtubs used as planters and some had wooden herb containers. The cars in driveways ranged from rusted-out old junk heaps, much like my car, to shiny newer models, much like Ralph's. The houses were everything from painted trailers, to modern frame bungalows, to century-old wooden farm houses. Although breaking up at the edges, the main road was paved. The centre of the road was raised and water pooled in the ruts made by cars and trucks too heavy for the roadbed. Every now and then, a wheel got caught in one of the pools, causing the vehicle to jerk across the highway, hydroplaning. Ralph didn't flinch and mostly kept us going in a straight line. The shoulder of the road was hard-packed gravel, now covered with water that was running off into ditches.

The Black Loyalist Heritage Centre appeared suddenly on our right. Remarkably out of place, it was a black-bricked, red-metal roofed building with manicured landscaping. It was one of those buildings that I personally didn't like much. It was too clever by half, with its slanted roof and plenty of glass placed in what some architect thought was an innovative design. The grounds were beautifully tended. The lawn was neatly mowed, and the trees were surrounded by circles of black mulch. To the left was a lovely old church, painted white with green trim, and ahead was a gravel path leading to an old footbridge. I saw flashes of molten-grey through the scraggly bush to my left. Water. Perhaps there were picnic grounds up the path by the sea. Ralph turned the wheel into the dirt parking lot beside the Centre and pulled up facing the building. Through the raindrops running down the windshield, I could see a tunnel, a curved entrance straight ahead; its rounded walls adorned with symbolic sayings mounted every few feet. Oddly, the path of interlocking brick to the entrance did not lead off the parking lot, but rather from the road.

This building worried me. Everything about it jangled my nerves. It was far too, far too, what was the word? It was far too *nice*.

I hadn't even stepped inside this Centre, and already I felt something was off. To me, the building was so out of place, so absurdly dropped in the middle of a seaside village, and so expensive to build, that I had to wonder about the incentive for such a structure. The architecture didn't fit in with the sombre contents. What were the architects' motivations? Was this a monument to guilt? I kept my thoughts to myself as I took a few pictures through the windshield with my phone.

Ralph sat back in the seat and looked at me. "Pictures?"

I shrugged it off. "The architecture is interesting," I said. "Maybe *The Express* would like to do a feature on small museum architecture. I can use the photos to sell the idea to Shirley." Man oh man, could I ever make stuff up in a hurry. Make stuff up? What a joke. That was a polite way of saying I could lie in a flash. Cindy had warned me that once I got good at being a crime reporter, I would be able to lie very quickly. She was right. Ralph looked at me. He knew. He always knew. I raised my shoulder in an acknowledging shrug. I knew that he knew.

The kids fell out of the van, and as a chattering group, traipsed across the wet grass to the entrance. The curved wall was covered with pithy sayings. I read: "*This is the place. BIRCHTOWN, haven of freedom.*" Underneath this was the question, "*Is this the place? Birchtown, the haven of freedom?*" Further along, I read: "*This is Birchtown. This is home.*" And underneath that was, "*Is this where your ship of hope was anchored?*"

I watched Winchester carefully as we headed to the front doors. He hadn't even glanced at the writings on the wall. Somehow, I knew in my heart of hearts that it was here that hope was lost, and that Birchtown was no haven. The writing, so to speak, was on the wall.

Ralph strode up to the fancy front desk and paid for the whole group before I could stop him. What a guy. First, the dinner last night and now the museum entrance fees? I wondered briefly if he was starting to feel a sense of responsibility for my family. And how did I feel about that? Part of me screeched, "*back off*," and yet another part of me nodded and thought, "*What a nice guy.*" Again, I wondered why I was so resistant to the idea of being a couple, why I had so much trouble trusting who he was. I'd known him for over a year now, and I heard a little voice in my head say, "Robin, either shit or get off the pot." He must have sensed that I was thinking about him and he turned to look at me, a question on his face. I smiled, and tried to look innocent.

Avoiding his eyes, I gazed around and saw through an open door across the foyer a spiffily tiled bathroom off to one side, which Maggie had also spied and was trotting towards. The reception desk was slightly curved and made of oiled teak. That must have set back the funding organization a few bucks. Behind it sat a black woman with sparkling green eyes. I'd talk to her later, after the visit, and do some research on the museum. There were several doors leading off the foyer and I assumed they led to meeting rooms. It was hard for me to get my bearings. The lights were so bright. Everything was shiny and on an angle. Where, exactly, was the museum part of the building? Ralph, however, wasn't mystified at all and led us to a doorway leading to a large room.

This was the museum? A single room?

The place seemed so vacant, so empty. I glanced everywhere and could see no other doors. It was just one large room. There was something about it that seemed so smoke and mirrors. The whole area was walled by touch screens, and had, weirdly in the centre, a floor made of glass blocks. Along the left-hand and back walls were about ten screens. There were a few shallow display cases filled with what I thought must have been easily found knick-knacks such as buttons and buckles, and on the far side, opposite me, there was a single larger display case. Because of the lights reflecting off the glass, I couldn't make out what it housed. Along the front wall were tributes to a few prominent black Nova Scotians pasted on what was likely bristol board from a local dollar store. The glue holding up printed information sheets had rippled the corners of the paper. There was plenty to read everywhere but little to actually look at. All the money, it seemed, had been spent on the building. I was getting angry. Was this a bullshit museum, pretending to be something it was not?

Above a case exhibiting trinkets, more buttons it looked like, was a large strip of orange paper printed with words proclaiming: "*But your black skin matters.*" The disparity between the emptiness of the room and the words above sickened me. Did no one else see how awful this was? How very sad? I felt rage building in me like I had never experienced before. I clenched my jaw to keep from shouting, "What the fuck? What kind of shit is this? How dare you?" If black skin mattered, they could have made a little more fucking effort. *Buttons* for Christ's sake. Surely a legacy of almost three hundred years had more to it than baubles. Is this all that was left behind? Couldn't they have at least found a pot? A handle from a wood-burning stove? A child's notebook? Some letters?

But then I took a deep breath and calmed myself down. Maybe this was all the archeologists had dug up. Maybe there was nothing much to begin with, so there was very little to find. Maybe that's what I should be angry about. The Black Loyalists lived in such grim poverty that they had no possessions beyond what was needed for survival. Clothing. This thought made me even angrier than what I had at first perceived as a lack of effort. But if that is the legacy, part of what has been left behind, then why is that rage-worthy? Artifacts like this are common in museums, I rationalized. Nevertheless, I felt myself almost vibrating from red-hot flames of fury coursing through my veins. I rubbed my arms, trying to put the fire out.

I walked on, tapping the touch screens and reading the story. With every word, the blaze within me was stoked. How could people treat people like this? There was a photo of a newspaper clipping about reward money offered by a man in Halifax for a young girl who had escaped her master. Money for a child? A child who was a slave? My heart pounded. There were descriptions of the abandonment of the promise for free land in exchange for fighting with the British in the American Revolution. There were stories of leaving behind the broken promises and the harshness of winter to go to a better life in Sierra Leone. From Africa back to Africa, with a Canadian black hole in-between that sucked out all dignity and humanity from a race. I was ashamed. I was sad. I was furious. I was mortified. And I learned.

Apparently, the Loyalist British in 1783 had promised free land and a better life to almost three thousand blacks who had pledged to fight with them. They arrived in boats from the American south and were documented in Sir Guy Carleton's *Book of Negros*. I had not read Lawrence Hill's prize-winning novel of the same name and was drawn to the printed and digital account of the original book on the far wall. I read the names of the people who had been on the ships with almost morbid curiosity. I scanned down the names, feeling the skin on my neck burn. What was I looking for?

And then, suddenly, a name jumped out at me. *Elliott*. Some with two t's, some with one. There were seven of them, and I knew, without a doubt, that these were Winchester's ancestors. I looked around the room for him. He and Maggie were sitting on a bench, snuggling and comparing stuff on their phones. Probably a good thing. I went back to the screen of the page in the book. The two vessels that carried the Elliotts, with two t's like Winchester's last name, to Nova Scotia were the *L'Abondance* and *Elijah*. Such hope in these names. These Elliotts were a man and a woman, Betsey and Daniel. I wondered if they were Winchester's great-great-grandparents. I thought it highly likely as their boats had arrived in a village called Port Mattoon, which was probably how Port Mouton was spelled then. He had said his family was originally from Port Mouton.

With this hot coal of information burning a hole in my chest, I moved to my right and stood in front of the single large display case. I took deep breaths as I tried to calm myself down. Something was happening with my eyes. The reflections on all the screens and the glass of this stand-alone case, the only one in the room, seemed to dance around. Was I going to faint? I tried hard to focus, to see what I was looking at through the shimmering lights.

In the case was a mannequin wearing the types of clothes that would have been worn by an original Black Loyalist. I looked at the frayed cuffs of a thin woollen coat, the layers of rags hanging below it, the yellowed shirt, the bent wire-rimmed glasses, and my heart was consumed with burning rage. How on earth were these poor people meant to survive a harsh Canadian winter dressed like this? My eye travelled down to the bottom of the case and I saw, lying in a jumbled heap, rusted and blackened metal.

I stared transfixed at the pile of forged steel links and tried to fathom what it was. There was a large metal circle that looked like a dog's collar. Some chains. And two smaller circles. This was for their animals? Their pets? What? And then with horrified recognition I knew what I was viewing. I could put a name to this random pile of metal that lay at the bottom of the display case.

Shackles.

With hot tears filling my eyes, I knew I had to get away from the horrible story of the Black Loyalist's heritage. I walked as quickly as I could to the exit, past the buttons, past the warning that I would not be readmitted, past the fancy bathroom, past the expensive teak reception desk, out through the heavy glass doors and down the circular path with the awful sayings on the wall. I hurried along the gravel path to the sea. Drizzle collected on my hair in droplets as I scurried away.

I scuttled over the footbridge and saw the ocean opening out in front of me. I stood at the edge of a grassy marsh area, looked far out to sea, and began my Nichiren Buddhist chant through my tears. My heart ached for these people who had come to this harsh land of ice and snow completely unprepared. How could they possibly cope with the cold? They had come from warm weather and soft breezes. I mumbled my chant under my breath over and over, hoping with all my heart for world peace, where all people would be treated with compassion and respect. I felt so entitled, and so guilty, that I had never experienced the kind of systemic racism the Black Loyalists had endured. The reality of the harsh truth rubbed my heart raw.

"Robin." I thought I heard my name off in the distance, sliding through the fog. Was it the wind moaning? No, definitely it was my name. Ralph had followed me out? Yes, it was his voice. He was calling me. I stopped chanting and wiped my sleeve across my eyes. He would not see me crying. I wouldn't allow it. Standing as tall as I could, I took calming breaths as I faced the ocean and waited until he caught up to me before I turned to look at him.

11.

"OH, ROBIN." HE TOOK ONE LOOK at me and wrapped me in his arms. Cold drizzle had soaked through my clothes, and I turned my head into his warm chest. The pain in my heart grew until I could no longer contain it. My pride evaporated, and I began sobbing again. This was the very first time since we'd been together that I had let Ralph see me cry. It was probably the first time in my life when I had been held while I cried. I had no experience with this kindness. Trevor had been judgemental if I cried, calling me weak, telling me to buck up, walking away as I struggled. And there had certainly been no time for tears growing up—my father had just told me to grow up. But here was Ralph, stroking my hair and rubbing my back. I felt like my heart was cracking apart. I had never been loved like this.

I had so much trouble wrapping my mind around those poor, poor people coming to this wretched land. They must have been so cold in those shackles on a reeling boat. How on earth had they survived? The wind blew around us, and I began to shiver. Ralph held me tighter. How did I ever deserve to be with such a kind man? He hadn't even asked me what was wrong. He held me simply because I was upset. There was no judgement, no criticism. He was completely in the here and now, taking care of me while I was crying. I wept even harder, crying for the Loyalists, crying for me. "You are so sad. Oh, Robin," he whispered, while stroking my head. "You are so sad."

And I was. I was so very sad that the Black Loyalists had suffered such broken dreams and promises. "They deserved better, Ralph. They deserved a better life. They deserved to have promises made to them honoured. They were subjected to so much humiliation."

"Yes."

"I hate this museum."

"Yes," he said again and rubbed my back.

He didn't say I was too sensitive or too political like Trevor or my father would have said. He simply took me at my word and held me tight. How had I met a man who was so accepting of my feelings? I rested in his arms for a long moment.

The drizzle was turning into a hard rain, and I began shaking with the cold. It was time to go back inside. I took a few deep breaths and once in possession of myself, said, "Let's go back in and round up the kids. Plus, I want to find out more about the museum."

"Okay Robin, it's up to you. I'm happy to wait out here with you. In the rain. Getting cold. Feeling a bit hungry. But take your time."

I laughed. He knew how to cheer me up. "C'mon," I said, tugging his hand, "let's go back in."

As we walked over the footbridge and along the gravel path to the museum, Ralph put a protective arm over my shoulders. I liked it. Did that make me weak? I didn't feel weak. I felt loved and cared for.

I was getting hungry, too. Of course I was. All this emotion burned up calories. I said, "Where would you like to eat?"

"Wherever you like."

"Let's see what the kids want to do."

My family and Winchester were gathered in the foyer, laughing and talking. They all looked up expectantly when Ralph and I entered through the heavy glass doors. Maggie, I saw, was nowhere to be seen. "Where's Maggie?" I asked no one in particular.

Winchester thumbed the washroom sign. "Oh," I said. I briefly wondered if she had an infection. That was the second time she'd gone to the bathroom while we'd been here. As soon as the thought crossed my mind, she rushed out to join us, beaming away.

After some discussion, we settled the agenda for the afternoon. We decided that we would go for a leisurely lunch in the town of Shelburne. Calvin googled the area and discovered a popular restaurant in a pretty lane that had excellent reviews. After that, we would have a toot around the town looking at sights, and then, later on, go for dinner at the restaurant we always ate at in Port Mouton for a goodbye meal. Later this evening, if we were lucky, the storm would blow itself out and we would be able to have a final campfire. It sounded like a great plan to me.

I wandered away from the family while they sorted out the details and headed over to the shiny brochures on the reception desk. I idly picked one up and noticed the staff member behind the desk watching me.

"I saw you run out, looking pretty upset," she said.

Oh, had I been that obvious? I could tell, even while she was sitting down, that she was a tall and strong woman. An African beauty with warm hazel eyes. I decided to be honest with her. "I *was* upset."

She tilted her head in a "go on" gesture.

"This building must have cost a fortune to build, hundreds of thousands of dollars, perhaps even more than a million, not to mention the price of the land, and yet the contents of the museum are pretty scarce. I don't mean to criticize, but it's mostly touch screens. A few buttons." I left out the shackles. I didn't want to lose it again. "It doesn't seem right to me. "

"Actually, the land was free."

"It was? Had it been a park or something that was donated by the government?"

"No, it was donated by the family of an original Loyalist.

They'd never had the title to the land anyway, so it's not like they'd ever even owned it."

"Wait a minute." I was trying to work this out. "I read in there," I jerked my thumb at the museum's main room, "that only a few of the Black Loyalists were given land in exchange for fighting for the British in the American Revolution. The head of all the families were meant to be given a hundred acres, and then fifty acres for each member of the family. But more often than not, that promise was broken. The gift of free land in exchange for military service didn't happen across the board. Just a few were given land. Are you saying those few weren't really given land at all? Not legally?"

"A few were given land to clear and farm, which frankly was impossible as the province is mostly rock, and they stayed on the land and paid taxes on it for almost three hundred years. But they weren't given the deeds. They had no title to the land."

I couldn't believe what I was hearing. "So, they didn't really own the land?"

"No. Despite paying taxes on it for three hundred years."

I was floored. I needed to clarify this. "They weren't given the deeds?"

"No."

"Why not?" I was sounding strident, my voice metallic. "Why hasn't anything been done by the government to correct this situation?"

The young woman shook her head. "There've been a few efforts at getting the titles to the people, but the trajectory goes nowhere. Maybe it just isn't that important." She shrugged, asking me to understand something, but I wasn't sure what.

I changed the topic, but I knew I'd come back to it later. "Where did the contents for the museum come from?"

She opened her hands wide in an encompassing gesture. "We worked hard to get what little we have. There had been digging on local land for years. Plus people from around here donated what they had hanging around. You know, in their sheds and attics. It wasn't much. That's why the displays are minimal. The people were so poor."

Oh God. Me with my entitled judgment. They really had done the best they could with what they had. My stomach cringed. "But who organized all this?" I flung my hand out, indicating the entire Centre.

"Do you mean, who was the driving force behind the creation of the museum?"

I guess that's what I meant. "Sure."

"The Black Loyalist Heritage Society. A founding member of the Society in 1989 was a woman, Dr. Elizabeth Cromwell, C.M., who has received honourary degrees from two Nova Scotian universities for her tireless work. A team of people, with her at the helm, worked, and continue to work for this." The receptionist spread her arms wide. "They wanted to make sure our story was known, that it was part of Canada's history, and that we would not be marginalized. We are very proud of this."

"People have worked very hard," I said. "It's quite the accomplishment." I could see now what they'd been up against.

"The Society raised the money. They lobbied various levels of government, prominent businesses, and some wealthy maritime families for funding to build the museum. It took years. You can see the list of donors over there," she gestured with her head across the foyer, "on that plaque. The Society also oversaw the construction. They set up the administrative structure as well. In fact, they run the museum today and work to educate people about our history in general. The Black Loyalist Heritage Society is a going concern."

"Who's in the Society? On the board?" I wanted to ask if it was a white or a black board, but that seemed a little awkward.

She looked at me as if I'd asked her the stupidest question on earth. "Mostly descendants of Black Loyalists, people who want the story of their black heritage told."

"Of course. I wasn't thinking. Sorry. Tell me, how was the museum received by the local community?"

The receptionist looked at me. In her lovely hazel eyes I saw her struggling to give me the politically correct answer or the truth. In the end she gave me both. "I can't speak for everyone in the black community or the local community, but generally people are pleased. People love the Centre. They are very proud of it."

"And for good reason," I said. "It's a very well-constructed building and it is very successful in telling the hardships and racism people experienced." Just because I personally didn't like the architecture didn't mean it wasn't good. I now knew that the meagre contents successfully conveyed the difficult heritage. They did that in spades.

"Was there a defining moment in time when the idea for this building was born?"

The woman pointed out the doors. "Did you see the white wooden church across the road before you came in?"

"Yes. So pretty."

"Wood burns so easily. That church housed some of the artifacts you see here. It was set on fire. Arson." She made sure I understood her meaning.

"Arson." I repeated.

"This building is brick."

I was deeply ashamed of my first impression that the building didn't fit into the local architecture. They wanted it to survive hatred. I felt terrible for my unthinking judgment.

The young woman must have sensed my inner distress. She smiled and handed me a brochure. "Here. If you want to read more about this…"

I took the glossy pamphlet and stuffed it in my purse. "Thanks," I said. "I'm a journalist. I am going to write about how the Black Loyalists were treated, especially about the land titles.""

"I doubt you will be able to change anything. The bureaucracy is slow and unwieldy, and systemic racism still runs deep." She was looking at me intently. I gave her a curt nod.

Yes, systemic racism, deep and unyielding. Shirley had mentioned this.

I thanked this astute young woman for her time and made my way back to my family who were grouped near the exit, waiting for me. I took deep breaths and did my best to control all the emotions swirling in my chest as I approached them. "Thanks for waiting for me. Let's go."

We hurried in the rain through the wet grass to the van and Ralph turned the heater on high. I leaned into the warmth, drying my damp clothes. What an experience. Resolve focused my mind: I would write about this.

The weather was such a contrast from yesterday. It crossed my mind that just one day ago I was lying on Summerville Beach, contentedly basking in the warm sunshine and eating sandwiches, and today I was upset, cold, and huddled around the air vent in the van. Thinking of the sandwiches from Saturday's picnic reminded me just how starving I was, and I looked out the window for a diner or something. But no, there were only scrubby coniferous trees on both sides of the road, and I didn't happen to have my recipe for boiling spruce bark with me.

Ralph drove along the Lighthouse Route until we came to an Irving gas station, where I could see through the window that they sold Lays potato chips—the kind I liked, with no additives. But there was no stopping Ralph who was on a mission, and we followed the road to the right. Thankfully, it was only minutes before we were parked on the main street near the café Calvin had researched. We walked down a cute lane, sided by cedar-shingled frame houses, one with a freshly painted white picket fence. At the end of the lane, I could see the water in Shelburne Harbour roiling a frothy grey, whipped up into white caps by the wind. We struggled against the gusts blowing up the street from the water and picked up our pace until we were outside the darling restaurant, which was painted a soft yellow and light purple. The overhead sign for the bistro creaked in the wind, and somewhere a shutter banged against wood siding. Ralph flung open the mauve-coloured door, and we all hustled inside out of the weather.

It was a small restaurant with about fifteen tables, all widely spaced out and covered in white tablecloths. There was a sense of colour here, a decorative care that was taken, giving a pleasing contrast from the grey day outside. Ochre walls and multi-hued dinnerware perked up my Home and Garden reporter's eyes. This instinct to admire something visual battled with the seductive smell of roasted garlic and frying onions. We waited by the front cash until we were led to a large round table in the back corner of the room. My mouth was watering. The place was packed.

As we wound through the tables to the back, I was careful to turn sideways so I wouldn't jostle any of the patrons with my hips. And then I came to a full stop. Seated at a table for four smack ahead of me was the MLA who had been at the lobster supper the night before. She was sitting opposite a woman with long, light brown hair that had frizzled in the dampness. What was the MLA doing here? Didn't she represent Queens County, and weren't we now in Shelburne County? Shouldn't she be supporting the businesses in her own constituency?

"Hi," I said, doing my best to smile openly, and hiding my suspicious nature. I just didn't trust politicians. Or anyone, really. Ralph was a case in point, although that nice hug on the marsh had melted my defenses a bit. The rest of my crowd followed the hostess to our table while I held back. "You were at the lobster supper in Queens County last night."

"Yes," the woman smiled warmly, although a spark of sharp pain flashed behind her eyes. "Wasn't that awful? Such a tragedy to lose a prominent member of Queen's County."

I couldn't hold back any longer. "But this is Shelburne County."

"Oh, I see your confusion," she laughed. "I represent both

counties. They amalgamated, and I'm here on business. I don't believe we've met," she said while standing up.

"Sorry." I held out my hand. "Robin MacFarland."

She took my hand. "Beverly Price. You can call me Bev, if you like. And this," she said, gesturing across the table, "is Meghan Oliver. Meghan is the director of the group that was finally successful in shutting down the Shelburne dump on the south side of town."

Meghan unravelled her lanky frame from the wooden chair and gripped my hand far too tightly. This was one aggressive babe. "It never ends," she almost shouted at me. "It's one thing to shut down the dump. It's another to get it cleaned up." She glared at the MLA.

Oops. Seems I'd opened a can of worms. In the far corner, I could see that everyone in my family was finding their seats and sitting down. I felt drawn to join them, but on the other hand, I could smell a rat, along with the garlic and onions. So, I was torn. There was something going on here and I wanted to know what it was. I smiled at Meghan. I followed their lead and sat down at the table without being asked. Sometimes, I was so brave.

But I would start by being light and casual. "Is there just one mayor then for the two towns, Liverpool and Shelburne?"

"Oh no," replied Beverly, "Thank heavens. Each town has their own mayor."

Why "Thank heavens?" I wondered.

"I noticed the Liverpool mayor kept his distance from you at the supper."

"Let's just say he's not colour-blind."

Oh.

"Plus, his daughter is going out with my son. Bradley, the mayor, is not happy about that."

I could read between the lines. Bradley was a racist. Best to leave that alone. I wondered how he kept a lid on his anger while his daughter was seeing Beverly's son. I quickly changed the topic back to the dump. "What's the story with shutting down the dump?"

Meghan was more than happy to oblige. "In a nutshell, the Canadian military base here was rented to the United States Navy, something to do with their submarines, and when the base was decommissioned, soldiers in hazmat suits dumped barrels and barrels of chemicals and waste into the Shelburne dump at the south end of town, where there is no town water or sewage system. The *black* people living there," she said, looking pointedly at Beverly Price, "have suffered illnesses way above the national average because they are drinking polluted water from their wells, polluted with what we will never know, and nothing has been done about it. Nothing. A flimsy lock on the wire gate closing the dump does not prevent chemicals from seeping into the groundwater. My group wants the dump cleaned up." She glared again at the MLA. "I'm trying to motivate the MLA," she spat out the initials, "to clean this mess up so people can live with dignity. So they can drink their well water."

I wasn't sorry I asked, loving a story the way I do, but still, she was so furious. And rightly so. There *was* a story here, I could smell it. Should I give my identity away? There were ethics about that, I was sure. I shouldn't be impersonating a hockey mom when I was a reporter. I had no trouble impersonating a police officer, but this was somehow different. The media was so powerful. The police were as well, sure, but there was that quote about nothing being mightier than a pen. Was that it? God, my mind was like cheesecloth in reverse, letting the facts slip through while I swam in the muddy gunk left behind. No, I remembered now: "The pen is mightier than the sword." A metonymic adage. Well, at least I could come up with a big word even if my brain was cheesecloth. I had to stop drinking. That binge last night had curdled my neurons. This was becoming serious.

"You sound angry," I said. What else could I say?

"Angry?" she hissed. "I'm fucking pissed off."

My kind of gal, I thought. She reminded me of Cindy, whom I'd be seeing tomorrow. I said, "How long did it take to get the dump shut down?"

"Years," she said, almost shouting. "Years! And I want it cleaned up now, which is why I'm having lunch in this fancy restaurant on the MLA's expense account."

Politics, politics. "Where exactly is the dump?" I was already planning a trip to it after we'd eaten lunch.

"On the black side of town, of course."

I waited for her to say more. I had no idea where the dump was located.

The MLA sighed. "It's all over the internet, if you want to find out more."

"I'll google it," I promised. "I'm from Toronto, not here, which is why I don't know where it is."

"Toronto?" asked Meghan, looking at me intently. "What sort of work do you do there?"

I didn't detect any of the animosity that some of the locals had for the people from Upper Canada. She seemed openly curious. Maybe she was from Ontario as well. So, I made a decision to reveal my profession. "I'm a reporter, actually," I said, almost apologetically, "for the Home and Garden section of *The Toronto Express*."

"A reporter?" asked the MLA. She sounded a bit alarmed, or maybe it was surprised.

Perhaps she was angling for some coverage. But maybe not. I thought I saw another brief spark of something in her eyes. But this time, it looked like fear. Or was it contempt? Did she hate reporters? Or did she see an opportunity? Or was she worried? I had to get better at reading people.

I laughed off the importance of my job, undermining what I do. "The Home and Garden section," I said derisively. "Wood flooring, pillows, new fabrics." I laughed as heartily as I could as I thought about the recent murder stories I had written.

Well, only two murder stories. I hoped they wouldn't google me. Sometimes, the internet was so annoying.

Meghan peered at me closely. "So, you write about how people live." It wasn't a question. "I guess plastics and other types of pollution come up. Air purifiers and the like."

Where was she going with this? I mean, she was right. A few months ago, I'd written a large piece on furnace filters. God, what a dumb job I had. Furnace filters. And then there was that scintillating article on air exchangers. Not to mention the bit I did on reverse osmosis water purifiers. "Yes, I've written on both air and water purifiers. Not that I'm an expert or anything." What was she wanting? Maybe she was hoping I'd be interested in writing an article about how to clean up the dump's pollution? I thought I'd better clarify my deficient level of expertise. "I don't know much about dumps."

And then Beverly startled me. She asked, "I guess you don't know anything about hoses. You've probably never written about that."

What? Where did that come from? Hoses had nothing to do with pollution. My ears perked up. This story was taking an interesting turn.

"In fact, I do. I know quite a bit about hoses." I knew a lot of stupid stuff.

12.

HOW DID THE CONVERSATION GO from air and water purification products to hoses? Was she baiting me because she knew I was a reporter? Naw. This politician was getting at something. I just couldn't guess what it was. Hoses, for heaven's sake. But I had liked the MLA from the moment I first laid eyes on her at the lobster supper last night. She seemed to be a hardworking and caring person, so I went with my initial instinct and remained friendly. Her question seemed genuine. Weird, but genuine.

"Funny you should ask," I said, "but I have written a few articles on hoses. Hoses have come a long way over the years. There are hoses that automatically curl up now, self-winding you know, although I understand they can get tangled up, so not recommended. And there are hoses that have holes in them for watering large areas. There are underground hoses that are as durable as pipes for sprinkler systems."

I stopped for a moment because I was losing my audience. Meghan was twitching a bit in her seat and the MLA was looking around, not really listening. "Beverly," I said, "What kind of hoses are you interested in?"

I was on pretty firm ground here because I knew my hoses. Whatever she had to throw at me, I could take it.

Beverly took a small bite of her dinner and said after swallowing, "Garden hoses. Green garden hoses. What do you know about them?"

"Ah," I said, "garden hoses. They have come under fire the last few years. I mean, we all drank from garden hoses as kids, right? I don't know about you, but me? As a kid one of my jobs was to water the garden. The hose was fun to play with. Water the garden, spray the dog. Water the garden, spray your brother. Water the garden, spray the house. Get hot, drink from the hose."

Beverly and Meghan both laughed in agreement.

"But nowadays, we know better. In fact, the water from a garden hose is full of all kinds of plastic and chemicals. It's a wonder we all don't have two heads. The water is not potable."

Beverly said, "That's my point."

Meghan was nodding seriously.

Now I was totally flummoxed. "The point? Sorry, but I don't quite see the connection between hoses and the dump."

Meghan pushed into the conversation. "It's environmental racism."

I nodded. "I get that the dump itself is an example of environmental racism. That started years ago when the toxic waste was placed near a black community that relied on wells for drinking water. But hoses...?"

Beverly said, "The story goes like this. We tried a year and a half ago to convince the town council to extend the town's water system to the south end. Everyone else is on town water, but not the black community in the south end. It was nixed. Too expensive. So, last year we tried to convince the town council to drill a central well where people could get fresh drinking water, just like they have in Liverpool."

I remembered Nan, our cottage landlady, telling me about that well. "I hear a lot of people use that well."

"That's right. People drive all the way from Shelburne to Liverpool, close to an hour away, to get good drinking water. But that was nixed as well. Why? Because, the council argued, there was already free drinking water at the old fire hall. But guess what?"

I could see where this was going. "The water at the fire hall comes from a hose."

"Bingo," Beverly sighed. "Non-potable."

Meghan closed her fist and gave a thump on the table. "Environmental racism is alive and well in Shelburne County." She was beginning to steam. She puffed out her lips and said, "Bottom line, I need the dump cleaned up. There are too many people dying in the south end of Shelburne. There are too many widows. There is too much cancer." Her voice rose a pitch. "It's environmental racism. That's what it is. Environmental racism. It's not being cleaned up because the people affected are *black*."

She was working herself into a lather and other diners around were shifting in their seats. I was having a bit of trouble figuring out why this white woman was beside herself with anger while the black politician was keeping quiet. Even so, quiet as she was, I could tell Beverly was also agitated. I could see she was upset by the way she was gripping her spoon. It was the only sign of internal distress. She was controlling herself, trying to appear composed.

Beverly smiled at Meghan and held out her hands in a tamping down gesture.

I could see that this infuriated Meghan even more—she was not going to be controlled or subdued. No one calms down when they're told to calm down. But she lowered her voice a notch. "Listen to me. The dump is full of industrial waste, of hospital waste, of military waste from all over the province. They burn it and people breathe it. It rains and they drink it. You have to think twice when workers wear hazmat suits fifty feet from your house. There are three brooks that travel through that dump and enter into Shelburne Harbour. These brooks seep into the earth, into peoples' wells. Those people, those *black* people who live in that area, are breathing and drinking poison."

Out of the corner of my eye, I saw that my family was

signalling for me to come over. Maybe they didn't want me involved in in local politics. Between them stressing me about having to walk away from something I was keenly interested in, and me spouting off about hoses, I didn't feel that great. I felt a bit like my father, who stuck his nose in everywhere and who lectured at the slightest provocation. He was always right. A spark of fury caught fire in my chest. Geezus. Where did that come from? I'd have to think about that later. In the meantime, I had two women in front of me who were telling me a great story. Shirley would like this one. I could see the headline: *Small town sullied by environmental racism.*

After Meghan's outburst, Beverly tried to dial back the conversation to restaurant hush. "We have had to struggle so hard to change the way things are. There is so much resistance to cleaning up the dump."

I interjected, "Resistance? Exactly where does the resistance come from?" Maybe she would give me names.

Beverly looked at me and sighed again. "From everywhere. There's resistance from all levels of government, but it's mostly from the town. Think about this: the previous mayor told the south end residents to move if they didn't like living near a dump. Can you imagine that? Three hundred years later and he's telling them to move?"

I said, "Wow. So hard-hearted." And what a racist prick I thought to myself. "It seems the current Liverpool mayor and the past Shelburne mayor are both..."

Meghan interjected, "Luckily, it's not most people. Most people around here don't think twice about the colour of someone's skin. But there are a few."

Beverly looked straight at Meghan. "I'm doing my best, Meghan, to get this dump cleaned up. But we know why I can't get anywhere. I try and try, but there is such opposition from everywhere. Such resistance. I can't even get an eight thousand dollar well drilled. I understand that cleaning up the dump is a huge environmental undertaking, costing millions, and installing a water system is expensive, but really, not even a central well?"

Meghan said softly, "I understand. I'm so sorry. We will work harder to get it done. I won't give up. You have my support."

Beverly said, "Thank you Meghan, that means a lot to me. Let's always remember that we are on the same side." Then she said, "Call it what you want, maybe it's environmental racism, but from where I sit, it's institutionalized, systemic racism."

And with that declaration, that summary, the air seemed to expand and loosen. It looked like the tension was over. Both women pecked at their plates and I moved my chair out, getting ready to go to my family.

But Beverly stopped me dead in my tracks when she said, "It explains a lot."

She bit her lower lip, breathed deeply, and wrung her hands, as if she didn't know what to do with them. Her eyes looked around the room, as if searching for someone. A bead of sweat appeared on her forehead. The woman looked truly frightened. Meghan was watching her attentively through half opened eyes. I could tell she was trying to understand what Beverly was trying to say.

I wanted to know too, but my family was now shifting in their seats. I was taking too long. But I didn't dare leave the table now. Something more was up here. Something sinister, from the sounds of it. I tried to add it up. Hazmat suits. Industrial waste. Hospital waste. The harbour. Wells. Fires. Air. Brooks. Resistance. So much resistance. I was trying to put it all together so that it would total this politician's dread. So that it would add up to this reaction of unbridled fear.

I asked softly, "What exactly does it explain?"

Beverly looked at me, her eyes wide with anxiety and her voice shaking. "I've been getting death threats."

"Death threats?" I was incredulous. I couldn't believe what I was hearing in this cute café in a small town in rural Nova

Scotia. Death threats? Wasn't that the sort of thing that existed in big cities like Toronto and Vancouver where there were gangs and mobsters?

The MLA, the elected official of the county, the hard-working Beverly Price, looked ashamed. As if she had done something to deserve the threats. "Yes. Death threats. Someone wants to kill me."

I knew a story existed somewhere in this mess of a conversation. Meghan Oliver looked contrite. I peered at her closely. Was that a contrite look or a guilty look? Maybe it was a shocked look. Had the threats come from her? Naw, she didn't look the type. Did she? I looked at her again. Her frizzy hair caught the glare of the overhead lights. Her black-framed glasses were smudged with what looked like butter. Her shirttails were hanging below her pullover. Perhaps I was naïve, but she really didn't look organized enough to send a death threat. And why would she? She had just said she supported Beverly. My mind was so suspicious.

Meghan reached across the table and put her hand over Beverly's clenched fist. "I'm sorry. Did you go to the police?"

Beverly slowly extricated her hand from under Meghan's and held it out for us to see. "No, what's the point? Look at me. See?"

I saw what she meant right away. But in this day and age, did she truly believe the police wouldn't take her seriously because she had cappuccino skin? Surely not. I knew that Ralph had run seminars on racial profiling, carding, various sensitivities, de-escalation. Didn't all police in Canada get this training? Of course, they'd pay attention, or risk bad press. She was an MLA. An elected representative of not one but two counties. Journalists would be all over any prejudice. I sure was.

I said, "I think you might be surprised by their reaction. Death threats are very serious. Where do you think they're coming from? And how are you receiving them?"

Beverly ran her fork around the edge of her dish. "I don't want to talk about it."

"Well, I do," I said firmly. My journalist hat was on. "Who do you think is sending them to you?"

She gave a one-shoulder shrug. "I don't really know. Perhaps from people who don't want me to clean up the dump, because it's too expensive. They don't want to spend tax dollars on a black community. Or maybe from people who think I'm not doing enough to clean up the dump. Or maybe they're from people who hate me simply because I'm black. Your guess is as good as mine."

I felt a tap on my shoulder. I jumped out of my skin and put my hand over my heart. I'd been listening so intently to Beverly that I was completely immersed in this world of burning garbage and death threats. It was Calvin. He said, "Sorry to interrupt, but Mom, should we go ahead and order?"

"Sure, Calvin, thanks. Ask Ralph to order for me." He went back to our table.

Beverly Price changed the topic. She was not going to talk about death threats anymore. "You have a nice family, Robin. My son Danny told me how Winchester and Maggie helped him after what happened last night."

Both the topic and I were being dismissed. "Thanks, they're good kids," I said. "Maybe we will talk about this later." I stood up to leave. "Nice meeting you Meghan, and seeing you again, Beverly."

Meghan smiled, her face opening up in sudden friendliness. "You too. Let's be in touch."

You betcha. If there was a story here, and I thought there was, she would be a good resource.

Beverly was focusing on her food. Scallops in some kind of creamy sauce dotted with parsley. I wanted them. Then she looked up. "And thanks for stopping by." It was a politician's statement, given by rote. A polite goodbye.

I wove through the crowd and sat down at our table beside

Ralph. "What was that all about?" he asked.

"I'm not sure, but nothing good. I'll talk to you about it later."

"Okay-y-y." He let it drop. "I ordered you soup and a sandwich. Hope that's okay. Tuna. And red lentil."

I couldn't wait. "Sounds perfect."

At that moment the waiter appeared, a sweet young woman with golden hair and rosy cheeks, balancing four plates up her arm. She laid them down in front of the right customers and then hurried back to the kitchen to get the remaining order. Eventually we all tucked in, savouring every bite. Although most of us had ordered what would be a regular lunch of soup and a sandwich anywhere else, the quality and attention to detail was exquisite. I tried not to moan in delight as I vacuumed up my moist and tasty sandwich. White albacore tuna with crispy lettuce on fresh rye. Who would have thought that such magic could be created by a tuna sandwich? Or maybe it was just me.

But unfortunately, all good things must end and this meal of scrumptiousness was no exception. As the waiter came by to clear our plates and pass around dessert menus, Winchester and Maggie stood up, holding hands. I wondered what this was about. They looked at each other, smiled, and then faced the table.

"We have an announcement to make," said Maggie, uncharacteristically serious.

An announcement? What on earth could they possibly be announcing?

"The two of us came to a decision a few months ago and now..." Winchester stopped talking as his throat choked up.

Oh my. A wedding? They'd been living together for about a year and now they had decided to get married? Is this what he was going to say? A wedding! A white dress for my darling! A large party! A beautiful ceremony! Oh my God. But oh no, my mother would be beside herself. And what would my racist father say? This could be tricky.

Maggie took over. "It's okay, Winnie, I'll tell them."

She called him "Winnie?" Well, I guess his irritation at breakfast was over something else.

Maggie held herself up to her full height and smiled at each of us, one by one. "A few months ago, we decided that we were meant for each other." She paused, maybe for effect, or maybe to gather her thoughts. "I know, I know," she said, "we are from different backgrounds, but I know we will be able to withstand all the hardships that will no doubt come our way. The world is changing now, and we feel confident that our relationship is solid and on a good foundation. We trust each other completely. We will be fine."

I could feel myself welling up. My first born was getting *married*. Oh, how I loved a wedding. I wondered what caterer I should use. Italian? Indian? Traditional British? French? I almost groaned as the various spices floated through my imagination. And where should we get her dress? What would be the best venue for the celebration? What music did I want? I had so many contacts from my job at *The Toronto Express*, this shouldn't be too hard. A tear escaped my bottom lid and slid down my cheek.

Maggie grinned. "We're pregnant. Winnie and I will be giving birth after the winter. Sometime around the middle of March."

13.

WHAT? WAIT. NO WEDDING? But I wanted a wedding. I really wanted one. I froze the smile on my face. I was determined to look pleased. But it was hard. I loved weddings. Oh, for Christ's sake, Robin, this wasn't about you. It was about these two darling people and what *they* wanted. It was their life, not yours.

I switched gears. Okay, no wedding. Gone were all the wedding thoughts. I threw it all out, as tantalizing as it was, and redirected my mind. This took a little effort—I felt like my brain was a derailed train as I tried to jump aboard a completely new set of tracks. Eventually, I got there. A wedding was out, but a baby was in.

A baby! A tiny little baby to hold and cuddle and to love and coo at. Oh my. I loved babies even more than I loved weddings. I instinctively hugged my body as the thought took root and my heart swelled. A new little baby! And then the tears flowed. I couldn't believe it. A joy I had never experienced before flooded my chest. "Oh, Maggie. Winchester. This is the best news I've had in a long time. I'm so happy to hear this. What a wonderful decision. You two will make fabulous parents."

My parents, on the other hand, would have a fit.

Maggie's constant peeing suddenly made perfect sense. It wasn't an infection. She was *pregnant*. I could have danced.

My middle child Evelyn said, "Congratulations. This is fantastic news." A frown crossed her face. "So, no wedding?"

My ever-practical middle daughter was worried about them not taking a conventional approach? That surprised me. She was the one covered with tattoos and piercings, who dyed her hair pink then blue, then pink and blue at the same time. The one who wore Doc Martens and dresses that were really slips from the thrift store. The one who told me she was gay, then bi, then gender-fluid. *This* kid was concerned that her older sister was pregnant and not married?

Maggie looked a bit sheepish. "Actually, we got married at City Hall a while ago. We had decided to not waste our money on one day in our lives. And we didn't want the stress of planning and executing a major event. We each had a friend to witness for us." She looked at me. "I'm sorry, Mom. I know you love weddings, but we had to do it this way financially and emotionally."

I admonished myself to pick my battles. A baby trumped a wedding in any event. I stifled a sigh. "Oh, honey, it is very smart to make decisions based on what works for you, not for what is good for other people. Besides, a baby? What could be better news than a baby?"

I meant what I said. Of course, I was disappointed about no fancy wedding, but perhaps I'd dodged a bullet. They were so expensive. Where would I find the money? My parents? I could not imagine asking my racist father for help. His face would turn bright red. And really, what was the point of a wedding? Trevor and I had had a lovely wedding with a five-tier cake, covered in little silver balls and pink icing roses. And look where that had got us.? That stupid cake had cost us hundreds of dollars. Weddings could be such a waste of time and money. Maggie and Winchester were right. Besides, a *baby*? Oh, how lucky was I!

Winchester said, "Thanks Mom, for understanding." He was smiling at me, his eyes shining with unshed tears.

Mom? Winchester had called me "Mom." How did I feel about that? He had a mom. How would she feel? But I looked at him standing beside my daughter, his lovely face beaming with pride at their news, and again my heart filled with sheer joy. Sure, I could be a mom to him. No problem. I was so overwhelmed with emotion I could hardly speak.

Ralph spoke up. "This is wonderful news, you two. Congratulations." He raised his glass. "Let's all toast the new parents. Congratulations," he said again.

After the toast and much clinking of glasses, the two sat down and the waiter proceeded to ask us if we wanted dessert while handing out the menus. Of course, I wanted dessert. In fact, I wanted ten desserts. This announcement called for a food celebration. I snatched up the menu from in front of me and saw immediately what would be perfect: Peanut Butter Cream Pie. Who on earth had created such a wonderful concoction? We all gave our dessert orders and chattered happily about the upcoming birth.

As I dug my fork through the chocolate drizzle on my pie, I thought about the news. Of course, they would be fine together. There were so many mixed couples in Toronto now that no one would even give it a second thought.

In just six months I would be a grandmother. Now there was a thought. Me? A grandmother? I would really have to stop drinking now. Imagine holding a baby with a bottle of wine coursing through my veins. Babies were slippery little things. Nope. Wasn't going to happen. Oh God, there was all that new research about DNA being altered by life events and passed down to generations. What if I had passed down a penchant for drinking in my DNA to Maggie and then from her to the new baby. What if the baby was trapped by my DNA? I hoped not. I would have to chant about that, that's for sure. If something about my karma needed changing, that was it.

Did being a grandmother make me old? I looked at my hands. Well, I certainly wasn't young. So many wrinkles. I'd done a lot of dishes. And were those age spots? I looked more closely. Nope, they were freckles. Right. Freckles. I was in denial. The grannies I knew all had short, curly, grey hair. I'd been dying my hair for years now. So, no biggie about that. But did I have the energy? I'd be racing around, working full-time plus taking care of babies on weekends while their parents did chores. I'd need way more energy than I had now. Drinking made me lethargic. I stayed up too late to have a party with only myself in attendance. I would have to stop, but that would be hard to do. I loved to drink. And I would really have to lose some weight if I was going to be chasing around after a crawling baby. Oh God. I would have to bend over to pick it up. Good luck with that. Right now, I could hardly bend over to put on my shoes. I loved to eat. That would have to stop too. Geezus. Maybe this wasn't such good news after all.

Ralph bumped my elbow. "What's up, sweetie? You're looking pensive."

I lowered my voice so only he could hear me. "I'm going to be a grandmother."

"Yes," he said. "Yes, you are."

"I'm going to have to make some changes in how I live."

"We both will."

I dragged my eyes away from my delicious peanut butter pie and locked eyes with him. "Thank you, Ralph. That means a lot."

"I do love you, Robin."

Were the kids watching? I kicked him under the table. He laughed.

In light of Maggie and Winchester's news, I resisted the urge to scrape up the remaining crumbs on my plate with my fork. The diet had begun. "I want to look at a garbage dump after lunch. It's been shut down. Is that okay with you?"

"Now there's a tourist attraction I would hate to miss." Ralph was joking, but when he looked at my face, he saw that I was serious. "No, it's okay. I don't have a problem with that." He looked like he did. But I knew it would be okay. Then he said to the table in general, "So, after lunch, what do you want to see in Shelburne, other than a dump?" He sounded like a tour guide.

Bertie was on his phone. "Okay, I've got a list of the tourist sights. Shelburne has some interesting things to see. There's the Dory Shop Museum, The Shelburne Museum Complex, The Sandy Point Lighthouse, Ross-Thomson House Museum, Boxing Rock Brewing Company. For the sporty types amongst us, there are boat tours in the harbour, a beach called Roseway Beach, and along the highway there's a trail called the Port L'Hebert Pocket Wilderness. And of course, the Black Loyalist Heritage Centre, which we've seen."

Evelyn said, "It's still pouring out, so let's do the indoor things."

Calvin parted the restaurant's net curtains on a window behind him. "It's really bucketing down now. Why don't we just drive around, so we don't get wet?"

A chorus of "No's" filled the air. He shrugged and smiled. "Okay, I'm overruled. That being the case, I'd like to park and look at the beach. Park and look at the lighthouse. Park and look at the wharf."

We all laughed.

Maggie said, "I'm all for going into the museums. They sound interesting."

I wanted to look at them, too. "Good idea, Maggie. I'd also like to see the dump in the south end."

"Sure, Robin." Winchester was rolling his eyes. No "Mom" while he was teasing me. "That sounds fascinating. I always wanted to look at a dump."

Maggie poked him. "Maybe there'll be bears."

He considered the idea. "Yeah, let's go to the dump. I can't *bare* the suspense."

Everyone grinned.

I got a little bit defensive. "I know it sounds boring, but it's for my work."

Was it? Beverly Price said she couldn't make changes because of systemic, institutional racism. Meghan Oliver was pretty adamant about the dump being an example of environmental racism. I had never heard of the term before and wanted to actually see what she meant. If I could. It was likely that you couldn't really see polluted groundwater. And the fires spewing toxins into the air hadn't burned for months. How the conversation had ended with the two women came back to me. I'd have to talk to Ralph about Beverly receiving death threats.

As we stood up from the table, I saw that the two women had already left, saving me an awkward moment when I had to walk by with a guy who was obviously a cop. No doubt about it, I would have to talk to Ralph about the death threats, and about his telling me he loved me in front of my kids. He was becoming quite brazen. I hoped the kick hurt him. Well, not really. Still. He shouldn't do that. But then again, why not? What on earth was wrong with me that I couldn't bear someone telling me they loved me?

Speaking of bears, I sure hoped there were none at the dump. After my exposure to bears at my cottage in May, I didn't want to see another one, ever again. We hung around a bit waiting for Maggie to have yet another visit to the washroom, and then we dashed as a group down the street to the museums by the water. We traipsed through them, leaving wet footprints, with me wanting to linger in the Dory Shop. I loved the smell of fresh cut wood there and would have spent hours, breathing it in.

Finally, we piled into the van. I googled the closed dump, found the location, and we headed off. A few minutes later, we were parked outside a chain-link fence that was padlocked shut. I saw through the rain dripping down the van's window a posted notice edged in red. It was attached to the wire gate with plastic zip ties, stating that the dump was shut. Behind the fence, there was a large grass-covered hill. No bears that I could see. It wasn't that kind of dump, filled with household trash. This dump contained garbage that was far more menacing than the potato peelings and crusts of bread that attracted bears.

What lurked below the dandelions and scrubby grass covering the mound was anybody's guess. I looked at it and shuddered. I swivelled my head and looked across the street. Everywhere there were signs of poverty. Trailers and ragged clothes hanging in the rain on sagging lines. "Let's go, Ralph." I'd seen enough. Meghan was right. This dump was far too close to where people lived. I was very upset.

He pulled away and drove slowly down the thin road until it became a mud track. He spied a driveway ahead. "I can turn the van around up there."

"Go for it," I said. I was feeling nauseous because of this place.

As we pulled into the opening in the bush, I saw a black man standing on a makeshift deck outside his trailer, smoking a cigarette in the drizzle. I wanted to warn him about the dangers of smoking, as I always wanted to do when I saw someone smoking. But what would be the point? The statistics were terrible. The people who lived around this dump were doomed to an early death, whether they smoked or not. They had been breathing the dump's air and drinking the dump's water for generations. Nobody had done a thing.

So this was environmental racism.

14.

WE DROVE BACK TO THE COTTAGE through alternating patches of fog and drizzle. As we passed the carved wooden sign for the pocket wilderness in Port L'Hebert, my head snapped around to look at it and I spotted a lone car parked in the gravel lot. A white pickup truck. What was someone doing here on a day like today? These Nova Scotians weren't held back by a rainy day.

I asked, "What on earth is a pocket wilderness? Old dryer lint in your pocket?" I thought I was being funny.

There was zero response. All I could hear in the car was the steady *whomp whomp* of the windshield wipers and the hum of the wheels on the wet road as we headed over hills and around sharp bends to our rented home. The miles ticked by. I looked in the rear-view mirror. Calvin, Bert, and Evelyn were in the row directly behind Ralph and me. They were in their own worlds, earbuds in and listening to music. Bert, in the middle, looked like he'd fallen asleep, his head lolled forward, bobbling up and down as if attached to his spine by a thin thread. Calvin was drumming his knee with his forefinger in time to some song or another as he gazed out the window. Evelyn was admiring what she was drawing in her moleskin journal, smiling as she tilted her head this way and that. She caught me looking at her in the mirror and held up what she'd been working on. It was a large heart full of Celtic-looking curlicues surrounding the word AUNT in capital letters. I smiled at her. She would be a fun-loving aunt.

Maggie and Winchester were sitting in the very back row. Maggie had fallen asleep, her head lying on Winchester's shoulder. His eyebrows were furrowed as he frowned out the window. I wondered what he was thinking about. He'd seemed okay in the museum. Well, when I thought about it, he'd seemed more than okay. He had seemed oblivious to the information. Surely, he saw his relatives' names in the *Book of Negroes*. Was that why he was looking so grim? Or maybe he was worried about his future with Maggie and their new little baby. He must have sensed that I was looking at him and met my eyes in the mirror. He smiled instantly and then tapped the air over Maggie's head with a long finger. Then he made a sleeping gesture with his hands, holding them together as if he were praying. Then he pretended to put his finger down his throat and gag. Oh, I got it. Maggie was sleeping because she felt ill. That's what he was worried about. I smiled back and shrugged. It was normal to feel ill in the first trimester.

Finally, we took the Port Mouton exit off the highway, turned left at the bottom of the ramp, and followed the road as it curved to Hunt's Point. We drove past a thin road that led to a pretty little church, and headed further left. The empty parking lot for Summerville Beach appeared, nestled in front of huge sand dunes. No one was there on a day like today. The wooden door of one of the outhouses was swinging in the wind. Ralph's hand snaked over the console and took mine. "Do you want to talk about it now?"

"Talk about what?" I knew damn well what he wanted to talk about.

"You know. The two women in the restaurant. What was that about?"

I didn't want to talk about it. I wanted to sleep. The wipers were hypnotizing me into la-la land. The sugar from the pie was zinging happily in my veins. Plus, we were almost home. I needed more time for what was going to be a longish conversation. "Maybe tonight." I did need to talk to him. Beverly's death threats had to be reported. I knew he'd do something about it. The weather seemed to clearing up a bit. I looked to the east and saw distinct outlines of clouds over the grey ocean. This was better than a solid bank of grey. "After the campfire."

"You're optimistic."

"I think it's clearing up. Plus, it would be nice to cap off the holiday with a final bonfire. The kids really like them. I'm sure we can have one."

He thought about that and then said, "Did you want to go to that same place for dinner tonight? You know, world's best fish and chips?"

"Of course! Remember? The kids already decided that." Did he miss that vote? Or was he double-checking with me?"

"I know that's what *they* wanted. I just wanted to make sure that's what *you* wanted."

"Yup. Delicious."

But my mind was wandering. The kids would have to get packed, and I was hoping they could help a bit with cleaning up the house before they left. I sure didn't want to do that job all by myself. If they each cleaned their own bedrooms, then it would leave just two bedrooms to clean when we left in a week. One for Cindy and one for Ralph and me.

I was looking forward to Cindy coming tomorrow. We'd kept in touch by text over the week. Plus, I knew where she was because of our app. She sounded like she was having fun, but I thought she was getting lonely. One of her texts read: *Awfully quiet here in Cape Breton. Just me and some trees.* She said she was going to show up after dinner on Monday. The kids' flight was midday, so I figured I'd easily be home from driving them to the airport to meet her at the cottage. We were just an hour and a half from the airport.

When we pulled up to the house the cloud cover had thinned enough that I could see a white orb shining behind the grey filaments. Perhaps this was the Nova Scotian version of a sun and cloud mix. In Ontario, a sun and cloud mix meant there were some clouds and bright sun. Here it meant thin clouds that the sun shone through. I turned around and said to the kids, "We have an hour or two before we head out for dinner. Why doesn't everyone pack and clean the house so that we can relax by a fire tonight?"

Maggie had woken up when we turned off the highway and replied, "Winnie and I have to get up before dawn if we want to get into Toronto in time for work on Tuesday, so let's do everything a little bit earlier than usual."

"Suits me," said Evelyn. "I'm already hungry for dinner."

Maggie turned a little pale at the thought of eating. "Maybe I'll be able to eat in an hour." She massaged her stomach.

Calvin slid open the van door. "I'm all for an early night. This kind of day makes me feel lazy."

"Everything makes you lazy," Bertie said, grinning.

I said, "Boys."

Soon after we got inside, I heard the sound of dresser drawers opening and shutting, the vacuum running over the pine floors, and the knock of the broom on the wooden stairs. Water was running, and I noticed the bucket was gone from beside the fridge. Someone must have grabbed it on the way upstairs. They were packing and cleaning. Ralph had taken Lucky out for a pee. Perfect.

Finally, I was alone. Peace and quiet. I could have a glass of wine before dinner. I plucked a bottle from the fridge along with some cheese and crackers. Why not? I was starving. All that sitting in the car. I laughed at myself. I plunked myself down at the kitchen table. It felt so good to sit in the quiet. My solitude lasted all of three minutes.

Ralph sauntered into the kitchen wiping his hands on the backs of his jeans, Lucky trotting behind him. "Just had to wash my hands at the outside tap after taking Lucky out. He found something disgusting around back and I had to pry it out of his mouth. Dead squirrel or something."

I tried to look interested, but I just needed a break to settle myself. "Oh yeah, he does that. If you say 'Drop it,' he usually does."

Ralph laughed, and said, "Now you tell me." He moved closer to the table. So much for my quality time with myself. "Do you mind if I join you?"

He was being so formal. Perhaps he sensed my hesitation. What was I going to say? "Yes, I mind? Go away, I need some private time?" Of course, I wasn't going to say that. "Not at all. Thanks for asking. Wine?"

He lowered his lanky frame onto the purple chair beside me at the table and poured himself a small glass. "So," he said, looking at me straight in the eye, "what was that conversation about with those two women?"

Geezus. He was like a dog with a bone. I bristled. I'd told him we could talk about it after the campfire. Now I wanted to drink wine, relax, and laugh a bit. The situation was so complicated. And serious. And it would take ages to explain. I wanted to do it justice. But maybe time was of the essence. Beverly was getting death threats. I had to talk to him about that, for sure, and I had to give him some context. It was important. How would I feel if I hadn't told him and she was killed? She didn't want the cops told, and he was a cop, but still... I took a deep breath and launched into my explanation.

"Meghan Oliver—the one with the fly-away frizzy hair—has been a long-time advocate for shutting down the Shelburne dump. It took years for that to happen. Her perseverance is amazing. Now she wants it cleaned up. It's full of military waste, industrial chemical, and hospital waste, from all over the province. There are three brooks that run from the dump into the harbour and along the way, the waste seeps into the earth and poisons peoples' wells. Nothing has been done about it. People are dying. It's primarily a black community that lives close by the dump."

Ralph nodded. "Right. Environmental racism."

I was surprised that he knew the term. At least I didn't have to explain *that*. But then, being in law enforcement, he probably knew all about it and the various issues that made people mad enough to kill. "Right," I repeated. "Environmental racism."

He noted my surprise. "I had a hint about it when I saw that guy on his porch. While Lucky was sniffing around, I went on my phone and looked up some of the Shelburne health statistics. There is an elevated risk of cancer and other diseases in the local population."

Maybe I should have talked to him earlier. "True. And Beverly Price, she was the black woman Meghan was sitting with, is the MLA for Queens and Shelburne counties."

Ralph lowered his eyelids as he worked out the meaning of the initials. "The Member for the Legislative Assembly. So, she's the one with the power to get the dump cleaned up. She was at the lobster supper last night."

"Right."

"But let me guess. She's running into opposition every time she tries to solve the issue, probably from the town council. Systemic racism. And this, in turn, results in environmental racism.

"How do you know all this?" I was surprised.

"We, and I mean the Toronto Police force, had to take an extensive course on race relations. This area around here," Ralph waved his arm in the air, "is known as the South Africa of Canada. Mississippi North. So, we spent some time looking at Shelburne County. And so it's easy for me to guess that the town council doesn't want to implement any changes because that would upset the applecart. They want to stay safe. They can't get out of the trap of tradition and take a risk of doing something new. It's like the story of the chained elephant."

"What do you mean, 'chained elephant?'"

He sat back and took a small sip of his wine. He knew he'd be driving to the restaurant in half an hour. His strict adherence to the law was a tad irritating. An inner rant rose up in my chest. He never went over the speed limit. He never swore. He never threw anything out the car window, not even his gum. Cause for divorce? Wait, that would mean we'd have to be married, and I wasn't going to do *that* again. So that was Ralph, Mr. Goody Two Shoes. Me, on the other hand, bring on the wine! I guzzled a gulp.

"Once," he said, "there was an elephant chained to a post in the ground. He strained at his chain but soon realized exactly how far he could go. After a month of this, his owners took off the chain and tied him up with a flimsy rope. The elephant didn't even try to break free, although he could have easily. He just walked to the end of where the old chain used to end. Do you see what I mean, Robin? There is an ingrained pattern of behaviour, a tradition of sorts, in the town council. For years they've blocked any effort to clean up the dump. It's like they've been conditioned to block it, you know, over time. Bottom line, I can understand why Beverly Price is meeting with some resistance to the notion of cleaning up the dump."

"Actually Ralph, a lot of resistance." Should I tell him? I had to. "She's been getting death threats."

There, I'd said it.

Ralph had been leaning back in his chair while we were talking, relaxed and eating my cheese and crackers. I didn't really care. There was more cheese in the fridge. But with my announcement about Beverly getting death threats, he threw himself forward. The chair legs hit the floor with a bang. "*What*?"

I gulped more wine. My tumbler was almost empty. "Yes, death threats. She hasn't gone to the police."

"Why not?"

"She thinks they won't take her seriously because she's black."

He frowned, looked at me quizzically, and pushed out his chair, as if to distance himself from what I'd said. "I tell you..." He shook his head. "I know things are different here than Toronto, but...." He stared out the kitchen window and shook his head again, as if trying to straighten out jumbled thoughts. "I can't leave this alone. I have to act."

"She didn't want the police involved."

Ralph made to stand up. "I have to make a call."

I put a hand on his arm. "Okay Ralph, I understand. But be careful. This isn't your jurisdiction. Who knows how they'll react to an outsider barging in. Plus, she didn't want the police involved. Plus, none of us are experts in race relations. Plus, this isn't Toronto. Things are different here. There's a different history. It's complicated."

"I don't care about any of that. Not in matters of life and death. I have a responsibility when people's lives are threatened. It's my job, Robin. It's just a phone call; it won't take up our whole last night here. We will still have fun." He was staring at my hand on his arm, waiting for me to remove it.

Well, it looked like this holiday was about to become a little more complicated. I kept my hand on his arm. I wanted to tell him again that she did not want the police to know, and I almost said so. But she was so frightened. And I was frightened for her. So I bit my tongue.

He said, "Look, it's just a call. All I'll do is report it. I won't pursue it. As you said, it's not my jurisdiction and I shouldn't interfere in a local case. I probably don't understand the local dynamics either, as you said. But Robin ... it's her life. Don't worry. It won't wreck our holiday. But I have to let the police here know. Her life is in danger, whether or not she's taking it seriously."

"Oh, I'm sure she's taking it seriously," I said grimly, recalling the sweat on her brow and the set of her mouth.

He was still looking at my hand on his arm. "I have to make a call."

"Okay, I understand." I removed my hand.

As he left the room, I thought about what had just happened. Ralph, unlike my dead husband Trevor, did not shake my hand off impatiently. He waited until I was ready to take it away. Did this make him a weakling or a respectful guy? I pondered this and drank some more. I loved the way the wine was making my veins yodel and shaking my neurons into a happy dance. It was going to my head, and frankly, I didn't really care if he was a weakling or a respectful guy. He had a big you-know, and that worked for me. I'd try and think about this tomorrow. If I remembered. He slouched back into the room, a bleak look on his face.

"What?"

"Less than helpful. The guy who took my call said that politicians get death threats all the time. Or threats to burn down their house. Or threats to have their tires slashed. He said it was they way people talked around here. That it wasn't serious."

"Oh." I took another gulp of my wine. "What do you think?"

"What do I think? I *think* you said she was taking it seriously. I *think* it is serious and that a death threat should always be followed up. I *think* I had better go into the station in Liverpool and make my point."

"Ralph." Really? But what about our last night with the kids? I shrugged the thought off, I knew he was right, but he read my mind.

"Robin, it's important. Life and death. I won't be gone long. Just an hour. I'll be back in time to get everyone to dinner." He looked at his watch. "It's just three-thirty now. I'll be home by four-thirty, we'll be in the restaurant by five, and back here by seven. Lots of time for a bonfire and an early night."

I nodded. "Okay, honey. Do what you have to do."

He sat down next to me and continued, his arm snug around my shoulder. "I know you're upset. But I could tell, even from where I was sitting in the restaurant, that something very disturbing was going on in your conversation. I'm sure Beverly has had threats before, just as the officer at the station said. But this feels different to me. And I think it felt different to her."

He was right. She was deeply upset. She was terrified. I could feel my resolve to keep the evening light-hearted dissolving. I sighed. "She was scared, Ralph. I know you're right to go in and make them take the threats seriously. I know it's selfish, but I just want to have a nice last evening with the family.

Ralph unfolded himself from the chair. "I know. Me too." He walked away while saying, "I'll be right back. Don't worry. This won't take very long."

I watched through the kitchen window as the van drove down the lane to the road, Ralph looking fixedly ahead. Sometimes he was such a nerd, but I loved him for it. Oh geezus, *liked* him for it. Not loved. *Liked*. He and I had a lot in common. He was as tied to his job as I was. He *had* to do what he was doing. I understood that. I was tied to my job, too. I was a nerdy type, as well. Damn. I should be writing an article about all these events. I got out my phone and started to make a list of the things that had happened since yesterday. I started with the death of that fish farm guy. What was his name again? I drank some more wine and then smiled at my empty glass. I needed more wine and cheese. I scooped out a new bottle and a new package of cheddar from the fridge. Geez, it was good to relax.

I sat down with my treasure and listened to the happy sounds of my family packing and cleaning. I even smelled bathroom cleaner. They were doing a great job. Wait. Chemicals? Bad for babies. Oh no! I jumped up.

"Maggie?" No answer. "Maggie?"

"Yes, Mom?"

"That's not you cleaning the bathroom, right? I don't want you near those chemicals, not while you're pregnant."

"It's me, Mom." Calvin.

"Oh, good. Thanks Calvin. Nice of you to do that job."

"No prob, Mom."

"You worry too much, Mom," Maggie said.

"That's a mother's job. Soon to be yours."

I heard her laugh as I sat back down and took a long swallow of my wine. A grandchild. I loved babies. More than weddings. Lucky uncurled himself from where he was sleeping in his crate and ambled over to me. He stood at the side of my chair, waiting for me to drop my hand and pat him. I stuffed the last cracker into my mouth and obliged.

My revelry was interrupted by the sound of a car crunching up the gravel driveway. What? Who could that be? Oh, it was Ralph. When he said he'd be back soon, I thought he meant in an hour. Maybe he forgot his phone or something.

The van door slammed and he dragged his feet into the house, looking steadfastly ahead. What was making him so morose? The skies were clearing and soon we'd be eating fish and chips.

"Hi, what did you forget?"

He stood in front of me, despair flitting in his eyes like a wounded bird.

My chest constricted. "What happened Ralph? Was there an accident on the highway?" My heart was pounding. Something had gone very wrong.

He said, "I was too late. She's dead. Murdered."

What was he talking about?

"Beverly. On my way up the ramp to the highway, a bunch of police cars were racing down. Sirens on. I turned around and followed them. They stopped outside a house in Port Mouton. Beverly's house. It was Beverly. Murdered."

"Beverly? No, it wasn't her. We just saw her at lunch a few hours ago. It wasn't her house."

"No, it's her. I asked. Someone killed her."

15.

"HOW?" I ASKED. "HOW DID SOMEONE KILL HER? And why? She was the MLA for Christ's sake."

Ralph looked out the window. "I don't know. Yet. But I will." A determined expression fixed his face into hard angles. "I wanted to come tell you in person, right away, before it got out on the news. I didn't want you to read it on your phone. But I'll go back to Port Mouton now and get more details."

"This is terrible. Why on earth would someone want to kill her?" I could hear my voice escalating. The world seemed to be whirling around me.

Winchester came into the kitchen, carrying a mop and broom. "Hiya. Almost done upstairs. Where do these go?" he asked, his voice trailing off as he saw our expressions. His head swung back and forth as he regarded us, questioningly. "What's up?"

I had to decide whether or not to impart this terrible news to my kids on their last night here. Oh geez, there was no debate. Of course, I had to tell them. They were adults now. I couldn't protect them from the world and all its ugliness. They had news feeds on their phones. Besides, the minute we sat down in the restaurant they would know. Danny, the MLA's son and our server for the past week, would be absent. Better if it came from me. I looked at Ralph. He was patting Lucky, pretending to be preoccupied, leaving the decision up to me. I carefully said, "Beverly Price was murdered."

Winchester was standing in front of the mess I'd made on the kitchen table. An empty plate covered with smudges. Cracker crumbs swimming in a splash of red wine on the vinyl placemat. An empty wineglass, with sticky purple residue on the inside. He stood a little taller. His chest expanded as he took a deep breath. A small tick vibrated below his right eye. A fist clenched. I felt anger and despair seep out of his pores as he contained himself.

"Winnie?" I asked.

"How?" he spat.

Ralph answered him. "I don't know. But I will find out." His voice thundered across the room. Murder enraged Ralph. His face had turned the colour of freezer burn on roast beef, pasty with blotches of red.

Maggie's singsong voice floated down the stairs. "Winchester? Can you help me bring down my suitcase?"

"I will in a minute. Can you come down here for a sec?"

Maggie appeared in the doorway to the kitchen. She stared at her new husband and knew right away that something was off. She ran to him. "What's wrong, Winchester? What's happened?"

Winchester answered, taking her hand. "Danny's mother was murdered. Today."

"Beverly? The MLA?" Maggie looked around the room at each of us, shaking her head. "That's impossible. We just saw her at that café at lunch. In Shelburne. She was eating with that woman with the frizzy hair." She looked at me accusingly as if I had created a conspiracy. "You were talking to her, Mom."

"I know. She told me she had been getting death threats."

A tear rolled down Maggie's face. She crossed her arms tightly in front of her chest. "This is terrible. I don't believe it. Did she go to the police? They would have protected her. Right? Wouldn't they Ralph?"

Ralph continued to pat Lucky. He wasn't going to answer.

He'd tried to get her protected and his efforts had failed. Stupid local cops.

I said, "She didn't want to involve the police."

Winchester spoke up. "I understand that."

Maggie looked at him. She was angry. "Oh, Winnie. It's a stupid black thing, right?"

Winchester planted his feet on the floor shoulder-width apart and drew himself up to his full height. God, I hoped these two were going to be okay. He said, "Yes, it's a stupid black thing." He opened his hands, "But please try to understand, Mags." His chest heaved as he let out a defeated sigh. "It's hard to explain." He looked through the kitchen window and saw a lobster trap leaning against Nan's woodshed. "It's like lobsters."

"Lobsters? Oh, right." She rolled her eyes. "Nice try." She wasn't going to let go of her frustration.

"Yeah, like lobsters." He gained momentum with his metaphor. "The police are like lobsters. Lobsters will go into a trap and even though the way out of the trap is wide open, they won't go out. They will stay trapped.

Elephants and now lobsters, I thought. Traps. I thought about traps.

Maggie stuck out her chin. "I don't get it. What do lobsters have to do with her not going to the police?"

"I'm not explaining it very well. It's like this. The police are so used to treating black people a certain way, and even though they've had training, they don't change how they *act*. They're like lobsters."

Maggie opened her eyes wide. "Oh, I get it. So, the police are in a trap. They could get out, but they don't. They don't change the way they behave. They are trapped by racism."

"Right." Winchester let out a relieved sigh. "It's complicated. I have trouble explaining it but you know what I mean. There's a way out, but they won't take the action to get out. That's why she wouldn't go to the police. She didn't think they'd *do* anything."

Well, she sure was right about that. They'd even dismissed Ralph, a white man, when he reported her threats. Deep systemic racism. My gut wrenched.

"Mom!" Calvin yelled from upstairs. "I was just looking at my phone and my news feed said that Beverly Price, that woman you were talking to at lunch, was dead. Wait..."

"Yes, Calvin," I called up the stairs, "I know."

Bertie, who was a faster reader than Calvin, shouted, "Oh my God. She was *murdered.*"

Footsteps pounded down the stairs. The boys burst into the kitchen. "What are we going to *do*?" asked Bertie, his palms facing up, his chest shaking, eyes wild.

Calvin looked at Winchester, as if for guidance. Winchester lifted one shoulder and bit the left side of his lip.

Evelyn had followed the boys down and was standing by the wood stove. Her arms were crossed over her chest. She was containing herself. "We are going to carry on. Cleaning, packing, going out for dinner, having a bonfire."

Bertie looked as if he was going to cry. "But she's *dead.* What about Danny? Huh? What about him? What's going to happen to him? He's not even finished high school. He's just a kid," he wailed. I thought he was going to hyperventilate. He was distraught.

Winchester took charge. "Bertie. Bertie, look at me." Bertie turned his head slowly until he faced Winchester. "He'll be okay. He'll live with his grandmother, like a lot of kids who have no parents. He told me he had lived with his grandmother all his life."

"She'll be too old to take care of him," he cried. Bertie's grandmother was certainly too old.

I thought about this and did some quick math. No, she'd be about my age. Did I figure that out right? I took out my phone and went to my calculator app. So, his mother was, say, forty-one or two. His grandmother could be about twenty years older, so she'd be about sixty-two. People had children younger then. Not much older than I was. Now there's a reality check. "She could be just five or six years older than I am, Bert. Plenty young enough to take care of him."

Bertie didn't look convinced that Danny was going to be fine. It hit me like a ton of bricks that he was reliving his reaction to his father's death. "He'll be okay, sweetheart. Just like you are. You're okay. "

Bertie's eyes were swimming with tears. "But what are we going to *do*?"

Ralph stood up while brushing crumbs off his hands. "I'll take care of it. I'm going to go back to the scene now. I'll do my best to make sure that the police here do everything possible to catch the killer. That's what we are going to do." With that, he manoeuvered around the kids crowded around the table. "I'll come back and let you know what I find out. In the meantime, you people finish up here. We'll have a good final dinner in Port Mouton and a nice bonfire afterwards." He slipped out the kitchen door, letting it bang shut behind him.

I watched him walk to the van through the kitchen window. His broad shoulders strained at his flannel shirt. What would he find out? The kids all looked at me expectantly. "I know what you know. Virtually nothing. But Ralph is a good cop. He works homicide. He's a detective. Don't worry. He'll make sure they get to the bottom of this. He'll help the local force if he has to and they will find the murderer."

"But what about *Danny*?" Bertie was still worried about Beverly's son. I could see his synapses were flashing as he worked out the details. "Oh no. Did he find her? *Dead*?" He grabbed his chest, as if trying to keep his heart inside his rib cage.

I sure as hell hoped not. That image would haunt that beautiful boy for the rest of his life. "He was probably working, sweetie. His shift probably began at eleven this morning so he'd be out of the house. He was probably working."

Bertie looked at his watch. "Cutting it pretty close. If he was doing the lunch shift. He'd probably be home by two.

could have seen the whole thing. The attack. *Everything.* Where is he now?"

Oh my God. He was catastrophizing.

Evelyn consoled him with practicality. "Bertie, don't worry. I'll call the restaurant and find out if he's there. Or when he was there. He probably had a shift from eleven to eight. Nine hours, with an hour off as a break. They close at eight."

She searched her phone for the number, dialled, and asked her questions. She tapped her phone off, ending the call, and looked at everyone. "It's okay. He was working during the time frame. An RCMP officer came to the restaurant and got him around three. So no, he didn't witness the attack, and he didn't find her dead body. The woman who answered the phone at the restaurant didn't know where he was taken, but she imagines he is somewhere with the grandmother, who he lives with in Port Mouton."

Winchester was right.

Maggie had crossed the room and put her arm around Bertie's shoulders. She hugged him close and was murmuring into his ear. She, being the oldest, had finished school and was looking for her first job when Trevor, her father, had been killed. Calvin was in his last year of university and Evelyn was just a year behind him. But Bertie was still in high school when it happened. He had only been sixteen, and his father's death had hit him hard. Maggie had helped take care of him when he was a baby, and she was helping now. She was going to be such a good mother.

I stood up and sopped up the wine spill on the table with a tissue. I brushed the remaining cracker crumbs off into my hand. The wine bottle went back into the fridge, the glass in the sink. "Winnie, the mop and broom go beside the fridge. Let's finish our cleaning and packing, everyone. It's three forty-five now and as soon as Ralph gets back, we will go out for dinner."

Lucky, sensing a change in the atmosphere, barked happily, his tail wagging. "Oh Lucky," Calvin said, and laughed. "You are one funny dog." He bent over and scratched his ears.

One by one, the kids left the room. Maggie led the way, her arm still around Bertie. In their wake was a vacuum of silence. I could hear my heart beating in my chest. A good indication that I was still alive. This was such a shock. Two deaths in two days. When on earth did that ever happen? What was going on in this lovely region of Nova Scotia? This harsh reality seemed incongrous with the soft, almost velvety landscape. I laughed at myself. It looked smooth and rolling, but it was hard rocks, worn down by wind and rain into deceiving contours.

What a disaster. The kids last night here and now this awful thing had happened. Maybe they'd get over it quickly. Really, they had only met Danny officially just the once, at the lobster supper, although he had been our waiter numerous nights in the Port Mouton restaurant. I guess just knowing him was enough for a bond to be created. No wonder they were upset, but hopefully it would pass by dinner. Dinner! Oh no. Should we go somewhere else for dinner? It might be too hard for them to be in the same village as the murder. To go to the same restaurant where Danny worked.

But maybe she was killed elsewhere. I knew so little. I'd have to wait for Ralph to get back to know the full story. I googled restaurants in the town of Liverpool and saw a few that looked good. But it was the Sunday night of a long weekend. I wondered if I should cancel our reservation in Port Mouton and make one elsewhere, and if I couldn't, if we should just go to McDonald's. Right. Like that would go over well. But what if they wanted to go to their usual place? Oh God. I looked longingly at my empty glass in the sink.

I had to get outside. "C'mon Lucky, we're going for a walk. Where's your leash?"

The dog danced around the kitchen in a state of euphoria while I searched coat hooks for his leash. Hopefully, the kids wouldn't forget their unworn jackets. Oh, there it was—Ralph had hung it on the doorknob. Lucky squirmed in enthusiastic anticipation while I tried to attach the leash to his collar. "You're a wiggly little thing," I said to him.

Once outside, I took some deep breaths. How had two deaths happened in two days? Unbelievable. I rested my eyes on the far horizon of the distant sea. Suddenly, I felt exhausted. Wine did that to me, sometimes. It slowed my blood down to a crawl. Or, conversely, sometimes it whipped it up into a froth. But this was a crawl kind of day. I had to stop drinking. I saw the way the kids had looked at the debris in front of me on the table. The crumbs, the bottle. I needed to be strong and reliable for them, not all over the joint like a staggering mess.

Joint. Hmmm. Now that marijuana was legal in Canada maybe I should start smoking it instead. I thought about all the advantages. First, it was easier to carry around. God, you could hide it in your pocket, unlike a huge bottle of wine. Although, believe me, I'd tried to sneak one past my kids just yesterday. My hoodie pouch bulged like I was the pregnant one. I didn't think they'd noticed, but I wasn't kidding myself. You couldn't cover up a bottle with clothing. A joint, though, was so little, so compact. A tiny fun bomb. And, I loved the smell of dope, that pervasive sweet odour. Did people still call it "dope?" I was getting so old, I'd lost touch with the lingo. Some people said it smelled disgusting, like skunk. Not me. If anyone in my cool Toronto neighbourhood was toking up outside, I'd follow the wisps of smoke down the street, sniffing deeply.

On the other hand, I cursed the stench of alcohol. After a night of knocking wine back, I smelled like a wino for hours, right to the next morning. Not that I had anything against winos, but really, I was going to be a *grandmother*. I couldn't smell like a wino. Wine breath was such a giveaway. But, if I blazed a spiff, the skunkish bouquet would linger on my clothes for about five minutes. I thought back to my university days, remembering the silly laughter and boxes of pizza. The blue clouds wafting in the room. Holding our breath until our faces turned purple. Coughing up a lung. Yeah, those were the good ole days.

Oh Robin, it was time to stop thinking about this need to alter my state of mind. Act. Don't be a lobster in a trap. Act and get out. Don't be the elephant. Stop eating so much. God, I needed therapy. It was something in my past that made me this way, probably something to do with my father. What a piece of shit he was. I knew I shouldn't think that way about my own father. He had provided me with a home, food, and paid for my university tuition. He had also barraged me with constant criticism, and dismissed me in favour of that jerk of a brother Andrew, who could do no wrong. Who was now living in Rosedale with a ton of money and his plastic wife. Whereas I, Robin MacFarland, was a lowly reporter, slumming it in Cabbagetown. Now I was whipping myself up. I decided I'd better see my naturopath as soon as we returned to Toronto. Sally would set me straight. I chanted my Buddhist mantra under my breath. That usually helped put me in touch with my power and compassion.

I walked around the property and breathed deeply as I chanted. I tried to rest my eyes on the beauty of nature. It wasn't that hard to do. This was such a pretty place, high on a hill, with a view over the treetops to the ocean beyond. Nan's lawn was beautiful. It was neatly trimmed all the way to the edge of the forest. I wondered what Mr. Whatshisname from next door was doing right now as my eyes passed over the break in the hedge he had come stomping through a week ago. What was that guy's name, anyway? It would come to me. What a nasty neighbour he was for poor Nan. Had he been at the lobster supper? I thought back. Yes. I remembered him sitting in the far corner of the cement driveway that had been cordoned off. He had been on his phone, though every now and then, he'd looked up. But then, he was suddenly gone. No wonder I hadn't noticed; I had been focused on the man dying in front of me. Had the neighbour been there afterwards? What was his

..me? I couldn't remember, but I sure remembered his vicious kick at my darling dog.

I could feel myself slipping into the grips of quicksand. My snake of anxiety had woken up from under its rock and was hissing in my ears. I was heading for trouble if I didn't turn the ship around. I took some more deep breaths, chanted as lively as I could, fought the urge to cry, and thought about my lovely children. On the whole it had been a great holiday with the kids. A whole week of sunshine and being at the beach. I hoped the kids would remember the fun times and not the terrible ending. There, now I felt a little better. *Chant chant chant.*

I walked around the wide expanse of lawn right up to the edge of the forest. This was a lovely rental. I smiled to myself at Nan's description that it had an ocean view. That two-inch ribbon of grey lying on top of the trees didn't really qualify as an "ocean view" in my books. But you knew the ocean was there. You could hear it, taste it, smell it. I wandered around the yard while Lucky peed on everything. I had never met a dog with such a pee capacity. He must have lifted his leg twenty times.

Drifting down from an upstairs window was a low drum beat. Someone had a radio on. No, it was probably a phone hooked up to speakers. Docking. That's what they called it now. The new lexicon. It was hard, keeping up with all the latest technology, though I did pretty well. I had apps on my phone and everything. I could hear laughter. I hoped it was Bertie, getting over his worries. Those kids were so nice with each other. I'd done something right. Maybe someone was poking him and making him laugh.

Our rental van turned into the driveway and chugged up the hill. Ralph was back. I looked at my watch. He had been gone longer than he'd said. But hopefully, he'd found out more. It was now just five o'clock. We'd be in the restaurant by five-thirty. I watched as he stretched a long leg out of the car, unwrapped himself from behind the steering wheel, and loped across the lawn. He embraced me tightly. I could hear his heart whacking against his ribs. It must have been awful.

I murmured into his shirt, "It was bad, right?"

He muttered, "Really bad." His breath blew on my hair as he exhaled. He let go of me. "Let's walk a bit."

Lucky was jumping at his leash towards a rustling in the woods. The neighbour? Ralph held my elbow and steered me in the opposite direction, keeping his voice low. "I've been a cop for a long time, and I don't think I've ever seen anything quite as brutal as what I saw today."

I shook off his elbow; I didn't like being led, but I didn't want to hurt his feelings, so I grabbed his hand instead. "Can you tell me about it?" Sometimes, Ralph had to keep information from me to protect an investigation.

"I don't see why not. It'll be in the news soon anyway. The cops did a useless job securing the scene. Not enough yellow tape for one. No cones barricading her driveway. No cars blocking off the street. Reporters all over the place."

Shit. Reporters? "I should have gone with you." Shirley, my editor at *The Express*, would be furious that I hadn't got the scoop. In any event, bye-bye holiday. I'd have to follow-up. "Tell me."

Ralph shuddered and looked over the trees to the ocean. "Her throat was slashed. There was blood spray dripping off the walls. But no discernible footprints. And her tongue?" He paused. "Her tongue had been cut out."

"Oh, Ralph."

"At least that detail was kept from the press, although I'm sure there'll be a leak in a small place like this."

But not from me. I pressed against him as I savoured the importance of the detail. Oh God, Robin. That was disgusting—to put your job, your stupid journalistic nose, ahead of a dead woman. I held tight onto Ralph.

16.

WE'D WALKED TO A FAR CORNER of the yard, away from where Mr. Henshaw—I'd finally remembered his name—usually lurked. Ralph wrapped his muscled arms around me, his chin resting heavily on the top of my head while the breeze in the yard blew around us. The kids' towels flapped on the line. This relationship was so different from the one I'd had with Trevor. It was almost as if there was a role reversal with Ralph right now, the way he was leaning on me. I was so used to the idea that the man was meant to bolster up the woman, but here Ralph was, physically using me for support. Well, I guessed that's one reason why I loved him; he was so sensitive. Oh no. I meant *like*. That's why I *liked* him.

Ralph continued with the story of Beverly's death, talking softly to the top of my head. "Anyway, her son, Danny, was spared the details. He didn't see anything pertaining to his mother's death. The house is divided into two parts: a granny flat and the main house. Beverly stayed in the granny flat, while the grandmother lived in the main house. Danny lived with the grandmother, ostensibly because Beverly was away a lot, but I gathered that Danny had always lived with the grandmother, ever since birth. His mother, Beverly, had just recently joined them after winning the election. Living there was more for her convenience than for Danny's sake. This house is closer to the town of Liverpool, where her office is. And, she only moved there after Beverly's own grandmother died, leaving the granny flat vacant. She'd been living down in Shelburne before moving up here."

Families. So, Danny didn't live with his mom. Sounded like there was a story there, too. Matching the quietness of his voice, I muttered, "Where is Danny now?

"I don't know. They weren't around, that's for sure."

"I'm sorry you had to see that," I whispered to Ralph. Despite his being a cop for his whole career, I knew how sensitive he was. "How was the tongue...?" I couldn't say it.

"Cut out? With a knife. Probably the same knife that slashed her throat." He held me a little tighter.

"And was it...?" My stomach was filling up with acid. I hadn't even seen the dead body, and here I was, feeling there was a high likelihood that I would toss my wine and cheese all over Nan's manicured lawn.

"What are you trying to say, Robin? Cut out before she was dead? Left at the scene? Mangled in any way?"

Even while talking quietly, his words were harsh. But I patted his bum because his tone was kind. "All of the above," I said, choking on my bile and talking into his chest. I felt like I was going to fall down and was grateful he had his arms around me.

"It was cut out after her throat was sliced, so I'm guessing she was already dead."

"Well at least that's a relief. She wasn't tortured."

"Maybe she was."

"Well, not without her tongue, anyway." I couldn't believe these words had come out of my mouth. Never in my wildest dreams had I thought I'd ever say a sentence like that. "Where was her tongue?"

Ralph coughed, swallowed, and said, "Her tongue was stuffed in her vagina."

Oh my God. I thought I was going to faint or throw up.

"I'm sorry. It's so awful Robin." He squeezed me. "You okay?"

Not at all. "Sure. I'm not going to faint. She must have been naked. " My knees were beginning to buckle, and my old friend snake was hissing in my ears. Darkness was pulsing at the edges of my vision. Ralph held me up.

"I didn't mention that? Yes, she was naked. Her legs were spread wide and her tongue was..."

I didn't want it spelled out for me. I moaned, "That poor woman. And you're sure Danny didn't see her."

"Absolutely positive. He was at work when it happened, and then he was whisked away by his grandmother while the scene was being processed."

"Did Danny's grandmother see her daughter like that?" I would never recover if I found my daughter dead and violated like that. But I felt the worst information had been given, and I was feeling a bit better. The snake had gone back into his hole, and my eyes were clearing. I pulled away from Ralph.

He breathed deeply, then added, "No, the grandmother was shopping for food in Liverpool, and the police reached her on her cell. She was told to pick up Danny and then to stay away from her house. The RCMP told me they were pretty clear about that. A guy named Porter. Seemed competent."

"Good thing." My suspicious mind began chewing through the facts. "But shopping? Really? On the Sunday of a long weekend? Maybe she was trying to create an alibi for herself."

"Believe it or not, the main stores are open. The liquor store, the large food chains, the Dollarama. And they are busy. It's a thriving tourist area."

"Oh, I just wondered. I mean, you can say you're anywhere when you use a cellphone. Seems like there was some family discord."

"That's all very true, but I'm sure the police will triangulate the call to see if she was lying. Besides, I don't think a mother would do that to her own child."

"You never know, Ralph. Families." I let the word hang in the air. He was the one who wouldn't talk about his family. Ever. "Families can have deep-rooted hatreds that lead people to despicable acts."

Ralph was nodding while he stared off above the trees. I could tell he knew what I meant. But I didn't know what it meant to him. His body had become very still.

"I mean," I continued, "my family is a case in point. I don't think anyone would murder anyone, although I've come close with Andrew. My brother. What a dickhead. A rich, arrogant prick." I was waiting for Ralph to add in his two cents about his family, but no, he just stood there, nodding, staring, standing still. Maybe I'd ask him tonight, after dinner, what exactly had gone wrong in his family. I knew he had children, whom he never saw. I didn't know how many. He also had an an ex-wife, someone else he also never saw. I'd try to get the story out of him later. We'd been together for a year; you'd think he would have told me at least something. But I guessed we both had our issues. Me, for example? I couldn't accept or say the word "love." And for Ralph, his family was definitely off-limits.

I said, "Why do you think she was killed?"

Ralph grunted, "Too early to tell, Robin."

"And who found her if not the grandmother?'

"A neighbour." He didn't say the neighbour's name.

Oh, so now he was keeping his cards close to his chest. Mr. Professional Detective. Being a dick and a dickhead. He whispered, "And forget I told you about her tongue being cut out and where it was found."

I smiled and pantomimed zipping my lips.

"I mean it, Robin. The police are keeping that bit of news to themselves. It's a point that only they and the murderer would know. It will help them find the real suspect."

I pantomimed zipping my lips again. I didn't care if it bugged him. This was a detail that the police, the murderer, and *I*, Robin MacFarland, crime reporter, would know. "Okay," I lied.

He looked away, exasperated. He knew I'd lied. "Let's go inside and get the dinner thing happening. Here, let me take Lucky." Lucky was pulling hard towards the gap in the bush t the neighbour had marched through a week ago, brandishing his newspaper.

Ralph's voice sounded extra loud after all our whispering when he called over to the bush. "Mr. Henshaw, remember what I said," he said, raising his voice even louder. "There will be big trouble if you harass Nan or the MacFarlands."

There was a scurrying in the dirt, and the sound of branches snapping.

"How did you know he was lurking?"

"I saw his stringy yellow hair through the leaves. And I was looking for him. That man makes me suspicious. I don't trust him. That's why I was talking so quietly."

"Do you think he had something to do with Beverly's murder?" I couldn't see it. Sure, the guy was a bully, but he was too scrawny to take on a substantial woman like Beverly. "He'd have to knock her out first. He'd be no match for her."

Ralph tilted his head. "Good point." His tone suggested he didn't mean it. "Let's see what the autopsy reveals. Maybe she'll have a dent in her skull. Or a pinprick injection site for poison. Or maybe the police will find a rag soaked in chloroform under her body."

"Don't make fun of me." I kind of laughed while I said this, but I meant it. "He's way too little. She would be able to fight him off with one swipe."

"Not if he attacked her from behind. Whoever slashed her was standing behind her. Let's go inside, face the music. I'm sure they'll ask me a hundred questions. I'm going to play it way down, so don't be surprised."

It wasn't an actual dismissal, but he hadn't really heard me about Henshaw being too short. I knew it wasn't Henshaw. I had known many bullies and what each one was capable of. Henshaw was not capable of murder. Kicking a dog, oh yes. But put a knife in his hand? No way. He might smack her hand with a newspaper, but cut her throat? He probably couldn't even reach up high enough. Ralph was heading to the kitchen door, marching ahead. I shouted out, "He's too short, for one."

He whipped around and put a finger to his lips. Geezus. Was I child? I hurried up to him and held my ground. My fists were clenched. "Don't tell me when and what to say." I kept my voice down, steely. He was pissing me off. First, he had dismissed me, now he was shushing me.

He said nothing until we got into the house. Then out it came. "Robin. You don't know what that man can or cannot do. You don't know the angle of the slash. You don't know what was around that he could stand on. But more importantly, you can't let him know he's even being considered as a suspect. That would put you in danger. I'm just trying to keep you safe."

"Oh."

"So please don't be mad at me. But I don't want you targeted. And if he is guilty, I don't want him taking off."

"Oh."

"So, are we okay?"

I'd made a mistake. It was time to own up. "Yes," I squeaked and then recovered my voice. "We're fine. I'm sorry Ralph. I made a mistake. And I won't say anything to anyone about the tongue."

He smiled at me and tilted my chin up. "We all make mistakes." Was he going to kiss me? I heard the stairs creaking as someone came down. Did I want one of my kids seeing us being intimate? Trevor and I had not been a touchy-feely kind of couple. In fact, I didn't think my kids had ever seen us snuggle, not even on the couch watching TV. Ralph gave me a quick peck on the lips and let me go, just as Calvin came into the kitchen carrying a suitcase.

"I saw that. Get a room, you two." He was laughing.

Hmmm. So my kids had grown up.

Calvin hoofed the suitcase to the kitchen door and let it drop with a thump. "Maggie's."

"That was nice of you Calvin." But I was puzzled. Why hadn't Winchester brought down her luggage?

Winchester's bringing down the rest."

Oh. It was as though he'd read my mind.

Just then, there was loud banging down the stairs. Winchester dragged a huge bag into the kitchen. He groaned under the weight of it. "That girl doesn't travel exactly light."

I laughed. "She's such a slave driver."

Oh my God. What had I just said?

"I'm sorry Winchester. I'm really sorry. It's just a figure of speech. I wasn't thinking."

He smiled at me, impervious to the insult. "Mom..."

"No really. I work with words all the time. I should be more careful. I'm sorry. I wasn't thinking. About what it meant. About where the figure of speech came from."

He was shaking his head and smiling. "Mom..."

"I'm so sorry, Winchester. It was thoughtless of me. The last thing on earth I'd want to do is hurt you."

He took a step over to me. "Mom. Let it go. It doesn't matter. I *know* it's a figure of speech. Language is fluid. The words have lost their original meaning. It now means, 'she knows how to make you work.' It's okay. Let it go. I'm not a slave, and she's not my driver." He paused for a second. "Most of the time." He laughed as he began pulling the suitcase out the door. He said to Calvin, "I'll come back for the one you brought down."

Calvin rushed over. "No, I'll do it."

I watched them drag the two suitcases out to Winchester's car, parked on the other side of the van. The wheels bumped over the lawn and then on the gravel in the driveway. The newlyweds would be ready to go, early in the morning.

Ralph had been jabbing at his phone with his large fingers but now looked at me. "Language can be tricky."

"His parents did a great job bringing him up. He seems so well-adjusted, so sure of himself."

"Yes, he's pretty solid. They're going to be leaving very early tomorrow morning. Let's get to that restaurant." He was looking down again, tapping on his phone as he talked.

My misstep was already forgotten, but not by me. I made a mental point of watching what came out of my mouth. I felt terrible about what I'd said. Ralph must have sensed that I was still upset. He put down his phone and hugged me. I leaned against him, hearing his heart beating in his chest, regular and strong.

"It's okay, sweetie, no harm done."

"Thanks, Ralph, thanks for..."

"I said, 'Get a room.'" Calvin was walking by, pretending to shield his eyes from a terrible sight.

I broke away from Ralph. "Tell the others to come down. It's dinnertime. We should head out to the restaurant now."

Calvin ran up the stairs, shouting, "Time to go, everyone. Fish and chips. Last night."

Ralph gathered me back into his arms. "Hey," I said, "no time for nookie. We have to get going. It's dinnertime."

He laughed into my hair. "I'm warming up my dinner now, saving it to eat later."

"Ralph! Don't." He was fondling my right cheek. The lower one.

Everyone traipsed down the stairs, and not long afterwards, we were seated at out favourite table. Danny came over to take our order. He was smiling, pencil poised. "And what do you want tonight, everyone? The same again? Seven orders of fish and chips? Two pieces for everyone?"

What the hell? I tried to keep my face impassive. What was Danny doing here? His mother had just been killed. Shouldn't he be with his grandmother? I looked around the table. Everyone was gawking at him.

"What?" he asked. "You want platters instead? The specialty is a seafood platter. Scallops and shrimp. Anyone for the special?"

I found my voice. "I think everyone wants the fish and chips for their last dinner here." I canvassed the table. "Right?" Startled faces nodded at me. "So, yes, seven orders of fish [illegible] chips. Two pieces each. And maybe a large order of sweet potato fries."

Danny frowned, "In addition to all the French fries?"

"Oh yes." I said. I was so hungry I knew I'd be able to eat two servings of chips, easily.

Evelyn was the brave one. She spoke up. "We are all very sorry to hear about your mom today, Danny."

Danny replied, "That's okay. I didn't really know her. I mean, I'm sad and everything. She was my mom, but I've lived with my gramma all my life. My mom lived in Shelburne taking care of her father. I hardly ever saw her. My mom and my gramma didn't get along, and my gramma and my grandpa didn't get along. My mom and dad didn't get along. And my dad had issues with his mom, who had issues with his dad. In fact, no one in my family got along with anybody, except me and my gramma. We get along just fine, so I'm fine." He left the table and headed to the kitchen, the yellow sheet from his order pad already ripped off to be handed to the chef, fluttering in his fist.

Wow, there sure was a story here. I pulled out my phone and mumbled the family history into my recording app. My kids were used to me doing this. To their frowns at my rudeness I said, "Just commenting on the unique style of restaurant furnishings here in Nova Scotia. I think it'll make a great article for the Home and Garden section of *The Toronto Express*." I was fibbing. They all nodded. Only Ralph caught on. I smiled sweetly at him.

My phone pinged with a text. I glanced at it. Shirley. That damn editor must never sleep. Even on a Sunday of a long weekend, bam, she was on a story like maple syrup on pancakes.

Bertie wagged his finger at me. "No phones at the table."

Thank heavens he was feeling better. Seeing Danny must have put his mind at ease. In deference to his admonishment, I slid the phone under the table, hiding it, but not really, and read her text. It said: *Heard about the MLA. Is it a good story? What's up?*

I texted back: *So many murder suspects. On it.*

There went the rest of my holiday.

17.

WE GORGED OURSELVES ON CRISPY FISH and chips, everything smothered in vinegar, ketchup, and tartar sauce. Usually, once the main course was over, we left the restaurant. But not tonight. Tonight, we all wanted dessert. We were celebrating the end of a fabulous holiday, and perhaps trying to ladle a layer of sweetness on this last troubling day. It had been a difficult day, and not just because of Beverly's gruesome murder. That museum in Birchtown had also shaken me up. How could people treat people so badly? The Black Loyalists had endured so many broken promises, had toiled on unforgiving land, had received such despicable treatment. No amount of food would erase the pain I felt for them, but I was never one to turn the away from the possibility of a fabulous dessert.

We all ordered the restaurant's well-known cheesecake. There were about ten different toppings to choose from: blueberry, strawberry, raspberry, caramel, and chocolate, to name a few. Most of us picked the blueberry topping, which I knew was homemade from local berries. It was, after all, blueberry season and the flavourful flavonoids were testimony to the freshness of the ingredients. After wiping our mouths, we thanked everyone in the restaurant for feeding us delicious food night after night. I even ventured through the swing door into the spotless kitchen and thanked the cook. I was so grateful we had found tasty food made from real ingredients. I was even more grateful that none of us had to cook dinner for a week. I couldn't wait to bring Cindy here.

We staggered outside with full bellies. Long evening shadows rippled across the gravel parking lot. There was a hint of autumn in the air, a crispness to the light. Some of the weed maples along the side of the road had already turned red and orange. I imagined the place would be beautiful with a blanket of colourful foliage in about four weeks. As we ambled across the unpaved lot, I took a deep breath. The air was so clean here, so pure. I loved the way the coolness entered my lungs. In it, I tasted traces of brine and seaweed, wafting in from the ocean just across the road. How would I ever readjust to the gas fumes at Parliament and Carlton in downtown Toronto?

That night, we sat around the campfire and sang mostly old folk songs while Ralph played his guitar. "Kumbaya," "Leaving on a Jet Plane," "Four Strong Winds," and "Greensleeves." Our voices intermingled in the night air, the bass baritones of the guys providing a rich foundation for the delicate female sopranos. The sparks floated high into the air and fizzled out, carried away on soft evening breezes. There was no risk of fire today, not after all that rain. The trees were still dripping and I'd had to wipe off all the plastic Muskoka chairs around the campfire before we sat down. We sipped on hot chocolate, roasted hot dogs and marshmallows, and recounted stories of our days on the beach. Calvin made dumb jokes to which we all laughed good-naturedly, although they weren't that funny. What was the ocean saying? Nothing, it was just waving goodbye. Such a silly pun that sent us into gales of laughter.

But soon, the blazing fire turned into glowing embers, and everyone began to drift away. Maggie and Winchester went first, holding hands and lifting their feet high in the dew-laden grass, trying to keep their running shoes from getting too wet. They had volunteered to take Lucky to his crate, and my little dog kept turning around, looking at me questioningly. But I needed him out of the way while I tidied up. As they headed

...he house, they each called out their "Love You" and "Safe trip." I hoped they'd make it to Toronto okay. It was a long drive, seventeen hours, and they were cramming it into one full day. I knew they'd take turns at the wheel, but still, I was a little worried.

"Be safe," I called to their retreating backs. Maggie turned around and in the glow from the kitchen door she looked positively radiant. My heart swelled. I loved my children so much. Maybe one day, I could admit I loved Ralph. My heart shrank into a tight little knot.

"Don't worry, Mom. We're good drivers."

"Text me when you get halfway, near Rivière-du-Loupe, and again when you get home."

She waved, and they disappeared into the house. With them gone, the miniature party wound down quickly with Ralph dousing the remaining embers with a bucket of water. I stirred the hissing coals with a stick until I was sure the fire was completely out. Smokey steam swirled into the air and enveloped me. I was going to stink with it and tried to move around the pit to get out of the soot. But no such luck; it followed me as I moved. Great. I smelled of Eau d'Ash. I would have to shower later, before getting into bed with Ralph. I poked at the earth in the firepit with my stick. Maybe he'd poke me with his stick. Oh Robin, I scolded myself, pay attention and put both fires out. I smiled to myself. Although it had rained, I knew from the hot and dry summer days at my own cottage that roots underground could smoulder and catch fire several feet away from the original bonfire. So, I was careful and stirred up the wet mud with vigour. It had been very dry for weeks.

Ralph and I stacked the plastic chairs neatly to one side of the pit and then scoured the area for bits of garbage. There was an empty marshmallow bag, some blackened sticks, and paper cups. Under some leaves, I found a wrapper that had contained vegetarian hot dogs. These were not my choice, but the kids had seen a documentary about the ingredients in meat hot dogs and had refused to touch one since. Me? I loved the oozing grease and burst of salt. I even liked the sudden hard pieces and wondered what they were. Beaks? Bones? Hooves? But in deference to the kids, and keeping in mind traditional bonfire activities, I'd purchased vegetarian hot dogs. What was a bonfire without roasting hot dogs? I picked up the empty packaging and read the ingredients: tofu and pea protein. It sounded preposterously healthy. I turned the plastic over and my eye snagged on the word *wiener.* I snuck a peek at Ralph's crotch. What a guy.

I gathered all the bits and pieces that we'd found and walked across the lawn to the two garbage pails behind the house. When I lifted the lid of the pail for garbage, rather than the pail for recycling, the smell of vomit accosted my nostrils. What the hell? Who had been sick? Maggie? From being pregnant? She hadn't mentioned that to me. And then I remembered. Calvin had put the bag of garbage from the lobster supper in our garbage. It was still at the side of the house.

Suddenly, the name of the fish farm owner popped into my head. Frank Statten. Right. That was his name. And now he was dead, after puking everywhere at the lobster supper at the fire hall in Liverpool. Not that I wished him dead, but the man had all the attraction of viral meningitis.

The stench was from the garbage I'd cleaned up at the lobster supper. I'd gathered some plates covered in puke from the head table. I'd scraped them into a plastic bag with a cleaner plate. I hadn't been able to find a garbage pail at the fire hall, so I'd taken the bag into the van to throw out at home. I remembered asking Calvin to throw the bag in the garbage bin behind the house. So, here it was, rotting away. I wondered when garbage collection was. Nan Littleton had probably made a note of it. I dumped what was in my hands on top of that bag from the lobster supper and went back to the fire pit, where Ralph was stacking some wood for our next fire, which would hopefully be tomorrow night with Cindy.

I finished tidying up and we meandered back into the house, arm in arm. As we walked, I felt our hips bump together, and I pressed his bicep against my breast. He looked down at what I was doing with his arm and then raised an eyebrow at me, his eyes sparkling. I waggled my brows back at him and picked up my pace. We fast-walked through the house to the bedroom, ripped off our clothes, and jumped into bed. I couldn't stop laughing.

I mumbled, "Just like in the movies," into his ear.

He said, breathing heavily, "I have a wiener for your buns."

I bit his ear and whispered, "My buns are steaming hot."

After we were done, Ralph sighed contentedly and moaned, "I love a roll in the hay with you." He caressed my head and ran his finger softly against my neck. I hoped it wouldn't get lost in my double chin. He was such a gentle lover.

But all these "love" words. Ugh. I really didn't want him getting all mushy on me. I responded, "I *love* a hot dog for my roll."

"Oh, Robin," he said, laughing at me. "I didn't even say that I loved you, although I do. I said I loved a roll in the hay with you."

"And I'm saying I'm rolling over now." I heaved myself over on to my side and tried not to grunt with the effort. We spooned together, and I listened to his breathing become slow and deep as he fell asleep. My mind, on the other hand, was whirring. Was this going to be one of those nights where I didn't fall asleep until three? I needed something to eat. A bowl of cereal maybe. I'd read that cereal can be very calming. I snuck out of bed as carefully as I could.

Ralph muttered, "Where're you going?"

I said, "To pee." I was turning into quite the liar. A closet cereal eater.

He snored. I crept into the kitchen, quietly opened the fridge door, and smelled the milk. Still good. I took down a box of Corn Flakes from above the fridge, found a bowl in the dish rack, and spooned the crunchy deliciousness into my mouth. As I was munching, I looked on my phone and went to The Weather Network. Great. No rain. Forecasted to be a nice day tomorrow. Good for driving. Winchester and Maggie would make good time. And Cindy hated driving in the rain, so this was good. I fired off a text to Cindy. *See you soon, ya' big baboon*. Feeling sleepier, I then rinsed out my bowl and crept back into bed.

Just as I was drifting off into never-never land, my phone pinged. Cindy. *See you later, alligator*. But instead of writing out the word alligator she'd stuck in an alligator emoji. I smiled. She was so funny. I zipped back, *In awhile, crocodile*. I used the same emoji as the alligator one for crocodile. She texted, *Copycat*. And, of course, she used a cat emoji.

Ralph stirred and slurred, "Robin, what are you doing?"

"Oh sorry," I murmured, "I'm having trouble falling asleep."

"It was a difficult day. But everything's okay." He rubbed my back. "Go to sleep now. Nighty-night."

The next thing I knew it was morning. After a little kissy-kissy with Ralph, I wove my way into the kitchen. When I looked out the window, I saw that Winchester's car was gone. So, they must have taken off okay in the night as planned. I hadn't heard a thing. I said to Ralph who had followed me, "Looks like Winchester and Maggie got off okay in the middle of the night."

He tickled me behind my ear as I was getting the cream out of the fridge for coffee. "I know we got off okay last night."

"Ralph." I playfully admonished him. "The kids will be down in a minute. Stop it." He was nuzzling my neck and making slurping sounds.

In actual fact, the kids didn't surface for a couple of hours. Ralph and I had our breakfast, showered—not together—walked the dog, and were chomping at the bit to get going to the airport. I wasn't that worried as I knew everyone was packed and ready to go. But still, by ten-thirty I was just about to shake them awake when I heard the mating call of a walrus coming from upstairs. It was a giant yawn.

Slowly but surely, the kids descended into the kitchen and gulped down bowls of cereal. No pancakes today. I threw a treat into Lucky's crate so he'd go in, shut his little door, and herded the kids into the van. Ralph was already outside, pacing around. He wasn't as good at waiting as I was, and I knew he'd be glad to set out. As we rounded the corner to the on-ramp of the highway, I looked down the road to Port Mouton. Yellow crime tape fluttered forlornly in the breeze around the first house I could see. Beverly's. Looked like the police were done, but no one had bothered to clean up the tape. Ralph's mouth set in a grim slash. He had seen it, too. We drove along for almost an hour in silence, both Ralph and I lost in our own thoughts about what had happened over the last two days.

Suddenly, Ralph spoke. "Leaving tape up like that? That's just not good enough."

I looked in the rear-view mirror to see if the kids were listening. No, they had nodded off in the back, listening to music through their earbuds.

"I don't think the kids noticed. It would have upset Bertie," I said in a low voice. "Even though he knows Danny is perfectly fine with his grandmother."

Ralph replied, "Seems like the mother had very little to do with him."

"I agree. Do you remember at the lobster supper and Beverly's reaction to seeing her son?"

"Yep, sure do. It was like he wasn't there."

So, Ralph had noticed the same thing. I added, "She didn't even ask him how he was or give him a big hug."

"No, she just thanked Winchester and Maggie for watching out for him."

"And before that? Did you notice, Ralph? Right after Frank Statten fell down, she looked all around. She seemed extremely upset. I thought she was looking for her son."

"Now that we know about the death threats, that sort of makes sense. She was being vigilant."

"Something seems off to me. I think I should be remembering something else, but I'm not sure what it is. I think it has something to do with traps."

"Oh, don't worry about it. Maybe it's the fish farm. It will come back to you. Look, here's the turn off for Hammonds Plains Road. Almost at the airport."

Ralph spun the wheel to the right, and we sailed off Highway103, up the ramp to the shortcut leading to the highway that went to the airport. Finally, I saw the control towers. As the van slowed down on the airport access road, the kids began to wake up and shuffle around in the back. We arrived at the departures for Air Canada door, where we dropped the kids off. After hugging and kissing everyone goodbye, we picked our way through the road maze around the airport and headed back to the cottage. I couldn't wait to change into my bathing suit and get to the beach for a few hours of quiet time. As much as I loved my kids, it was nice to be quiet.

Ralph and I had the nicest time at Summerville. After an afternoon of swimming in the icy cold Atlantic and then warming up in the slanted early September afternoon sun, we went back to the cottage, relaxed and happy. Ralph and I broke with our dinner tradition and went into the town of Liverpool for a change of scenery. We ate in a corner pizza joint, got ice cream cones at the convenience store on Old Port Mouton Road, and took our time driving home on old Highway 3 as the sun was setting. When we pulled up to our house atop the hill in Hunt's point, it was almost dark. Cindy's rental, a white Honda Civic—she only ever drove a Honda—was parked where Winchester's car had been a day ago. As we came to a stop beside it, I saw through the kitchen window that she was at the sink, her red hair like a beacon in the gloaming. It was so nice to see my friend, although I was pretty sure Ralph didn't share the same sentiment. But for me? It was good to see her.

She looked up from whatever she was doing and waved.

Ralph groaned, "I guess our party's over. There's your friend." He saw the hurt look on my face and quickly amended, "Sorry. I'll do better to get along with her. It's not that I don't like her. I just don't like journalists."

That stopped me dead in my tracks. Wasn't I a journalist?

He realized his gaffe, and added, "I mean to say, crime reporters."

What the effing hell? I reported crime. On the front page, I might add. "Really?"

"Oh geez," he said. "Sorry. It's just that I have to be careful around her, you know, with information."

"Oh, like Beverly's tongue, which was carved out and stuffed you-know-where?" I couldn't bring myself to say "vagina."

"Robin, please forget I said anything. I'm really screwing up here."

"Yes, yes you are."

I marched on ahead. He said to my back, "I'll get some wood for the stove. I think it's going to be cool tonight. You go on ahead and see your friend," he said weakly.

"Cool, bordering on cold," I huffed.

I swung open the kitchen door and gave Cindy a nice big hug. It was so good to see her.

"How have you been?" she asked.

"We've had a great time. The kids got along really well, and you'll never guess..."

"Guess what?"

"Maggie's pregnant. And *married*. She married Winchester."

"Oh my God." Cindy's green eyes danced in the light, and she pressed her hands against her chest. "A baby. You'll be a grandmother. Oh, you are so lucky."

"I know," I said.

"But you look tired. What else has been going on?"

"I'm so glad you're here." I burst into tears.

18.

"OH, ROBIN. PLEASE DON'T CRY." Cindy took two long steps to me. "Why are you crying, Robin?" She wrapped her long arms around me and held me tight. "Tell me. What's happened? You can tell me. It's okay." She guided me to the table where we both sat down.

"It's not okay," I said, sniffling. The disastrous events over the past two days, plus saying goodbye to my kids after a really nice family holiday, were all pushing me over the edge.

"Start at the beginning. Is it Ralph? Did you fight?" She looked a little hopeful. The feeling between them was mutual.

I took a deep breath and pulled myself together. "No such luck, Cindy. We are really good together." Except for the last five minutes, which I didn't go into. "No, it's nothing to do with him. It's..."

"The kids? Is something wrong? Are you really okay Maggie is married and pregnant?" She had leaned into me, her eyes wide with worry.

"Of course. It's the best news I've had in years. I love Winnie. And they are so nice together. They'll do just fine over the course of their lives. And I love the idea of being a grandmother."

Cindy looked skeptical. "Really? It doesn't make you feel old?"

"Can't stop the march of time, Cindy." Age spots be damned. "Soon I'll have a little wee baby to hold."

"Well, let's hope they let you."

She sounded so bitter. So angry. But I knew that underneath

that negative energy lurked deep hurt. Cindy was estranged from her oldest daughter, and I'm sure she thought she would never get to hold her grandchildren. I tried to console her. "There's always hope your relationship will be repaired."

Cindy looked off into the distance. "I don't know what I ever did to deserve being shut out."

Well, I did. Cindy had divorced spectacularly and then announced to everyone that she was only ever going to have gay relationships. Sure, people divorce, and sure, gender can be fluid, but she hadn't informed her kids kindly about all the changes heading their way. It must have been shocking, to say the least. One minute you had—at least what you thought you had— two loving parents, and the next minute your dad was gone from the house while your mom was decked out in rainbow-coloured clothing. Cindy adjusted quickly to new information and she probably expected others to be capable of the same mental calisthenics.

"We can talk about that if you want," I said, cautiously.

"Anyway," she said, sighing, "it's good to be here. Tell me what's made you upset."

I was actually feeling much better. When I saw my friend, there had been such a sudden rush of emotion that I couldn't control. It was like a dam had broken inside me. Right now, I felt quite rational. A novel feeling for me, but still, I relished it. "A lot has happened."

Cindy looked into my eyes. "So, tell me."

I sighed. This was going to be a long haul. "Two deaths and racial prejudice."

"Sounds like front-page news, but I need a bit more to go on that that."

I took a deep breath. "Okay. On Saturday night, we all went to the town of Liverpool. There was a lobster supper being held at the fire hall to raise money for the hospital..."

Cindy gushed, "I would have loved to go to a lobster supper. I wonder if there'll be another. I love lobster."

Was this all about her? Now, she was pissing me off. "No, you wouldn't have loved it. Believe me. A guy died right in the middle of the meal. I'd hardly had anything to eat."

She pursed her lips. "I think losing one's life is a bit more serious than not getting to eat your dinner."

Wow. We were jousting already. I refocused. "I know, I know. But it was awful. The guy had taken just a few mouthfuls of his lobster, and when he was being introduced by the mayor, he keeled over dead."

"Heart attack?"

"No, they're saying a stroke."

"Who was the guy?"

"It was in the news. You didn't read about it?" That was so unlike Cindy. She was always a step ahead in the media department.

"God, no. I've taken a real holiday from all current events."

What? Was this my friend? She was probably lying. "Oh. Good idea." Wish I'd done the same. "Well, anyway, the guy was Frank Statten, and he was a hotshot in the community, a big philanthropist."

"What made him so rich?"

"He was owner of a few fish farms, one right here, in the next little town over, in Port Mouton."

"Fucker."

That Cindy, she sure called it as she saw it.

"Don't say that, Cindy. He's dead."

"*Yada, yada*," she sang, "Don't speak ill of the dead." She wagged her finger at me. "Fuck that shit. Fish farms destroy oceans. Period. Did you read that Nova Scotia just passed a bill to protect biospheres? What hypocrites."

So, she *had* been reading her newsfeed. Liar. I let it go. "Anyway, he kicked the bucket while he was handing over a big fat cheque to the hospital."

"He deserved it."

"*Cindy*. Stop. It was a shocker. He was in great condition.

I think he was a runner. So, it made me very aware that a stroke can happen to anyone. My parents. It reminded me of my own mortality."

"Yeah, well, maybe someone murdered him. I know I'd want to."

I laughed. "Naw, it was a stroke."

"A *stroke* of genius to get rid of that shithead."

Even though I agreed with her, I said, "C'mon Cindy. He was probably a good person, underneath. He gave money away like it was water."

"Guilt money. I still say someone probably killed him."

"That's ridiculous. I was right there. No one was around him but the mayor. Besides, it clearly was a stroke. Paralysis. Vomit. Slurring words. The whole bit. You just want a story. You've been on holiday too long and you're bored. Tell me the truth."

She put on a fake shocked look and held her hand over her heart. "*Moi?*"

But she'd given me something to think about. Many people wanted Statten dead. Had he been murdered? But how could he have been killed? I was right there. I saw him die. Nope, the idea was stupid. I dismissed that thought.

"Anyway, the next morning we all went to the Black Loyalist Heritage Centre in Birchtown."

"Really? You've been there? I want to see it. I read up on all the racist shit here in the province before I came. It's unbelievable. So, nice of them to expose it."

Little did she know. "Yeah, well, I won't go again. You can go by yourself."

"That bad, huh?"

"Worse than bad. The racism then was so terrible. The story of the Black Loyalists is disgusting. The Black Loyalist Heritage Society worked miracles raising the money to tell their story, to make it part of Canada's history. Hundreds of thousands of dollars were spent on that building, maybe more than a million. It was built out of brick so it couldn't be burned, unlike the wooden church where the artifacts were displayed previously.

"I found it so upsetting. Imagine setting fire to someone's history, someone's roots. The land was free as it was donated by one of the black families in the community. And there's irony for you. That land, which was supposedly given to the black supporters of the British troops way back when, was never registered to the supposed owners. The Black Loyalists never got titles to the land they were given. So, in essence, they were giving back to the province something that was never theirs.

"I am enraged, Cindy. I am so angry about the whole thing. Those goddamn piece-of-shit bureaucrats, after almost three hundred years, couldn't be bothered to sign over the title to the land and these black families have been paying taxes on it all along. The systemic racism is so deep it's..." I couldn't think of the word or even the concept. "...It's sort of like it's *everywhere*, no, that's not right, it's *not noticed*, no, that's not right either, its like it's seeped into the soul of the society. It's been absorbed. That's what I mean."

Cindy had cocked her head to one side. "Wait a minute. Here, let me look something up." She dug in her pocket for her phone and started thumbing through sites as she spoke. "I think I read just a few weeks ago that the government has now put aside some money to hire land surveyors so the titles of the land can be given to the people." She tapped away and then stopped. "Here it is." She showed me a picture of a black woman clasping her hands together with a big smile on her face. She read some of the article out to me, what she thought were key bits.

"There, see? Some effort is being made to correct the wrongs made over time."

Geezus. Had her critical thought process flown out the window? I said, "So, there are over one thousand and six hundred properties that they're looking at. Right? Is that what the article said?"

"Close enough."

"Okay, and how many Black Loyalists were promised land? That fact is not in the article. But it sure is advertised at the museum. Around three thousand. Maybe more. So, where's the retribution money for them?"

"Retribution money? "Cindy looked flummoxed.

"You know, money to reimburse them for the broken promise?" I was getting pretty whipped up. "All of them were promised land and most of them didn't get it. "

Cindy said, "I didn't know that."

"It's true. Tons of the Black Loyalists that had been brought by ship to the South Shore of Nova Scotia left for Sierra Leone. From Africa to Africa, via slavery in the United States and a terrible time in Canada. I find that very ironic. And awful. I can't imagine the despair. The waste of life and time. But that's not the point here. No. The point is, how many land surveyors were hired?"

Cindy scrolled through the article and found the fact. She looked at me, eyes wide. "One."

"Right!" I shouted, "*One* land surveyor. Oh, isn't that just *great*. One surveyor to measure up more than sixteen hundred properties. How long do you think *that's* going to take? Five years? Ten? Twenty?"

"Well, I guess a pretty long time. Years and years."

"That's my point. So has anything really changed? Are those families being treated with any dignity at all? Any respect? Is there really *any* intention to treat them well? I don't think so." I was yelling.

"So maybe best if I give it a pass, you know, going there? To the cultural centre? Might be too upsetting?"

I grunted as I got up from the table and headed to the fridge for a bottle of white. I whipped it off the shelf like a baseball bat.

"Oh thanks. I'd love a glass," Ralph said as he stomped heavily into the kitchen, carrying an armful of logs. "The campfire is all ready to go. And now the wood stove is too." He let the wood tumble out of his arms into an old lobster crate by the stove and then brushed bark off his sleeves.

"Oh, hi Ralph. How are you doing? Having a nice time here?" Cindy was being so polite.

He grunted, "So far."

I was still revved up from talking abut Birchtown. "Oh, for Christ's sake you two. None of that. Just bloody get along."

Ralph had the good grace to look guilty and put up his palms in a gesture of peace. "Sorry." He turned to Cindy and said pleasantly, "Nice to see you. Did you have a good drive here?"

"See, that wasn't so hard," I said. While they were busy sizing each other up, I took a swig directly out of the bottle. I wiped my mouth with the back of my hand before they turned to look at me.

"Just fine, thank you, Ralph." Cindy was smiling sweetly. "It was a long drive, about four hours from Baddeck, but very beautiful."

He looked thoughtful and put a finger on his chin. He was pretend-thinking. "Four hours? You had time to look at scenery? That's easily a five-hour trip. How fast were you going?"

"Slipping, Ralph. Play nice," I said. God, he'd only managed one pleasant sentence.

Cindy's cheeks turned a light shade of pink, but she kept her mouth shut.

I put the bottle on the table, got some glasses out of the cupboard, and sat down. "Cindy was asking me about the events of the past few days."

Ralph let some air out of his chest. "It's been a bit rough. A death. A murder."

Cindy almost choked on her wine. "Murder?" she squealed like a rat in death throes. "Robin, you never said anything about a murder." She whipped around to Ralph. "She told me about that Birchtown experience. About Frank Stiple."

"Statten," he corrected her. "Yes, the cultural centre really upset her. Robin hates it when people aren't treated well."

He put a protective hand on my arm. Cindy looked at it and something shifted in her eyes. What was she thinking? God, I didn't need that right now. I wanted her to feel welcome and loved. It wasn't easy being gay in your fifties with no partner. With one kid who didn't talk to you and three more who barely tolerated your presence. I slowly moved my arm away from Ralph's hand. He didn't notice. She did. I saw some of the tension seep out of her chest.

I said calmly, "I didn't get up to the murder. That just happened. Anyway, the MLA for Queens and Shelburne counties was killed yesterday afternoon."

Cindy straightened up. She was all business. "How?"

Ralph interjected. "This isn't a story for your paper, Cindy."

Cindy ignored him and looked at me. "How?"

I tried to downplay it. "Oh, just a slashed throat." I looked at Ralph. For what? Permission? God, I needed my head examined. I drank some wine.

Ralph shook his head impatiently. "You don't need me to give you a go-ahead, Robin. Tell her. It's been in the news already. It's not like it's a big secret or anything."

Cindy crossed her arms and waited for me to spill the beans.

19.

IN THE MIDDLE OF THE CONVERSATION about Beverly's murder, my phone pinged. Maggie. I'd completely forgotten to worry about her and Winchester driving across the country. She'd texted: *Made it to Montreal. Great weather. But the long weekend traffic is getting heavy. Might take more than five hours to Toronto.*

I texted her back: *Just watch for brake lights ahead, in case there's a sudden traffic jam. Be safe. Love you.*

"Maggie," I said by way of an explanation to Ralph and Cindy, while putting my phone back down on the table.

Cindy wasn't going to be distracted, oh no. "So, the murder. What's the scoop? Give me the deets. Who, what, where, when and how?" Cindy looked at me, not Ralph. She was still a little pissed off at him.

I answered, "Okay-y-y." I took a deep breath to begin the saga. "Beverly Price was the MLA for Queens and Shelburne counties." Cindy looked at me questioningly. "'MLA' means Member of the Legislative Assembly. Sort of like our MPP's. Our Members of Provincial Parliament representatives in the Legislative Assembly in Ontario." I couldn't believe that tripped off my tongue. I knew a ton of shit.

"I get it." She was impatient for the murder story and had no time for politics 101.

"I'm just giving you the background. Be patient." God, save me. "Beverly is the mother of Danny, a fourteen-year-old."

Cindy did a double take. "A child? Where's he now? With his father?"

She caught on quickly to the important facts. "No, his grandmother. Apparently, he's lived with her all his life."

"That's interesting."

I could see her mind was connecting some dots. "I know. Nobody in his family gets along, except for him and his gramma. The rest of them, grandparents included on both sides, all live pretty much separately. Up and down the South Shore here."

"So, animosity?"

"Yup."

"Lots of murder suspects." Oh yeah, she caught on quickly.

Ralph interjected, "I don't think this was a family dispute."

Cindy tilted her head and cocked one eyebrow at him. Sneered a bit. Turned back to me. "Robin, go on." He was being dismissed. She'd make up her own mind about what was relevant.

"We first saw Beverly at the lobster supper in Liverpool. The one I was telling you about where Frank Statten died. The fish farm guy." I made sure she was following me along. "She was sitting at the head table along with other bigwigs. In fact, she was sitting right beside Statten."

"Ah ha! So maybe she was the target, not him. Somebody missed. Maybe it was a drive-by-shooting and someone had bad aim."

"Cindy, c'mon. He wasn't shot. He died of a stroke. There was no gun. He had all the signs of a stroke."

"Yeah, yeah, you told me that." Like it wasn't important.

Ralph said, "The local doctor pronounced him dead *from a stroke*. There was no drive-by-shooting. This isn't Toronto. There are no gangs here doing that sort of thing. He was pronounced dead from a stroke. Not shot by some gang. No gangs here." His words popped out of his mouth like bullets, punctuated with little head nods. This was Ralph being emphatic.

Cindy's mouth stretched over her teeth like a smile on a wolf.

"You'd be surprised." She spoke with the confidence of one who knew everything about gangs. And to her credit, she did know a lot, having written an award-winning series of articles about Toronto gangs.

"If you say so." And with that, he snapped his mouth shut.

She'd won that round. "I do." She looked at me expectantly. "Anyway, go on. *We* can figure out what really happened." Implying that Ralph could not.

Ralph snarled. "It was a *stroke*. I saw it with my own eyes." To make his point, he put his hand on the table a little harder than he needed to. At least it wasn't a slam.

"We'll see," Cindy said, wiggling her bum on the chair.

"Anyhoo," I said, breaking up their immature tussle, "Danny was one of the servers at the supper, and he hit it off with my kids." I thought for a minute. "In particular, with Maggie and Winchester. I think he saw Winnie as an older brother figure."

Cindy was puzzled. "Why would he think that? Why Winchester, say, over Calvin?"

"They're both black."

"Ohhh." Cindy nodded with sudden comprehension. "I see. That changes things. You never mentioned that Beverly was a *black* woman."

I felt my spine straighten. Was Cindy being racist? "Why does that change things?"

"It broadens the suspect list. It could have been a hate crime."

Oh. I hadn't thought of that.

Ralph leaned forward. "There was certainly hatred in her murder, but I'm not sure it was a racially motivated kind of hate crime."

Cindy was curious. "Why not?"

He hemmed and hawed, probably wondering how much detail to give her, a rabid journalist. "Because of the nature of the murder."

"Which was...?" She beckoned with her curled fingers, encouraging him to talk to her.

He sighed, then said, "Okay, this is off the record."

She smiled like a coyote at a lamb. He noticed.

"I mean it. I've told Robin the same thing. No one can know these details." His eyes ping-ponged from Cindy to me.

Cindy had been thumbing her phone. She found what she wanted and looked up. "So, her tongue was cut out."

Ralph gagged. "How the hell...?"

"There was a leak. But it was worse than that," Cindy said. She looked like she'd swallowed a slice of lemon. "What's worse than that? Someone clearly wanted her to stop talking."

"You think?" Ralph was being sarcastic.

"So, what's worse than having your tongue cut out?" Cindy was looking first at Ralph and then at me.

I grimaced before I volunteered the missing piece. "Having it stuffed in a body orifice." I still couldn't bring myself to say the word, "vagina."

Cindy thought for a minute. She was running through various body orifices in her mind. Her eyes suddenly opened wide like saucers. She'd figured it out. "What the hell does *that* mean? A cut-out tongue has a clear symbolism, but stuffed in her...?" She was truly puzzled. "Maybe sexual hatred. Was she gay?"

I hadn't thought of that either. "I don't know. I don't think so. There seems to be more tolerance for gays around here than you'd think. I doubt it's a homophobic crime."

"You'd be surprised," she said, again, only this time at me. "People hide their hatred pretty well, you know, if it's uncool to be against the general consensus."

"I guess you would know."

"Oh yeah, do I ever."

"Me too," I said. "Remember those two murders of those two gay guys? Who worked at Everwave? The water cooling business that air-conditioned downtown Toronto? Definitely hate crimes."

Cindy added, "Not to mention the blowing up of my car,

that darling Honda Accord. I'm sure that was homophobia, although the police never did a thing, thinking it was because I was a journalist."

Ralph leaned back in his chair, affronted. "I'm sorry you believe that the police don't protect journalists like they do the rest of the citizenry. I personally don't like journalists much, especially pushy ones..."

"Really? Could've fooled me." Cindy's foot was jumping.

He continued, "But I try to protect *all* life, even if it is low." He cast her a meaningful glance.

I knew it was true; he was highly compassionate and moral, even though Cindy was doing a "whatever" sort of snort.

"Knock it off, you two." I was getting tired of this. "There is no such thing as a low life. All life is high."

"Oh, now I get it," crooned Cindy, "I have to be high to appreciate how great the police are."

"Well, ladies," he said. "Enough of this speculation."

Cindy snickered. "I'm not a *lady*."

"You're telling me."

"Geezus," I said, "I mean it. Get along." They were like teenaged siblings, harping at each other's throats. How was I ever going to last a week with these two?

They were suitably chastised, and I continued from where I'd left off in my story. "So, anyway, the day after the lobster supper, yesterday, Sunday, we went to that cultural centre, which I've told you about, and then had lunch in a cute café in Shelburne. When I walked in, I saw Beverly Price sitting and eating a meal with another woman."

"Who was who?" asked Cindy. "A lover? Maybe it *was* a gay crime."

"No," I said, shaking my head slightly, although maybe she was a lover. "She was an advocate who had fought for several years to get the Shelburne dump closed."

"Why did it need to be closed?"

"The usual reason why dumps need to be closed. It had been

...ed as a catch-all for all kinds of waste: industrial waste, hospital waste, military waste. You name it. The dump was chock full of chemicals. An infectious cocktail. The people who lived nearby were experiencing much higher than average incidents of cancer, heart disease, diabetes. Their wells had virtually been poisoned by the dump. So, it needed to be shut."

"But the dump was in a town? Shelburne you say? Why were the people on wells? Why not on town water?"

That Cindy really paid attention with her mind churning along.

Ralph stood up. "Racism. In particular, environmental racism," he said as he walked over to the fridge.

"Oh," she said. "It was a *black* community. So, no town services, and the dump is near their homes."

"Yup," I said as I guzzled the rest of my wine. This whole story scraped my nerves raw.

Ralph wandered back to the table with a new bottle. He unscrewed the cap with a flourish and refilled my glass. He half-apologized to Cindy for my overindulgence. "It's been a rough two days," he said, looking at her while pouring the wine right to the top of my glass. Bless him, my darling enabler.

I took another swig. "So, as I was saying, Beverly was sitting in that café with Meghan Oliver, she's the advocate person, and I decided to sit down and talk to them."

Cindy nodded approvingly while Ralph scowled.

"To cut a long story short..."

"Too late," Cindy cackled. It was her favourite joke.

I threw her a look and kept going. "Beverly said she was getting death threats."

Cindy absorbed this news. "Death threats." She nodded once or twice. "But she didn't want to go to the police."

I was surprised that this was a statement and not a question. "Why do you say that?"

"Well, she's black, isn't she? If I were black, I sure wouldn't want to go to the police. No offence, Ralphie."

"None taken. I'm well aware of the statistics."

Cindy's head slowly went up and down in appreciation of his honesty. "Your honesty is refreshing."

Ah, was a truce in the works? Before they started to squabble again, I quickly said, "Anyway, she didn't want to go to the police. She wouldn't go. Period."

After a suitably respectful pause, Cindy asked, "When you were talking to her, did she say she where she thought the threats were coming from?"

"She made some pretty broad hints. She'd had a lot of opposition from the town council to have the dump cleaned up. They argued the cost was prohibitive."

Cindy barked a laugh. "More like they didn't want to spend tax dollars on a black community."

I nodded. "The council wouldn't even approve a central well so they could have clean water. They told them to drink out of a hose at the fire hall."

"But that's undrinkable."

"Anyway," I continued, "she thought the threats might be coming from someone who didn't want the dump cleaned up, or someone who felt she wasn't cleaning it up fast enough. Or someone who hated her because she was black."

Cindy looked at the now pitch-black kitchen window, as if she were trying suck out from the darkness beyond the glass some rational meaning to what I was saying. "Humph," she said, finally. "Well, I can understand that."

"You can?" It was a taunt from Ralph.

"Well, duh."

I thought she was going to stick her tongue out at him, so I nudged her knee and butted in. "Okay, can we just leave it there?"

Cindy nodded, her eyes flashing at Ralph, and said, "Okay, so let's make a list of suspects."

Ralph thinned his lips. Maybe it was a smile. "Let's not and say we did."

"Spoilsport."

No, this is a job for the local police, not me, not Robin, and certainly not you, Cindy."

Cindy grabbed the bottle and headed to the kitchen door. "Ralph said he stacked the wood by the firepit. Coming?"

I jumped up. "Sure. Campfire?"

The screen door thwacked shut behind her. "Let's do it," she called from the yard.

My chair squeaked on the linoleum as I stood up. "C'mon Ralph, let's have a bonfire. Some good old-fashioned fun."

He looked at me bleary-eyed. I'd forgotten he'd driven all the way to the airport and back today. He was probably tired. Also, he'd hoofed suitcases around, walked the dog, driven into Liverpool and back, and dealt with the woodpiles. No doubt about it, he'd be exhausted. But I wanted him to join us and strum a bit on his guitar while we wound down from the day.

"Naw, you two have fun. Catch up with each other."

"No, come. I need you to build the fire. You do it so much better than I do. I need you to supply the music." I put on my best female-in-distress, tone. "Please? Ralphie?"

Although I was sure Cindy could put us both to shame in the fire building department—she had a lot of camping experience—I needed a change of scene. All this kitchen table yattering was making me itchy for something a little livelier. I watched him go over his options in his mind.

Ralph put his hands on the table, pushed himself up, and slowly got to his feet. "Oh, okay," he said, sighing.

"That's more like my Ralphie." I grinned at him as I headed to the door.

"Sure," he said following me. Then he was patting my bum. I yelped as he goosed me. "Sounds like fun. I'll put my log in your fire."

"Oh, Ralph. Stop it. Cindy will hear you." I slapped his hand away. He laughed.

20.

THE KITCHEN DOOR SLAMMED BEHIND RALPH as I aimed for an energetic fire already glowing in the pit. How did Cindy get a blaze going so quickly? She was a regular girl scout. I saw her sitting in one of the plastic Adirondack chairs, out of the wind, and talking to someone sitting beside her. I squinted my eyes, but in the shadows of the fire, I couldn't make out who it was. I could see Cindy was leaning forward aggressively, her back stiff, her hands making choppy slashes in the air. Oh no. Something was pissing her off. What else was new?

At least she had put a pail of water beside the fire. Maybe I should throw it on her to put out her bad temper. As I lifted my feet high over the wet grass, I noticed that there was another bucket close to the foot of the stranger. It was a man. Nan had warned me that people would get water from her the tap outside the kitchen during droughts. But now? After all that rain? Didn't make a whole lot of sense. Maybe Cindy had put two buckets of water out, being a girl scout and all.

As Ralph and I approached, she waved at two empty chairs beside her. "Pull up a chair Robin, Ralph." She had now leaned back and was on her best behaviour, although she was breathing rapidly. Something had set her off.

As I got even closer, I could tell that the person beside Cindy wasn't anyone I'd met before. Even when he stood up to greet us, I didn't recognize him. But Ralph did. He strode over to the fellow, hand extended.

"Hello, nice to see you again," he said. They shook hands and then Ralph turned to me and Cindy. "This is the RCMP detective heading up a team on Beverly's murder, Hans Schroeder."

Hans spoke, his deep voice just a little too loud. "Hi, just thought I'd drop by and see how you all are doing. Ask a few questions." He sounded like he had been fighting a round in the boxing ring. Cindy was looking smug.

Hans was just shy of a foot shorter than Ralph, which made him about five feet, seven inches. His nearly bald head—punctuated by wisps of crinkly, red hair—shone in the glow from the fire. His nose was dented with the effects of rosacea, and his cheeks were spidered with criss-crossing red veins. A fair-headed man who'd been out too long in the wind and sun. He was wearing blue jeans and an Adidas running jacket, rolled up at the sleeves. I could tell from his thick forearms that what he didn't have in height, he made up for in wiry muscles.

"Call me Hans," he said, his deep growly voice at odds with his short stature. When he sat down, I saw that he had a short torso—his head only came up to Cindy's ear. Mind you, she was close to six feet tall. He obviously didn't like the disparity. To make up for the height difference, he didn't sit back in the chair like a normal person, but perched on the edge, giving him a few inches.

Ralph took a seat two chairs away from Cindy, making it evident where he thought I should sit, and crossed his legs. Perhaps he felt it was important in present company to show distance from the reporter. His foot dangled in the air and cast a long shadow on the cut grass. I was surprised to see that Hans's foot was nearly the size of Ralph's, and I looked at him with a new respect, remembering what they say about large feet as an indicator of you-know-what.

"Hans," I said, "nice to meet you. Terrible what happened to Beverly."

"Yes. Yes, it was. We don't get many murders like that around here."

Cindy sat up straight. Oh joy, Cindy was about to go off and antagonize the police.

"Actually, I looked up the stats. You haven't had a single murder around here in forty years. So best to say, 'We don't get murders around here.' Given your age, you probably haven't handled one, ever."

Hans held his body up as straight as he could while balanced on the edge of the seat in the Adirondack chair. His face contorted, revealing dirty yellow teeth. He was smiling. "But we do have mysteries, and I have a very good solve rate."

Ralph's foot was boinging up and down. Was Cindy bugging him or something else? Had he had a conflict with this guy earlier, maybe at the crime scene? Or maybe this was the same guy who had dismissed Beverly's death threats.

Cindy leaned back in her chair. While smiling at him, she said, "I'm sure you do." Although to an outsider it would look like she was placating him, I knew better. She was *goading* him to show how inexperienced he was.

He fell for it. Or so I thought. "Just last week, we put security cameras in a tree opposite a house in Port Mouton. A woman there was selling baked goods from a kiosk, and someone wasn't putting money in the jar, taking bread and pie without paying."

Cindy smirked. She'd made her point.

He continued, "And the week before that, my team busted an international drug trafficking ring. Ten guys in jail and three million dollars worth of cocaine."

He looked smug, as well he should. It was a good bust. The next point went to him.

Cindy quickly wiped the satisfied look off her face and replaced it with grudging homage. Was she still playing him? I couldn't tell. I wasn't a master at these sorts of manipulative games. "That wasn't in the news," she said, head held high. I looked at her carefully, trying to figure out if she was presenting authentic admiration or baiting him.

Ralph gestured to Hans with an open palm. "Hans is well-respected in the community. He has many accolades to his name, and I'm sure he will have a quick result on this case."

I wasn't too sure about that, he seemed a bit doltish, but I let Ralph have his say. Ralph was being a tad too sycophantic to my ears. I wasn't sure Hans knew what "accolades" meant, although he was preening from the praise given by a homicide detective from Toronto, Canada's largest city. Cindy, on the other hand, had stifled a guffaw. I gave her the same look I gave my kids when they were bickering in the back seat of the car, and to her credit, she tried to hide her rudeness by covering her spluttering with a fake yawn. No one was fooled, but I appreciated her gesture. There were no points for irritating the locals.

"And how do you think the two murders this past week are connected?" she asked.

"Two murders?" Hans looked completely flummoxed. "There's only been the one."

"In my books, there have been two. Frank Stiple, and now Beverly."

I corrected her, again. "Statten. Frank Statten."

"Whatever." She flicked the air with her hand.

Ralph yipped a fake laugh at her.

Really? Why would he do that? Perhaps he was trying to show solidarity with Hans by crudely dismissing Cindy. That wasn't really his style. He was a lone dog, following his own morality. It was something I admired about him. Maybe he had just had enough of her. "Statten had a stroke. I told you that, Cindy. The doctor, the head of Queens General Hospital in Liverpool, mind you, pronounced him dead *from a stroke.*"

"Yeah," she said, "and pigs fly out of my ass."

Oh God. Did she really say that? This was turning into a carnival hour.

Hans' eyes bugged out. I guessed he'd never met anyone quite like Cindy. Then again, neither had I. I glanced at Ralph.

Oh dear. His jaw was clenched. I could see the muscles in his cheeks bulging. Yup, he'd had enough of her. Panic lurched around in my chest and crawled up my throat. There was a real fight brewing here. I had to stop it. I didn't know what to do. Damn. I wished I hadn't asked her to come.

Oh, but I loved my friend. She was smart, witty, and sassy. I admired her feistiness. Of course, I wanted her to come. Her potty mouth didn't bother me a bit. I had to admit I kind of liked it. "Pigs flying out of an ass" was a very funny image. I could just see them: tiny pink pigs tumbling in the air, propelled by a dark wind.… Oh God. So funny. My panic turned to giggles bubbling in my chest. Now, laughter was creeping up my throat. I had to stop it, so I took a deep breath.

I got a grip. But unlike Ralph and Hans, I was mentally applauding her. Not that I believed her. I had seen Statten die, and it had had all the classic features of a stroke. But she was clearly thinking he'd been murdered. She'd brought that up a few times. Maybe I should think about it. Was it, in fact, a stroke? I relived the scene: frozen mouth, jerky movements, paralysis, sweat, falling down, and vomit. Sure looked like a stroke to me. But when I thought about it, he was young, fit, and successful. He was clearly a fine, physical specimen. Why would a guy like that stroke out? On the other hand, you heard of young fit people having strokes all the time. Even MacKenzie had mentioned a kid having a stroke the week before. It must have been a stroke.

I asked Cindy, "Why do you think he was murdered as well?"

Cindy shrugged a "duh" and gave her head a scornful little shake, the palms of her hands open wide. We all got the point, including me. She thought we were stupid.

"No really, why do you think that?"

Ralph was doing his best to look earnestly interested. "Yes, tell me. I'm curious."

He was lying, or waiting for her to look dopey.

Even Hans chipped in. "I read the death certificate, so why

e you contradicting it?" His mouth made a malignant moue.

Pompous asshole.

Now that she had our attention, she said, "Everybody hates fish farms. They destroy the beautiful oceans and all creatures that live in them. No one wants them. The product is infected with sea lice. Fish farms are disgusting. And the people who profit from them? They hate those people even more. Enough to kill, I would say. Especially if you make a living from fishing and your fish are dying because of the pollution farms create."

I had to concede, she had a point. There sure were enough people who held him in contempt. There wasn't a single person at that head table who had looked at Statten fondly. That scientist, in particular, was vibrating with hatred. Although Beverly Price had kept her expression stiffly neutral. Politicians were pretty hard to read.

Hans put his hands on his knees and sat back in his chair, feigning nonchalance. He proceeded to lie. I could tell he was lying because his rosacea was now blushing vermilion. "Interesting theory, which my team will pursue."

Cindy wasn't fooled. "Sure you will."

He lifted a shoulder and shrugged her off. "I actually came here tonight to specifically ask Robin a few questions about Beverly." He angled his body away from Cindy, shutting her out, and looked at me. "I understand you had quite the chat with her yesterday in Shelburne."

I stared at him. "Quite the chat?" Where the hell was he going with this? Oh God, of course I was of interest to the police. I had been seen talking to her hours before she was killed. Was I a suspect? I said nothing, giving him a pause to trip over.

Hans appeared nonplussed. "Creston here told me that you had told him that she had said she was getting death threats."

I puzzled through that convoluted sentence. I really needed to drink less to help focus my mind. To celebrate my determination to quit, I took a gulp from the wineglass resting in my hand. It bought me some time.

What was I supposed to say here? I wasn't like Cindy. My mouth had a filter. Hers had a sieve that words leaked through. Right now, she'd probably say, "Asshole cop." He looked so pretentious, and he was so conceited. I really didn't like cops. Except of course, Ralph. But right now, even he was bugging me. Sitting there, leg crossed like a know-it-all, looking regal. Maybe that's why the "L" word rattled my brain so much. Did I have *doubts*? I swilled my wine.

I nodded. "Yes sir." Shit, did I actually say "Sir?" I was getting drunk. How much had I had, anyway? "We were talking about cleaning up the Shelburne dump, and she told me she was getting death threats."

"Did anyone else hear her say that?"

"Yes, Meghan Oliver, the person who…"

"I know who she is." He was making a note on his phone. "I'll talk to her as well."

What a shithead, interrupting me like that. "I'm sure she had nothing to do with her murder."

"Let *us* figure that out, Miss MacFarland."

So, it was "Miss MacFarland" now, was it? I could feel Cindy tensing up. Ralph made a tamping down gesture with his hand low down beside his chair while looking at her. He knew what she thought about "Miss."

I waited a second. Nobody told Cindy how to behave. There just might be an explosion. I waited a bit, but all was clear. Phew. I spoke up. "I asked her if she went to the police."

"I don't have a record of her doing that," Hans said, while nonchalantly scrolling on his phone.

"For good reason," said Cindy. "She said no, she wasn't going to go to the police."

Hans looked at her as if she were dog shit on his shoe. "I was talking to Robin."

So, now we were back to "Robin?" No more "Miss MacFarland?"

I was feeling feisty, so I copied Cindy, right down to the

-pping foot. "For good reason. She said no, she wasn't going to go to the police."

Cindy smiled.

Hans put his phone in his pocket and stood to go. Ralph followed suit. Cindy and I stayed seated. I don't know why. Perhaps I just felt like being rude. Hans was a jerk.

Hans said, "Well, if you're not going to go to the police, then I guess you get what's coming to you."

What the hell? He was blaming the victim? I looked up at Ralph. To my relief, even he looked shocked. His eyes were so wide his eyelashes were practically touching his eyebrows. Then I looked over at Cindy. To my surprise, and maybe horror, she was smiling sweetly at Hans. Something was up. I'd ask her later. Or maybe I'd find out soon. She was probably planning something. If there was one thing she couldn't tolerate, it was blaming the victim.

Ralph spoke up. "Now Hans, I'm sure she had very good reasons why she didn't want to go to the police. It's probably not a good idea to blame her for what happened to her. No one deserves to be killed. Maybe she wasn't convinced she was in danger. Maybe she didn't want to waste resources. Maybe she knew who was threatening her and felt she could handle it." A spark flashed from Ralph's eyes. He then said, again, "It's not a good idea to blame the victim."

Hans just laughed and slapped Ralph on the back in a good ole boy's gesture, "Now, you know and I know that stupid is as stupid does."

Geezus. I wondered if Ralph was going to forget it. But his smile had stiffened on his face, and his teeth gleamed white in the glow from the fire. Cindy, on the other hand, was examining her cuticles. What was that about? I started to breathe deeply to ward off a panic attack. The old snake was back, hissing in my ears. My feet were vibrating. Were they going numb? Maybe the circulation to my legs was being cut off by the edge of the chair? I had to lose weight. Maybe if I stopped drinking the pounds would fall off. I took a small sip.

Everything seemed to move forward in slow motion. I watched from afar with a buzz in my ears and my body disappearing. What on earth had set me off to this extent? Two cops were simply talking. What had he asked me that had disturbed me? Maybe it had to do with reliving the lobster supper, which had been so traumatic. I was definitely forgetting something there. Or maybe the atrocity of blaming the victim made me feel powerless and overwhelmed with fear. I hated my panic attacks.

How would Ralph react to all this? It suddenly seemed very important to me. Two minutes ago, he had sat in his chair looking like such a know-it-all. Was he going to make nice and play along with Hans's version of victim behaviour? God, I hoped not. Ralph towered over Hans, and I watched in fascination as he pumped up his chest. He thrust his chin forward and was practically breathing down Hans's neck. So no, he wasn't going to let this dumbass cop get away with that attitude.

"Victim blaming went out of style years ago, Hans." Although the actual words were mildly instructive, Ralph had spoken with a quiet authority. He would not be questioned.

But Hans smiled cockily and waggled his head contemptuously while he spun on his heels in the wet grass. I heard mud squish and hoped it was seeping into his New Balance running shoes. "You guys from Ontario think you're such cool hotshots. Around here? Things are done right."

As he strode into the night, his feet squelched in the mud. Over the sound of the fire crackling and the crickets chirping, I heard him mumbling to himself. I distinctly heard the words "black bitch."

Cindy, who had been hemming and hawing, examining her nails and picking at lint on her jeans, catapulted out of her chair like a spring uncoiling. She caught up to him in three long strides on her rangy legs. When she was right behind him, she screamed in his ear at the top of her lungs. "WHAT?"

He recoiled as if she'd hit him. "I'll charge you with assault," he shrieked, hand clamped to his ear.

Ralph was suddenly beside the two of them. "No, no you won't. She didn't touch you. But if I ever hear you say that again, I will report you."

Hans put his hands on his hips, his right hovering over his gun. "Say exactly what again?" Hans challenged, chin thrust forward, malice shining in his eyes. "Say exactly what? That it was black as pitch tonight?"

He tilted his head belligerently and stalked off. The grinding sound of his car door opening ripped through the night and the overhead light sparked on, illuminating his hardened features. Hatred screwed his mouth into a tight knot and turned his eyes into slits. He adjusted his body in the seat and reached for the door handle, slamming it shut. The sound echoed through the dark like a pistol shot. The low vibration of his exhaust thrummed down the long driveway. The air behind him slowly filled with the summer sound of humming insects.

"Well," I called, from the safety of my chair by the fire, "that went well."

21.

CINDY WAS SILHOUETTED AGAINST THE COTTAGE, her hands on her hips, as she watched the cop's rear lights fade into the distance.

"Fucking prick," she said to no one in particular. "No wonder Beverly didn't want to go to the police. Racist jerk."

Ralph was standing beside her, his chin still thrust out, his jaw muscles working. God, I'd never seen him so mad. Even from the chair I was sitting in, I could feel the angry energy oozing out of his pores. "You know what Cindy? For once I agree with you."

Wow. He agreed with Cindy? I couldn't believe my ears. Maybe some good would come out of that disastrous exchange with Hans Schroeder. I called out, "Nice to see you two getting along."

Ralph harrumphed. "Won't last."

Cindy walked back to the circle of chairs, slouched into one, stretched a long arm for the wine at her feet, and took a swig directly from the bottle. Geezus. I wished she hadn't done that. Her manners were abominable. I knew I'd done the same thing lots of times, but it seemed different somehow. At least I was trying to hide it. I simply didn't want to drink from a bottle that she'd been drinking from. I wasn't as bad as my prissy brother in the germophobe department, but honestly, her glass was on the armrest, right there. She could have easily filled it. She was being deliberately offensive.

And Ralph was duly offended. He glowered at her with distaste. "I don't want your germs."

She licked her lips. "Get your own fucking bottle."

"And there's no call to use language like that."

"Oh, piss off, Ralphie."

So much for that brief moment of peaceful accord.

I hoisted myself out of the chair and lurched to the kitchen. "I'll get a new bottle," I said, wheezing. Fall allergies were kicking in. Or maybe it was residue from that panic attack. On my way, I wondered what Ralph would do now. Would he completely back off from the investigation, or would he throw himself into it, butting in where he definitely wasn't welcome? Hans had made his opinion of people from Ontario pretty clear. He was also a racist, sexist, prejudiced pig. Ralph would undeniably be an intrusion.

I flung open the kitchen cupboard door, swiped a bottle of wine from the cupboard, red this time, unscrewed the cap, and knocked back a swig. God, I was as bad as Cindy. Well, not really—at least my bad manners were clandestine. Then I rummaged in the fridge for whatever cheddar my kids hadn't scarfed, bit off a corner, sliced off some chunks, inhaled a few, and then threw the rest on a plate with some crackers and a knife. I wobbled back to the fire, careful not to slip on the wet grass with my precious booty.

Cindy and Ralph were staring into the blaze, mesmerized by the sparking logs. Lucky was at Cindy's feet, his head tilted at her adoringly as she absent-mindedly played with his ears. Ralph was glaring at the flickering flames, his arms crossed over his chest. I clunked the plate of cheese and crackers on the arm of my chair and passed the bottle to Ralph. I noticed that he was certainly keeping up with me in the guzzling department. His glass was drained dry and looked like it had been for awhile. The outside was smudged with opaque fingerprints and I thought I saw a mosquito floating in the dregs, although maybe it was just ash from the fire. He didn't care and poured himself a glass. Cindy was happily nursing her bottle.

We all settled into being hypnotized by the flames. Finally, I couldn't take the silence any longer and ventured, "So... Now what?"

Cindy looked at me as if I were living in a parallel universe. "We find the killer. Write a great story. What did you think was going to happen?"

Ralph sighed. "Cindy." He sighed again. "It's not our business."

Cindy shot back, "I'm a crime reporter. *Everything* is my business."

Oh God. Those two. I didn't think I could take their constant quibbling, their animosity, their one-up-man-ship. What on earth had I been thinking inviting Cindy to join us? I felt like crying. I crammed my gob with a mouthful of cheese and crackers. Great. Now, I was emotional eating. I'd been doing that for years, ever since Trevor died. I wolfed down more cheese and crackers, and washed it down with the rest of my wine. This whole situation was upsetting. I floated out of my food reverie into the present. At least the panic was gone. Cindy was looking at me funny.

"What?" I said, although I knew she knew what I was doing and why.

"It'll be okay, Robin. I'll try harder to get along with Ralph. I know he loves you, and he is a good guy."

Geezus. I wasn't expecting quite that. What was this? *Dr. Phil*?

Ralph muttered, "Sounds good."

I was out of my depth here. I smiled a little woodenly. "That's great."

Cindy looked off into the trees. "I mean it."

Silence floated down over the three of us once again. The hiss of the fire mingled with the hum of the night insects. A firefly sparked in the corner of the yard.

Wait a sec. Firefly? In early September? Naw. But I had

definitely seen a flash. I nudged Ralph and gestured with my head over to the bushes.

I whispered, "Henshaw?"

Lucky suddenly started barking in the direction of the flash. Cindy hurtled up, unhooked his leash from under her chair leg, hushed him, and stalked toward the bush, Lucky straining at his collar ahead of her, pulling like a dog at a fire hydrant convention.

"Scat," she yelled. "Scat." The branches shook and feet scuttled in the dry earth like rodents scattering.

"There. Gone." Cindy marched back. "Was that the neighbour? What's with him?"

"Just nosy," I said, although I wasn't so sure about that. He gave me the creeps.

Ralph stood up and yawned. "He's gone and I'm done. It's been a long day, I need to get some sleep. See you guys later. I'm going to hit the sack."

Cindy snickered. "And then go to bed?"

Sometimes, she was so gross.

"That joke is old, Cindy." Ralph headed to the kitchen door. "Night. Don't be too late."

The screen door thwacked shut. Cindy and I were alone. The flames from the fire leapt and danced while smoke curled into the darkness. Hot embers crackled and sparked while I sipped my wine.

Cindy said, "I'm sorry, Robin. I don't know why I feel so compelled to bug him. I'll try to stop."

"Thanks," I said. "It's a little bit stressful."

"And I don't really think Frank Stiple was murdered. I was just getting Ralph's goat."

"Statten. Frank Statten. And I saw him keel over. Sure looked like a stroke." But now that the murder seed had been planted, I had my doubts. I said, "But he easily could have been killed. I mean, even you said that. Many people hate fish farms with a passion. They threaten the livelihoods of the local fishermen.

The people around that head table sure gave him a wide berth. The animosity was palpable. Plus, he was in great shape, so not really stroke material."

Cindy raised the bottle high and toasted the fire. "Here's to people destroying the environment." Her sarcasm sliced through the smoke like razor wire.

I lifted my glass with her. "Cheers," I said. "But you know, not everyone was wary of him. Beverly, the MLA who definitely was murdered, sat right next to him." I thought about the dinner. "She even gave him her lobster."

"She gave him her lobster? Why on earth would she do that?" Cindy's head was tilted as she processed the information.

"I don't know? Maybe she was trying to butter him up or something." I laughed. "There were bowls of melted butter on the table. You know, to dip the lobster in. If I were going to butter him up, I'd just pour it over him."

Cindy said, deadpan, "No, Robin, you wouldn't. You'd drink it first."

She knew me so well.

Cindy continued thoughtfully, "Maybe he'd promised a large donation to a school or something, which would let the government off the financial hook."

I thought about that and remembered him standing at the head table, shaking the director of the hospital's hand. "You're right. He handed over a big cheque to the director of the hospital for an MRI machine. The MLA literally beamed up at him as he shook hands with the doctor."

"So, there you have it. Money talks."

"And she's a politician, so when her son gave her the biggest lobster around, and Statten wanted it, no wonder she gave it to him."

"Wait a sec. Did you say her son gave her the biggest lobster?"

"Yeah, Danny. He was one of the servers. A beautiful boy. Mocha skin and flashing green eyes. Sort of like yours, Cindy."

Cindy batted her eyelashes.

I added, "Statten got a gaunt little skeleton, a one-pounder it looked like, and she got this plump three-pounder. He asked her for it."

"And then he took a few bites and died." Cindy laughed. "Talk about karma."

"I don't think karma works that way, Cindy."

"Oh, look at you, the Buddhist expert."

"Cindy." She should keep her trap shut when it came to my Buddhist practice. She knew nothing about it.

"Sorry," she sang.

"I mean it. You know nothing about Buddhism, so don't mouth off about it."

"C'mon, you got to admit it's pretty funny. He asks for something that he's destroying in the ocean, a lobster, and then it kills him."

"I'd call that irony, not karma." Although maybe she was right; maybe it was karma. I should go to more study meetings, learn what was what. I had to admit my Buddhist knowledge was pretty thin, unlike me. "And besides, the lobster didn't kill him. He had a stroke."

"How do you know the lobster didn't kill him? Maybe it was a bad lobster. Maybe it pinched his jugular vein." She laughed and pinched the air with her fingers shaped into a claw. "Maybe it had a weird poison in it. Maybe it had a killer bacteria." Her fingers chomped the air.

"At a lobster supper? Where at least a hundred people are served? How unlucky would that be that he got the one poisoned lobster?"

"And maybe," Cindy continued, "just maybe that lobster, that *poisoned* lobster, was meant for the MLA. What was her name again?"

"Beverly. Beverly Price."

"So, furthering that thought, maybe the poisoned lobster was meant for her, for something she had or hadn't done, but it didn't kill her because she gave it away to him. So, she had to be murdered a different way." Cindy chewed over her conjecture while I chewed more cheese and crackers. "Yeah, I like it," she nodded in agreement with herself. "This is what happened. So doubly ironic."

"It's all speculation. Not reality." I didn't say anything for a minute and thought about it. "Well ... there are some things that add up. And then again, there are some things that don't."

"Like what? I love my theory."

"Okay, let's say Statten was murdered. You've said that before, right?"

Her curls bounced a golden red in the firelight as she waggled her head and spread her palms. "Right."

We were just shooting the shit.

"So maybe the lobster has nothing to do with it. I mean, how could it? Maybe he was shot with a poisonous dart that dissolved." I was being deliberately silly.

"Oh, come on, Robin."

"I'm just saying. A poisoned dart makes as much sense as a poisoned lobster. Or maybe someone wafted some poisonous gas under his nose."

"Robin. Be real."

"I am being real. I like the idea that he was murdered. Let's go with that." I laughed. This was a fun game. "I'm trying to figure out how. A poisoned lobster at a huge supper? You have to admit Cindy, it's pretty random."

She literally dug her heels into the wet earth at her feet. "Could be done." She sounded like a petulant six-year-old.

I ignored her. "On the one hand, everyone hated Statten, except maybe Beverly who loved his money. So, he was a good candidate for being exterminated by some hate group. But it didn't make sense then that *she* was given the poisoned lobster. If it had been poisoned. Who'd want to kill her?"

"She'd been getting death threats." Cindy wagged her finger at me. "Don't forget that pesky detail."

I rolled my eyes. "Of course she was. No one loves politicians but actually murdering one? Naw. We aren't that violent of a people. Not here in Canada."

"We are so. And maybe it had nothing to do with her being a politician. Maybe it was because she was female." She took another swig. "What about that van driving on the sidewalk in North York and killing so many, mostly women? That was definitely an attack motivated by hate against women. Women are vulnerable targets of violence, Robin."

"I know that, Cindy." I imitated her teacher voice. "But that happened in Toronto. Big city. Way more violence. It's not the peaceful Maritimes."

"You are so wrong. There's violence here. And where there's violence, there's violence against women. You wanna talk about violence in your perfect Maritimes? What about that shooting in Fredericton that killed four people, including two police officers? Fredericton is definitely in the Maritimes. And violence against women? Over fifty women have been killed by their partners in New Brunswick alone since the Montreal Massacre in 1989. One in eleven women here will experience violence against them. These are the 'peaceful Maritime' facts."

"All right. You've made your point People are capable of extreme violence, even in the Maritimes. But let's stay on topic. She could have been a target because she's a politician. And I agree, maybe because she was a woman. But why are we even arguing about this? I think this whole lobster thing is bullshit. No one poisoned a lobster."

"Really? Bullshit? I don't think so." She hurled the bottle to her mouth and gulped ferociously.

Oops. I must have said the wrong thing because Cindy was now going on a rampage. I took another look at her—she was the epitome of another reason to quit drinking. It made some people angry. Not me. I just became morose and stupid, and, well, hungry.

She ground the bottle into the damp earth at her feet so

it wouldn't tip over and continued. "Nope. It's not bullshit. Forget the whole Beverly as target argument. How is it that a very hated man in the province, a man who destroys the ocean and everything that lives in it, suddenly dies in the prime of his youth? And by a *stroke*? It just doesn't make sense. A *stroke*? He probably ate an anti-stroke diet all his life. Fish. Even you said he was in great shape."

"You're right. Although people do have strokes for no reason at all."

"Pulleeze. Not this guy." She was running her words together. Some people just couldn't hold their liquor.

"Okay, saying he was murdered, just how? By a lobster? The only way that works is if Beverly, the person sitting next to him, killed him. And wanted him dead."

Cindy looked at the fire. I could see her mind was zigzagging crazily through the possibilities. "Okay. Here's an idea. Maybe she had somehow organized a nice fat juicy poisoned lobster to be given to her. Maybe, somehow, she knew him well enough to know that he, a greedy pig, would ask for it."

"How would she know that?"

"I don't know. He was a capitalist pig, wasn't he? Aren't they all wanting more than anyone else?"

I thought of my brother. Yup. She was right. "Okay-y-y."

But then Cindy started second-guessing her theory. "But why would she kill a clash scow? I mean, a cash cow?"

"Right. Exactly. So maybe he wasn't murdered. Not by her or anyone else."

"Or maybe he was."

"Let it go, Cindy."

"No, really. I think I'm on to something. I think that lobster was poisoned and he ate it and died. We just have to figure out how it happened."

My head was reeling with all the conjecture. "Maybe she was meant to die."

"Well, she did."

I argued, "Look, there's something fundamentally wrong with your theory. It's bullshit. The main assumption here is that the lobster was poisoned. We can't prove that. On top of that, how does a murderer ensure that a poisoned lobster gets to the right person out of a hundred at a dinner? Besides all that," I raised my voice, "who exactly was the target?"

Cindy's long fingers wrapped tightly around the neck of her bottle. She raised it high in the air, drained it with one gulp, and announced, "I'm going to bed."

She teetered up and poured a bucket of water on the fire. It hissed in rebellion, sparks circling in the coiling steam above the drowning embers. "This fire needs two buckets. Here—you do the second one."

Oh, so the fun party was over? I tried to winch myself out of the chair and grunted. Between the extra weight I carried and the amount that I'd drunk that night, getting up was impossible. I sank back down, trapped by the chair. Maybe I'd spend the night here. I could lick the remaining cracker crumbs off the plate for breakfast in the morning. Cindy was bent over the fire, stirring it with a stick. She tilted her head and watched my efforts, gluing her lips together so she wouldn't laugh. Seeing I wasn't moving, she tossed the second bucket of water on the sparking embers. And then a laugh blasted from her lips.

"Oh, go ahead and laugh. I've eaten too much this holiday."

My friend straightened up and extended a hand to me. "Come on, fatty."

She said it like it was a term of endearment. I gave her my hand, and she pulled while I unbent my knees. Off we staggered to the house, arm in arm, laughing our heads off.

22.

I LOWERED MYSELF GINGERLY INTO BED, trying not to wake Ralph, and slowly drew the duvet over my body. His toasty temperature had already heated up the bedding, and I curled the duvet around my neck, snuggling in the warmth. It was so good to lie down. What a day. I stared at the ceiling, waiting for the room to stop reeling. I had had way too much to drink. A lump of digested cheese and crackers rose in my chest. I gulped it back down, willing myself not to throw up. I took deep breaths, trying to tame the spinning room, and succeeded in burping twice.

Oopsy daisy. I giggled and quickly put my hand over my mouth. Don't wake up Ralphie. But my body was floating and then falling on giddy waves of disorientation. Then I felt that I was slowly slipping towards the centre of the sagging mattress where Ralph lay, snoring away. My skin, I knew, was icy cold from sitting outside for so long, and my addled neurons also knew if I brushed against him, it would wake him up. Trapped by the duvet and the lumps in the mattress, I grunted and squirmed towards the edge of the bed, careful not to jostle him. Of course, it woke him up.

"Arrhumph."

"Sorry, sweetie." I floundered and flopped to the edge of the bed, my fingernails grasping at the sheets.

"Where are you going?" he said, his voice slurry with sleep. "You're freezing. Come here."

He wrapped his cozy arms around me, and I burrowed into his chest, blowing away a curly hair that was jabbing up my nose.

"Love you," he muttered into my hair.

"Nighty-night, darling," I replied. It was the best I could do. None of this *love* business.

He was back asleep in a second, soft puffs of toothpaste-scented air floating over me. I disentangled myself from his arms and hoisted my body over to my other side. Eventually, I must have passed out.

When I woke up the next morning, I heard Ralph banging around in the kitchen. The smell of coffee wafted into the bedroom, and I smacked my lips together. My mouth tasted like the rear end of a donkey. But no headache. It was a miracle. I should check the brand of wine and get more of it. I tumbled out of bed and staggered into the bathroom to brush the fuzz off my teeth. When I looked in the mirror, I nearly shrieked. I leaned closer to take a better look.

When the hell did *that* happen? What had happened to my cheeks? They were sagging over my jaw bone. I stood on tiptoe and peered at my face again. Holy shit. I had *jowls*. Geezus. I was only fifty-seven, or was it fifty-eight? No, I was only fifty-six. And I had jowls? I looked at them more closely. Oh my God. There were wrinkles on my jowls. God save me. I was now a bulldog that had caught its face in closing elevator doors.

I put a hand on each cheek and pressed upwards, lifting the skin. There! No more jowls. If I could walk around like this, I would be fine. But no, that would look stupid. I finished in the bathroom and hurried away from the betraying mirror into the kitchen.

Trying to sound merry, I said, "Hi Ralph. How'd you sleep?"

"Mostly on my back."

"Oh, aren't you the chipper one this morning." He was stirring pancake batter. Such a cute little bum.

"There's a high wind today. I don't know about the beach."

Wind? Sounded good to me. I could sit on the beach facing the gale and let it flatten the skin on my cheeks—a cheap facelift.

But instead, I said, "We can rig up some umbrellas to block it. It'll be warm in the sun."

Cindy straggled into the kitchen. She looked kind of cute in her terry bathrobe with the loose threads. "Morning guys. The wind sure was howling last night. What are you making there Ralph?"

"Pancakes," he replied, a bit snippily, I thought.

The master of the one-word sentence.

"Delicious. Thanks." She walked over to the coffee pot and poured herself a mugful. "This is some five-star hotel."

I set the table and got the maple syrup out of the fridge, glancing at the label on the wine so I would know what to buy next time. There was a picture of a heron on it, so it was probably a local wine. I hoped it would be available in Ontario. Geez. What was I thinking? I was going to stop my nighttime charade. I said, "What do you want to do today, Cindy?"

"After all that looking at trees in Cape Breton, I think I just want to sit still. Is there a nice beach nearby?" She picked up her phone and was probably Googling, "beach near me."

The pancake batter hissed as Ralph ladled it into the pan. "Pretty windy out today."

Cindy ignored him, thumbing through her phone. "Wow. There are so many. Rissers. Crescent. Beach Meadows. Here's one that's really close. We can almost walk there. Summerville Beach."

"It's beautiful. That's the one we've been going to."

"How cold is the water?"

Ralph grunted, "It's the Atlantic." He flipped the pancakes.

"So, basically, cold water and a very windy beach. Sand blowing in my eyes, pinpricking my face. Perfect."

Blowing sand? In addition to a facelift, I was thinking derm-abrasion. Might be helpful for eliminating wrinkles.

Ralph placed a stack of pancakes on a trivet in the middle

of the table and we dug in. Lucky sniffed around our feet, looking for crumbs. He'd eat anything. What was that saying? "Like master, like dog." I slathered mine with butter and syrup while Cindy and Ralph just poured on a few drops of syrup, no butter. I guess that explained why they were both so trim. But I loved butter. And syrup.

Somewhere, a phone rang.

"Not mine." Cindy waved hers in the air.

Ralph pushed his chair away from the table and ambled into the bedroom. "I think it's mine."

Cindy and I sat at the table, unabashedly doing our best to hear what he was saying. I didn't like the sound of it. His voice was raised. What on earth? The call was over as soon as it started, and he stomped into the kitchen, red-faced.

"Ralph? Who was it?"

He shovelled in some pancakes. "My ex's lawyer. She needs something from storage. Says it's hers."

I didn't know what to say. He never talked about his ex-wife. Never. Cindy looked at me, eyes wide. I gave an imperceptible shake of my head that told her not to say anything. She looked down and concentrated on her food.

"So?" I let the question drift into the silence. He didn't answer.

I mustered up some bravery. "So why doesn't she go get it?"

"I have the only key."

"You could mail it to her," I suggested. This sure was shaky ground.

"Nope. She's not allowed to go into the unit. I'm the only one who can."

This sounded pretty nasty. What kind of court case had he been through?

"Oh." What else could I say?

"So, it looks like I have to go."

"What she needs is important?"

"She thinks so."

He scrolled through his phone while finishing off the rest of his pancakes, and then pushed away from the table. "There's a flight at two. I'll hop on that and then get what she wants from the unit delivered to her as soon as possible."

"Can't she meet you there? Might save a little time and the money for delivery," Cindy said, ever helpful.

He scowled at her. "Nope. Restraining order."

What? He had a restraining order against him? No, that couldn't be. He was a police officer. They had to have a pristine background, which probably included no restraining orders. So, it was her. He had a restraining order against her. Oh my God, this was terrible. What had she done to deserve a restraining order? I knew they were immensely difficult to get against someone. The police didn't just hand them out. There had to be a documented risk to life or property. God. And I thought I had baggage.

Ralph was pitching things into a bag in the bedroom. He was furious. "I'll be back tonight, late, or tomorrow morning, depending on how it goes."

"I'll drive you to the airport," I said.

"Thanks, Robin, but I'll take the shuttle, so don't worry. You need to have a car here, and it's a long drive there and back."

"No," said Cindy, contradicting both of us. "He can drive himself and leave the car at the airport. Don't forget, I have a car. We can use my car while he's gone."

I heard Ralph's bag being zipped. He called from the bedroom, "Thanks, Cindy. Sounds like a good plan."

She buffed her nails on her chest. "Not just a pretty face."

There was no comment from Ralph, which was to be expected. He marched into the kitchen, nodded at Cindy, and then cupped my chin in his hands, kissing me lightly on the lips. "If I hurry, I'll catch that flight today and get there in time to deal with the storage depot. Sorry to run off. But I'll do my best to be back by as soon as possible."

"I hope so," I said. He was the best kisser.

"Take your time," Cindy yodelled to his departing back.

I gave her a look.

She said, "People have accidents when they rush, so I'm just saying...."

Ralph laughed as he opened the kitchen door. "Good save, Cindy."

And then he was gone, his cute bum and gym bag heading to the van. I stood at the kitchen window and waved as he slowly backed down the driveway. Me, I would have done a three-pointer and zoomed. If he stuck to the speed limit, and I knew he would, there was an outside chance he would make it in time.

When I turned around, Cindy was bent over and reading a newspaper, while absent-mindedly chewing on her pancakes. "I picked up the Halifax paper on the way through Liverpool last night, so it's pretty current. Good little rag. Lots of coverage, seems to encompass the whole province. There's even an article here from the South Shore. Some poor kid died suddenly from eating a poisoned lobster. A fourteen-year-old boy named Billy Schnare."

The name rang a bell with me. Where had I heard it before? "Sounds familiar. Did they say where he was from?"

She rustled the paper, shaking it out. "Yes."

"C'mon, Cindy. Don't be like that."

"Oh, you wanted to know where he was from?"

"Cindy."

She laughed and pretended to scan the type. "Oh, here it is. Lockeport."

I was pouring myself another cup of coffee. "Lockeport? That's near here. I saw it on a highway sign on our way home from our lunch in Shelburne yesterday. God, was that just yesterday? No, it was the day before. When the hell was it?"

"How time flies when you're having fun."

Suddenly, I remembered where I'd heard the name Billy Schnare. "Get this. At the lobster supper on the weekend, the director of the hospital, a Dr. MacKenzie, said that he'd lost a boy to a stroke this week. He was making the point that virtually anyone could have a stroke, like the man who died at the supper. He said the boy's name was Billy Schnare."

"A stroke? No, this article definitely says the boy died from eating a bad lobster."

"What? That doesn't make sense."

Cindy was scanning the article while I sat down with my second cup of coffee. "No," she said, reading intently, "it definitely says the lobster infected with toxin—saxitoxin—killed the boy. Apparently, this toxin is rarely seen in lobster, but still, it exists. It's more common in other types of shellfish. This toxin causes 'paralytic shellfish poisoning," which, in turn, causes parathesias, coordination loss, speech defects, nausea, vomiting, and in extreme cases, death." She'd rhymed off the symptoms while holding up a finger for each one.

"So," I replied, "six symptoms. And they all look like stroke symptoms to me. So that explains why Dr. MacKenzie thought the boy had died from a stroke." I thought for a minute. "But how did it go from a stroke to the correct diagnosis?"

Cindy threw me a look. "Lab work"

"But wait a sec. If the lab work was done in the hospital in Liverpool, then why did MacKenzie say the boy died of a stroke? MacKenzie would know he'd been poisoned."

"Hang on," Cindy said as she read. "Maybe the lab work was done in Halifax. Maybe the lab in Liverpool doesn't have the resources to pinpoint various toxins. Maybe they had to send the samples to Halifax, so maybe your doctor hadn't yet got the results."

"Hmmm. No. Something about this isn't right, Cindy. If there was enough time to get the results to the newspaper, there was certainly enough time to get the results to MacKenzie's hospital."

Cindy stared at me. I could see her mind churning away, just as mine was. "So," she said, "MacKenzie was making the point that anyone, even healthy young kids, can have strokes.

And he was doing this while knowing Billy Schnare had died from saxitoxin."

I added, "While explaining Frank's death as being a stroke. Let's face it. The symptoms of saxitoxin poisoning mimic the symptoms of a stroke."

"And Stopple had just eaten lobster?"

"Statten. Frank Statten."

She laughed. She was getting his name wrong to rankle me. It worked.

"Cut it out, Cindy."

"Okay, so Stiple was eating lobster..."

I groaned.

"...and then he keeled over as if he were having a stroke. Right? And then MacKenzie pronounced him dead from a stroke."

I nodded. She'd got the sequence exactly right. "But even Ralph and the cop, what's-her-name...? Oh, Baxter. No, Branson.... Even she said it was a stroke. And it wasn't just MacKenzie. The paramedics said so as well."

"And let me guess. MacKenzie made sure everyone concurred." Cindy was trying to fit the pieces together.

"Yup."

"Okay. This is looking a little weird."

"I agree." It was sort of beginning to make sense to me. MacKenzie was covering up his tracks. "But let's just say MacKenzie wanted Statten dead. How would he ensure he got a poisoned lobster? Same question as last night. There were about a hundred people there, and each one got a lobster."

"Easy-peasy. Bribe the waiter to give him a specific lobster."

"Of course. You know your criminals, Cindy."

"I have to, being a crime reporter."

Was I supposed to be thinking about an article for Shirley? But something wasn't right here. What was I forgetting? I replayed the supper in my mind on fast-forward. "But wait. The lobster that Statten ate was really meant for the MLA. Beverly Price."

"How do you know that?" Cindy said sharply.

"Remember? I told you that last night. Don't tell me the wine erased your mind. It was because her son, Danny, who was the waiter for the head table, gave the big fat juicy lobster to his mom."

"So, if he'd been bribed, it was to give his *mother* the best lobster."

"Right."

"So, *she* was the target. Now I remember. As I said before, this explains why she was murdered later. The first attempt failed."

"I think so."

"If that's the case, then why did Stouply die?"

"She gave her lobster to Stamper." Two could play this game. "He was a greedy pig and wanted the big fat juicy one."

"Well now, that's a good example of a victim asking for it." Cindy laughed. She absolutely hated victims being blamed for whatever had happened to them. "But why would she give her lobster to him? That just doesn't make any sense."

"She's a politician, and he's rich. She probably wanted to butter him up so he'd make donations. But still...." I'd gotten snagged on the mention of butter and my mind momentarily turned in on itself.

"A bunch of barf is some donation."

My derailed train of thought got back on track. "But why would MacKenzie want to murder the MLA?"

Cindy reached for the butter and lathered some on her third pancake. Drowned it in maple syrup. Her previous reticence had vanished. How could she eat like that and be so thin? She pointed at me with her fork and mumbled with her mouth full, "It's either money or sex, Robin. Money or sex."

"Okay," I said, turning my face away so I wouldn't tell her not to talk with her mouth full. "I definitely think there's a story here. Something is going on."

"I'll tag along, Robin, but it's your story. I'm on holiday. I really don't want to write a thing. Especially about a crime."

I didn't either; crime was so distressing. My area of expertise had to do with homes and gardens: LED lightbulbs, afghans, soaps. I'd just written about the butter dishes from France that helped to preserve it for long periods of time. Frankly my butter never lasted long enough to go bad.

But honestly, people shouldn't get away with murder. I pulled out my phone and texted Shirley. *I think there might be a story here. Murder.*

She texted right back. *Go for it. But be careful. Is Ralph with you?*

I replied: *Yes.*

It was a small white lie. He'd be back soon. "I just lied to Shirley," I said to Cindy.

"And so, it begins. A new crime article."

My phone dinged. *Murderers are dangerous.*

Cindy looked up from sopping up the lake of syrup on her plate. "Shirley again?" I nodded. "What did she say?"

"First she said I was to go for it. And then that murderers are dangerous."

"Duh."

23.

WITH RALPH GONE, IT WAS UP TO CINDY and me to tidy up the kitchen. He was the best housekeeper of the three of us. She was washing the dishes and I was drying. "Cindy, how do you think I should approach this?"

"If I help you, I get a credit."

"Of course you do." Hard-nosed bitch. "I'm only asking because you've done way, way more crime stories than I have. I've only done two."

"But they were pretty sensational Robin. That Everwave business! Homophobia times ten. And what about the actor molesting the stagehand and then killing her? You were brilliant figuring both those crimes out."

Not such a hard-nosed bitch.

Her eyes were ablaze with excitement. "What do you think you should do first?"

She thought I was getting the hang of crime writing? Or was she forcing me to figure it out? "I don't know. Maybe talk to some people?"

"Bingo. But who?"

"Well. I'd like to talk to the mother of the boy who died of paralytic shellfish poisoning from a lobster. If I remember correctly, it was at his birthday party. They must have served lobster. Where and when did she send the food to a lab? Was it to Halifax? When did she get the results? Did she contact the newspaper in Halifax?"

"Good questions, Robin. But if she didn't send the lobster to Halifax, or if no one did, and the lab work was done in Liverpool, then that Dr. Fuckenzie is pulling a fast one."

I laughed at her new name for the old geezer. But I actually hadn't thought of the idea that MacKenzie was hiding something. I was more interested in figuring out the timing of the information. "My thought exactly," I fibbed.

"Because the doctor might say he sent it to Halifax, but in fact, he didn't. People lie all the time, Robin. All the time."

She had tilted her head back and was examining me. So, she knew.

"You don't miss a trick."

"Nope. But it would be best if you didn't lie to *me*, Robin. I'm your friend and we need to work together." She shook her fiery curls.

I didn't want to get on the bad side of this warrior and resolved to be more honest. "Who else should you talk to? Let's assume someone murdered Statten with a rotten lobster."

"The lobster that was meant for Beverly? Don't forget the irritating little fact that blows holes in your theory."

Nonetheless, I gave it some thought. "But I'll play along for a bit. That scientist at the head table was pretty happy that Statten keeled over dead." I paused while I dried a glass. "In fact, she looked pretty ecstatic."

"Really? That's pretty uncouth."

"I know. Everyone else seemed to be upset, you know, jaws hanging open and all the rest of it. But not her. She was pleased as punch."

"What's her name?"

"Um, I forget. Wait." I put down the tea towel and rummaged through the newspapers on a chair that had been pushed underneath the kitchen table.

"What are you looking for?"

"There was an advertisement for the lobster supper that had mug shots and names of the bigwigs that were going to be there. I've forgotten her name, so I'm looking it up." I finally put my hands on *The Breaker* from last week. "Here it is." I rustled through the pages until I saw the ad. "Here's the ad. Elizabeth Morely, Ph.D." I held the page up under Cindy's eyes. She was up to her elbows in soap suds.

"Hold it away a bit. I can't focus on something that close."

I obliged.

Cindy squinted at the page. "Sour-looking bitch, isn't she? And so skinny. I hate that. But is she a murderer? I mean—Robin, you can put it down now—Ms. Morely would definitely know saxitoxin. See, it says here under her name that she's a marine biologist. She'd probably know how to administer it so it caused what looked like a natural death, say in a lobster, and she certainly had a motive. But I like MacKenzie for it."

I resumed drying the dishes. "Yes, she would. Most marine biologists hate fish farms. They know how destructive they are to the biosphere of the ocean."

Cindy mimicked me. "'Biosphere? Aren't you the well-educated one, using a big word like that."

"Oh, shut up," I said and poked her bum.

"Oh my," she said in a falsetto, "that might be construed as sexual assault."

I ignored her. "That woman was filled with hatred for Statten. I was watching her and wondering what she ate, if anything, being so skinny. Also, I wondered how she could be so hateful. Maybe she had been malnourished as a child. I was actually feeling sorry for her. She was so obviously unhappy."

Cindy singsonged her reply. "Oh, you and your Buddhist practice. 'There's Buddhahood in everyone.' Why don't you chant for her happiness?"

"Knock it off, Cindy."

"Just saying. Some people are plain miserable. And that woman," Cindy turned and poked the nose of the scientist's photograph with a wet finger, "is one of them. Look at her tight thin mouth. Those lips fused together."

"Whatever. Anyway, I think I should interview her. As well."

"*We* should. We should interview her. If I'm helping, say 'we.'"

"You know what I mean."

Cindy pulled the plug and the water gurgled down the drain. "And who else?"

"Maybe the mayor, but mayors are usually decent people. Not murderers."

"I'm not that keen on mayors," said Cindy. She wiped out the sink. "They always have another agenda. Crooked people, usually."

"C'mon, Cindy. Not all mayors are bad. Toronto has a good one right now. The person after that awful crackhead mayor is doing a more than adequate job."

She shook her hands, spraying water all over the floor. Lucky sniffed around, hoping it was food. "Oh, you mean the guy who hems and haws about putting extra shelter beds in empty buildings when the temperature goes below minus twenty? So, the homeless people can freeze on the streets? That guy?" She grabbed the tea towel from me and struck her hands with it. She was a tad angry. "The fella who blames the police and doesn't help the force when Toronto has over a hundred murders in one year? That guy?"

Her voice was rising. She really didn't like the current mayor. She was now slapping the tea towel around her arms.

She spat, "You mean the fat cat who struts around in Armani suits and polished loafers with *tassels* while some kids don't even have mittens? That guy?"

"Okay, I get your point. I'll talk to the mayor. His name was..." I looked at the ad on the kitchen table, "...Dave Bradley."

Cindy threw the tea towel over the back of a chair. I straightened it out so it would dry. She shook her head, tossing her coiled springs of copper hair. "And don't forget MacKenzie."

"I really don't think so, Cindy. He's so old."

"What? You think old people don't kill?"

"Well...." I was dubious.

"Of course they do. Poisoning is a perfect crime for someone who hasn't enough strength to strangle a person with their hands. And injecting a little poison into a lobster? Oh boy, *that* an old person can do."

"But he's a doctor. Doctor's heal. They don't kill."

"The pro-life people would disagree."

"We won't get into that. You know what I mean."

"Robin. You have to admit, he would know how to *doctor* the lobster. He would have access to the toxin from the young boy's lobster. And he would know the symptoms it would produce. That they would point to a stroke."

"So would the scientist."

"Yes. That's why you're talking to both of them."

"What? You're not helping me? I thought this was a 'we' endeavour."

Cindy looked sheepish, which was a very rare sight. "Alright. I stand corrected. *We're* talking to both of them."

"And do not forget," I said, shaking a finger at her, "do not forget that the lobster was meant for Beverly Price. We should be thinking about why someone would want to murder her, not Statten."

Cindy cocked her head. "Statten is a perfect target. Even I want to murder him and I've never met him."

I poured myself another cup of coffee, my third, and sat at the table. "Here. Let's make a list of people to talk to. Maybe some new information will come to light that points to a motive for killing Beverly."

"What? You can't remember a few names?"

No, I really couldn't. What was wrong with my brain? I needed to eat walnuts or cauliflower. Foods that looked like a brain. Or I needed to stop with the wine. "I like to be organized," I said.

I grabbed a pad of paper off the table—it was there for people to leave messages or make grocery lists—and wrote "Interview" in big letters at the top of the page. Then I looked

. Cindy for the information. "MacKenzie," she said. "I'd put him at the top. I like him for this."

I didn't write his name down. "He's too old. And what motive does he have for killing Beverly?"

She bypassed my objection with the precision of a heart surgeon. "Add Bradley, the mayor. He's a close second. The scientist, Elizabeth Morley. She looks mean enough."

I was busily writing. "Who else?"

"You tell me. And write down MacKenzie."

I kept her happy and scribbled his name below Morley's. "I'd like to talk to that Branson cop. I mean, she was pretty quick to not insist for an autopsy. I want to find out if she knew about the death of Billy Schnare. And if she did, why wasn't she suspicious of Statten's death?"

Cindy tapped the paper. "So write her name down. Who else?"

"I don't know. Maybe the reporter for *The Breaker*? She might have something interesting to say."

She tapped the paper again. I obligingly wrote down "Reporter."

"Who else?"

'I think that's it. No, there was the fellow who was starting the cannabis farm and manufacturing business." I looked at the ad, found his photo and wrote on my list, Brian Dawson.

Cindy read upside down. "What possible motive could Brian Dawson have?"

"I have no idea, but then, I don't know why any of the people here," I said, thumping the paper with my fist, "would have a specific motive to kill Beverly."

"Well, I'm talking about Statten, and they all hated him. Who wouldn't?"

I shook my head and rolled my eyes. She was so wrong. The lobster was meant for Beverly.

"So far, you have three legit suspects. Morley. MacKenzie. Bradley." She bent back her fingers as she counted.

"Four, including Dawson."

"Right, four. But he's on the fringes. Anyone else?

"The two academics from Dalhousie. I mean, unlikely, but they were there."

Cindy said, "They'd really hate Statten, knowing what he was doing to the ocean and the food supply."

"It's not about him, Cindy."

"Maybe it is, just maybe it is. So write them down too." Cindy grabbed the paper and read out their names to me. "John Bigelow and Nathan Cook. Bigelow is the older one. Ph.D."

I scratched at the paper. The pen was running out of ink. I gave it a shake. "There, that's it. Quite a long list of suspects. But no motive."

"Sure there is." She was still on about Statten. "A long list of suspects is what happens when a lot of people think you are a disgusting human being with no moral compass." She changed her voice to that of a smarmy cartoon character. "But I'm sure you'll find their Buddhahood."

"I said, knock it off Cindy. Leave my practice out of this."

She laughed. "But there's one more person you should interview."

"Really?" I looked at the paper. "I think I've included everyone."

"Think, Robin."

I hated when she got like this. Like she was my teacher or something. Oh wait. She was. "Ummmm...."

"Give up?"

I shrugged.

"Danny."

"Danny?" Why should I talk to him?

"Yes, Danny. You have to talk to him. He's the one person who connects the two murders together. What does he know? He was there at the supper, and he lived in the same house as the MLA."

"Not really the same house. They lived in two houses joined together, under the same roof. He lived in the front of the house with his grandmother, and Beverly lived in the granny flat at the back."

"You're splitting hairs. He was no doubt in and out of his mother's place."

"But he's just a kid, Cindy. I don't feel good about talking to a kid. Grilling him for answers. He's a sensitive young boy."

"Then I'll do it. He has to be talked to. He just might be key to the whole business. Maybe he did it? We need to find out how it happened that he delivered to his mother a poisonous lobster. That lobster was deliberately given to her. To kill her. Did Danny want to kill his mother? Did he cut her throat later? Was he a friend of Billy Schnare'? Did he go to Billy's party and scoop up some of the lobster Billy was eating? Did he obtain the toxin from the dinner? So many questions, Robin. And Danny knows the answers. He must be interviewed. A key person."

"I can't see how he'd be a suspect," I said, horrified at the thought of a young teenager killing his mother.

But Cindy was blasé. "Kids do stuff like that. They lose control. I've seen it tons of times. They have no emotional filter, no frontal lobe. They blow a gasket and in a fit of rage, kill someone. It's a phenomenon. A thing. Believe me, it happens."

She was right. I'd seen my kids fly off the handle when they were in their early teens. But it just didn't seem to fit this scenario. "There was no fit of rage here, Cindy. If the same person murdered both Statten and Price, then it was calculated murder. When the murder of Beverly Price failed because she gave her poisoned lobster to Statten, then the murderer simply tried again, with a different MO."

"Look at you using the copspeak."

"I'm just saying, this doesn't seem to be the act of a kid. Especially a boy like Danny. He's very sweet. I just can't picture it. He's mature beyond his years, a little philosopher. Besides, I don't think he'd have the strength to cut his mother's throat."

"Doesn't take much strength with a sharp enough knife. Even an old person could do it with a razor-sharp scalpel. Like an old *doctor*."

She was still on about MacKenzie, but I knew it wasn't him.

Cindy continued, "And besides, she would let him come up behind her. It's not as if she would be expecting her son to slice her neck."

I thought about this. "True, but who would she let get behind her? It's a good question. I'm sure it was someone she knew. And knew well. Someone she trusted. But not Danny. No, he wouldn't do this."

Cindy was like a dog with a bone. "How was he after Statten died?"

"Inconsolable." I remembered how Winchester and Maggie had clustered around him after the supper, supporting him physically while he wept.

"Do you think that was an appropriate reaction to the death of someone no one liked?" She had a point.

I stuttered, "I don't know. Maybe...."

"Well, I don't. I think it's the reaction of a kid whose plans were foiled. He was beside himself because his mother gave the poisoned lobster to an innocent person, who then died."

"Not so innocent, Cindy."

"Well, at least not the intended victim."

"You're certainly throwing a lot of theories around with different intended victims."

Cindy stood up. "Don't forget to put Billy Schnare's mother on the list. I didn't see you write her name down. She's not a suspect, obviously, but she knows stuff we need to know."

"Oh right." I put her name at the very top. "She'll be a good starting point. If anything happened at all, if Statten was killed with saxitoxin, then it started at her son's birthday party. I like the idea of beginning at the beginning. Although I really don't want to talk to a woman whose son has just died. On his birthday. Ugh."

Cindy stood up straight and towered over me. "I'll go with you," she said firmly. "In fact, I have to go everywhere with you. I'm the driver. My car's a rental, and you're not on the agreement. She's from Lockeport, right? Not too far from here. What are you waiting for? Time is ticking. You can make calls while I drive."

"I just need a few minutes to get myself together."

"Me too," Cindy called. She was already taking the stairs two at a time, heading up to get dressed.

I threw on some clothes and searched around for my phone. I wanted to text my editor before Cindy came back down, raring to go. It was under a pair of Ralph's jeans.

I wiped off a smudge of cheese from last night and texted Shirley. *There is definitely a major story here. Fish farms. Politics. Murder. I'm on it.*

She called me right back. "Robin?"

"Hi Shirley." I could hear her puffing on a cigarette. Her ever present plastic beads around her neck clattered as she took a breath. I could envision them rising and falling on her enormous chest.

"Listen hard," she said, puffing. "Remember to be safe at all times. This isn't an escapade, you know. Is Ralph really there with you?"

"Ahhh." What? She could read minds a thousand kilometres away? She knew I'd spoken a mistruth? I came clean. "No. He had to return to Toronto for a day." I couldn't continue to lie, face to face, so to speak.

"But he's coming back?"

"Yes. Tomorrow."

"Well, I'd feel better if you waited for him to return before you pursued this story. I don't like it that you're there all alone. Murder is a dangerous business." A long drag. Rattling beads.

She was my mother? I blurted, "Cindy's here with me."

"Cindy? You're kidding me. But that makes sense. She was going to Nova Scotia as well. Right." Another puff. "Don't let her steal this story. You know what she's like."

I did know what she was like. "I mentioned her because she's here. I'm not alone."

"Not that you can't take care of yourself. Remember, this is your story. Not hers. Yours. Don't let her control you. Or steal your story. I'll clear it with her editor."

"Don't worry. She and I have established a good division of labour. You don't have to bother Doug."

"Never a bother," she gushed. "I don't know Robin. I wish Ralph were with you."

"Nothing much happens here, Shirley. This is peaceful Nova Scotia."

"Except a murder or two."

"Besides that. These are the first two murders in decades. And the police don't even think there are two. They think only the MLA was killed. It's just me and Cindy thinking there were two murders."

"You talked to the local cops?"

"Not really. One guy dropped by last night to ask me questions. RCMP detective. Hans Schroeder."

"You were questioned? Do you need a lawyer? We'll supply one if you do."

"Oh no, it was pretty informal. Ralph was there."

"Okay, good. What did you think of the detective on the case?"

"He's a pencil dick."

There was silence on the phone. I should watch my mouth.

"Robin. Please don't talk like that around me. I really don't like it."

"Yes, Shirley."

"The size of one's penis doesn't make a person a good or bad cop." She was breathless.

"Yes, Shirley. I know that." I was suitably chastised.

"If you're going to allude to the size of a man's penis because the said man is an idiot, at the very least refer to him as miniature Vienna sausage. Give the fellow an international reputation."

I put a lid on my guffaw. "Yes, Shirley."

"So, it's you and Cindy there. No Ralph." I could hear her nails tapping at her computer.

"Yes, Shirley." She loved to be exactly accurate. And she loved for me to agree with her.

"Knowledge can be dangerous, Robin. Be careful. But I've looked it up and crime is pretty absent. The figures are low. Especially murder. I mean it. Be careful. If you even think there's danger, call that Hans guy, even if he has a tiny sausage pecker."

"Yes, Shirley. I understand. But nothing much happens around here."

If only I knew.

24.

WHEN I HUNG UP FROM SHIRLEY, Cindy was standing at my bedroom door. She was wearing black jeans with a neon-pink T-shirt so bright that it would jangle a hangover. And it did. On her feet were white Adidas, loosely tied with matching pink laces. No socks. She was impatient to get going, her arms crossed and her right hand tapping against her left bicep.

"Who were you talking to? Ralph?"

I debated on saying "yes," but decided to tell the truth. "No, Shirley. I wanted her to know that there was definitely a story here and that you and I were going to pursue it."

"And I bet she told you not to let me steal the story."

"My darling Cindy. She'd never think that of you." I was being sarcastic.

Cindy flicked my comment off with a toss of her head. "Did you tell her we were the only ones who thought there were two murders? Not just one?"

"Yeah." I slipped on my runners, grabbed my phone, and stood up. "I told her that not even the local detective believed there were two murders. I called Hans Schroeder a pencil dick."

"You did what? Robin! She wouldn't like that. You know how prudish she is, despite being a bitch. Don't antagonize her. You never know when you'll need her. Try to be on her good side. What did she say?"

"She was pretty funny."

"'Shirley' and 'funny' aren't two words that usually go together. What did she say?"

"She told me to call an incompetent cop a 'miniature Vienna sausage.' To give him an international reputation."

Cindy cheeks puffed out as she tried to restrain a laugh. "Unbelievable. That's hilarious. Shirley is a dark horse. Let's get going. I've google-mapped Lockeport. It isn't far." She strode on her long legs out the kitchen door, leaving me scrambling for my purse and a bottle of water.

"Shouldn't we call first?" I shouted through the screen door as I filled up my water.

"No, not if you want to speak to her. Otherwise, she'll just slam down the phone."

"Oh, right."

"But take the dog," Cindy called over her shoulder. "People love dogs. It will open her up and make her feel calm."

"Good idea."

I searched around for Lucky's leash. "Where's your leash, sweetie?" Lucky looked at me, his tail wagging madly. "Want to go in the car?" He yipped twice. "But where's your leash? Where did Ralph put it this time after taking you out?" He ran back and forth. "Oh, here it is." It was hanging over the back of a chair. I clipped him to it and followed Cindy to her car. She'd already started the white Honda Civic and turned it around. Of course she had. Highly efficient was our Cindy. Didn't waste a minute.

I lifted Lucky into the back seat and then got in. It had that new car smell that was said to cause cancer, so I opened the window as I patted the dash. "Nice wheels. Brand new."

"I asked specifically for a Honda. I always drive a Honda. They work great. Speedy little devils too, when you need it. I love speed."

Didn't I know it.

She plunked her sunglasses on her nose and we were off, kicking up dust as we sped down the driveway to the main road. Little dirt devils whirled behind us.

"Okay, you made your point. You can slow down now."

She just smiled, her foot on the gas. We zoomed past the little beach in Hunt's Point, dodged potholes like a drunken driver, screamed around the corner just past Summerville Beach, and finally rounded the bend to get onto the highway ramp. I pointed down the Port Mouton road where Beverly Price had been killed.

"See that little pale green house? That's were the MLA lived. There's still a bit of crime scene tape tied to a bush. See it?"

Cindy briefly took her eye off the road and gave a quick glance down the road. "Yes. Pretty house, with that wraparound porch and those carved gables."

"Ralph was mightily pissed off that the cops left the tape up when they were done."

"He likes to do things by the book."

She said it as if it were a failing.

I was usually an agreeable type, one who didn't want to make waves, which perhaps explained a lot about how my life had gone. Not everything in my life had been in my best interest. But this was going to change. So now, I spoke up. "I like it that he's methodical. It feels solid and sturdy. A good foundation for a relationship. He says what he means."

"Oh, listen to you." She sang, "Ralph and Robin sitting in a tree, k-i-s-s-i-n-g"

"Give me a break. The relationship is still new."

"No, Robin, it's not. It's been a full year. Clearly, he's in love with you."

"Oh, shut up."

Cindy cemented her lips together and looked at me, a twinkle in her green eyes.

"Keep your eyes on the road."

We drove along in silence until just past the next exit, the Port Joli turnoff. Cindy said, "Down there is one of the most beautiful beaches in the world, Port Joli Beach. It's in the Kejimkujik National Park Seaside. Down there." She gestured with her thumb as we roared past the exit. "I hear it's beautiful and there are seals singing on the rocks at the end of a hike. Worth it, if you ask me."

"How long is the hike?" I wasn't that keen on hikes. Walks, okay, but a hike was in a whole different ballpark.

"The guidebook said about twenty minutes if you go the short way."

"Sounds doable."

"Yeah, let's go on a cloudy day. You know me. I burn like a crisp in hot sunshine. Also, there's a working fish wharf on the other side of the peninsula. Port L'Hebert. I'd like to see that, too."

Suddenly, the car slowed down. I glanced at the speedometer and saw that Cindy was going a steady one hundred kilometers an hour, exactly the speed limit. This was not like her. She was usually a speed demon. "You on cruise control?"

"Oh yeah."

"You're poking along," I said.

"Don't want a ticket. They watch this highway."

Aha. "Did you get stopped?"

"Yuppers. Some bitch gave me a whopper. She was so, so ... words escape me. So military."

I thought I knew who it was. How many female cops could there be in a small community?

Cindy suggested, "Maybe while we're driving you could make some calls. You know, to people on your list. Like the academics. Or the cannabis guy. Even the scientist. Or that cop lady you mentioned who was at the supper after Statten died. What was her name? Barter?"

"No, Branson. I'll look up the station's number and try to get her. She'd be a good place to start."

It took just one call to be connected to her. I put her on speakerphone. I said into some static, "Hello? Hello? Officer Branson?"

"Speaking."

I recognized her voice immediately. And so did Cindy. She put her finger down her throat and made a gagging noise.

"Oh, hi. It's Robin MacFarland. We met at the lobster supper?"

"I met lots of people at that supper."

Still a cranky old crab. Cindy shook her head and imitated her, mouthing the words and wiggling her tush as if she had a stick up her bum.

I was stuck on how to identify myself. I sure wasn't going to say I was Ralph Creston's *partner*. If he wanted to say that I was his partner, fine, but not me, I wouldn't say it. "I was with Ralph Creston? The detective from Toronto?"

"Oh yes, I remember you." Her voice was clipped.

"Right. I just have a few questions about that night. I'm trying to make sense of it."

"Guy had a stroke and died. What's so hard about that?"

"Well, I'm wondering if he actually, you know, had a stroke. You heard about that boy, Billy Schnare? Dr. MacKenzie mentioned him? Said that he had a stroke too?"

Cindy was hissing at me. "Stop talking as if you're asking questions. Be definitive. Make points."

Branson said, "Could happen to anyone." She'd relaxed her façade significantly.

I took a deep breath and tried to find my power. Cindy was right. I was coming across like a wimp. "Yesterday's *Halifax Herald* reported that Billy died of food poisoning. From eating a lobster."

Dead silence.

I continued. "Billy ate a lobster infected with saxitoxin, which kills. It causes symptoms that look like those of a stroke."

I could hear her breathing.

"He didn't have a stroke."

Branson said nothing.

"So," I said, filling the void, "I was wondering about Frank

Statten. Maybe it should be considered that he died from the same thing."

Branson coughed and adjusted her voice to being officious. "I doubt it. First of all, Statten's been cremated already, so no way to check. Secondly, that's a very rare occurrence, that toxin in lobster. Sure, it's in other shellfish, but lobster? Hardly ever. Thirdly, does it really matter? The guy is dead. By an accident or by a medical event, it doesn't matter."

"Matters to him. Matters to his family."

"What? You going to report me for not insisting on an autopsy?"

Hadn't crossed my mind, but now it did.

Cindy was drawing her finger across her neck. End the call.

"Thanks for your time." I clicked off before she said goodbye. My mother wouldn't approve, but Cindy was smiling away.

"You're getting good at this," she said. "Be strong Robin. It looks good on you. Call the academic. Don't bother with the younger guy, just talk to the older one."

"Okay." I crossed off Branson on my list of people to interview and found the Dalhousie people. "That would be Bigelow. Dr. John Bigelow." I thumbed my phone. "Here he is, on Connaught Avenue in Halifax. Maybe he'll be home. Classes haven't officially started yet. There's only one Bigelow. What am I supposed to ask him?"

Cindy looked at me. "Don't be stupid. Think. Ask him anything. Find out where he stands on fish farms. Where he stands on black female politicians. Whatever."

"I didn't even talk to him at the supper. How do I start off the conversation?"

"Oh, for Christ's sake, Robin. Give me the number. I'll call."

"No, no, I'll do it. Hang on." I dialled and waited. The phone rang five times before it was picked up.

"Dr. Bigelow."

His voice was deep with the grating undertones of a smoker. Maybe he smoked a pipe, in one of those tweed jackets with leather patches on his elbows. He had smudged out his Nova Scotian accent with carefully modulated vowels. He probably thought it gave him authority or something. I thought it sounded like he had hemorrhoids. Okay, Robin. The time was now. I was no delicate shrinking violet. I put him on speaker.

"Robin MacFarland here from *The Toronto Express*."

Cindy nodded in approval.

"I was at the lobster supper in Liverpool and wanted to get your feedback on what had happened." A nice easy general statement.

"My dear girl," he said.

Cindy put her finger down her throat and pretended to gag again. God forbid anyone should call her a "girl." Me, I didn't care so much. I was fifty something and being called a "girl" was sort of a good thing. Or maybe it wasn't. I'd have to think about it, later.

Dr. Bigelow went on: "That was a terrible thing. Poor man, having a stroke like that. And after he'd given such an exceptional cheque to the hospital. Talk about timing."

He was going to ramble on, I could tell, so I butted in. "Tell me what you think about the MLA who was there. Beverly Price."

"You're a reporter you say? From *The Toronto Express*? I had better be careful here, then. You can quote me, if you like, in your article." He cleared his throat as if getting ready for a speech. "Ms. Price is a wonderful, caring MLA. I'm sure she's devastated by Frank Statten's death."

He didn't know she was dead, and I wasn't about to tell him and listen to his well-modulated concern. I didn't think he'd murdered her in any event. He was too far away, up in Halifax. I asked him, "And what's your opinion of fish farms?"

He cleared his throat again. "I'll keep this simple. As a professor of all things environmental, the interconnectedness of all life, I do have an opinion. I've been to Port Mouton, Liverpool, and all the surrounding areas, studying the health of the ocean. There has been a decline in the lobster fishing industry in particular. I've read the newly released study. I would have to say fish farms are a hazard to the ocean biology in general."

"A hazard? Can I quote you on this?" I pretended I was writing down his words.

"Of course. I mean what I say. They are a hazard." He raised his voice. The carefully rounded vowels flew out the window. The local accent flattened his words. "Fish farms are more than a hazard. Much more. They are a…" he paused while searching for the right word, "…a scourge. A *scourge*." He was almost shouting. Then I heard him taking a breath, calming himself down. "But now I must get back to my research." *Click*.

"Geezus, Cindy. That went to hell in a handbasket pretty quickly."

"People are passionate about the beauty of the ocean. Threaten it at your own risk."

"Did I blow it?"

"Oh, Robin, grow a pair. It's not personal. You did fine." She was so harsh sometimes. "Don't speak to me like that. I'm doing my best."

"Sorry." She wasn't.

"Did you catch that he had no idea Beverly Price was dead?"

"Yes. But people lie, so keep an open mind. He was filled with passion and passion kills. He could have done it."

She was such a cynic. I said, "From Halifax?" No reply. "How much further?"

"Time for two more phone calls. Try the cannabis guy. He's probably in the office now."

I found the number and tapped my phone for a connection to Weedlot. It rang and rang. The guy was probably blazing. It was finally picked up.

"Weedlot."

It was the young CEO for sure. I recognized his low chainsaw voice from the argument he was having at the lobster supper with Dr. MacKenzie. I must have paused for too long as he said, "Hello?"

"Oh," I said, startled. "Hi."

"No, I'm not high."

He sounded defensive. I laughed. "Good joke." Cindy gave me a thumbs-up. "I'm Robin MacFarland. I'm calling from *The Toronto Express* and wanted to know your reaction to the lobster supper in Liverpool on the weekend."

"What? Did Dr. MacKenzie complain about me? Weed is legal in Canada now. That doesn't give the police the right to hassle people even more than before. So maddening. And no, the research says it's not addictive."

But he hadn't answered my question. I tried a new one. "Does Beverly Price support your new business?"

"Are you kidding? She loves it. Anything that employs people around here is a good thing. I showed her a business plan that includes over a hundred employees."

"Sounds like a positive thing to me." I wanted to get in his good books. He probably had all kinds of connections to the younger people in Liverpool.

"Most everyone, of all ages, support the business. Marijuana is great for pain control. Believe you me, the people around here work outdoors in all kinds of weather. Their bones hurt by the time they're in their fifties. So yes, she is a good support. She backed my proposal to council and is helping me get funding for the start-up."

Clearly, he didn't know she'd been murdered. I looked at Cindy for a little advice. Should I tell him?

She shook her head.

"How did you feel about Frank Statten's death?"

"Fuck him." He spat out the words.

I was shocked. I mean, I swore all the time but not in the company of people I didn't know. Unlike Cindy. I tried not to let it show, keeping my voice calm. "You sound angry."

"He was a scumbag wrecking our ocean. I'm glad he's dead, and I hope his fish farms die with him. We don't want his infected fish. We don't need his infected fish. Ask anyone around here. Trust me, no one eats his fucking farmed salmon."

Righto, then. "Thank you for your time. Good luck with your venture. I'll try to give you some good press in Toronto."

"Yeah, those Upper Canada tourists will be good for my business. Thanks."

Cindy turned off the highway and headed to the town of Lockeport. Pretty water vistas flew by on the winding road. "How do you know where you're going? We don't have Billy Schnare's address."

"I do. I googled it and then google-mapped it while you were talking to Shirley this morning. We'll be there in about five minutes. But call the scientist."

I searched for Elizabeth Morley's number and saw she was living in New Brunswick, even further away than the academics. Thank heavens for long-distance plans. I tapped her number into my phone. When she picked up, I identified myself as a reporter who'd been at the lobster supper when Statten had died.

Her voice was low and throaty, belching out words from the smokestack of her mouth. You'd think a scientist would know better than to smoke. "Yes, I'm happy he's dead."

I wasn't surprised. Her face at the supper told that story already.

"But, of course, no one deserves to die like that. It looked to me like he'd been poisoned, and not a stroke."

"Oh," I said, cool and collected. "Why's that?"

"You're asking me?"

I played along. So, I was stupid. "Tell me."

"He eats; he dies. Lots of poisonous bacterium in shellfish."

"You're right," I said. "Tell me about your study."

"Eleven years, it took. Eleven years for anyone to act on the information that lobsters are harmed by fish farms. The whole lobster industry is harmed by fish farms. No one listened to the lobster fishermen, saying the lobsters wouldn't even go into their traps, that they couldn't smell the bait because of all the smell in the water from the farms. Talk about prejudice against uneducated people. Believe me, those lobster guys are smart. Smarter than the politicians, that's for sure. Did you know that a lobster can smell up to five kilometres under water? Imagine how sensitive they are. Imagine what the stinking food and antibiotics are doing to them. Of course they are harmed. I hate those fish farms. They're not even needed. We have lots to eat. We don't need fish farms. And if you're going to have them, put them on the goddamn land." She was shouting.

Cindy threw her hand across the centre console and whacked me on the thigh. I took the hint. "Thanks for your time, Dr. Morley." And I snapped the phone off.

"I didn't mean you should end it *that* quickly," Cindy said, laughing. "That was quite the rant. She is infuriated by the farms. But anyhow, she didn't do it. If she had, she wouldn't suggest the possibility that he'd been poisoned."

"People who say 'bacterium' and not bacteria bug me."

"Well, it is the plural. And you say it. Do you bug yourself?"

Yes, yes I do, I thought.

"Anyway, we're here." She pulled up in front of a very large two-storey frame house painted white with green trim. Green shutters adorned the many windows and a gravel driveway ran down one side. There was a lovely covered porch with planters and white wicker chairs. A few Canada lilies were still in bloom under the lower windows. Cindy hopped out of the car and was already knocking on the front door while I was gathering my things together. I got the dog from the back seat and scooted after her.

The door slowly opened to reveal a red-eyed stump of a blonde woman. Poking out from behind her stood two preschool kids, gripping on to her track pants, eyes wide in coffee-coloured faces.

25.

MRS. SCHNARE FILLED THE DOOR FRAME. "Yes?" Her voice was raw from crying. She tucked a lock of her flaxen hair behind her ear.

One of the kids squealed, "Oh look, Amanda, a puppy." She crept out from behind her mother's pant leg onto the porch, holding out her hand to the dog's wet nose. Lucky obliged by licking the little girl's fingers and wagging his tail. She giggled, and said, "He's kissing me."

"The pup likes kids," I said.

She begged, "Mommy, can we get a puppy?" Her big brown eyes then looked up at me. "What's her name?"

"It's a he, and his name is Lucky."

"Nothing lucky around here," the woman said, sighing.

I let the comment hang in the air a respectful second and then said, "My friend, Cindy Dale and I are here from *The Toronto Express*. We're journalists. My name is Robin MacFarland."

Mrs. Schnare looked at me and then at Cindy. "Nice to meet you. Please, call me Linda." Her head ping-ponged back and forth from Cindy and me. "What on earth would reporters want to do with me?"

"Can we come in?" Cindy was already moving closer to the woman, forcing her to back up into the house in order to maintain her personal space.

"Sure, I guess so."

We followed her into a sun-filled living room, the kids fawning over Lucky as they both trailed behind me.

"Have a seat," Linda said, gesturing to a couch covered with a blanket.

Lucky jumped up on the sofa to sit beside me, and I tried to shoo him off by poking at his hind legs. God, that dog was so stubborn.

"Oh, don't worry about the dog. Our old dog just died about three weeks ago, and I'm used to animals being on the furniture."

Amanda, the little girl, was standing beside Lucky, stroking his head. "He's so velvety and furry. I wish I had a new little puppy."

"All in good time, Amanda," said her mom. She gazed at me, her eyes bloodshot. "It's been hard on the kids, these past few weeks. So much loss. Now, how can I help you?"

Cindy had been right. Lucky was an icebreaker in this very sad household. I was glad I'd brought him. Still, Linda seemed very upset. Not that I blamed her, losing her son. I wanted to put her at ease. "How do you like living in Lockeport?"

"Lockeport? Way better than Liverpool. We've only lived here a year, and the community is very accepting." She tilted her head at her tawny-coloured children. "Not like Liverpool. That mayor? I have never met a more racist man. I hope you never run into him."

Her words were spoken with such venom. I'd had a hint that the mayor was racist when I talked to the MLA in that café. So, it was pretty widely known. "Do you mean Dave Bradley?"

"Him." The word exploded out of her mouth.

She continued, "Serves him right that his lily-white daughter is going out with a black boy. Maybe it will teach him something. People are people. All blood is red. My mixed marriage has worked out very well." She shook her head and clicked her tongue in disgust.

I computed the information. Linda had been in Lockeport

for a year. That would mean that Danny's relationship with Bradley's daughter had been fairly long-standing, at least a year. Lots of time for rage to flourish in his father. I'd have to think about Dave Bradley as a suspect. It seemed so unlikely. A mayor? Who'd vote for a racist mayor? But I couldn't dwell on that right now. Now, I had to somehow get the conversation back on topic. Linda was sitting ramrod straight, full of tension. So much for my putting her at ease. She was now stoked up with anger. I guessed that was better than sorrow. I looked at Cindy. She had way more experience at interviews than I did. Obviously I was screwing up this one.

Cindy looked at me, read my silent message, and took over. "Dr. MacKenzie said at the lobster supper on the weekend that Billy had died of a stroke."

"He did? Well that's just wrong. Billy died of food poisoning." Before she launched into Billy's final hours, she turned to her kids and said, "Go outside now and play in the backyard, not on the street. And watch out for ticks. I'll call you in when it's lunchtime."

I'd written about ticks and their diseases for the paper. They were disgusting. Luckily, I hadn't had one on me yet. Thank God. The idea of a tick burrowing into my skin nauseated me.

"Ticks?" I asked, gasping as the kids scampered out of the room, headlong to Lyme's Disease.

"There aren't many now, but Lockeport has more than our fair share. This is a red zone."

I surreptitiously checked my pant legs. It felt like a thousand bugs were crawling in my scalp.

"Anyway," Mrs. Schnare continued, "We were having a birthday party for Billy, who was turning fourteen. He was my second oldest. Suddenly, he couldn't talk, threw up, and fell over. It was awful. My husband and I shut down the party and raced him to the hospital in Liverpool, but he died on the way. The on-call there said it was a stroke, but I thought it looked more like a reaction to the lobster. Made sense. He had just been eating it. Allergic or something, although he'd certainly eaten lobster before with no problems."

Cindy interrupted her. "Allergies can suddenly show up, so good thinking."

Linda gave her a look. She didn't need her self-confidence bolstered. "I'd grabbed the lobster he'd been eating before we left the house and put it in a cooler bag. I handed it into the lab, insisting they examine it. Good thing, too. They knew within hours that it had saxitoxin, a reportable toxin because of its seriousness, sort of like *E. Coli.* That was reported to Public Health, and then the Halifax paper got hold of the findings."

Well, that answered my question on how it was reported so quickly by the *Halifax Herald*. But I still didn't know if Dr. MacKenzie knew it was food poisoning when he brought up the conflicting information that Billy had had a stroke.

Cindy had the same question. She leaned forward in her chair, trying to look innocently friendly. "So, do you think Dr. MacKenzie knew Billy had food poisoning?"

"Why are you asking that?" Linda wasn't fooled and looked suspiciously at Cindy. This woman was not to be underestimated.

Cindy said, "I'm just trying to figure out the timelines."

My friend was acting all casual, but I knew what she was after. She was trying to prove that MacKenzie murdered Beverly. She wanted to prove he had known the lobster that killed Billy was highly toxic, had taken a bit of it, injected it into a lobster, and bribed the waiter for the head table, Danny, to give it to her. The fact that the MLA gave the lobster away didn't matter to her. Cindy just wanted to prove MacKenzie wanted Beverly dead. Sure, I could see it happening like that. But it didn't follow through. It all fell apart. I knew it wasn't him. He may have had the wherewithal to kill her with poison, but when that didn't work, he sliced her throat? No. I didn't think so. The poor man could barely stand up. Besides, what could possibly be his motive?

Mrs. Schnare looked thoughtful. "Yes, I would imagine that he did know Billy had been poisoned. Even though MacKenzie wasn't the attending physician in the ER, it would have gotten back to him that I took the lobster to the lab and demanded an analysis. Plus, he's a pretty hands-on type of guy. I'm sure he reads the Public Health alerts daily."

Cindy tried not to look smug. She was on her way with her theory.

I changed the topic. "This is a lovely home you have here, Mrs. Schnare."

"Linda. Thanks. We were lucky to find it, having five children."

"Five?" Cindy was disbelieving. "But you look so young."

"Oh, Brad and I started out early. I had my first when I was just eighteen. So, we needed a big house when we were desperate to get out of Liverpool, and found this one. I'd rather be in Lockeport as I said."

"Where does your husband work?"

"He's a lobster fisherman. His boat's registered in Shelburne."

I stood up. I'd found out everything I needed to know. "Mrs. Schnare, Linda, I'm terribly sorry for your loss."

"Thank you." She looked down, a tear escaping her right eye. And then she looked up, her eyes shining with wet. "Are you going to write about all this in your paper? In Toronto? That people should be aware of this terrible poison in shellfish?"

Cindy pushed Lucky off the couch. "If we do, I'll be sure to let you know."

I stomped on Lucky's leash before he took off across the room. "Thank you so much for agreeing to talk to us."

Linda looked truly puzzled. "Why wouldn't I?"

Hadn't she heard that people hate journalists? Maybe not here, in this pretty part of Canada where communities were strong and people helped each other, most of the time. "Well, thank you just the same."

She waved goodbye from the porch as we climbed into Cindy's rental. Cindy punched the air as we drove away. "I knew it." She punched the air again. "I knew it. I knew he knew. I *like* him for this."

Lucky barked from the bask seat, caught up in her enthusiasm.

Honestly. She had to control herself. "Cindy, it wasn't him. He didn't murder Beverly."

"We will see," she argued. "I'm pretty sure I'm right. I'd place a bet on it. He poisoned the lobster. Bribed Danny to give it to her. Then Beverly gave it to Statten. He died by accident. So, then, MacKenzie had to kill her by slicing her throat."

"He's too old Cindy. He couldn't have done it. I saw him at the supper. He walks with a cane."

"Sure he could. With a sharp enough blade, it would be easy. Slice." She zipped her forefinger across her neck to illustrate her point. "Just like that."

God.

We drove along in silence, up the same winding road to the main highway. "Are you hungry?" she asked.

Dumb question. I was always hungry. "I could eat."

"Did I hear you say there was a good restaurant in Port Mouton?"

"Sure. Let's go there. And then maybe look at the fishing boats on the wharf there? You said you wanted to look at some boats."

"Sounds like a good plan. Fish and chippies, here we come."

We drove along in silence, both of us lost in our thoughts about what we'd just learned. I knew that Cindy's take-away from the interview was very different than mine. I couldn't for the life of me see Dr. MacKenzie slicing a blade across a throat. He simply wouldn't have the strength. And I was now suspicious of Dave Bradley, the mayor. Did he hate black people so much that he would kill? There was the complicating and enraging factor that his daughter had surely defied him and dated Beverly's son, Danny. That would be intolerable to a racist. It could be a motive.

I moved from these thoughts into the state of the world. I

..s so grateful for my Buddhist practice where every day I chanted for world peace and the happiness of all living beings. It looked to me like I would have to chant harder with people like Bradley around. If everyone could treat others with respect and dignity, then awful wars wouldn't happen. Violence against others would be a long-ago nightmare. But, in the meantime, there was so much hatred everywhere.

Had Bradley murdered Beverly Price? Had Bradley bribed Danny to give his mother a juicy lobster? One that had been poisoned? This was all so terrible. I put my hand on my heart. Imagine how Danny would feel if years later he discovered that he had murdered his own mother. As it was, if the lobster had been poisoned, then he had carried it to the table. He had been involved in a murder. How old was Danny anyway? Fourteen? It was hard to peg his age. My mind leapt around all these thoughts while Cindy drove.

She was no doubt constructing a scenario in her mind where MacKenzie had poisoned the lobster, and when his attempt to murder Beverly failed, he went after her with a knife. I was surprised that Cindy didn't even entertain the idea that Bradley could be a suspect. She hadn't mentioned him at all. If anyone understood how others could hate others, it would be her. She had been the target of a bomb under her car just a year and a half ago. I believed, like she did, that it was a hate crime, that her being gay had caused this horrific act against her. Why didn't she see Beverly's murder as a hate crime? I certainly believed that. Maybe Ralph did too.

The miles whizzed by, and we were soon pulling into the gravel parking lot of what had recently become my favourite restaurant in the world. Cindy flung the gearshift into park and smiled at me. "Okay, we disagree on a few things, but let's have lunch. I'm starving."

"Me too," I said as I lowered the window to let some air in for Lucky while we ate. "Good thing it's cool out today, otherwise, we'd have to go home and put Lucky in the house."

"Oh, he'll be fine. Don't be such a worrywart."

Oh screw off, I wanted to say, but didn't. He was my dog, and I didn't want other people to tell me how to take care of him.

"Dogs cannot be left in hot cars, Cindy."

She rolled her eyes. "There's a cool breeze here. Let's go." She hurled open her car door and started to get out.

"You know what?" I said, "I'm not comfortable leaving him in the car here with the sun beating down. Let's find some shade. There's some trees out front. Let's park under their shade."

Cindy shut the car door, revved the engine, and squealed out of the lot to a spot under a tree. "There. You happy?"

"Oh, come on Cindy." She was irritating me.

She grabbed her purse, and I followed her up the wheelchair ramp into the icy coolness of the air-conditioned restaurant. She'd stopped right inside the front door. She muttered to me under her breath, "I thought this was a restaurant?"

To our right were metal shelves filled with convenience store items: loaves of bread, dish detergent, cans of dog food, soup. A stocky man brushed around us, carrying a case of beer.

"It's multi-purpose. The restaurant's to the left, through the swing doors."

"Oh."

We pushed through the doors, and I spied a free table for two in the alcove at the very back. Good, we could be seated there. I saw Danny hovering near the far wall, waiting for an order to come up from the kitchen. As my eyes passed over the crowd chowing down on their massive plates of steaming food, I noticed Dave Bradley, sitting immediately to my right. He was alone and staring at the menu. I poked Cindy in the ribs with my elbow and whispered, "Speak of the devil. There's the mayor. Dave Bradley."

She nodded and took a quick inconspicuous look. "The fat-cat racist asshole?"

I nodded back. "Yup, one and the same."

Meanwhile, Danny delivered two enormous seafood platters

to a young couple holding hands across their table immediately to my left. When the boy looked up, he saw me.

"Hi, Mrs. Creston. Did Winchester and Maggie leave yet?"

Mrs. Creston? Geezus. I wasn't *married* to Ralph. "Hi Danny, just call me Robin. Ralph and I aren't married. And yes, they're gone. My friend Cindy is staying with me right now."

"Hi Cindy. You two can take that back table in the alcove. I'll bring you some water in a second. I just have this order to take."

Danny turned away and stood in front of Dave Bradley. "Afternoon, sir. Have you decided on your order?"

Bradley didn't look up.

Danny looked around, colour rising into his cheeks. "Sir, can I take your order?"

Cindy had stopped midstride and turned to watch the exchange.

Bradley huddled over his menu, refusing to acknowledge Danny. The boy looked around, his eyes flooded with pain, and then walked away. He approached an older woman standing by the kitchen doors and whispered to her. She then went back to Dave Bradley and said, "Can I take your order?"

He looked up and said, "Three pieces of fish and chips, thanks. And coffee. I like it black, like that boy over there."

The waiter's eyes widened.

Cindy had had enough. The coffee comment had thrown a control switch in her. Her face was livid with rage. She marched over to his table and said, loudly enough for everyone in the restaurant to hear, "You're the mayor of Liverpool, right? Well I'm a reporter for the largest paper in Canada, *The Toronto Express*. And trust me, your name is going to be all over the paper as a racist. How dare you treat this young boy as if he didn't exist. That's so disgusting. I'm going to ruin you."

Sometimes, Cindy said just the right thing. The restaurant patrons were shifting in their seats. Some of them were smiling.

The mayor shifted in his seat. "You threatening me?"

"Oh no, *sir*. I don't threaten. I act."

Meanwhile, Danny was huddled by the kitchen door. The waiter who'd taken the order was now standing in front of the boy, protecting him, whispering to him, putting her arm around his shoulder. I wondered if this had happened to him before.

The mayor threw down his napkin and pushed his chair back angrily. Cindy was knocked backwards. "Serves you right, bitch." He bustled to the door and called over his shoulder, "I'm not going to eat in an establishment that hires jungle bunnies. And you, you stupid redhead, you're going to hear from me."

"I'll quote you on that," Cindy shouted to his retreating back.

So, she'd been threatened as well. I didn't like the sound of that. Shirley's words echoed in my ears. *Murderers are very dangerous*. I shuddered.

The tension hung in the air for a moment or two, and then the silence was suddenly filled with clattering silverware and small talk. Everyone had gone back to eating their delicious food. Was this business as usual in Port Mouton? Maybe it was the way it was everywhere. Only a brave few, like Cindy, challenged the status quo.

Cindy and I continued to the table in the alcove and sat down on the metal chairs. I could feel the cold seeping through my pants. Danny walked over self-consciously, menus tucked under his arm, and two glasses of water on a tray. He put the water down in front of us, condensation dripping down the sides.

"Thanks," he said, to Cindy. "It's the first time he's been in here. But we all know what he's like. He hates me because his daughter and I are, you know...."

"Dating?" I asked helpfully.

"Yes. And he can't stand the idea of whiteness being polluted by this." He pulled some of the skin on his arm to make the point.

A very aware young man. "So, a white supremacist?"

"I didn't want to say so, but yes. That's what he is. Everyone knows it. He hated my mother, too. She was dating Statten, you know, the guy who died. I didn't like him anyway, fish farms, you know, but still. That mayor is full of hate. His daughter doesn't know what to do."

"I'm sorry Danny. It must be very hard for you." Cindy touched his arm.

Holy smokes. I was reeling with the information that Beverly Price had been dating Frank Statten. That explained her smiling at him. That explained why she was looking around, all upset at the lobster supper. That explained why she gave him the lobster. And here I thought she was searching the crowd for her son. Or that she was buttering Statten up because he gave the town money. The situation was getting more and more complicated.

"I'm used to it. There are a few around." A ding was heard in the distance. "I got to go. That's my order coming up. I'll be back in a moment to take your order. Belinda told me to tell you it's on the house. No one has spoken up like that to the mayor before."

Danny rushed off to the kitchen door to get his order, and Cindy and I opened the menus. "Why am I even looking?" I said, trying to be lighthearted. "I always order the same thing. Fish and chips."

Cindy looked up from the menu and spat, "I'm not kidding. I'm going to write about that shithead."

"It's okay Cindy. I think his term is coming up."

"He won't be re-elected."

"You never know. Some people are full of hate, and they'll vote for a person who hates. What are you going to have?"

She didn't answer. She was writing up the story on her phone. God, she was rabid. One day it was going to get her in big trouble.

And she still didn't think of the mayor as a suspect in Beverly's murder? Unbelievable.

26.

WE RECOVERED FROM THE AWFUL ENCOUNTER with Bradley in the restaurant and thoroughly enjoyed our meal. We were licking our chops as we walked back to the car. The fish and the chips had been cooked to perfection; crunchy on the outside and soft and fluffy on the inside. That lunch was so good, I could eat those fish and chips a dozen times in a row. But wait—that's exactly what I had done. I wondered how much weight I'd gained. My zipper still did up on my pants, so I guessed I was doing okay.

I peered in through the car window and saw that Lucky was curled into a little ball, snoozing on the back seat. Cindy plipped the locks, and when I opened the car door, I immediately fanned the air, checking the temperature. Nice and cool. Lucky wasn't even panting. I stroked his soft head as he woke from his nap.

"Let's go look at the boats on the wharf," said Cindy, folding her long body into the car as I patted Lucky. "I'm dying to see a real lobster fishing boat. What do they call them? Cape Islanders?"

"I have no idea. There's also a pretty beach up the road here. Carter's Beach. We could go there after and check it out."

"Naw. I read that the water there's freezing. Plus there's no parking. Let's go to Summerville Beach, like we planned to. The tide's going out now, so the water will warm up when it comes back in."

"How do you know the tide's going out?"

She waved her phone at me. "I have an app."

Of course she did.

When I stopped patting Lucky and stood up, I noticed that Danny was sitting at a picnic table at the far end of the parking lot. He was staring out across the road and eating a plate of restaurant food absent-mindedly. Looked like a hot turkey sandwich. The poor kid. His mother was dead, and he had just been harassed by one of the most important men in Liverpool, the mayor. I said to Cindy, "Hang on just a sec. I'm going to talk to Danny. You know, cheer him up. He looks so despondent."

Cindy looked over to the picnic table and saw what I saw: a skinny kid with a big mop of curly brown hair staring off into the distance. He was dealing with emotions that no child his age should have to cope with.

"I'll come too," she said, releasing her seatbelt and throwing it off.

We waved as we walked over to him across the parking lot. He swiped a hand across his eyes. My heart broke as I saw he'd been crying.

Cindy swung her legs over the picnic table bench opposite Danny. I tried to do the same but utterly failed. I ended up lifting my right leg over the bench with my hand and straddling it. No way was I going to get both legs facing the same way. I really needed to control the calories. These unsolicited thoughts ended the minute I looked at Danny. Cindy was holding his hand as he silently wept. Tears coursed down his cheeks, leaving wet tracks. Finally, things had hit him.

Cindy crooned at him while stroking his hand with her thumb. Despite her brash approach to life, she had a soft side, a mothering instinct that took over when she saw anyone hurt, except for her own kids. For them, she had a different standard. People were sometimes like that. My father was highly critical of me and Andrew but wouldn't say a bad word about my four kids. Some people thought people mellowed with age. In his case, it was probably dementia.

"It's okay. Danny," she whispered, "it's going to be okay. Your grandmother is going to take care of you."

He looked at her, tears welling up and over his eyelids, "She always has. It's not that."

Not that? Why would he be crying then? What was the cause of his sobs? Bradley?

Cindy caught on. "What is it then, Danny? What's upsetting you? Bradley?"

He looked down and whispered, "No, not him. It's just that I delivered the lobster that killed Mr. Statten first to my mom."

"You couldn't have known that it would kill anyone," I said, trying to console him.

"It could have killed my mom, but she died anyway," he wailed.

But Cindy, the reporter, was hot on the trail. "Who told you to deliver the lobster?"

I shot her a glance. She was taking a risk here, assuming someone had told him to deliver the lobster.

He looked at her, his eyes pleading for understanding. He muttered, "Dr. MacKenzie."

Cindy squirmed with triumph. She smiled smugly at me. She had been right about MacKenzie. Because he had asked Danny to deliver it to his mom, and that attempt had failed, he had killed her another way. He had killed both Beverly and Statten. "Dr. MacKenzie gave you the lobster?"

"Yes, it was all warm and cooked. Dr. MacKenzie had it in a Sobeys bag. It was huge."

"And he told you where to take it."

"Yes." Danny was so ashamed.

"Danny," I said, "You couldn't have known it was poisoned. How could you have known? Did Dr. MacKenzie promise you something to deliver it?"

"He hinted that I was smart in school and to make sure I

applied for the big university award. The sixty-thousand-dollar scholarship. That I would really enjoy free tuition."

"That's quite the hint."

Danny looked up again. "But you don't understand." He was crying in earnest now.

"What don't we understand, Danny?" Cindy's voice was as soft as she could make it. "You can tell us."

He stuttered. "I didn't obey Dr. MacKenzie. But I'm still going to get the money."

"You didn't obey him?" Cindy was truly puzzled. Danny had taken the lobster to his mother as instructed, hadn't he? "What didn't you do? You delivered the lobster."

"Yes, but not to the right person. Dr. MacKenzie told me to deliver it to Frank Statten, not to my mother. He said it was a nice juicy lobster for the fellow who was donating so much to the hospital. It was his way of thanking him."

Cindy looked at me, totally flummoxed. This didn't suit her theory at all. Her current theory was that Dr. MacKenzie wanted the poisoned lobster to be delivered to Beverly Price, but when she gave it away, Frank Statten died instead, an innocent bystander. According to her theory, Dr. MacKenzie had to then kill her another way. He wanted her dead. That was her theory and she was sticking to it.

Me, on the other hand, couldn't figure out why Dr. MacKenzie would want anyone dead, especially not Frank Statten, who was his cash cow. Statten was the goose that had kept laying golden eggs for his hospital. I didn't get it.

"Danny," I said, "why would Dr. MacKenzie want Frank Statten dead?"

Danny looked at me as if I had rocks in my head. "Fishing."

"I know I'm fishing here, but why..."

"*Lobster* fishing. Dr. MacKenzie's son owns the largest holding tank in Nova Scotia." He thumbed at the wharf. "The fish farms are destroying the catch."

"Oh," I said. It was suddenly making sense to me. Dr.

MacKenzie's allegiance was first and foremost to his family, not the hospital. His motive was to save his son's business. MacKenzie was at the end of his life and wanted to ensure his son's success.

Cindy was a step behind. "So, you're saying that Dr. MacKenzie took a lobster from a grocery store bag, told you to take it to Frank Statten because he was so helpful to the hospital, and hinted if you did this you could get free university tuition from a scholarship,"

Dany was so ashamed of himself. He sighed, and said softly, "Yes."

Cindy was dotting all the 'i's.' "He didn't ask you to take it to your mother. Statten was his target all along. But you took it to your mother."

"Yes," he said and sighed again.

"Why did you take it to your mom, Danny?" she asked.

He looked at her. "I wanted her to have the largest lobster. She's my mom. She should have the best lobster."

I interjected here. It looked to me as if Cindy was making him feel badly for defying a murderer, which was not a good thing to do. "I would have done the same thing, Danny," I said.

"But now," he cried, "Dr. MacKenzie's going to make sure I get the award. Because the right person died. I need the award. I need to go to university. That's why I'm working now. To save up. I want to go to Acadia and take chemistry. It's a really good program."

"Danny," I said gently, "look at me."

He lifted his sad eyes to my face.

"First of all, you don't have to accept the award if you don't want it. You can apply for a student loan and pay it off when you get a great job as a chemist. Secondly, Dr. MacKenzie probably won't be around to fix the scholarship books, if they need fixing, two years from now, when you're applying. He did a very bad thing." Hell, the man would shortly be wanted for murder. He'd be in jail.

Oh my God. I just realized that I'd better call that awful jerk Hans Schroeder, the detective that so mightily pissed Cindy off. Danny had just identified a murderer. The police should know. In the meantime, we had one very upset teenager on our hands.

I tried to lift Danny's spirits. "I'm sure you're a good student and you'll probably win a scholarship anyway. Just keep at your studies."

"That's what my gramma says."

"You talked to her about all this?"

"Of course. I tell her everything."

Cindy patted Danny's hand one last time. "Danny, you're just a kid. What are you? Fourteen?"

"Almost fifteen," he said proudly.

"Still, just a kid. You've done nothing wrong. You were used, that's all. Don't worry about any of this. Robin and I will take care of it. Robin will tell her boyfriend, Ralph, that MacKenzie wanted to kill Statten. He's a cop."

Danny looked at me, shaking his head. "I could tell he was a cop at the lobster supper. But don't tell Winchester. I don't want him to know."

I was puzzled. "Know what?"

"That I took a bribe."

"Oh Danny, anyone would have done what you did. Dr. MacKenzie is a big shot in the community. You had no idea he was trying to kill someone. Besides, was it really a bribe? Think. What exactly did he say when he handed you the lobster?"

"He said that I was a smart kid and would go far if I won the big university scholarship."

"There. See what I mean? He didn't say, if you do this, I'll help you win. What he said doesn't sound like a bribe to me. Stop worrying."

"I didn't take a bribe?" He looked at me hopefully.

"Not legally, not from where I sit."

Cindy, sensing the crisis was over, stood up and stretched, her long arms going on for miles. "Beautiful day."

"I have to get back to work," Danny said. He gathered up his paper plate with its uneaten French fries and headed over the parking lot to the restaurant. "Thanks for the pep talk." He turned and flashed me a wide smile. What a beautiful young man he was. I hoped he'd get over this nastiness soon.

Cindy watched me struggling to lift my leg out from under the picnic table and over the immovable bench. "Here, Robin, let me give you a hand."

She reached down and helped me up from straddling the bench. "Don't worry," she said, "he'll do fine. School starts next week, and he'll forget all about it."

"But he won't have a mother," I said.

"Sounds to me like he never did. I hate to admit it, but if MacKenzie told Danny to give the lobster to Statten, then he probably didn't murder Beverly. She was never his target in the first place. Let's face it, Robin. You're right. An old geezer like that probably couldn't knife someone."

I'd been saying that all along. But I didn't rub it in.

Cindy slung her purse over her shoulder. "I can't believe she was having an affair with Statten. Not good optics, that's for sure. Not if her platform was against the fish farms. And that Bradley guy? What a dickhead." She shook her head as if to clear it, and then said, "Robin, let's have some fun. Let's go look at some boats."

"Sure," I said. She put her arm around me as we walked back to the car. People in the restaurant were watching as we crossed in front of the window. I didn't give a shit what they thought. I loved my friend.

Lucky barked excitedly as we slammed the car doors and headed to the wharf. That dog was such a handful sometimes. I put my phone in the glove compartment where it would be safe and turned to pat the dog. I could barely think with the racket, but still, there was one question that kept zapping around my skull. If MacKenzie hadn't murdered Beverly Price, who had?

When we got to the wharf, I opened the back door and grabbed

Lucky's leash as he leapt out. He immediately started barking at seagulls. Cindy laughed at him as she stood beside me.

"Well, I guess I was right. Dr. MacKenzie was a murderer, like I said." She was trying to rescue her dignity.

"Yeah, well, you got the wrong victim. He was aiming for Statten all along." I wasn't going to let her get away with it.

She changed the topic. "We should call that asshole Hans Schroeder. The Vienna sausage."

"Yeah, I'll do it. I think he'll be less antagonistic towards me."

"No wait." Cindy thought for a moment. "He hates all women. I think we should ask Ralph to call. That would be sure to get some action."

I looked at my watch. It was just after two. "Ralph is in the air right now. I can't call him. And we definitely should let the cops know about MacKenzie right away."

Cindy shook her head. "But Schroeder? He won't believe us mere females."

"You're right." What to do, what to do? "Listen, I think that Branson woman will pay attention to us. She hesitated when I told her that the lobster had been poisoned, like she was thinking about it. I think she'd at least look into it. But Schroeder, no. He wouldn't act. You're right. He's obviously a woman hater."

"Or maybe a gay woman hater."

"Aw Cindy, he was pretty rude to me too."

"Not really."

"Well, you did shout in his ear." I laughed. "That was a pretty good tactic. No physical assault but an assault nonetheless."

"I think it should be me to call Branson," said Cindy. "I was very polite to her on the highway. Plus, I think she plays for my team."

Cindy polite to a cop? Like hell she was. Or maybe she had been. Maybe she even pretend-cried, trying to get out of the ticket. And there was the gay factor. "Okay, you do it."

She took out her phone, "Here, give me the number."

"My phone's in the car, in the glove compartment. Look it up."

Cindy walked away from me on the wharf, out of earshot as she made the call, and I let Lucky go where he wanted to go. He pulled me along as he snuffled discarded shells on the wharf. I looked around feigning innocence as he lifted his leg and peed on a rope. Phew, no one was watching. In fact, the wharf looked completely deserted. There was only Cindy and me, and she was looking over the edge of the wharf at the seaweed undulating below as she talked. The tide was out, just as she said it would be, and the boats were straining at their ropes, low in the water. I took a deep breath of the air scented with brine. It was so nice here. A seagull cawed from the top of a high mast, and a few barn swallows dipped and flew between the boats.

"Robin?" Cindy was tucking her phone into her jean pocket as she sauntered back to me. "I was right. Same team. She was flirting with me. Anyway, I'm pretty sure she'll look into it."

"Why, what did she say?" Lucky kept tugging at his leash. "Lucky."

"Here, let me take Lucky."

I handed the leash to her. I was tired of restraining him as he pulled, his nails scrabbling on the wooden pier towards everything new, including seagull poop. "Thanks. But what did she say?"

"She said she was worried about the lobster at the lobster supper being poisoned after you had called her with the information that Billy Schnare had died from saxitoxin. She asked me if I was *with* you." Cindy winked, her meaning clear.

"What did you say?"

"I told her the truth. I said you were *with* Ralph Creston, the Toronto homicide detective. That you were partners."

Something in my gut tied in a knot.

"Cindy."

"Face it, Robin. You are partners. Anyway, Officer Branson, *Marilyn*, said she was in the neighbourhood and she'd stop here at the wharf to talk to us both. Take a statement. She's like five minutes away, if that. I'm going to take some pictures of the boats. They are so pretty, bobbing in the water." She grabbed her phone from her pocket and held it away from her, filming the scene. "My kids will love this video."

All of a sudden, Lucky started barking and charging in the other direction, jerking the leash. Cindy's phone flew out of her hand and skittered across the wharf. "Stupid dog," she said as she leaned over to pick it up. Cindy had been holding Lucky's leash in her fist and the handle slipped from her grasp. "And there he goes." Lucky charged down the wharf barking his little head off at a man striding over to us. Cindy aimed her phone at the action.

I squinted my eyes. Who was it? Oh damn. Dave Bradley. What was he doing here? Had he followed us?

"Oh shit," said Cindy. She dropped her hand and held the phone at her side.

I called Lucky, and he looked at me sideways, ignored my command, and kept barking at the mayor. Bradley paid zero attention to him and marched in our direction. When he was a couple of metres away, Lucky ran by my side, and stood, feet planted, ears back. A low growl curled up from his throat. My dog didn't like this man. Wise dog. Neither did I.

Bradley snarled at Cindy, "You effing cunt. Embarrassing me in front of my constituents. You have no idea what's right around here. That black MLA was having an affair with Statten. She deserved what was coming to her. And so do you. Keep your nose out of our business."

Was that an admission that he'd killed Beverly? And he could say "cunt" but not "fuck?" I couldn't believe I was thinking about word choice at a time like this.

Cindy fumed, "Oh aren't you the hotshot mayor, trying to order me around. Forget it, buster." She poked him in the chest. "No one"—poke—"and I repeat, *no one*"—poke—"can act like a racist around me. Because that's what you are. A white supremacist. And I will expose you. The article has already been submitted." She poked him in the chest again.

That was a lie, but Bradley didn't know it. He took a step closer to Cindy and forced her to back up to the edge of the wharf. "I'm going to sue you for slander if anything is printed about me. My beliefs are right. We can't muddy the water with black dirt." His face was in hers. "You deserve the same as that mother of the pickaninny." I watched in horror as his right shoulder jerked forward and knocked her off balance. Her phone flew out of her hand as she tumbled backwards over the edge of the pier, her face white with shock. On the way down her head clunked against the bow of one of the boats. I looked over the edge and saw her body floating, seaweed wrapping around her lifeless limbs.

27.

"WHAT HAVE YOU DONE?" I screamed as I gaped at the water below. Cindy looked dead. Her long, white arms were floating over her head. I shouted again at Bradley. "What have you done?" My words echoed in the stillness of the shore. I turned back to look at Cindy. She was slowly sinking under the waves.

"I hope I killed her," he yelled as he ran off the pier, head down low, fists pumping and feet churning up the gravel at the end of the wharf.

I hooked Lucky's leash over a wooden post at the edge of the pier and hoped he wouldn't be stupid enough to jump in after me. He'd dangle from the post and choke to death.

I jumped between two boats into the frigid Atlantic water and gasped with shock at the cold. Cindy's feet were sinking and her head was rapidly following. My lifeguard training from forty years ago at summer camp kicked in. I reached down and grabbed a handful of her curly red hair. I yanked her back up, madly treading water. I hooked my hand under her chin and started scissor kicking toward shore, dragging her behind me. I never worked so hard in my life. The water was freezing, and although I was a very good swimmer, I wasn't that strong. Her weight was already tiring me out. I knew I needed help. The rocks on the shore seemed so far away. Could I make it? I had to. I wasn't going to let my friend drown.

I could hear Lucky's high-pitched bark above me. *Please don't jump in*, I prayed. And then I heard someone talking to him.

"Help!" I cried. "Help. Down here." I was panting.

Officer Branson peered over the edge of the wharf. She quickly disappeared, shouting that she was coming. I could hear her footsteps pounding on the wooden slats of the wharf above me. I kicked and kicked as I dragged Cindy to shore. Officer Branson scrambled over the rocks and waded in the water to me. I hadn't realized I'd reached a spot where I could stand up.

I put my feet on the sand and tugged Cindy through the icy water to Branson, who was paddling with her arms as she walked, trying to go faster. "Is she breathing?" she shouted.

"I don't know." I sure hoped so.

Officer Branson hooked her arms under Cindy's and lifted her head up out of the water. It lolled sideways, and I was gripped with fear. Had she been killed when she hit her head on the boat's gunwale? Broken her neck? Branson put her face over Cindy's, checking for breath.

I asked the officer, "Is she dead?"

"No, I don't think so. She's breathing. I think she's just knocked out. But let's get her out of the water."

I took hold of her feet while Officer Branson took her head. Between the two of us, we managed to lift her out of the water and over the boulders, our feet slipping on the slimy seaweed. Branson stopped climbing backwards for a moment and put her ear to Cindy's mouth. "She's still breathing just fine." She looked at me appraisingly. "You saved her from drowning with your quick actions. I don't think she even got a mouthful. Did she hit her head?"

I would never forget the sound of the hollow clunk of her head bouncing off the side of the boat. "Yes, on the bow of a boat after she was pushed over the wharf."

Branson looked at me, miscomprehension etching a question mark on her face. "She was pushed? Who pushed her? No one's around."

"Bradley. The mayor. He took off," I said, huffing. Cindy was large, and the going was tough, even though I had the lighter end of her body. "They were arguing, and he backed her to the edge of the wharf and then knocked her with his shoulder. She fell over."

Finally, we made it to the top of the rocks at the foot of the wharf. Branson and I gently laid Cindy down on the sparse grass. She regarded me seriously. "That's attempted murder."

Boy oh boy, did I know that.

"We need an ambulance." Where was my phone? I patted my pockets. Not there. "Do you have a phone? I can't find mine."

Had it fallen to the bottom of the sea? No, now I remembered. I'd put it in the glovebox in Cindy's car.

"You stay here," Officer Branson said. "I'm going to get a blanket and I'll radio EHS from my car. Emergency Health Services," she said for my benefit. "That will bring them faster than a call from a civilian. Depending on where they are, it might take a while. She'll be in shock." I watched her canter across the lot to her car, sit in it for a minute talking into her radio, and then head out the wharf.

Cindy was starting to move. She was trying to speak. "Robin?" she whispered. "Robin? What happened?"

I started crying as if my heart would burst. She was alive. She could talk. "Oh Cindy, you fell off the side of the pier. You whacked your head."

She opened her big green eyes and looked up at me. "No. I did not."

Arguing already? Definitely back in the land of the living. "Yes, you did."

Propping herself on one elbow, she said, "I did not. I didn't fall. That asshole Bradley pushed me. He tried to kill me. And stop crying, you big baby. I'm fine."

She tried to get a leg underneath her but fell back on the ground. "Not perfect, but okay. I'm a little dizzy."

"Just lie still." I patted her head, smoothing down her wild hair. "An ambulance is coming. And I'm not a baby."

She suddenly became agitated and started patting her hips. "My phone. Where's my phone? I need to write this up. That man tried to kill me. There's some kind of movement about journalists being killed while working. This is a hot story."

Geezus. Here she was at death's door, already thinking about the next article she was going to write. She was going to type it out on her tiny phone.

"Where's my phone?"

"I'm sure it's on the dock." I remembered seeing it fly out of her hand when Bradley pushed her.

"Wharf. It's called a wharf. A dock is where you sit in a Muskoka chair."

I wasn't sure we needed an ambulance. All her cylinders were firing.

Her eyes lost focus for a moment.

"Cindy, just rest. You've had a terrible head injury. Maybe you have a concussion."

"Naw, I have a skull made of steel. I faint whenever I hurt my knee."

"You hurt your knee?"

"It's killing me."

I looked down and sure enough, her jeans were ripped and there was a big gash in her knee. She must have hit that as well as her head. I looked at the cut closely. It needed stitches, that's for sure. I thought I could see bone. Nausea lurched in my chest. "You need stitches. It's a deep wound."

"Whatever."

Branson came back with a blanket and Lucky. "The ambulance will be here soon. Apparently, there was a heart attack in Milton so as soon as they deal with that, they'll be here." She covered Cindy with an old grey army blanket. "Here. You're shivering."

Cindy said, "I'm usually hot."

Oh God. She was making googly eyes at the cop.

Branson reached into her back pocket and held out Cindy's phone to her. "I found this on the wharf."

Lucky was licking Cindy's wounded knee. I pulled him back.

"Give it to Robin, please," Cindy said to Branson.

She handed the phone to me, and I pushed the home button. The screen lit up, and the grass and pebbles below me came into focus. Oh my God. It was still videotaping. "It's still working."

I clicked the camera feature off and then played the video back from her camera roll. It looked like her phone had captured the whole exchange between her and Bradley. When she fell over the edge of the wharf, she'd tossed the phone in the air. I watched the film of upside-down boats and loopy birds cascading in circles on the screen. Then the screen went black. I figured it had fallen face down. I held it to my ear, and I could still hear faint voices. I pressed the volume button up and listened to all the things he'd said. The audio had still been recording.

Branson was standing close to me and listening as well. She pulled a small plastic bag out of her pocket and held it open. Oh no. Cindy wasn't going to like this. Her phone taken into custody? Branson gestured with her head for me to deposit the phone in the bag. Cindy was not going to be happy about this.

"It's evidence," Branson said. "Put it in the bag."

Cindy opened her eyes. "No. Wait. That's my phone. I have to have it."

Branson smiled grimly. "Nope. It's evidence. Really good evidence, too. Finally, we'll get rid of the man. He's so full of hate. I have no idea how he got elected."

Cindy said, "Quite a few people are full of hate." That was my line. "But I need my phone. I have a story to write."

Branson held it tightly in her hand. "Nope," she said again.

I scrunched down on my haunches and spoke softly to my friend. "Cindy, you almost lost your life. Losing a phone is nothing. You can replace a phone. We'll go into town and get you a new one."

She let her head fall back, defeated. "Oh, okay."

In the distance, I heard the wail of the ambulance. Good. The sooner this mess was dealt with the better.

"I don't need an ambulance. I just hurt my knee. I can still drive."

Who was she kidding? She could hardly lift her head.

"Or Robin can," said Branson, crouching down beside Cindy.

I spoke up. "I'm not allowed to drive that car. It's rented in Cindy's name. I'm not on the insurance."

Cindy sighed. "I don't need to go anywhere. I can drive."

But Officer Branson was adamant. "You need to go to the hospital. Who knows what you've hurt. You need to be looked at by a doctor." She stood up and waved the ambulance over to where we were.

The ambulance crunched over the rocks and gravel and stopped three metres from us. Two young kids jumped out, a Mutt and Jeff team, one short and stocky, the other a beanpole. They surged over to where we were on the grass but then slowed down when they took in Cindy's wet clothes, the gash in her leg, and her sitting up on her elbow.

"Fall in, did ya'?" said Beanpole.

Cindy glared at him. "Pushed. I was *pushed* in."

He laughed. "Yeah, that's what they all say."

Officer Branson stood up and stuck out her chest. "That's enough of that. She was definitely pushed. And fell pretty far down off the wharf at low tide."

Chastised, the stocky fellow said, "The tide was out? She hit bottom?"

I interrupted. "She hit her head badly on the way down on the side of a boat. Plus, as you can see, she's sliced her knee and needs stitches."

They quickly returned to the back of the ambulance, opened the doors, and took out a collapsed gurney. They didn't bother erecting it and lay it on the grass beside Cindy. She started to climb on when Beanpole held her down. "No, we don't know where else you're hurt. Let us lift you onto the gurney. Our backboard is at the hospital with the heart attack victim on it. He fell off a ladder. We can all lift you carefully by making like a fireman's chair without causing any more damage. You carried her over these?" His head nodded at the rocks.

"Come on," Cindy said as the four of us slid our hands under her body and hoisted her onto the gurney. "I only hurt my knee."

"And your head," said Officer Branson. "We need to be careful you didn't crack a bone in your neck."

I looked at Cindy's long, graceful neck and remembered how it had canted to the side when Officer Branson lifted her shoulders out of the water. I hoped she hadn't hurt her neck. That would really annoy her when she got old.

What was I saying? We were old.

I followed the boys carrying the gurney to the back of the ambulance. "Is it okay if I come too? And my cute pup?"

"Ahhh, no. Sorry. Regulations. We can only have patients in the bus. And definitely no dogs," said Mutt.

I was indignant. "In Ontario, caregivers can ride in the ambulance."

"I'll follow in my car," said Officer Branson as she squelched toward her car, still dripping wet. "You can come with me. Lucky too. Might as well make the car seats really wet."

Beanpole looked at her questioningly. "That's okay, Marilyn. You can go home and change. We can take it from here. She and the dog can grab a lift with someone here on the wharf."

From whom was a mystery to me.

"Thanks," said Officer Branson, "but I need to take a statement from Cindy. Soon, before she forgets any details. As I said, she was pushed. That's attempted murder when the tide is low like that. She could have broken her neck in the shallow water."

"It's not that shallow," I said, and then realized I sounded argumentative. "But she sure did hit her head hard, which could have killed her instantly. Or she could have drowned."

Cindy waved an arm in the air. "Stop talking about me. I hurt my *knee*. My head is made of rock." The boys lifted her into the ambulance while she was making her point.

"In you go," Mutt said, as he shut the doors on her sentence. They climbed into the cab and took off slowly, without the siren.

I turned to Branson. "Thanks for the offer of a lift to the hospital. I think I need to be with Cindy." I saw a movement out of the corner of my eye. Lucky started barking hysterically and pulling at his leash. I held on tightly. Bradley. "Bradley." I shook the officer's arm. "He's over there, behind that building."

Officer Branson took off, her black oxford shoes sliding on the pebbly gravel, her short figure disappearing behind the building. I could hear her shouting, "Stop, Bradley. Stop. You're making it worse for yourself."

I heard a motor start up and watched helplessly as a dinghy sped out of the harbour, rounded the far island where the fish farm was, and disappeared from view. Officer Branson appeared from behind the fish shack, shaking her head with disgust at herself. "He was so close. I almost had him."

"Never mind," I said. "He'll show up soon. He has to. He's the mayor."

"Let's get to the hospital." She headed to the back of her car. "I have green garbage bags in my trunk for us to sit on. No point in wrecking the municipality's property."

I hurried to the rental.

"No, you can come with me. You're not on the insurance."

"I know." I tried to not sound irritated. Of course I knew. "But I have to get my phone. It's in the glove compartment."

As I walked back to the cop car with my phone in hand, I saw Branson talking quickly on her phone, holding it to her ear with one hand. Who was she talking to? She finished the call and then carefully laid green garbage bags over the seats like she was covering a baby. That officious act at the lobster supper was just that. An act. Today, she had stepped up to the plate, and there'd been absolutely no political incorrectness, unlike with Schroeder. I hoped she'd go far in the organization, but I didn't think the RCMP had a good track record with the way they treated women, or black people, for that matter. With assholes like Schroeder around, it would be awhile before all people had dignity in that organization. I didn't envy her career path.

Speaking of careers, I thought as I walked, I should get in touch with Shirley and let her know that all hell had broken loose. I pushed my phone's home button and was alerted to two texts. When I checked my messages, I saw one was from Ralph and the other from Shirley. Speak of the devil. I looked at Shirley's first. *Hope you're being careful. Remember, murderers are very dangerous. Should you go to the police?* Too late for *that* text, I thought. I wrote back, *I am, I know, I have.*

Ralph's text was a bit more involved: *Arrived safely. I love you. I miss you. Will be back tonight, late. Hope you're having fun on the beach and in the water with your friend.*

If only he knew. I wrote back: *Bradley pushed Cindy off the Port Mouton wharf. Rescued her. She's in the hospital. He virtually admitted to killing Price. On video. He's loose.*

I got into Branson's car, the garbage bag slippery under my wet pants. Lucky curled up beside me. I said to her, "My pants are pretty wet. Sorry."

I looked at her profile and saw her lips twitch. But she said nothing.

My phone dinged. Ralph. *Do not, I repeat,* DO NOT, *under any conditions, go after Bradley. Tell the police.*

"Who's that from?" Branson was making conversation as she shut her car door.

"Ralph. He's told me to let the police look for Bradley."

"Oh, and we will. Don't worry. Or at least *I* will."

"Don't like Schroeder much?" I asked, looking for gossip.

"He's my boss," she said, starting up her car. It purred like a kitten.

So, she wasn't going to yap about him. "Nice new car," I said. I was truly impressed. "Ralph often brings home elderly Ford sedans, often containing computer equipment powered by coal."

"Let's not talk about Ford Nation politics."

I laughed as I texted Ralph back. *I'm with the police right now. Officer Branson. She helped save Cindy. She'll go after Bradley. On my way to the hospital in Branson's car. Cindy is going by ambulance.*

God, there was so much he didn't know. He knew nothing about MacKenzie giving the lobster to Danny either. What time was it? Four-thirty already? He'd only been gone for a few hours, since ten this morning. I tried to picture where he was. Let's see, his plane would have landed, and he'd probably caught a cab into the city, right to the storage unit. Yes, that's where he likely was, with literally all his past baggage of which I knew very little.

He and I would have to sort out our secrets if we wanted this relationship to last. It was a good relationship, I knew that, better than the previous one I'd had, and better than most I'd seen. We had fun, talked, played. It was all good.

But did I love him? Every time I looked at him my heart did a little leap and felt all soft and silky. I pictured him in front of a storage unit, sending me texts on his phone. I could see his lovely kind eyes, square jaw, dark wavy hair, cute little bum. Yeah, I loved him.

I held the thought close to my heart like it was a precious jewel.

But I wouldn't tell him just yet. I wanted to savour my epiphany. "Epiphany" was probably the wrong word. Not a sudden revelation at all. It was more like my heart had been inside a hard rock, protected from all emotion. Now that rock was breaking apart, letting fresh air travel between the pieces to nourish the place where love grows.

I daydreamed out the car window as Branson and I drove

along in silence. I felt as if a flower was blossoming in my chest, its petals softly caressing my heart. As the landscape passed by, I knew it was the truth. I did love him. And I knew for certain he loved me. He cherished who I was. He didn't complain that I was too fat, or too stupid, or too weak, or too anything. I was loved for who I was. Ralph was the kindest, gentlest soul I had ever met. He was so *good*. Was he too good for me? Oh, God. I knew myself—now I'd worry about this.

"Here we are." Branson's voice startled me.

She pulled up in front of a low brick building that crouched at the top of a hill. An ambulance was parked to the side of the emergency entrance, probably the one that had brought Cindy. Beside it was a low black hearse. The funeral home? I wondered who'd died as I disentangled my sticky legs and got out of the car. The garbage bag was stuck to my wet bum and flapped around my legs as I walked. It was so attractive. Branson saw it and turned her head, trying not to laugh.

"It's okay," I said. "I know it's funny, Officer Branson." I peeled the bag off and crumpled it into a ball.

"Call me Marilyn. And I didn't say anything." She took the bag and threw it into the trunk. Only then did she let her laughter rip.

We walked through the hospital door, and I immediately saw Cindy lying on the gurney by a nurse's station, eyes closed. Marilyn walked over to a male nurse, and I headed to Cindy. She still looked very pale. I didn't care what she said about how hard her head was, I was worried. But she must have sensed me being next to her because her eyes snapped open, wide and green in her white face.

"Don't look so worried. I tell you, it's my knee. They just stitched it up. Anything goes wrong with my knees and I feel like fainting."

I said, "Oh."

"Where's Officer Branson? Marilyn?"

"Talking to a nurse."

"Well Robin, you're not going to believe this."

"What?"

"The heart attack victim? The person who fell?"

"Yes?"

"It was Dr. MacKenzie."

Oh God. What a day.

"He died." Cindy looked at me and laughed.

"It's not funny, Cindy."

She laughed harder.

28.

DR. MACKENZIE WAS DEAD? And Cindy was laughing about it? You were not supposed to laugh if someone suddenly dies, especially if they were wanted for murder. Maybe she *was* a little doolally. She *had* hit her head. As unobtrusively as I could, I tried to inspect her pupils.

"This isn't funny, Cindy. It's a mess. That's what it is. A big stupid mess." Her pupils were little pinpricks. "Now Statten's murder will be buried, along with MacKenzie. And the doctor will go down as an upstanding citizen of the town."

"Oh, don't be such a tight-ass. Who cares? Aren't you going to say 'karma'? I mean, he was a very nasty fella."

"This has nothing to do with karma. And I've told you a hundred times, don't diss my spiritual practice."

She mimicked me. "My spiritual practice."

"Oh, eat shit." I didn't mean it. Sort of. This was a crusty old fight.

A female nurse approached. "Now, now. We need to stay quiet for the next twenty minutes or so. We have to rest." She waltzed off down the hall, her words of wisdom falling on stony ground. Cindy stuck out her tongue at her swaying back.

Branson loped over to us. She inspected Cindy's eyes. "Feeling better, are *we*? Like the painkillers?"

Cindy laughed. Everything was a big joke to her. I guessed she was happy she hadn't died. The outcome could have been so different. The image of her head sinking under water flashed across my eyes. She had almost died; my best friend had almost drowned. The hospital's fluorescent strip lighting flickered as people moved, leaving an iridescent halo around their bodies. The nurse's voice seemed to echo in my head. The greasy white tiles were shining and vibrating from the overhead lights. Oh God, there was that snake hissing in my ears. I was going to faint. I grabbed the edge of Cindy's stretcher and slid to the ground.

Next thing I knew, I heard my name being called. It sounded far-off, whirling around in a tin room, a staccato reverberation. Where was I? I could smell bleach. Had I died? Was that formaldehyde? Was I being embalmed? My cheek was pressed against something cold and flat. A coffin? But there was grit pressing into my forearm. My clothes were wet. Had I swum the River Jordan? What the hell had happened to me? Was that God calling my name?

I opened my eyes. I was staring at a small black wheel. There was a silver lever pressed against it. A brake? My eyes travelled up a thin strut to a metal shelf that had wet Adidas on it, the colour of puke. Cindy's. I recognized the neon-pink laces. I turned my head and saw a white sheet draped over a body. Oh, I was looking at a hospital stretcher. Green eyes looked over the edge.

"Cindy?"

"Robin, you fainted." She giggled. "You're okay."

Officer Branson bent over to help me up.

Cindy said, "No Marilyn. Give her a minute. She does this. Robin's a fainter when things get to be a bit much. She needs to lie there for a minute, otherwise, she'll just keel over again."

Marilyn said, "Oh, okay. Should I get her a blanket?"

"Naw, she'll be fine." She giggled again.

God, they were discussing me like I wasn't there. "I'm okay," I said to the black rubber wheel.

"Sure, you are," Cindy said, laughing.

"No, really. Stop being so bratty. I'm feeling better. I can get up now." To prove my point, I sat up. The room swam around me, but I refused to lie back down.

"Here, I'll help you get up," said Branson.

She grabbed under one of my arms and lifted me as if I were a beach ball. A honking, big round beach ball. That woman was strong. "Thanks."

I brushed off my damp pants. I still felt a little light-headed and took a couple of deep breaths. They didn't help, but I tried to act normal. "Cindy? Are they letting you go home today? That was a terrible fall."

"Oh sure. They're just making sure my knee isn't bleeding. Only a few more minutes to wait and then I'm good to go. I'm fine, Robin. But are you?"

Her pupils had expanded. The drug was wearing off. "I'm okay," I said, wiping my clammy hands on my jeans. "Yeah, I'm good. I'll call a taxi. Let's get home, and get changed while the driver's waiting. Then, we'll take the cab to pick up your car."

Marilyn interjected, "No, no. I'll drive you home. I called in earlier about Bradley escaping in a boat, right after he took off in the dinghy. The police boat is out now, after him, so there's nothing much for me to do."

Oh, so that's who she'd been talking to before she spread out the garbage bags on the back seat with such care. And great that they had a boat. That made sense, what with so much water around. I hoped they caught him.

"Thanks, Officer Branson."

"Please, call me Marilyn. Everyone else does."

I wasn't sure I'd be able to do that. She had forged a strong impression in my mind at the lobster supper as being professional to the max. Marilyn, on the other hand, was a soft, powdery sort of name that didn't jive with that image. But I would try. I had now seen another side of her. She was a truly kind person. It was probably hard being female in the RCMP. One probably had to go overboard in the power department to gain any sort of acceptance into the ranks.

After getting into the police car, it soon became apparent to me that Marilyn wasn't taking the highway home. She'd opted for White Point Road from Liverpool. I wondered if she thought the road along the shore was faster than taking the highway to the Port Mouton exit and then backtracking to Hunt's Point. The road twisted and turned, and we bounced over potholes and rocks that had poked through the asphalt. We travelled through scrubby forest, thick with spruce trees and rocks. Every now and then, a rushing brook coursed away into the bush, yellow foam bubbling over rocks. But soon the forest opened up, and lovely ocean vistas sparkled though the tree trunks. The sun was low in the sky and flashes of white light played across the water. Frame cottages dotted the shore—some built only a foot or two from the edge of the ocean. As beautiful as it was, I thought about the destructive power of storm surges and erosion.

As we drove along, Cindy and I told Officer Branson about Danny and his revelations about MacKenzie. Cindy asked Marilyn, "What's going to happen about MacKenzie poisoning Frank Statten? I'm guessing that case is over before it even started."

So now she was singing a different tune, taking the impact of his death on the case seriously. I stared at Cindy and mouthed, "Tight-ass."

She smiled and looked away.

Marilyn glanced over her shoulder at Cindy on the back seat. "Are you kidding? No way." She talked, almost as if to herself, as she negotiated the potholes and rocks on the twisting road. "MacKenzie is going down for the murder of Statten. I started the investigation before I knew what Danny had said, even though Hans.... Anyway, enough about him. I've already confirmed that the doctor knew Billy's death was caused by food poisoning. He gets the Public Health alerts."

I knew that. We'd learned that already from Billy Schnare's mother.

"While I was at the hospital with you guys, I asked about security in the lab and if anyone had wandered into the lab recently, anyone who was not a regular. I was told there was just hallway video coverage, but also that MacKenzie was in there last week, just poking around. He'd come before lunch, saying he'd like a look-see, and was left in the lab alone when everyone went out to eat."

Cindy interrupted. "Lots of time then for him to steal from the fridge."

"Yes, you're exactly right." She smiled coyly at Cindy over her shoulder. "Plenty of time for him to get some of the poisoned lobster flesh out of the refrigerator. I haven't looked at the hallway tapes yet, but I know he'll be on them. With Danny's testimony, it'll pretty much be a wrap. I hope. Unfortunately, we have no way to prove that Statten actually ate some of the lobster and that it was poisoned. It's one thing to steal toxin, it's another to prove it was administered. And don't forget, there's no proof that he stole the toxin. Just because he happened to be there doesn't mean he took it. I'm hoping Danny's testimony will get around that."

I was listening intently, making mental notes for my story. I *knew* Statten had eaten the poisoned lobster. I replayed in my mind the sequence of events at the supper. I clearly saw the fluttering flags dangling from the ropes enclosing the cement patio covered with picnic tables. My family was sitting right in front of the head table. Calvin was standing up. What was he doing? Right. Filming! Calvin was filming! And so was I!

I was excited. I knew I had been right to document the event. "My son filmed the whole thing. He filmed the lobster being brought to the table by Danny and being placed in front of his mother. He filmed her giving the lobster to Statten. He filmed him eating it. He filmed him quote—'having a stroke'—unquote. He even filmed him throwing up. And I filmed him under the table, dying."

Marilyn frowned. Her head tilted to one side. "I don't mean

to contradict you, but I asked at the supper if anyone had video of the event. You and your whole family said no."

Oops.

"Were you lying to a police officer?"

The knuckles on Marilyn's fingers had turned white as she gripped the steering wheel. She was angry.

Cindy looked at me, her mouth pulled back in a grimace.

Yes, yes, I'd lied. I was protecting my story. I was getting good at lying, but clearly, not good enough. "No, not lying, not really. I'd never lie to the police." Cindy kicked me and pretended to write with a pretend pen. "I was just trying to get a story for *The Toronto Express*."

"*The Toronto Express* is more important than a person's death?" She'd turned her head, glared at me, and then turned away, shaking her head in disgust.

Just shit. I'd blown it this time. "Of course not." I hoped I sounded penitent.

Cindy was mouthing something at me, her mouth opening and shutting like a goldfish's. What was she saying? Oh, "stroke."

"I mean it. I'm not like that. Of course not. We all thought at the time that he'd only had a stroke. I was thinking of doing a piece on strokes for the Home and Garden section. It didn't seem important." I said, as I lied to the police.

"Okay. That makes sense. I see where you were coming from." Her fingers relaxed and turned pink.

That was a close call. "I really appreciate you driving us home. It's been a bad day." This was my idea of an olive branch.

"No problem. I live out this way anyway, and I have to change into dry clothes as well."

The loud sound of a phone ringing reverberated in the car. Marilyn clicked a button on her steering wheel. "Officer Branson."

She'd lowered her voice and had suddenly become officious.

A disembodied voice swirled around us. "We got him. He hadn't got far, was heading down the coast, probably to the next port with a wharf. Port L'Hebert."

Marilyn sighed with relief. It was just a colleague, not the brass. Not Hans Schroeder who she obviously had trouble with. "Thank heavens. He could have headed into the woods and we would have lost him. What's he saying?"

"He's acting all innocent, saying he was just out for a ride. Puffed all up like a pompous dick."

"Did you ask him why he ran from me?"

"Sure did. He said, 'Officer who?' Like he hadn't run from you."

"Don't tell him we have a videotape of his confession. Not until he lies that he wasn't even on the wharf." She turned to me and admonished, "It's not good to lie to the police."

I smiled sweetly at her.

"Got it." The guy clicked off.

"Good," Cindy said. "Good. I'm glad he's caught. He tried to kill me. And he did kill Beverly."

Marilyn nodded. "I'm working on that murder too. That guy on the phone? I asked him to write up a search warrant on Bradley's house this morning. Hopefully, we'll find the murder weapon. Knowing how arrogant Bradley is, he probably used one of his own kitchen knives and then put it back, thinking we'd never in a million years suspect a mayor."

Finally, we turned into the long driveway leading up the hill to our lovely rented cottage. I couldn't wait to get out of my wet clothes.

"Thanks for the drive here. We won't be but a second." I grabbed Lucky from the back seat and almost raced inside, followed by Cindy.

Next thing I heard was the washing machine chugging away. "What?" I asked Lucky as I threw on some warm socks. "Who has time to do laundry?" He wagged his tail. I came out of my bedroom and Cindy was already in the kitchen, sporting a tight new pair of jeans and a T-shirt. She was also wearing sports sandals.

"What are you washing?"

"My Adidas. They'll stain if I don't get them clean before they dry. Let's go."

I marched out ahead of her. "I'm going to leave Lucky here, so pull the snapper around so he can't get out."

She looked at me dumbly. "The snapper?"

"Oh, for heavens sake." I reached behind her and twisted the door slammer, the snapper, whatever you wanted to call it, so the door couldn't be opened from the inside. It was jammed shut.

On my way to the car, I went to the garbage bin and retrieved the bag with Statten's vomit in it. It stunk to high heaven. Cindy looked at me with her eyebrows raised. I carried it at arm's length to the waiting car.

"Here Marilyn," I said, as I held up the bag in front of her car window. "You need proof that Statten ate poisoned lobster? Well, here it is. There were no garbage bins at the supper, so I brought home what we tried to clean up. I don't know if the toxin will still be good, but this has Statten's vomit in it."

Marilyn eyed the bag with distaste and got out of the car. She walked around to the trunk and opened it. "Here, throw it in the trunk. It just reeks. We'll see if it's got any merit as evidence. There might be a chain of custody and decomposition issues. Thanks for remembering you had it. If it's all good with the lawyers, it'll be really good evidence." She slammed down the trunk lid and slid into the driver's seat while waving her hand under her nose. The stench had permeated the whole vehicle.

We buzzed down our windows as Marilyn drove us slowly along the Lighthouse Route, past Summerville Beach, past the restaurant we always ate at, and then veered left toward the centre of Port Mouton. The wharf appeared and Cindy's white Honda Civic still sat perkily on the gravel.

"Here you go." The car slowed to a stop beside Cindy's rental.

Marilyn turned to us. "I'm sorry all this happened to you both today. I know everything's come out in the wash, so to speak, but if we'd been on the ball then Bradley would have at least been watched as a suspect."

"We're all okay, Marilyn, so don't fret. I just wish that Hans Schroeder had believed me when I said there had been two murders."

Marilyn looked surprised. "He didn't?"

Cindy launched into a tirade. "What's with that guy? Is he a woman hater, or is it just gay women? Or black women?"

"Well," said Marilyn, "he certainly hates me."

"Why is he in his job if he's so full of hate?" I asked.

Marilyn shook her head and said, "Bradley ... Hans...." But she didn't finish the sentence.

I wondered if she was going to say that Bradley, a racist, had ensured that the primary detective in the community was racist as well and that systemic racism was everywhere.

Officer Branson continued, "What an awful mayor. I think he'll be charged with a hate crime as well as murder. He'll never get out of prison. I just can't figure out why he cut off her tongue and shoved it where he did."

I guessed she didn't know that the MLA was going out with Frank Statten, that a black woman was seeing a white guy. Plus, she was Danny's mother, and Danny was going out with Bradley's daughter.

"Well," I said, coughing, "you know he was a white supremacist, right?"

"Oh?" Was she pretending she didn't know? Was she being sarcastic?

"His daughter was going out with Danny, Beverly's son." From the look on her face, I could tell she definitely didn't know that.

"I see." She sucked in her cheeks. "That would be a big no-no for him. He'd work up a raging head of steam."

"And," Cindy added, "on top of that, Beverly was going out with Frank Statten."

Marilyn was incredulous. "She *was*? But she didn't support

fish farms. I don't understand that. How could she go out with him? How did she keep that a secret?"

Cindy rubbed her sore knee. "Well, she was. So, I guess her saying she didn't support fish farms was a big fat lie."

"Hence the tongue. First, he cut it out because she was a liar. Then he shoved it inside her because she was having a sexual relationship with a white man."

I needed to get away from the conversation and the stench in the car before I fainted again. "Thanks for the lift, Marilyn. Maybe see you around. We're here for the rest of the week."

"Where's your husband?"

"Partner," I said, correcting her. "We're not married."

"Not yet," interjected Cindy.

I rolled my eyes and changed the subject as Cindy and I got out of the police car. I said, "Good luck with wrapping up the two murders, Marilyn. And thanks for the ride here."

"Thank *you*." She put the car in gear and talked to us through her open window as she pulled away. A cloud of vomit-scented air roiled past me. "I couldn't have done it without your involvement," she said. "And now to face Schroeder. Wish me luck."

That night, after a delicious pizza in the town of Liverpool, Cindy and I sat around the fire, polishing off a bottle of wine. And then another.

"When's Ralphie getting back?" she asked.

"Ralph. Sometime after twelve. He said he'd be late and I checked the flights. One's coming in around nine, so add about three hours to that. He has to get the car and then drive here. I'm guessing around twelve."

Right that second, my phone pinged. Ralph. I looked at my watch. It was around nine. *Just landed. See you soon. But don't wait up.*

No worries about that. I could barely keep my eyes open. "How are you doing Cindy? Do you have a headache or anything?"

"My knee throbs a bit, but I'll take one of the pills they gave me before I head up." She yawned. "In fact, I think I'll head up now. I know it's early, but I'm zonked."

"Okay. Night." I watched her teeter off to the kitchen door.

I threw some water on the fire and it steamed into the night. I called, "I'll make sure the fire's out. And don't mix painkillers with alcohol."

Cindy waved a toodle-oo in the air over her head as she went into the house but didn't turn around. She'd had quite the day. I didn't blame her for wanting to crawl into bed.

I gathered up the bottles, the dog, bits of garbage, and followed her into the kitchen. No way was I going to sit out there all by myself. Who knew if that awful Mr. Henshaw was watching me, or a wild cat or something. I fell into bed, absolutely exhausted and barely woke up when Ralph snuck between the sheets.

"Hi sweetie," I mumbled into his ear. His skin was icy cold.

He ran his frosty fingers all over my body, and I leaned into him. He whispered, "I missed you today, Robin MacFarland."

I could feel his heart beating next to my breast. I said, "Me too. I'm so glad you're home. I have a major story to write. Shirley's going to love it. It was a very bad day, Ralph. I'll tell you about it in the morning." I kissed his cheek and said, "There's so much hatred in the world."

"But not from me. I love you with all my heart."

"I love you too, Ralph."

There, I'd said it. I fell asleep with a soft silky feeling wrapping around my heart.

Acknowledgements

I am very grateful to all the people who helped me write this book, including my friends and family. For me the subject matter was very difficult: I was enraged to discover the extent of the historical racism in the province of Nova Scotia and how it lingers to this day. I was also repeatedly shocked by the wanton destruction of the beautiful ocean biosphere by greedy individuals, wanting to make a buck from fish farming. The environmental theme of the book, fish farming, was suggested to me by Anne and Kurt Sarty one sunny day while we were watching the tide go out on a South Shore beach. I would like to thank them for their insight into a serious South Shore issue. Marine Biologist Inka Milewski provided me with the terrible details that were revealed from her eleven-year study on the impact of fish farms on the South Shore lobster fishing industry and the ocean. Kim Masland, the MLA for Queen's and Shelburne County, outlined the responsibilities and jurisdiction of her elected position.

Several people helped me understand the racial issues along the shore. The Black Loyalist Heritage Centre was very forthcoming with information about the history of Black people in Nova Scotia. Mary Manning, a member of Shelburne's South End Environmental Injustice Society, a committee dedicated to correcting environmental racism, talked to me at length about the toxic waste in the Shelburne dump and the devastating consequences on the health of the surrounding black community. A special thanks to Calvin Lawrence, a descendant of Black Empire Loyalists and a retired police officer, who was encouraging at all times throughout the writing of the book, answering my many questions.

I would also like to thank all the people at Inanna Publications for their editorial, administrative, and promotional support. In particular, I am grateful to Editor-in-Chief, Luciana Ricciutelli, for her dedication to feminist books and her loyal support to writers. I sincerely appreciate Publicist/Marketing Manager, Renée Knapp, and cover designer, Val Fullard, for keeping Inanna's books in the public's eye and attractive. I am very proud to be an Inanna writer.

Photo: Phil Brennen

Sky Curtis divides her time between Northern Ontario, Nova Scotia, and Toronto. She has worked as an editor, author, software designer, magazine writer, scriptwriter, poet, teacher, and children's writer. Sky has published over a dozen books and is passionate about social justice issues and the environment. Her poetry has appeared in several literary journals, including *The Antigonish Review, Canadian Forum*, and *This Magazine*. Her debut novel, and the first in the Robin MacFarland series, *Flush: A Robin MacFarland Mystery,* was published in 2017 and was short-listed for the 2018 Arthur Ellis Award for Debut Crime Fiction. The second in the series, *Plots: A Robin MacFarland Mystery,* was published in 2018.